The Fire God Tour

Michele Sims

The Fire God Tour. Copyright © 2019 by Michele Sims. All rights reserved. Printed in the United States of America. No part of this book may be used or reproduced in any manner whatsoever without written permission.

ISBN 978-1-7347567-3-9 print book

ISBN 978-1-7347567-2-2 ebook

Publisher: Green Publishing, LLC

Editing: RQ Editing, LLC and Nick May

Cover design:- J.L. Woodson
jlwoodsonwoodsonstudio.com

TABLE OF CONTENTS

PROLOGUE

Just keep pushing, Bella Aliyah Wahlberg reminded herself for the tenth time as she rushed around her bedroom trying to get ready for her teleconference with Mr. Hansen, the new Vice President of International Marketing at World Music, LLC. She had completed a fellowship with the company three months earlier, and her parting with the organization had been less than amiable.

What could he tell me at this point? She huffed and furrowed her brows, dissatisfied with her reflection in the mirror. She rubbed her fingers along the crescent-shaped shadows under her brown eyes and felt a lack of the usual smoothness. Before pulling the thick locks of her auburn-colored hair back in a tight bun, she examined the ends of her ponytail, which could use a much-needed trim.

Watch the frown lines Bella. Her mother's voice echoed in her head, and the fact she had to remind herself on a daily basis to smile at work provided a snapshot of her life for the last six months. She knew she had spent too many long days and late nights preparing for Ari Moore's upcoming international Fire God Tour and her life lacked balance.

"I have to prove I can do my job—and there's nothing a little concealer can't hide," she assured herself as she smoothed the loose strands of hair and applied the finishing touches of her makeup. The starched white shirt and black pencil skirt were hanging on the door of her closet as she walked across the room and shimmied into her outfit for the day, ready for battle in the male-dominated music industry in Los Angeles.

Working at home was a luxury for her as a marketing consultant for Ari Moore's entertainment company, AriMusic. Even though her family's modest and recently renovated early twentieth-century craftsman-style home was not as plush as the mansion Ari Moore had converted into the studio home of his growing entertainment empire, she liked that she could get things done at home with minimal interruptions.

Her phone rang, and she saw Darien Grayson's smiling face on the screen. He was Ari's executive assistant. She answered the call on speaker.

"Good morning Darien." Her voice was less than enthusiastic.

"And a good morning to you too, Bella. Did we not get a good night's rest last night?" He said it with mirth, but she wasn't amused.

"What's a good night sleep, Darien? I don't think I've had one since I became a consultant for Ari Moore."

"Ari can be a taskmaster, but his bark is worse than his bite. You'll figure that out soon enough—and I'm not sure why you're not calling him Miles at this point."

"We don't have that kind of relationship and calling him Ari is a reminder to use his stage name when we're out in the public." She slipped on her matching black leather pumps.

"Have it your way, but the reason I'm calling so early is to let you know that you and…Ari have a packed schedule today. The radio stations have confirmed the time for the interviews you requested, and the local nightclubs owners are thrilled you convinced Ari to agree to more meet and greets. I'm not sure how you did it; he hates a packed schedule." She rolled her eyes as he spoke. Ari had told her a thousand times he didn't want every minute of his day planned with one obligation after another. Her mind wandered as she thought of the number of engagements, she had to attend with him. "And Reagan—"

She tuned at the mention of Reagan Madison's name, the lead dancer at AriMusic and one of her favorites...well, her only, gal pal. "What about Reagan?"

"Are you listening Bella?"

"Yes Darien." She sighed.

"I was about to say Reagan wanted me to remind you that your girl time with her is over dinner at seven o'clock tonight. You've been working hard, Bella, and you need to take a break." She blew out a breath of air instead of protesting. She knew he was right.

"Again, I don't know how you arranged the coup, but Ari has agreed to give Reagan an audition as a lead singer for a group he is considering forming after they return from the tour. Bella, your girl Reagan is a great dancer, but that doesn't mean she can handle a mike."

"Darien, I've heard her sing many times, and I think she can handle a mike. All she needs is a chance. Besides, I need to pay it forward because even though I have the training, I lacked the experience of a seasoned marketing consultant and I know if it wasn't for you, his trusted assistant," she smiled as he cleared his throat, "and Parker using his influence as the CFO, Ari wouldn't have given me a chance."

"No problem Bella. Parker told me you've exceeded his expectations and your wonderful mother, Chief Wahlberg, also put in a good word for you. Having you around girl, has made my life bearable as we prepare for this world tour. Someone needed to convince Miles that if we continued our expansion in the music industry, we needed to run a tighter organization with schedules and more structure. Speaking of structure, have you returned Scott Hansen's call—Mister Uptight himself?"

Bella looked at the time on her cell phone as she walked down the hallway and into the room at the end of the hall that her mother had turned into a home office, with modern gray painted walls accented with white trim and filled with sleek furniture. Bella especially liked the modern look of the pewter and steel light fixtures and accessories on her desk. She took in a breath and sat down in the chair in front of the camera on her computer.

"I have a teleconference with him in a few minutes, but before you go, have you finished compiling the list of all the VIP and press passes for AriMusic that are floating around this city? I know many of the members of the press corps who cover musicians, and I only recognized a few of the names on the list you gave me."

"Yes, I sent you the completed list that Bradley in security gave me, and I looked at it before sending it to you. Many of the names were Miles's former girlfriends or associates. I'll tell Bradley to tighten up the list before we launch the tour."

"Bradley has enough to do, and I wanted to go over the list so that only members of the press will have press passes for the tour. I'll run it by Ari before I request that Bradley disarm the passes of those who are not members of the press and limit the number of VIPs who are allowed backstage."

"Bella, I'm telling you this as a friend: I think you should stay in your lane with the passes, which have been a sticky situation for his former press agents. There are women on the list who feel they deserve an all-access pass to Ari and he's allowed it. They're his uberfans and some of them are scary."

"Consider me warned. I have to take this meeting. Bye Darien, and thanks."

"Bye Bella and good luck." She ended the phone call with Darien and activated the hook up on her computer, which was buzzing to begin the conference with the VP at World Music. The computer screen lit up with the image of one of the receptionists she knew from her time there.

"Good morning Brianna. I have a teleconference with Mr. Hansen."

"Good morning Bella. We really miss you around here, and someone asks me almost every week when was the last time I heard from you." She pouted while arranging her headset over her ears.

"I miss seeing you too Brianna and tell the team I said hello."

"I will. Mr. Hansen is expecting your call. Hold on as I prepare to transfer you to his office." The screen went blank for a few seconds, followed by a view of an office with a large mahogany desk and a gold nameplate with the name Scott Hansen, VP of Global Marketing, etched on it. She assumed the unfamiliar, tall, distinguished man seated behind the desk unbuttoning his shirt and loosening his tie was him.

"Good morning Miss Wahlberg. I'm Scott Hansen. You're one busy person, and I didn't realize it would be so difficult to catch up with you. I guess I should have had my people contact your people, but I wanted us to talk on a personal, friendly note." He chuckled as Bella placed her hands on her lap and sat straight with confidence before replying to him.

"Good morning Mr. Hansen."

"Call me Scott." He widened his smile and leaned into the camera.

"Okay, and I'm Bella." She forced a smile. "I've been very busy, and I didn't recognize your name on my caller ID. Have we met before?" She leaned in a little for a closer view of his face.

"No, we haven't. During your time here at World Music, they assigned me overseas to head our expansion into the European and Asian markets. I understand that you worked under Brett Watkins, the director of new employee development for the marketing fellowship."

"Yes, that's correct," she responded with a slight tilt of her head.

"It's a great program, and I heard your presentations were excellent, but let me get right to the point. The artists on the team you promoted weren't pleased with the marketing plans that Michael Monroe came up with after you left, and many of them have told me they liked your ideas better. There are rumors that they gave Michael the position as team leader on the project instead of you because his father is the director of marketing, West Coast division."

Bella's lips tightened and her posture stiffened.

What? Nepotism and sexism at World Music? It can't be so. Her sarcasm didn't lessen the heavy weight of hurt and disappointment that had settled in the pit of her stomach. She placed her hand against her belly and applied light pressure as she looked down and pursed her lips.

"Sir, I'm not sure what that has to do with me at this point. You're aware I'm no longer affiliated with World Music."

Let me see where he's going with this. She relaxed her posture.

"Bella, I wasn't in this position at the time they made those decisions, but I want to make things right. I've done my homework, and is it true you're a consultant with the startup record company AriMusic?"

"Yes but—"

"Hear me out. I'm offering you a full-time position with my organization, a world class entertainment conglomerate, and I'll match any offer AriMusic proposes to keep you."

Bella sat back and crossed her legs as she pondered his offer.

"So, Mr. Hansen…Scott, let me understand this. You said that you did your homework, so you're aware that Michael and I were assigned to the same marketing team, where he took credit for my ideas and got the position I worked hard for, and now you want me to consider accepting a position at World Music?"

"Bella, again, that's in the past, and yes, I would like you to come and work with us at World. I want to assign you to work with some of our artists, like Young Robb, and there are several others who want to work with you again. But here's the full disclosure."

Bella focused her attention on the screen, avoiding the chance of a dismissive eye roll.

"We have a delicate situation here. For the time being, I need to assign you to Michael's team." She tightened her grip on the arms of her chair as she saw his Adam's apple moving in a hard swallow.

"But you'll answer to me during the transition, and I'll approve all of your performance appraisals until you're transferred to another team. Of course, we'll need you to sign a contract with a non-compete clause if you leave. We can't risk having you take our information or procedures to competitors. You didn't by any chance sign a non-compete while you were here, did you?"

"No, I didn't. Scott. I've done my homework too, and I understand that there are several lawsuits against the marketing department for its numerous cases of bias in its hiring practices. You don't have to worry about me joining in a class-action suit, although someone has approached me about it. Second, I already work with several of the artists that left World Music and have recently signed with AriMusic, which is more than a startup. Thanks for the offer, but I plan to stay where I am."

"Bella, you're new to this industry and your decision is either a boss move or is ill-advised, if I may offer my professional opinion. The music industry out here is…interesting. I can only make this offer to you once, and if you refuse, I must take you out of my contacts. I would hate that later on in your career you discovered you've made a mistake."

Here we go. We're leaving ultimatum and heading to Threat Level 1.

"Scott, I think we both like to minimize mistakes, but…." She took in a breath to slow down the accelerating beats of her heart and to let the pause in her statement emphasize what she was about to say. "Do it." She looked directly into the camera.

"Let's be clear and careful about this, Bella. Do what?" He leaned to the side and waited.

"Remove my name from your contacts." Undeterred, she stuck her chest out. Her decision was made.

Viewing his image on the screen, she saw his jaw drop and his eyes blink as if the weight of her words were an affront to what he thought was sensible.

"All right Bella, but in this town, our decisions have consequences." His fake smile was a thin veil, covering the possibilities of his not-so-subtle intent. "Goodbye Bella."

"Goodbye Scott." She hit the power button on the computer and the screen faded to black as she folded her arms and processed her thoughts about the meeting.

"So I'm supposed to work like a dog and then accept the scraps from the table as a reward? Not today, dude. Not today." Her phone buzzed with an alert of her next appointment.

"Just enough time to freshen up before I meet Ari at the studio for an interview this morning. Startup? Scott, you haven't seen what I plan to accomplish at AriMusic."

She rose from her chair, invigorated that she had made the right choice and ready for the day's adventures.

Michele Sims

CHAPTER ONE

The engine raced as Miles Aridio Tavares Moore—Ari to
his fans and Miles to people in his inner circle—
downshifted on a banked curve in his new, candy-apple-red
Ferrari. His heart rate seemed to increase with the roar of
the engine as he regained speed on a straightaway. Tall and
handsome, with brooding good looks and a well-toned
physique, Miles Moore turned the heads of many when he
entered a space. His smooth brown skin and his soulful,
alluring brown eyes the color of cognac, attracted the
attention of many of his female followers.

As a mega hip-hop star, he preferred spending long
hours cutting tracks in the studio instead of getting up at 7
a.m., but given the chance to show off his skills on this
high-performance race track, he'd go with little sleep. Oh
yeah, it was worth it. The fellas in his crew had told him he
was crazy to get up so early this morning. They'd planned
on spending their time relaxing and chilling, but not
Miles—he was an adrenaline junkie and liked heart-
stopping experiences. When he'd arrived at the speedway
in Irwindale, the pit crew had already been there to show
him how they'd rigged the car for maximum speed. He
practiced his favorite maneuver: accelerating hard with a
wide-open throttle and then quickly sliding his feet off the
accelerator to snap the throttle shut. The crew had figured
out how to create the right air-fuel mixture to dump into the
exhaust and ignite the hot pipes. The sight of the red,

yellow, and orange flames streaming from his pipes always turned him on. It was almost orgasmic. Today—a very rare day off from recording and touring—was his to spend with fast cars and even faster women.

Taking a few laps around the race track was more than exhilarating, and he decided he'd talk to his business manager, Parker Middleton, tomorrow to make additional funds available to give the pit crew a bonus.

He got out of the car after rolling into the pit and spoke to the crew manager. "You guys really stepped up your game this morning. I haven't had an adrenaline rush like that in a long time." He slapped the crew chief on the back and shared a laugh before walking around the car to shake the hands of each man on the crew.

"See you guys later. Thanks for everything."

Waving goodbye, he headed to the parking lot to retrieve his car: a black Audi R8. He pulled out his shades as he moved slowly across the black asphalt and contemplated the weird dream, he'd had last night. Thoughts of Bella Wahlberg, his chief consultant for marketing and publicity, had invaded his dreams again.

Imagine me turning down a date with Angel to stay at the office and go over media plans with Bella? That's absurd. She's good at her job, but I'd never spend the evening with her, the original Ice Princess, and pass on spending time with Angel. He laughed out loud, still amused by the strange unconscious thoughts in his dreams.

Nah, I don't have a thing for Bella. She's not my type.

He shrugged it off and attributed the dream to probable confusion and fatigue from long nights of rehearsals in preparation for his upcoming world tour.

After wiping smoke residue off his clothes, he jumped in his car and started the engine. The video panel lit up, revealing options for beating as much traffic as possible on the busy LA freeways. The 605 South from Irwindale was less congested, and he hoped for a quick ride into downtown LA.

Driving home, he contemplated the rest of his day—and his evening—with his "fallen angel." First, a shower to wash off the odor of sweat and car fumes, then a nap for a few hours before getting ready for some real heat. He almost passed through a red light thinking about all the things he planned to do tonight, which included seeing Angel in the new red bikini he'd had his assistant, Darien Grayson, purchase for her.

Miles loved the feel of Angel's soft, unblemished skin and noticed even the slightest physical details while having sex. He appreciated that Angel could take as much as she gave, and there was no denying the heat between the two of them. Most importantly, though, Angel didn't have a problem with the rules he had imposed. He needed passion…without commitment.

He cleared his throat and swallowed; his throat felt a little sore from the intense studio session the day before, so he sent Darien a voice message to have a strong hot toddy waiting for him. His world tour would start soon, and the last thing he needed was a defective voice.

The phone rang, and Darien's name came up on the car's Bluetooth display. He had been working for Miles for three years, and he knew his moods and his routine.

"How was the ride, Miles?" Darien's voice filled the interior of the car after Miles pressed the *accept* button on the steering wheel.

Miles sensed a slight tension in Darien's voice.

"It was good." He kept his response subdued to avoid gushing about his experience this morning. "What do you need Darien?" His voice seeped with a need to have him spill it, and Darien knew better than to waste his time with idle chatter.

He spoke fast. "There has been a change in plans. Angel can't make it tonight."

Miles glared at the road in silence as he contemplated his response.

"How long have I had these plans for tonight? And wasn't it you Darien who convinced me to give her another chance after she cancelled on me last month? It's not like I don't know that Angel only wants to have fun, but I've had enough of her cancelling at the last minute. I don't have time for this shit."

His skin heated, and his heart raced. Gripping the steering wheel tighter, he hoped the pain would distract him from his growing anger over the news. He didn't care that the muscles in his arms were quivering as he held on to the wheel. Distracted and almost lost in his thoughts, it took him a few seconds to notice that the car in front of him had stopped, causing him to slam on the brakes.

Forget her. I'd better keep my eyes on the road.

"Damn her. I meant damn it."

"Miles, are you alright?"

"Yeah."

"I'm sorry this has happened again. I really thought Angel had changed her ways after she begged me to speak to you. I knew you would be disappointed, so I called Felicia before I called to tell you the news. You remember Felicia, right? She has been dying to spend some time with you. I told her you were in town, and she came over in record time to sign the nondisclosure papers." A nervous laugh escaped him. "You remember how she likes a good time."

"I'm supposed to be happy with a consolation prize?"

"No, Miles. Felicia is better at having fun than consoling anyone."

"I thought we were doing away with nondisclosures Darien?"

"Well, if you want to maintain your privacy and not make the news before starting the tour, I recommend you have her sign it this time."

He let out a loud grunt and an audible sigh to acknowledge he was still listening but not convinced Felicia was the best choice for tonight. The drive down the streets, lined with tall palm trees with their full crowns flowing in the wind, calmed him. He needed to accept his assistant had done everything possible to ensure he enjoyed his day off. He understood better than anyone that shit happened.

"Say something. What can I do to make things right?"

Working hard to keep his focus on the road, he continued to fume.

Nothing can make it right. Angel isn't going to be in my bed tonight. He gripped the steering wheel tighter. He knew he needed to regroup now that his initial plans for tonight weren't going to happen, and he turned his attention back to the phone.

"If Felicia is still there, let her know that you're sorry but something came up and we'll need to reschedule."

"Yes, she's still here Miles, but I don't think cancelling the plan is a good idea."

"I'm not in the mood for the twenty questions game she likes to play. You're good at coming up with something—give her my regrets. I'm tired and I've let you and Bella make too many changes in my schedule without first consulting me."

"Miles I know you're tired from all the work you've been putting in preparing for the tour, but some days, so many things are happening in real time around here, it's impossible to run everything by you."

"No more excuses Darien. I want most things like my appearances and major changes in my schedule run by me first."

"Alright Miles. Will do. I know things have been stressful with the Fire God Tour being bigger than the last one and with more overseas dates. Don't worry, I'll handle the matter with Felicia, and I won't add anything else in your schedule today. You deserve some time off. Just don't blame me when Parker cuts into your time."

Parker Middleton was the chief financial officer for Miles's music company.

"One more thing, Darien. I'm making some personnel changes."

Darien was generally calm in his dealings with Miles, but he began to stutter. "B-but... but... Miles—

I know you like Angel, but I want you to delete her name and number from all of my contacts. There's no need to discuss this. My decision is final. Goodbye, Darien."

He ended the call. The humming of the engine provided a cadence to slow the thoughts racing through his mind. He needed time to deal with his current reality, and he refused to let his irritation ruin his rare day off.

Before reaching his exit, he looked in his rearview mirror and the driver behind him was flashing its lights. Miles slowed down, and a sporty silver Lexus cruised alongside him, filled with young women waving and motioning him to pull off the freeway.

Lowering the window on the driver's side and flipping his dark shades to the top of his head to get a better view of the women, he smiled and threw a few kisses their way. Despite his intent to acknowledge them and urge them to move on, his actions were met with more screams as the women fangirling him leaned out of the car on the busy freeway.

"We love you Ari. Let's have some fun hanging out," one of them yelled as their driver continued to pursue him.

*They're fans, and I know it comes with the territory, but I'm not in the mood for a stalking tod*ay. He shook his head and sped up.

"Better take the backroads down through the canyon. He turned off the freeway at the next exit and decided to take a more circuitous route home. The scenery on the isolated road, dotted with parched trees and the brown and gray bushes, became a brief blur as he took the sharp turns at fast speeds down the steep hills. He held his breath, then let out a sigh of relief, having evaded attempts to follow him.

"She's not going to follow me on this road." He laughed knowing that most people unfamiliar with the route, with its twists and stretches of well-worn two lanes, would give up.

Driving along the roads now marred by wildfires, but still with sweeping views, he looked at the blackened earth all around him. To his right were the charred remains of a once-stately home surrounded by scorched earth covering acres caught in the random path of natural fire, which made him wonder how some areas, such as his home, were untouched by wildfires, while others had been destroyed. His neighbors had fled their homes onto roads clogged with frightened Angelinos as he watched from his patio, ignoring recommendations to evacuate so he could enjoy Mother Nature's majestic destruction. Of course, he hoped no harm came to anyone and property loss was minimal, but he just couldn't turn away from a natural wildfire blazing out of control. The dancing embers, floating through the air like fireflies and mixed with the heat of the flames and the smell of burning timber, were intoxicating to him. For anyone else, the scene naturally evoked fear and a need to flee—but not for him. The power of nature in all its fury mesmerized him.

He liked fire in all its forms, and because of his interest in wildfires, he gave generously to fire prevention programs and local firefighter funds. He once gave an impromptu concert and donated all the proceeds to firefighters and law enforcement charities. It didn't hurt that the law enforcement community knew him, which made it easier for them to overlook his frequent refusal to obey mandatory evacuation orders during wildfires. They knew he didn't expect anyone to risk their lives if he decided to remain in his home. His excuse that he was capturing scenes to include in his shows to create an authentic visualization of fire seemed plausible, but the first responders probably knew he was obsessed.

The sound of a loud car horn disturbed his thoughts. He looked into the rearview mirror again, and the same silver car was in quick pursuit. He was about to hit the accelerator when he looked in front of him at a car that had swerved into his lane and was quickly approaching.

"Shit. What's going on?" He flashed his lights and the car kept coming toward him as the Lexus sped up behind him. Miles pounded his fist on the horn with a long, loud blast, hoping to get the attention of the driver in front of him. His shirt was drenched with sweat and his heart was drumming in his ears as he tried to figure out what to do when a familiar voice came over the Bluetooth.

"Miles. This is James." He jerked his head toward the console, distracted by the voice, then swerved into the left lane and the driver also swerved and kept coming, closing the distance between them.

"Abort Miles. Abort." He had just enough time to jerk the car back into the right lane without crashing into the women still pursuing him. The road had narrowed again and there was a deep ravine to the right of the road that the silver car slid into, its brakes screeching as it left the road.

"Abort? This ass is going to kill us all." Miles yelled before tightening his jaw and extending his arm out of the window to throw a fireball at the car in front of him, causing it to lift off the road as it went airborne upon impact. Flipping and bursting into flames after it landed into the ravine, the car set the dried underbrush and debris on fire. He jerked his head and watched as the line of flames spreading rapidly by the gusts of wind headed toward the silver car.

Miles hit the brakes hard, causing his car to spin before coming to a complete stop on the road. He unbuckled his seatbelt and ran full speed out of his car, following the black skid marks on the road leading down the ravine. Two of the girls had gotten out of the car, weaving and unsteady on their feet before stopping on the shoulder of the highway, looking dazed and confused.

"Help us!" They pointed toward the car with the driver still inside, the door crushed with deep indentations by the impact of landing on the hard, dry soil.

"Get back away from the car," he yelled as he ran to the car and struggled to rescue their friend.

He was able to open the door and cut the motor before helping the driver out of the car as she moaned and grimaced, but she was able to move her arms and legs. She leaned in and rested her head on his shoulder as he helped her away from the vehicle.

Miles attempted to see if he could rescue the driver of the other car, who moments earlier had tried to kill him, but the vehicle blew up in flames, forcing him to retreat. A black sedan came up, and its occupants, in dark clothing and sunglasses, ran to assist him as flashing red lights and the sound of emergency vehicle sirens were heard in the background.

"Are you all alright? We're here to help you Mr. Moore," one of the men stated while the other went to block off the road and secure the scene.

"These women need medical attention, and I'm alright, but I'm not sure about the driver of the other vehicle." Miles was kneeling on the ground surrounded by the girls, who looked at him like emojis with heart eyes. He had a woman wrapped around each bicep, and the driver encircled his waist as she placed her head on his chest. Miles took in a breath and slowly shook his head, as he didn't know where to place his hands- eventually he decided to pat the driver on the back.

"Don't move. Help is on the way," The man with the dark glasses tried to mask a slight smile as he viewed Miles's discomfort in the clutches of the women.

"Let me handle this Mr. Moore. I'll talk to the EMTs." Miles gave him a side-eyed glance but decided not to challenge his directions.

He's got to be with the Network, Miles thought as he sized the man up.

"Ari, you saved our lives. What happened?" The female driver of the Lexus raised her hand to the bump forming on her head and the other girls were examining the bruises on their arms when emergency personnel arrived on the scene.

"We're Mr. Moore's security detail." The second man came and tried to help Miles to his feet, but he had to loosen the women's grips before the EMTs could take over their care.

"We'll need to take all of you in for an evaluation," one of the EMTs informed them as the scene quickly filled with policemen fanning out around the scene, firemen running to put out the burning vehicle, and helicopters flying overhead. "What are your names?"

"I'm Lisa Dixon," said the driver.

"I'm Brittany Lawson, and she's Amber Odom."

"And he's Ari Moore, our hero," Lisa said, pointing at Miles as she offered a coy smile, lifted her shoulders to her ears, and swooned.

"I won't need to go in. I'm fine." Miles got up and brushed the dirt off his clothes as both men in dark suits flanked him.

"Mr. Moore is preparing for a world tour, and we're here to take care of his needs. My partner will drive him home, and I'll stay here to answer any questions you may have. We witnessed the whole thing."

"Mr. Moore, will you be available if we have additional questions?" one of the policemen asked him.

"Sure, I'll be available until the tour launches, and I'm happy to cooperate." He looked over his shoulder at the women looking doe-eyed at him as they were being placed in the ambulance. "Please make sure they get the best care." Miles smiled at them.

"Will do," one of the EMTs responded before closing the door of the ambulance and hopping in to take the women to the hospital.

"Mr. Moore, it's time for us to go." Miles followed one of the men in black, and after they had gotten into his car, away from all the activity, he questioned him.

"Let me guess, Network operative?"

"Yes sir Mr. Moore, I'm with the Network, and your father will be expecting to speak with you after I get you home."

"Hell. Now all I need is the Kaiden Moore inquisition." Miles leaned his head back against the cool leather seat and closed his eyes.

The Network, an international clandestine organization of former military men, captains of industry, and government officials, was unknown except to a select few on the planet. They had a long reach and access to intelligence most countries would kill—yes kill—to have. Miles had come to their attention as a result of his genetic condition; his father, Kaiden Moore, and his uncle Vincent Moore had also been affiliated with The Network before he was born.

"Was that you yelling 'abort' earlier? I never forget a voice, James—James Bond." Miles looked at the driver and saw him smirk as he turned into the estate.

"Yeah that was me." He kept his eyes on the driveway.

"What's your real name? And when did y'all hijack my car's audio system?"

"You know I can't answer either question, Miles. Your father will brief you on everything you need to know."

Miles frowned as the car made its way up the hill toward his sprawling estate, past the manicured gardens and the Olympic-size swimming pool in the rear of the mansion. The driver turned off the motor and parked in the private garage while Miles pulled out his phone and called his father, Kaiden—or Cade as the family called him. He exited the car and took the elevator, which opened in the master bedroom at his home.

"Might as well get this over with now." He waited for his father to pick up.

"What took you all so long to get back home?" *Here come the questions.* Miles blew out a breath.

"Pops, we couldn't leave without answering some of the questions from the police, and the road was backed up because of the accident."

"Of course. I've already been briefed by the operative you left behind at the scene, but I was getting concerned when I didn't hear from you." Miles could hear his father's heavy breathing as he looked at the phone, waiting for the next question. "Son, are you alright?"

"Yes, Pops I'm fine, and before you ask, the answer is no. I'm not going to the doctor, but I have a question for you."

"What is it?" Cade asked.

"When did you authorize the surveillance on me? I'm not a little boy anymore, and I have my own security."

"I'm aware you're not a little boy Miles. Your mother, my wife, gave birth to you twenty-six years ago. One of the happiest days of my life."

"Quit stalling, Pops. I need some answers. I don't want to have my every move monitored, and my security team already follows me as close as I choose to be followed. The Network operatives don't take orders from me, and I won't be treated like a kid ever again."

"Where are you Miles? Are you alone so that we can talk freely?"

"Yes Pops, I'm alone in my bedroom." He placed the phone on his table and began taking off his clothes, down to his underwear. He threw the clothes, soiled with dirt, oil fumes, and sweat, on the floor; he was anxious to get the smells off of him. Darien had preset the temperature so his room would be a balmy 88 degrees when he arrived.

His chest was throbbing, as it had hit the steering wheel when he spun out of control, and he went to the mirror to view the light blue mark that covered the smooth brown skin on his breast bone. He rubbed the stubble on his chiseled jaw before examining his chest, broad and hardened by well-defined muscles.

"I'm waiting Pops. What happened that made the Network resume monitoring me closely?"

"Miles, I just found out that they were receiving intelligence reports that the paramilitary group, the Alt Knights, was sending a hit squad to kidnap or kill you if necessary, and I'm sorry that I didn't share it with you, but it was out of my hands. The Network insisted on following you, and I agreed with their call." Cade's tone of voice and the thud in the background as if his father had pounded a desk with his fist added to the gravity of the situation.

"I know you've got to take all information about the AKs seriously, but I've not known them to employ suicidal assassins. I agree Pops—this is different." He sat in a chair and continued the conversation.

"This wasn't a job for Bradley and the other members of your security team son. The Network had to step in to counter their moves."

"Pops, I've been giving this a lot of thought, and I think I should call a press conference and let the world know about my condition. I think the fact that we've tried to keep this a secret has made me more of a target."

"No Miles! Your disclosure is going to make you more of a target, and we shouldn't change the plans before your world tour. Can you imagine the amount of security we'll need on an international scale? And we won't be able to guarantee the safety of your fans."

Miles rubbed his chest again and scrunched his face, unable to deny the pain from the bruise on his chest.

"No, I don't want to jeopardize anyone's safety. I love my fans." His breath caught.

"Miles, are you sure you're alright?"

"Yeah Pops, it was a cramp in my leg that's all."

"Speaking of your fans, was that fan love that had you joyriding with those women? Darien told me you've been a little more demanding, crankier, and even more impulsive lately."

"No crankier than usual, and he knows how I get before a big tour. Did Darien share with you that sometimes he talks too much?"

"No Miles, but you may be proving his point." Miles let out another deep sigh.

"To set the record straight, I don't know those women. They were having a fanatic moment and chose to follow me. It was their impulsive behavior that could have gotten us all killed."

"Hmm, that's interesting, but it doesn't explain how the assassin knew they were following you. We'll do background checks on them. Who knows, they could have been working with the AKs—you're sure you've never met them before?"

"Not as I can recall Pops, but I was impressed at how well the driver handled her ride—like she was a pro driver."

"Well, we'll check on it and tell your new press agent...Bella is her name?"

"Yes, its Bella, she's my marketing and publicity consultant, and I'm not going to ask why you know her name." He chuckled.

"I've known you longer than you've known yourself Miles, and it's important how we handle this. You can't afford to be nonchalant about this…. Better yet, I'll tell Darien to communicate to Bella that this should be reported as if you were a good Samaritan, not a hero. You offered assistance to the young ladies because it was the right thing to do, and don't let anyone in your organization comment on the story after it's released to the public. We need to let this die before someone starts snooping around. The Network will make sure the story is buried in the back pages."

"Bella has me scheduled for a lot of events despite my protests, and now I'm back under the Network's thumb? I feel like I'm losing control of my life."

"Son, we need you to cooperate for now until we can infiltrate the AKs and find out their intent. Just act like it's business as usual and play it cool. I don't want to worry about you while you're on the road."

"Fine Pops. As usual, we'll do it *your* way." He rolled his eyes.

"And no more fireballs in public Miles—that we won't be able to explain."

"I had no choice Pops. It was either me, the girls, or the man in the car coming toward me."

"I know you had no choice Miles. I'm not criticizing but advising you."

"You won't have to worry about me." He rose from the chair and grabbed the phone. "Pops, I'll handle the spin on this situation after I talk to Bella." His cock twitched and tented his underwear as he spoke her name.

"Alright, you talk to Bella, but I need to talk to Bradley about this. Goodbye Miles, I love you son." There was silence as he looked at his cock thickening.

This has been a weird day.

"Miles are you still there?"

"Yeah, Pops. Love you and say hello to Mami and the girls."

"Tell her yourself. You should call your mother sometimes to say hello. She worries about you too."

"Bye Pops." He didn't want to get into it now with his father that he had made the hard decision to distance himself from his mother and his sisters for their safety and also to live his life on his own terms.

"Goodbye son."

Miles ended the call and placed the phone back on the desk before heading to the bathroom for a long shower. Afterward, he drank his hot toddy and sat back in one of the chairs in his bedroom to close his eyes for a few minutes but fell asleep unintentionally. When he woke up, he was relieved to find that his throat felt better. He got up and dressed in a tailored polo-styled white shirt, a pair of casual shorts, and sandals.

"Miles?" A voice called from outside was followed by a knock, and he turned his head toward the door.

"You're late for our meeting." It was Parker Middleton, his business manager and chief financial officer.

"I'm coming, Parker."

"Please don't keep us waiting Miles, and by the way, NeNe has been trying to get in touch with you. She said she'll be in town before the end of the week."

Miles pulled out the phone flashing in his pocket and NeNe's name came up on the screen.

"It's NeNe." He sighed and placed the phone back in his pocket before taking care of business in the bathroom.

"She'll have to wait. Nature calls."

After washing his hands, he came out of the bathroom and there was another knock at the door.

"Miles, what's taking you so long? I'm not coming back to remind you again. We need you downstairs in the study."

"I heard you the first time, Parker." He placed the magazine he'd been reading in the bathroom, on his desk.

"I'll be downstairs waiting for you. There's a line forming of people who need to talk to you. NeNe called again. She said she was having trouble reaching you." He listened to the sound of Parker's footsteps as he retreated from the door. Parker didn't know about his genetic condition or about his family's connection with the Network, so he decided not to share the morning's events with him. He would give Darien and Bella the briefest rundown possible later and they would handle it.

No harm, no foul.

He decided he'd better call his cousin, NeNe Moore, before he went downstairs to the meeting. It wasn't a stretch that she would call for an all-points bulletin on him. He took a deep breath before dialing her number.

I don't know what she wants, but she'll understand I'm busy and need to get back to work.

He placed the phone on speaker and let it ring. He breathed a sigh of relief when she didn't immediately answer. He was off the hook—at least for now. NeNe never let her phone ring more than three times before it went to voicemail. He prepared to leave a message letting her know he was in a meeting and would check with her later. In fact, he planned to give her plenty of time to forget the idea she needed to check on him.

"Hello, Miles, is that you?"

He took a deep breath before answering her question and decided to take control of the conversation, since there was no way to redirect NeNe once she decided he needed her help. He knew she was patient with him, despite the storms of his fiery temper, which often collided with her take-charge personality.

"Yes, NeNe, it's me. What rumors are you hearing about me now? I can answer any concerns you have over the phone."

"I need to discuss my concerns with you in person Miles." He paced as he held the phone to his ear.

"We aren't kids anymore, and you don't need to come across the country to check on me. You know I'm preparing for a world tour with my band, and I'm sorry, but I probably won't be able to spend much time with you. In fact, my people are waiting for me right now. I'll call you later."

"Miles Aridio Moore." Her tone stopped him before he could hang up. "This is serious, and I'm concerned about you. I've already talked to your people, and I know you won't be leaving before the end of the month. My plans are made, and I'll see you soon. Goodbye."

"NeNe!"

There was no answer from the other end of the phone.

He ended the call, still uncertain of what or who had NeNe so concerned about him that she would leave the comfort of her home and career in New York to come to California. She knew he didn't like uninvited guests, and he'd reminded her numerous times that he liked the distance from the family. It was the main reason why he'd moved out west to one of the homes owned by his parents. His parents were satisfied with the excuse that it was easier to launch his tours from the West Coast than the East Coast. If they checked his tour dates, they would've known most of his tours overseas often extended to Europe instead of Asia. He wasn't going to give too much thought to the possibility that maybe his parents needed a break from him more than he needed a break from them. Maybe that was why they'd given the property to him when he first started out.

Parker's voice came from downstairs. "Miles, you're paying people to look at each other. Get your ass down here, man."

"Parker you're getting on my nerves." He yelled back at him. They had known one another since they were boys and had been best friends since their college days, when he'd been an engineering student and Parker had been a business major.

He turned his attention to those waiting for him downstairs and headed for the door.

Wasn't he the one always reminding others he could take the heat? His declaration at this point was debatable, since he couldn't recall the urgency for all these damn meetings.

Eventually it dawned on him that Parker had reminded him last night that he needed to talk about the revenue projections and to get him to sign off on all the merchandising contracts for the tour. He hadn't pressed it, but he thought they were things Parker was accustomed to handling without him. He entered the room and Parker was seated at the table by himself.

"Where are the other team members?"

"We don't have time for bullshit, Miles. They left to attend to things since this wouldn't have been the first time you stood us up to get laid."

"You're mistaken buddy. I wasn't getting laid, and that's why I'm paying all of them to handle things, isn't it?" Parker bristled at Miles's cavalier attitude and laid his hands on the table.

"Miles, you gotta stop this, buddy. Your behavior is costing me lost time and your money."

"Like I said, that's why I have you, my friend, to keep an eye on the money and..." He lowered his eyes. "I'm sorry this time about making you wait. Is there something else before I leave?"

Parker looked at him, unaccustomed to Miles being contrite about anything.

"Yes, and I'll be direct with you Miles. I'm monitoring the expenses for this tour, which is growing, and on my way over here, I got a call from Bradley that he needs more money for security." He pulled out his pen and pushed the spreadsheet in front of him for Miles to review.

"Give it to him. If he says he needs it, he needs it." Miles looked at the report and shrugged.

"I'll need to shift some money around, and in the past, I would have done it without discussing it with you, but Darien said you've been complaining lately about all the changes and that we're not keeping you in the loop. Your little organization has grown, buddy, and it's becoming difficult to tell you everything that goes on around here, but I agree, we can do better."

"I guess I need to get used to the growing pains. AriMusic is no longer a small operation." He rubbed his chest and his lips tightened.

"You okay?" Parker frowned. "You've been working hard preparing for this tour—maybe too hard."

"I had a longer workout at the gym and I'm sore, that's all." Miles smiled to reassure him, and Parker leaned forward and narrowed his eyes. Miles could tell he wasn't buying his explanation. Parker had a way of seeing through him—but he was better at distracting Parker.

"I want more fire in the shows." He sat back and waited for a response.

"I'm glad you brought it up Miles, and this is a good a time to discuss that. First, there's the cost of more special effects and there are safety issues. I know you're going to say that's why we hired Chief Wahlberg as a fire safety consultant for the tour, right?"

"Yeah, so we're addressing the safety issues." He nodded.

"It's out of my field of expertise, but I know our pyro-technical guys devise and set up designs that come out of your twisted mind, and we can push the limits because Chief Wahlberg lets us know what is and isn't safe. She's good at what she does."

"Every tour has had costs overruns, and The Fire God Tour is no different. You know that better than I do, and I've addressed the safety issues…so what else is it Parker?"

"Why are you agreeing to play venues in cities with terrorist threats, especially since you're going to need more security?"

"The answer is simple. I have a growing fan base in those cities, and I go where my fans are." He crossed his arms over his chest and sat back in his chair.

"I guess there's no convincing you to limit your appearances." Parker tapped his pen on the table.

"Not unless you want to waste your time. Anything else?"

"Yes, there's one more thing." He cleared his throat, "It has to do with Bella."

"What about Bella?" Caught off guard, Miles raised an eyebrow.

"Since she's been working here, she's proven herself to be competent, smart with great marketing ideas, and a kind woman. She came up with the idea of having a charity gala to kick off the world tour. Instead of contributing your own money to charity, she lined up sponsors who made large donations just to talk to you at the meet and greet. The money we're getting from the gala will cover the usual obligations to your charities and some of the tour costs."

Miles raised his hands to his face, tenting his fingers and covering his mouth, then leaned back in his chair.

"Again, what's your point?"

"My point is you need to stop antagonizing her. Dammit, you speak three different languages. You're the one who hired her, so I don't understand why you can't remember the name Bella? Not Elsa or Belsa. And stop whistling Disney tunes when she's around."

"You have to admit the tunes are catchy. Is it my fault Bella has the warmth of an ice cube? She's frozen."

"I'm just asking that you treat her like the professional she is. She brings a lot to the team."

"Fine, I'll treat her like I treat the rest of you who walk around here like you have a hot poker up your ass. My conversations with her will be limited to the numbers, the optics related to her ideas, and projections. Nothing more."

"I'm glad we had a chance to talk about Bella. I'll see you tomorrow. Bye."

"Bye Parker." Miles looked at him and grunted as he walked out the door. He shifted his thoughts to the bevy of beauties Darien had scheduled for dates leading up to the start of the tour to distract himself from the events earlier in the day, but he remembers that he had planned to hit the town tonight for nonstop partying in downtown LA. Who knew what adventures the night held for him?

Parker's right. I've been working hard, and maybe spending time with the ladies will help reduce my stress.

In the meantime, he still had a couple of hours before he got dressed for the night, so he decided to get out of the house and enjoy the afternoon on a nature walk with his favorite buddy, his dog Bosco, a half collie and German shepherd mix.

Miles awoke in his own bed alone at his estate, instead of the bed in his penthouse apartment downtown. His date last night at the party had been beautiful and sexually appealing, but his desire to have sex with her was just not there. He stretched and rubbed his chest. The over-the-counter pain med he bought from the drugstore had kicked in and he was no longer sore.

He recognized that for the past week he hadn't been his usual uptight and intense Ari persona who kept everyone hopping just before the start of a tour. Especially when Bella was at work at the estate, he didn't like scantily clad women walking around the house. He even waited for Reagan Madison, his principal dancer on the tour, and Darien to finish their yoga practice with Bella before starting rehearsals one morning. They all knew he didn't wait for anyone, but he had to admit rehearsals went smoother and were more enjoyable when the dancers were more relaxed after meditation and yoga. Parker had given the approval to pay for yoga instructors after Bella discussed the benefits of a calmer environment with him, and Miles had agreed to the changes. He was the last one to argue with success, and he had to admit he was more creative when he wasn't raging at others or creating his own intense atmosphere. Even Bosco was more relaxed and growled less when he didn't want to take a bath.

Bella had clearly impacted the way he did business. Last week, he'd had to hide his growing erection in a meeting with her. She'd been discussing figures with him, and all he'd thought about was *her* naked figure.

Hell, his erection was growing thicker and harder as he thought about her now. He shook his head to bring himself back to reality. He knew she had a boyfriend, and while she was attractive in an academic sort of way, he realized she would never be happy in a relationship with a player like him, and he wasn't a man who could commit to one woman. He needed to remember that. Before Bella had come into his life as a business consultant, he'd loved his freedom to come and go as he chose and make his own decisions. He never felt the need to question the morality of his behavior.

I'm a single man in my prime. He looked up at the ceiling and quickly shook off the idea of changing how often he satisfied his libido before throwing back the covers and heading to the bathroom for a shower. He needed to cool off and stop thinking about Bella in order to calm down his cock, which was growing harder.

What? Bella turning me on? I must be working too hard.

He turned on the water, and instead of his normal steaming hot shower, he intentionally kept the water cool. He jumped in and let the water stream down his body.

For a fleeting moment, he considered his need for sexual variety. Could he ever change his ways and give his heart to only one woman? He'd never before questioned the fact that he had an insatiable desire for sex with multiple partners. Was it possible his priorities were changing? He smiled as he compared his pleasure with multiple partners to his enjoyment of multiple flavors of ice cream. He liked his women sometimes hard, sometimes soft, sometimes sweet or maybe strong as chocolate, sometimes sticky and dripping off him. He scrubbed his body with his favorite body wash.

He had to admit his thoughts on women were changing, and what was previously very important to him no longer mattered as much. Women were once only objects of pleasure to him—but maybe, not anymore.

CHAPTER TWO

It was times like these Bella knew she needed a best friend her age. She and Reagan, the lead dancer at AriMusic, with her sunburst of tightly coiled curls crowning her head and her lean, graceful body, had grown close since Bella started consulting with Ari's company, but she didn't feel comfortable sharing her deepest feelings about working there, especially her feelings about Ari Moore. Chief Joan Wahlberg was her mother and had also been her best friend as far back as her adolescent years. Her mother knew Ari better than she did, and she needed her advice about the mercurial Ari, who seemed more subdued ever since he'd shared the news about the road rage incident, he was caught in days ago. Baffled that he didn't want her to grant requests for interviews about the incident, she stopped asking questions about it.

"Let's stay focused on the music," he'd responded the last time she'd asked, and it also peaked her curiosity that he didn't want her to contact the women involved after he helped pay for their medical expenses.

"Miles, they wanted to say thank you and that's it," she'd relayed.

"No more meetings Bella. Please." She'd agreed, not wanting to add to his stress. *At least I got him to sign the get well soon cards.*

Bella looked at her reflection as she passed the mirror in her bedroom. Like her mother, she was a curvy girl with a svelte waist and well-toned legs. She'd inherited her proud chin, bronze skin, and thick, long hair from her father, who'd been of Scottish and Native American descent. Back in Texas, she was known as the daughter of Chief John Wahlberg and Assistant Chief Joan Wahlberg. John, a striking physical contrast to Joan, had been built solid, with a ruddy complexion and straight black hair. He'd commanded attention when he'd entered a room: tall, self-assured, and muscular. His voice had boomed, hiding his gentle heart and the tenderness he'd reserved for his wife and daughter. Her mother was tall, with long legs and delicate features. She'd been a Texas beauty in her day, with mocha-colored smooth skin and thick curly hair she still wore just above her shoulders.

"Bella, come and get your breakfast."

Her mother's voice broke through her recollections while she placed the final touches on her hair and light makeup.

Game face on.

She patted her stomach and hurried out of the bathroom as the smell of food cooking was causing her stomach to growl.

"I'll be there in a few minutes."

She stood in the center of her bedroom, unsure where she last saw her hiking boots. She looked around the gilded shrine to her father, a connection to a time long ago when she'd felt safe and protected. She loved the warm memories of being showered with kisses on both cheeks by her parents.

One wall of her room held the trophies she had won as a junior archer, a skill her father had taught her, and next to those was a collage of pictures of her and her father spending some of the most memorable times of her life together. There were pictures of her with white paint on her cheeks and nose, pictures of her father hugging her, and pictures of the two of them admiring their finished project. She teared up a little as she looked at the pink and white silken fabric on the canopy, in the shape of a golden crown hanging high above her bed; that her father had designed.

Mom has really been on me about renovating my room. I guess she doesn't understand that I worry about losing my memories of Dad. She always says we need to move on with our lives, but she hasn't had a date in the years since he died.

She shrugged her shoulders and continued searching. She finally saw the brown boots that matched her hiking outfit on the other side of the bed and placed them on her feet, before walking out of the room to join her mother in the kitchen, which was brightened by streams of yellow sunlight. Her mother stood at the center island, wearing her robe over a black A-line dress with matching black pumps.

"Good morning sweetheart. I woke up with a taste for pancakes and bacon, and if I say so myself, they are good. I left a few pancakes on top of the stove if you want some."

"Good morning, Mom, but no thanks. I'll have my usual smoothie."

"Suit yourself. I finished cutting the kale, and the pineapple and apple slices are in the refrigerator. Did you leave a note in my room telling me we needed to talk? I hope you're ready to submit the plans to renovate your room. You've had plenty of time to think about it," Joan reminded her as she finished wiping down the center island.

Enough already about my room, Mom. It's my private space, and it will look the way I want it to look. She took a deep breath. *Hold your peace. You need her help, not an argument.* "It's not about the room Mom. Did you sleep well last night?" She poured them both a cup of coffee from the hot pot on the table. The aroma filled the room with the smell of hazelnut. Joan joined her and sat at the table. Bella hadn't told her mother about her plans to go over to Ari's house this morning at Darien's request, but before then, she needed to talk to her about him.

"I did, and it's a good thing I got some rest. I have two meetings scheduled for today, one of them out of town, remember?" Joan stirred her coffee.

"Yes but, I need your advice, and this shouldn't take long." Bella poured a little cream in her coffee and stirred it while she spoke. "You know Ari, and he respects and admires you. Maybe you can help me work better with him. I'm really not comfortable with the way he's treating me."

"So, this isn't about your room?" She sipped the coffee from her cup as Bella averted her gaze and looked into her coffee.

"No, but I promise I'll decide on new colors soon."

"What's it about then? Are you being harassed?" Joan looked up, concerned.

"No, it's not that. It's the little things he does."

"Does he disrespect you or demean you in any way? Or does he discount your advice or belittle the recommendations you make in the meetings?"

"No, it's not that either. He has taken my advice on many occasions over the recommendations of his friends and closest advisors."

"I see you working hard at home, and I know you always go beyond expectations for your clients. So, what is it?" Joan asked, perplexed.

"For the first six months of my contract with him, he called me Belsa or Elsa, and once I heard him call me 'the frozen princess.'"

"Is there anything else? Have you asked him to stop it since it bothers you?"

"I didn't have to ask him to stop it. He stopped doing things like that suddenly a few days ago. It's just that the easygoing banter he has with others around the house is absent in our encounters. He keeps it professional, yet he always seems to be interacting with me at a distance. Even Bosco pays more attention to me than Ari."

"I think it's best to maintain a professional distance with Miles. He's very busy right now, and he may realize it's best to maintain firm boundaries with his consultants. He has to make physical contact with the dancers; it's a part of his job. Other than his cousin and lawyer, NeNe Moore, there aren't any other women in his close professional circle." She placed her elbows on the table and leaned forward.

"I need to share something with you, Bella." Joan pulled her chair closer and placed a hand on top of Bella's as she spoke her concerns.

"I wouldn't label Miles a pyromaniac, but he has a preoccupation with fire, and he doesn't need to know you're afraid of it. Let's maintain some discretion about it. You're doing a good job promoting the tour, and he has complimented you many times. I'm sorry I didn't share this with you earlier." Bella furrowed her brow in response to her mother's advice.

"I can't imagine that my fear of fire would come up in usual conversation."

"I don't either, but he's quite perceptive and can be difficult, but he isn't a mean man. I'm certain he meant no disrespect to you. In fact, he hasn't hidden his appetite for women, and let's face it, Miles Moore knows how to seduce women."

"It's not like I'm romantically interested in Ari. I just want to have a better working relationship with him."

"I'm glad to hear you want to keep it professional. Don't you have a date with Corey today?" She noticed her mother had tried to change the subject and was hastily rising from the table to place her dishes in the dishwasher.

"I didn't tell you that Darien called to ask me to swing by the estate and scan missing contract papers to him. He's very busy, and I don't mind doing it for him. Darien and I have become good friends, and besides, Corey needed more time to prepare for the upcoming acquisitions of two additional stores and to complete inventory of the merchandise. He's okay with changing the time to start our hike later this morning and to go on a shorter hike. Darien is sending a driver to take me to Ari's. I'll scan the documents, and Corey will pick me up from there."

"Why don't you call him Miles instead of Ari? All of his friends and family call him Miles. He'll probably let his guard down a little if you refer to him by that name. I've been calling him Miles for a while."

"Thanks, Mom. I want to get a good recommendation from Ari—I mean Miles. It's easy for me to call him Ari because it reminds me, he's a charismatic public figure, and I should expect to see different women surrounding him at his home. He's a bit too temperamental for my comfort, but I can't deny his talent, his refusal to sing misogynistic lyrics, and his outstanding showmanship. He's the real deal, and I should be grateful I at least have a good working relationship with the guys in his inner circle."

"Let me know Bella if I can help in any way. I need to get out of here to get to my meetings on time." Joan kissed her and gave her a supportive hug before departing, and Bella cleaned up the kitchen a little before the driver arrived. She hoped only a few members of Miles's staff at the estate would be on duty today, since this was her day off and she was in her hiking gear. She turned on her computer, reviewed her documents, and sent out a few emails in preparation for the meeting early next week, with Miles and his executive team.

Maybe her mother was right. She shouldn't worry about his cool demeanor. She wasn't attracted to him, and he would never be attracted to someone like her. She saw him as just another rich man; one who was used to having his way with women. He probably changed his female companions more often than he changed his underwear. She chuckled at her assessment of Miles and their relationship with one another. She was growing comfortable with the thought that, as long as the quality of her work remained above reproach, she would have a job.

She powered down her computer in time to see her phone buzzing with a message: the limo driver was minutes away. She locked up the house just as the driver pulled up and she waited while he parked and got out of the car to open the door for her.

"Thank you." She got in and sighed, feeling torn that she had work to do on her day off instead of enjoying a long hike; yet also wanting to be seen as a team player. She resolved that even though she'd agreed to do this favor for Darien, she would accomplish it as quickly as possible so she could get out and enjoy nature.

She loved hiking, and even though Corey often spent their time together talking about the store or himself, she enjoyed having someone on the trail with her. She'd learned to tune him out when she wanted to enjoy her own thoughts without leaving him concerned, she wasn't listening to him.

"Bella are you listening to me?" he'd asked the last time they'd hiked. She discovered that repeating his last statement was often enough to make him think she was listening and even interested in what he was saying. *Men can be so self-absorbed.*

The car arrived at the estate quicker than she expected. She was happy traffic was relatively light. The butler, Mr. Curtis, dressed in a black suit with a starched white shirt, dark tie, and spit-shined black shoes, greeted her at the door. She sensed he disapproved of her casual attire as he looked her over, jutting out his chin, and gave her a loud sniff.

"Good morning, Bella. Darien left instructions to take you to Miles's bedroom to get the papers."

She hesitated a bit but followed him as he walked up the stairs to the space regarded as off limits.

"This is quite unusual, since Mr. Moore rarely allows employees other than Parker, Darien, or myself in his personal space, but I was assured it would be okay for you to go into his private suite of rooms to search for the contracts in question."

She was also uncomfortable being in Miles's private space, but Darien had been frantic when he'd called. He knew NeNe would be angry if all the documents weren't there for her review even if she was on a conference call with them and not there in person. He assured her Miles wouldn't be at the house and he would handle any fallout if he discovered she had been in his bedroom without his permission.

"He had a date last night and planned to stay at his penthouse in the city," Darien had assured her on the phone before she'd agreed to do him the favor.

Bella and Mr. Curtis were at the top of the stairs when she began wondering if changing her plans with Corey was such a good idea. She liked the hardware store entrepreneur and was glad things were working out between them. He seemed okay with her work obligations in general, but she shrugged at the gnawing idea that Corey might not be okay with anything out of the ordinary at AriMusic, especially if it involved close collaborations with its CEO.

Mr. Curtis opened the door to the bedroom, and she took in the view of the massive mahogany bed, with etches of rams carved into the posts. Tastefully decorated, the room had touches of black and bold red accents. There was a very masculine feel to the room. A massive fireplace covered one entire wall, and there were windows on two walls, which allowed for an impressive view of the city. She entered the space alone to search the room, as Mr. Curtis had retreated down the stairs.

Money can buy many things, but it's a pity his views are now marred by the wildfires where thick forests once stood. She shuddered at the reminder of the devastating effects of fire.

Looking around the room, she discovered his desk with papers on top of it. What piqued her curiosity was the old-style lamp filled with oil next to an ornate candle on his desk. There was also a container filled with individually wrapped mounds of red wax, and a heavy metal seal located beside the mounds of wax had an impression of a ram carved in it at the bottom. She began looking for the papers Darien had asked her to find and didn't notice the bathroom door opening or the presence of someone else in the room.

"What the fu—" The loud verbal bomb startled her, causing her to spin around and throw the papers in the air.

Miles abruptly cut off the f-bomb and stood still, a few feet away from her, while she froze as she viewed his nude body. She knew he had a great body, but she'd never imagined she would meet Adonis in this lifetime. His beautiful pecs, six-pack abs, and oh, his large cock, even in a flaccid state, and his thick muscular legs had her face feeling hot and her heart racing.

"Why are you here, Bella?" He initially made no effort to cover himself.

The papers scattered across the floor, blown by the air currents from the ceiling fan whirling above. She broke her gaze, embarrassed by the impropriety of their meeting, and knelt to pick up the papers.

"Darien asked for a favor, and he said you wouldn't be at home. He needed these papers for a meeting later today," she stammered and tried but couldn't hide her tremulous voice or the shaking of her hands as she tried to gather the papers.

Surely the sight of a naked man should've caused little Miss Goody Two-Shoes to flee down the canyon, frightened out of her wits.

He was surprised; he'd underestimated her. However, he didn't miss her appraising look at him before she quickly turned away.

Oblivious to the discomfort he'd caused her by his nakedness—and too busy fantasizing about how pleasurable it would be if she dropped to her knees for him—he continued to stand before her naked. He had never seen her in tight shorts before, and her current position gave him the opportunity to observe the tops of her full breasts in her tank top, but his growing cock brought him back to reality. He grabbed the towel around his neck and wrapped it around his waist while she rose to her feet.

"This is…so embarrassing," she stumbled over her words.

Blushing and attempting to make the situation a little less awkward for her, he knew he had to explain his part in the misunderstanding.

"I just got back from downtown and came up the back stairway. I came directly to my room and was finishing my shower when I thought I heard someone in the space and didn't hear a knock at the door. I'm sorry about my irritation, but no one comes to my room without permission. This is my private space. It's where I come to unwind."

He smoothed off the droplets of water on his chest, which glistened in the rays of sunlight streaming into the room.

"Since you're here, maybe we could use this as an opportunity to go over some marketing ideas about the tour after I get more presentable?"

Yes, she likes talking about marketing, but damn if this isn't awkward. He raked his hand through his hair as he waited for her to answer, but she didn't.

"I have some questions for you—if you could give me a moment to get dressed?"

This time she looked up at him.

"I'm sorry I didn't knock before I entered your private space, but Mr. Curtis let me in. I'll finish gathering the papers, and we can talk downstairs." She let out a breath and took a few steps away from him.

"Let me put some clothes on and I'll be down shortly."

"Alright, I'll wait for you."

"I won't be long." He turned and hurried to get dressed.

She looked around and hoped she had gathered the papers scattered throughout the room despite her trembling hands, which betrayed her attempts to remain calm and in control. Her vision was blurred with panic that her actions would either cost her the contract with Ari or cost Darien his job. She knew he could be ruthless and unforgiving, even if his outward demeanor was calm, and she was aware how much he guarded his privacy.

"Everyone knows not to go in Miles's rooms!" she mumbled, angry with herself and Darien for talking her into something that was obviously a mistake.

She was surprised again by Miles, who returned to the bedroom, wearing a shirt and casual pants, before she could escape downstairs to scan the documents.

"I need to get these to Darien before my friend Corey Baker comes for me. I'm not sure how long we'll have to talk about things before he arrives, but I'll have my phone with me if you want to send your questions." She smoothed back her hair, a little flustered by the continuation of their unexpected encounter and began backing away. She hurried to the door and hoped Corey had arrived to take her on a much-needed nature break.

"Wait, I'll meet you downstairs after I find my belt and put on my shoes. We can wait for your friend to arrive, and you can introduce the two of us. I'll have the staff provide us with something to eat or drink if you would like. Or, if that doesn't work for you, maybe we can talk business later. Are you free this evening? We can talk then."

She hesitated before replying to his request and shifted her weight on unsteady feet as she stood before him. He was looking at her as if he could see right through her. She held the papers in front of her to hide her anxieties.

"I'm free tonight. My boyfriend will be busy going over inventory and acquisition reports probably for the next few weeks." She frowned before she caught herself giving up too much information.

"So, this Corey is your boyfriend?" He raised his eyebrows.

"Well, yes."

"I see. What about your mother? Could she join us for dinner—in preparation for the tour of course?"

"She went to a fire safety meeting, and then she has plans to fly out to Texas for a presentation and bid on a new contract. She's been very busy."

"So, it will be just the two of us then." He leaned forward and waited for her response.

"Yes, just the two of us, unless Darien or Parker will be joining us?"

"No, they can't make it; too many contracts to finalize. I'll tell Mr. Curtis to prepare a meal."

Her cell buzzed in her pocket. She held her index finger in the air to signify she needed a moment to answer the text before pulling out her phone. Corey was outside.

"Will seven o'clock tonight work for you? Corey and I are going on a short hike this morning. It shouldn't last more than a couple hours."

Although his eyes hadn't left her, she noticed he'd widened the space between them.

"Yes, seven o'clock will work for me, and please accept my apologies again if I startled you. I hope you didn't find my nudity offensive."

She sighed; a bit relieved by his attempts to make their encounter feel less difficult.

"I accept your apology, Miles. I'd better get going," she reminded him before scurrying out of the room.

CHAPTER THREE

Corey was seated in the sitting room off the foyer after she finished scanning the documents.

"Good, you're here."

"A staff member said you were expecting me and let me in through the security gate."

He rose to meet her, dressed in a light blue polo-styled shirt, khaki shorts, and hiking boots. He placed his hand on her elbow and directed her toward the door before she had a chance to tell him of the brief meeting with Miles.

"Corey, if you can give me a moment, I need to tell Miles the documents were successfully scanned. Remember, I told you I needed to scan some documents for Darien. He'll be downstairs shortly. Do you want something to drink in the meantime?" She motioned toward the bar, where a glass pitcher filled with water, ice, and assorted citrus fruits had been placed.

"Bella, my time is important too. No, I don't want something to drink. Doesn't he have enough people on staff to check if his documents scanned successfully? Have I ever asked you to scan documents for me or to do things for my stores outside of promotions?"

She cocked her head and gave him the *do you really want me to answer that* look.

"It's not like I work for you, Corey, and I wouldn't have done it if someone else could have handled it." She blinked her eyes and pursed her lips while he backed away and said nothing further. Hearing someone, probably Miles descending the stairs, she turned her head and hoped he hadn't overheard their conversation. They were standing in front of each other when he entered the room, but the tension remained.

"Welcome to my home. I'm Ari Moore but call me Miles. You must be Corey."

"Yes, Corey Baker is my name." Corey motioned to give him a fist bump, but Miles kept his palm open for a traditional handshake. Bella looked at the awkward exchange as Corey shook Miles's hand.

"Hey, bro, I hear you're a famous rapper."

She mouthed a silent question to Corey. *What are you doing*?

Miles had turned to receive a cup of hot tea with lemon and honey from Mr. Curtis, who'd entered the room after him. She had seen him drink a lot of tea to coat his throat in preparation for one of his concerts.

"I hear you're a shopkeeper," Miles responded between sips of his tea. He sat down in a large chair near them and crossed his legs. His cool demeanor emphasized his position as master of this estate.

"I own my own stores," Corey told him. "I built them from the ground up." He jutted his chin in the air.

"Shopkeeper indeed." Corey curled his lips, smiling contemptuously as he looked at Miles, unaware that Bella was frowning beside him.

The muscles in her shoulders tensed as she witnessed the verbal volley between the two men. She knew they both worked hard and were proud of their businesses, built with a lot of toil and dedication.

I thought they would get along better than this. Looking at both of them, she saw them as men driven by their passion for their businesses.

"I plan to franchise my stores up and down the West Coast. As a matter of fact, I'm finishing the acquisition of several new stores this month."

"You should be proud of your accomplishments. I'm proud that I built my entertainment enterprise, AriMusic, from the ground up. It's hard work being a business owner."

She was relieved Miles had chosen to take the high road with Corey, whose cash flow didn't come close to his income from one large concert.

She took Corey by the hand, leading him toward the door.

"Miles, the contracts scanned successfully, and Darien should have them for the meeting this afternoon."

She hoped he wouldn't mention she would be meeting with him tonight, and before she could continue the conversation, she felt her phone buzz in her left pocket again and pulled it out. It was a text from Darien.

```
Darien: Thanks. Got the
documents. Sorry about encounter
with Miles. He called minutes
ago to tell me what happened. He
isn't angry about finding you in
his bedroom. He's planning
something informal so wear
something casual tonight. You
agreed to meet him for dinner at
seven o'clock tonight, right?
Wear something black.

Bella: Yes, to dinner & MYOB

Darien: I do mind my own
business and my friends R my
business.
```

She looked up at Miles and sighed. Dropping her shoulders before releasing her lower lip from between her teeth, she was relieved he didn't want to provoke Corey by telling him about their meeting as payback for the way he had antagonized him. She planned to talk to Corey about the encounter. *Why did he need to act like that with Miles?*

"We'd better get going. See you later."

"Yes, see you—"

She shook her head to interrupt him.

"Enjoy your hike, the two of you."

"Thanks Miles."

She quickly led Corey to the door and closed it behind them.

Corey talked about his stores the entire time they were hiking the Santa Monica mountains, with its rolling hills, and she was glad he wanted to cut their hike short. When they got in the car for the drive back to her place, she used the time to voice her feelings.

"I didn't appreciate your behavior this morning with Miles. Not only is his contract with my mother's firm important to our family, I'm working hard to build my own clientele. You know how much I want my own marketing firm someday. Ari is a big fish; he can really help me build my career."

Corey kept his eyes on the road, nodded in agreement, but said very little.

"I'm supportive of your business aspirations, and I know how much you want a chain of hardware stores. I support your dreams, and I expect you to do the same for me. I would never be rude to one of your customers or potential investors, so please don't be rude to my clients." She sat back in her seat and crossed her arms.

"I understand your ambition, Bella, but why am I the villain here? I can't believe you're calling me rude. Have you listened to some of Ari's lyrics? I don't care if he was acting like a gentleman today. He uses a lot of profanity; are you telling me he can say whatever he wants because he's a rapper? Why do you even work for NMM, new money Miles?" He threw his head back and let out a hearty laugh.

"You know I don't like when you call him that." She jerked her head and narrowed her eyes, shooting daggers at him.

"You may not like Miles, but you don't have to be a snob. Miles's family has money, but unlike your—you, they don't feel the need to flaunt it."

"Fine, Bella. You don't have to involve my family in this. All I'm asking is why can't your mother work for him while you focus on building your own clientele?"

She took a deep breath, trying to remain calm. She knew this was a conversation they needed to have.

"Ari...Miles is the real thing. He owns his own record company. He's a lyricist, a singer, a rapper, a musician, and a multi-millionaire. He has a degree in mechanical engineering and has multiple patents. And did I forget to mention...he pays really well?"

He clutched the wheel of the car; his eyes narrowed, and he drew his jaw tight. After pulling up in front of her house, he jerked the car into park before cutting the engine and turned to look at her. His chest heaved as he managed to get out his words. "Are you sleeping with him? I need to know the truth." He searched her eyes for answers.

"I'm not sleeping with Miles. We're not each other's type. I have a professional relationship with him and nothing else. You have no reason to be jealous or to falsely accuse me." She kept eye contact with him, refusing to back down from an uncomfortable discussion.

"I'm not accusing you of anything, but I needed to know the truth. You've always been honest with me, and I believe you. I'll work on being polite to him. Maybe I'm a little jealous of him, but I still think you should end your professional relationship with him when he goes on tour."

"Corey, I respect your opinion, but the decisions about the terms of my professional relationship with Miles aren't yours to make. You know, your focus should be on getting through your big acquisitions and inventory this month."

His mood shifted now that she had returned the focus back to the stores.

"Yes, I'm looking forward to reviewing the papers tonight. I'll be busier most of this month. Do you mind if we touch base with each other by phone next week?"

"That sounds like a plan. I'll be very busy this week too."

She leaned over to give him a chaste kiss on the lips, since both were sweaty from their morning hike.

"Goodbye Bella." He stroked her arm and smiled.

"Goodnight Corey." She opened the door of the car and went into the house as he pulled away from the curb.

Her stomach growled and she headed for the kitchen, where she saw a note her mother had left on the refrigerator, telling her she'd left early for the airport and promising to text her when she arrived in Texas.

Looking at the time on her phone, she saw she still had a few hours before she got together with Miles. Darien had sent her a text while she was out hiking to remind her of the agreed-upon time. She smiled slowly, becoming excited about her evening with Ari as she opened the refrigerator and pulled out food for a light snack before she sat to review the research notes she'd left on the table that morning. She knew her plans for fan giveaways, merchandise options, and media appearances were good. She planned to discuss a new option called Where's Ari, to tap into the fan craze of dressing up like Ari and uploading the photos in Ari attire to a thread on the AriMusic site. Fans would pick the person most resembling Ari, who would then receive a weekly fan pack of AriMusic merchandise. She hoped he liked the idea.

Her attention to her work was broken by a text she received from her mother, telling her she had arrived safely. The text came with an attachment giving her information on the hotel and the conference site.

Engrossed in her reviews of data about the tour, she hadn't realized several hours had past. She looked at the time and stretched before she got up from her chair to go to her room; with just enough time to shower and change into her black skinny jeans with the matching black baby-doll top with a cold shoulder-cut design and new strappy sandals she'd purchased last week. She pulled her hair up in a high ponytail and rimmed her brown eyes in kohl-colored eyeliner and mascara for the popular smoky-eyed look. Darien had given her red lipstick in a swag bag from a promotional event; he thought the color would look great on her. She applied the lipstick, and the shade of red *was*

surprisingly attractive on her. She had seen Miles in black so often, she didn't have to wonder if he liked the color.

Is that why Darien encouraged me to wear black?

She shook her head no. This wasn't a date; it was a business meeting. She looked at her phone and reviewed the instructions Darien had sent earlier concerning the meeting:

```
Darien: The driver will pick you
up at 6:30 pm. A light dinner
with wine at the estate has been
planned, followed by a meeting
in the conference room to
discuss promotional plans. The
driver will also be available to
make sure you get back home
safely.
```

The sky was darkened by clouds as she looked out the window and waited for the driver, who showed up promptly and rang the doorbell. She gathered the bag containing her materials for her presentation and locked her door while he waited at the car beside the door he had opened for her. She had ridden to meetings with Miles on several occasions, but tonight, the car sent for her was more luxurious. The driver informed her that drinks were in compartments in the back seat while music played softly in the background throughout the ride to the estate. A song came on with a singer who sounded like Miles accompanied by only an acoustic guitar. The song was sweet, and, unlike his usual songs, it lacked hard driving beats and aggressive lyrics. She realized there was a lot she didn't know about him.

The driver reached the long driveway leading to the estate on top of the hill. She looked out the window and saw that black smoke stains still remained on the side of some of the houses abandoned by his neighbors.

"What a pity the fire destroyed so much of the landscape in the neighborhood," she commented to the driver as she surveyed the carbonized tree stumps and scars on the landscape from last year's fire.

"Yes, ma'am, it is unfortunate that the native plants, camellias, and the jacaranda trees were all destroyed. Some of the neighbors still haven't fully restored their homes."

The clouds were now darker, more ominous, and droplets of rain started to fall before she exited the car. Miles was standing in the doorway in black casual slacks, a dark gray shirt, and black designer moccasins to match. He came to the side of the parked car, took her into a light embrace, and led her into his home.

"You look great, Bella. It's nice seeing you in party attire. I hope you're hungry. My cook prepared a light dinner for us. We should eat before we discuss promotional details of the tour.

"Sounds good. I'm hungry, but you didn't have to go to so much trouble."

"It was no trouble at all, and I'm looking forward to hearing your ideas." He placed his hand on the small of her back to escort her to the dining room. She smiled but said nothing as a frisson of excitement ran down her spine at the touch of his hand. *Calm down girl. This is business!* She spoke once the tingling in her back where he touched her had subsided.

"An unplugged version of a song by you was playing in the car while I was riding over here. The hook of the song is "After the fire is over, you'll hurt no more."

He nodded. "The name of the song is 'No More.'"

"It is hauntingly beautiful. Did you write the lyrics? You should open at least some of the tour stops with that song. I can obtain some downloaded stats of where that piece is the most popular. It would be a great opening song."

"I like how you think, Bella." He nodded his head in approval. "You do your research, but you also understand the power of music to move people. Good music should evoke feelings."

Your touch seems to have the same power. "Thanks, I agree with you about the power of music to move people. Music is often used in marketing for that very reason."

She followed his lead as they walked into the dining room, and he offered her a seat at the table, set with a thick porcelain place setting and enough stemware for wine, champagne, or any drink of choice. She placed her bag on the chair next to the one she was seated in. Mr. Curtis came in the room, placed their meals on the table, and closed the door behind him to allow them privacy. After a meal of red snapper, fingerling potatoes, and vegetables, they had a few more glasses of wine.

"So Bella, what do you like to do besides hiking in your free time?" She looked up at him with a slight smile.

"I like listening to music, and I do pro bono work for a few charities."

"Do you like to go out dancing?" She looked at her hands, moist with sweat, and for a few seconds kept her eyes focused on her lap.

"I do like dancing even though I'm not good at it, and besides that, I don't get out much these days." She recalled the way Miles walked into a room, chose one of the dancers practicing her moves, and before long everyone was dancing and laughing. Corey, on the other hand, didn't like dancing. He preferred spending a quiet night together, just the two of them.

"Given the right music and the right partner, I'm sure you could burn up the dance floor too. We're young, Bella, and don't tell me you're too busy to enjoy life and have some fun." He placed his hand on the table on top of hers as she hesitated in responding to his question and looked down to hide her sadness.

"Did I say something wrong? Or am I getting too personal for your comfort?" He removed his hand and gave her a little more space.

"No, I'm glad we're getting to know one another a little better. Tell me, how do you spend your free time when you get it, Miles?"

"I like that you're finally calling me Miles." He flashed her a bright smile.

"Well, I like hopping on my bike and taking long rides to clear my head. Do you want to take our drinks to the conference room?"

"Sure, let me grab my bag." She smiled at him and he paused, looking at her.

"You have a very nice smile Bella. Sad that I don't get to see you smile more at work. While you gather your things, I'll take our glasses."

"Are you saying I don't smile when I'm at work? I wasn't aware that you only see my serious side." She grabbed her leather bag and followed him down the hall.

"I guess we've both been so busy that we forgot to enjoy our work and smile with the people around us."

"I do enjoy my work, Miles, and I promise I'll make more of an effort to be less reserved."

They entered the room, with a table large enough to spread out her marketing materials. She placed the bag on the table and pulled out a chair.

There were two large windows in the conference room, with the draperies pulled to the side to allow for maximum views of the hillside. A sharp bolt of lightning followed by the sounds of thunder caught her attention as rain began to pelt the windows. The wind started blowing, and charred underbrush passed by the window.

Drawn to the developing activity outside, Miles took her right hand and led her to view nature in a dance of fury outside the window. The lights in the room blinked temporarily, and despite the fierce drumming of her heart and her growing apprehension about standing in front of a large window during a thunderstorm, she remained in place. She raised her left hand and placed it on her chest to mute the thumps she swore could be heard throughout the room.

"Aren't the forces of nature fascinating?" He didn't see her left hand shaking at her side. The thunder roared and lightning struck two trees, causing them to burst into flames. The proximity of the strike led her to jerk abruptly away from the window. She bit her lips to stop them from quivering, and her palms grew sweaty as the rain continued to come down in a blinding fury. He didn't say anything but gave her hand a firm, supportive squeeze and stood there mesmerized and unable to move away from the window.

Her hands, moistened from sweat, slipped out of his grasp with ease and she bolted back to the dining room, located in the interior of the home, and fell into a wing-back chair in the corner. She placed her head between her legs, trying to calm her breathing, fast and shallow from adrenaline.

Walking slowly toward her, he meant to avoid startling her again.

"Bella, I'm here. Don't be afraid; I'm here for you."

She watched him go to the table and dip a cloth napkin into a glass of ice water. He placed the cloth at the back of her neck, cooling the heat of her skin and slowing the thumping of her heart drumming in her ears. The scrape of the chair as he moved it to close the space between them initially annoyed her, but she was distracted by the tender warmth of his large hands enveloping hers in a firm grip while soothing her with intermittent rubs on the top of her knuckles with his thumbs.

Her breathing slowed, but her hands were still trembling.

"Tell me what's wrong." He tried to look into her eyes, but she turned her head to avoid his gaze.

"I'm so embarrassed, but I don't feel the same way you do about storms. They may be interesting to you, but they scare the hell out of me."

She slowly turned her head to look into his eyes while she spoke.

"My mother advised me not to tell you, but I'm going to be honest with you even if you think less of me. My father was a firefighter, and he lost his life responding to a fire caused by a lightning strike. I've been afraid of sudden storms and raging fires since his death." She had never displayed her emotions in front of others following the loss of her father—she preferred to appear as strong as her mother.

"I'm sorry for your loss, Bella. I didn't know your father was a firefighter, and your fears don't make me think less of you." He absently stroked her reddened cheek, searching for something else to say. "I use pyrotechnics when I perform, and now I understand why you've never come to any of my shows or accepted the free tickets. I thought you didn't like the music or the sensual nature of my shows."

"I love your music, but the fire displays…I just can't handle it. My mother is good at what she does, and I know safety measures are in place, but there's still the element of danger with fire in an indoor setting."

"You're right about the risk. So tell me, my marketing genius, how do I appeal to people like you who want to see me perform live?" He smiled as he spoke to her.

"That's a good question." Her heartbeats slowed as she focused on his question, which provided her with a needed distraction from the storm raging outside.

"I think it would be great if you played more outdoor venues here in the States and also overseas. Or—and I know you don't want to consider this as an option—you could choose not to use fire in your shows." She looked directly at him to measure his response.

He held her hands, apparently contemplating her suggestion. The storm had started to subside, and the rain no longer pounded the house in torrential sheets.

"Let's run the idea of adding more outdoor venues by Parker and Justin tomorrow. You may be right, but not using fire in my shows isn't an option for me. We can talk more about concert dates later. Right now, I'm more concerned about you."

He released her hands, pulled out his phone, and checked his weather app. "There's going to be scattered severe storms throughout the night. You said your mother is out of town, and maybe this isn't the night to be alone.

We don't have these kinds of storms in LA very often, and it's clear you're not comfortable in this kind of weather. Why don't you stay in one of the guest rooms tonight?"

She was wary about traveling home in the storm; she didn't want to put herself or the driver in danger. *But hmm, not sure about staying here tonight.* She wrinkled her forehead as she thought about how to handle this.

"I don't want to inconvenience you, and I didn't come prepared to stay here tonight." Concerned that he might think she didn't appreciate his hospitality, especially since he'd been the perfect gentleman all evening, she felt she needed to tread lightly.

"It's not a problem. You can stay here tonight in the guest room of your choice. This place is so big, you won't even know I'm here.

"Miles, you weren't expecting me to stay and I can't."

"Why not? Do you change into a werewolf at midnight?"

She surprised herself by bursting into laughter as he gave her the most charming smile.

"Surely you don't want to leave because you're afraid of me, are you?" He tilted his head.

"No, I won't turn into a werewolf, and no, I don't fear you." She giggled. "I may not understand you, but I don't fear you." Goosebumps formed on her arms, and she rubbed them to generate some heat.

"Good. It's settled then, I'm safe having you here, but I'm going to lock my bedroom door just in case." He laughed again and offered her his arm.

"Come and join me in the grand hall. You're shivering."

Reluctantly, she followed him.

"Do you mind if I start a small fire in the fireplace?"

"No, I'm okay with a fire in a fireplace." She smirked. " It's the ones that rage out of control that frighten me."

He took her hand and led her to one of the couches in the grand hall and started a fire with the remote before going to the bar to pour two more glasses of wine. The rain returned, at times in torrential downpours, but the claps of thunder and the lightning weren't so scary while nestled on a couch with Miles, sharing a bottle of wine.

The time passed with shared laughter and a little friendly banter between the two of them.

"So what kind of charities are you involved with?"

"I provide publicity for groups who work with kids who have experienced early parental loss."

"That sounds interesting."

"It is—and quite rewarding." She was thankful that she had gotten a chance to know him a little better. "You're one of the good guys Miles. Thanks for your understanding."

"You are welcome and thank you for your company tonight. It's getting late, so I'll have one of the housekeepers come and lead you to an available room. I need to look over a few remixes I'll be using in the concert before I hit the sack. Will you excuse me?"

"Sure, you go ahead, and I'll be fine." He left, and shortly afterwards, a member of his staff came to assist her.

"Hi, I'm Carrie. This way to the guest room, ma'am. I'll be providing whatever you need for your comfort tonight."

"Thank you, Carrie." She grabbed her bag and followed her upstairs.

He awoke the next morning with thoughts of Bella on his mind that had nothing to do with business.

I'd never take advantage of her, not while she's fearful and vulnerable. But boy was she smoking hot last night in her black jeans. And I loved how her black top draped across her boobs.

He would have welcomed dinner and a night of sex with her, but he knew he had more to lose if he played with her feelings, and he'd heard from every member of his staff that she was a sweet woman. "Sweet" wasn't the word used for the women who had paraded through his life.

He also knew the chief wouldn't be happy with him, and for the first time in their friendship, he risked breaking a promise to Parker if he pursued Bella. His friend had implored him to avoid any attempt to mix business and pleasure when it came to her. If he didn't know how much Parker loved his wife Jen, he would've thought Parker wanted her for himself.

In order to block the desires of his growing cock, he channeled his thoughts to the possibility of a showdown with NeNe Moore. NeNe had concerns about Bella's marketing ideas to capitalize on his love of fire, which was interesting now that he knew how much she feared fire. If NeNe knew of his fleeting desires to sleep with Bella, he would have to hear about the legal ramifications of possible sexual harassment and so on and so forth.

NeNe has always been a cock blocker.

He finished dressing and checked himself in the mirror in his bedroom before heading downstairs.

Michele Sims

CHAPTER FOUR

Loud music thumped in the background as Miles moved downstairs to attend yet another meeting with his tour management team three days later. He passed the glass-encased studio where the dancers practiced their moves. Eric, the choreographer on the tour and creator of Miles's moves, stood front and center on the dance floor. They waved at each other after he briefly stopped and mimicked Eric's sensual hip-gyrating. He gave them a smile of approval and a thumbs up. The dancers smiled back as they continued to practice their routine.

Although charismatic, he demanded perfection from those around him, and the people in his inner circle wanted to keep him happy. He entered the room where Parker, Darien, Bella, Justin Peterson, his concert tour manager, and Bradley Marshall, his security manager, were sitting around the table mulling over folders containing dates and potential revenue from the upcoming tour. He took his seat at the head of the table, and all of them looked up and nodded to acknowledge his presence. He wasn't disappointed that NeNe, his cousin and contract lawyer, wasn't able to attend since something had come up with a case she had in New York. NeNe was excellent at her job, but when it came to him, she had difficulty maintaining boundaries. Somehow, it always ended up being personal.

"Okay, I'm listening, what have you got?"

Looking at the members of his executive team sitting around the table, Miles sat back in his chair and crossed his legs as he made eye contact with each of them.

"Make it quick, will you. We've only got a little more than two weeks left before the start of the tour, and I still have to remaster some of the songs for the live performances."

"I can go first." Bella cleared her throat, straightened the papers in front of her, and looked directly at him before speaking up.

"I spoke to Parker about some of my marketing ideas, and he assured me we've got the money for additional publicity, despite the added security costs. I think we should take advantage of the growing media buzz by arranging more meet and greets for you and members of the tour. Darien said he would help with the arrangements since he already maintains your schedule." She took another breath before proceeding with her marketing plans.

"I'm alright with more meet and greets. What else do you have Bella?"

"Miles, I can't tell you how many organizations contact me weekly to ask if they can auction you off for a date night for charity. I thought we could hold our own auction for dates with you, like maybe a dinner date, maybe an afternoon watching you practice for the tour or possibly a personal autograph session with you for a group of their friends. We could give most of the money to your charities and use the publicity to add to the buzz." She cast her gaze directly on him.

"I don't know about that. Sounds like you're trying to make me the beefcake on the menu." The guys around the table laughed at his joke while Bella looked up at the ceiling in a vain attempt to stop rolling her eyes.

"Miles, hear me out. I said—in jest, of course—to a group of reporters last week that you might be interested in an auction, and this check came in the mail yesterday."

She took a check out of the envelope sitting on the table beside her papers and slid it to him.

"Impressive." Looking at the number of zeros on the check, he seemed to consider it before frowning and sliding the check back to her.

"No, Bella, not interested." She gripped the check as if to draw strength from it.

"It may interest you that the man who signed the check is Isabelle Bronson's father. He told her she could have whatever she wanted for her twenty-fifth birthday, and she chose a week with you."

"I can't do it Bella. I'm too busy to be a plaything for a spoiled brat," he asserted. "But give me a moment to understand this. On one hand, I've heard you like that I don't use words like bitches and hoes in my songs, and now you want to pimp me out?" Her back straightened.

Oops, too much. His shoulders slumped and he closed his mouth as he sensed he had hit a nerve. The rest of the team remained quiet, and no one tried to get him out of the mess he had stepped in while Bella contemplated her next response.

"I didn't consider my ideas to hold an auction the same as pimping you out. I see it as a shrewd business move. Her father is also willing to produce a trailer for the tour at his expense and make sure it's shown on his television stations throughout the country. You know he's a media mogul, and the amount of coverage he could provide will translate to increased ticket sales and greater profits."

"Yeah, that's interesting." He raised his eyebrow.

"Isabelle is a beautiful and talented young woman who's looking for a break in the music industry. Her career hasn't taken off the way her father hoped it would've by this point. If she's photographed with someone as successful as you, it might help her record sales. It couldn't hurt her career or yours, and besides, you'll have a very powerful man grateful to you for helping his daughter. Please reconsider before you say no."

Parker piped in to help her convince him it was a good financial move.

"Miles, Mr. Bronson's people also contacted me with a very lucrative contract for exclusive marketing rights in several large venues they own throughout the world. The contract alone would put the tour in the black before you sing your first note, and it would allow Bradley to hire more security. I also need to let you know there are some unexpected additional costs, more than I originally anticipated, with providing enough security in the cities we've booked, especially the ones that have had recent terror attacks." Bradley raised his hand to get Miles's attention.

"I understand the need to maintain a budget, but I also wanted to talk to you about bringing in even more security, especially for the western European leg of the tour. I think it would be money well spent."

"If you think we need more security, hire them. I told Parker to give you the funds you needed. Isn't that correct Parker?" Miles always approved of keeping everyone on the tour safe.

"Yes, that's correct. I am still running the numbers Miles."

" Great. I need to take care of that now if you'll excuse me." Bradley rose from his seat and left the room while Parker continued the meeting.

"And Miles, Justin could hire more musicians and dancers, and you could also have more pyrotechnics in the show, provided we get the approval from the fire marshals at the large indoor venues." He looked around the room at the team and placed his hands firmly on the table.

"Why didn't you say that at the beginning of your pitch? The idea of having a bigger, more dramatic show has placed me in the mood for some fun. When is my first date with the fair Miss Bronson? "

"Tonight."

"Tonight? I'm sure I have plans. Have y'all considered how busy I am?"

"Darien has your schedule on hold pending your decision," she continued. "Everything previously scheduled for tonight can be rescheduled. I'll alert the media tomorrow of the plans and confirm tonight's date with Isabelle's assistant. Don't worry, Darien and I will take care of everything. So, can we proceed?"

"Go ahead." Outwardly, he frowned. Inside, he felt the excitement of sexual stirrings. Isabelle wasn't a strong singer, but she had the look and she was hot. Justin cleared his throat to get his attention before he spoke.

"You won't regret this. Remember I told you about two gifted dancers just completing a world tour with another artist last month? They're rested and ready to hit the road again. With the additional funds Mr. Bronson promised, I could hire them tomorrow and have them here by the end of the week for practice sessions. They're very good and are familiar with some of routines. If you agree, I can have them signed and under contract by tomorrow."

"Fine. Why do I feel as if all of you conspired to get my approval?" He looked around the room and frowned.

"I'd never conspire against you. You're my boy. Excuse me, but I gotta go." Justin pushed away from the table, eager to get the dancers under contract.

"I need to get going too." Bella pushed away from the table, turned toward the door, and looking over her shoulder one last time, saw Miles staring at her rear. She shook her head and closed the door behind her, leaving Miles and Parker in the room alone.

"Miles, what's wrong with you?"

"What are you talking about?"

"I told you to watch yourself with Bella."

"Watch myself?"

"Yes, she saw you watching her and focusing on her ass. Do you want to end up in a harassment suit?"

"She has a fine ass, and we both know that brother. I'm not doing anything unethical. Contrary to what you may believe, I respect her as a professional woman, but I'm not blind. And besides, didn't I agree to go out on a date she's arranging with another woman?"

"Just be careful. That's all I want to say about you and Bella. We're taking this organization to another level, and I don't want any major stumbles along the way." He smiled and raised his closed hand to bump fists.

"This deal is sweet, man. Do you know the financial projections for this tour? Your talent and skills with the ladies have allowed us to hit the mother lode. After this tour, if you wanted to take a year off to watch all the volcanoes on the planet erupt, you could do it and still be a very wealthy man. Bringing Bella into the organization was one of the best things we've done in a long time. I'm your best friend and would do anything for you, but I need some time off after this tour to spend with my family. After the second baby gets here, Jen will need some help, and I'd like to get to know my kids while they still want to be around me."

"We both could use some time off." Miles threw his head back. "I'm tired, but I guess I'd better go to the studio to get some work done before my week of dates with Isabelle. This had better work out, or I'm going to beat the shit out of you. And you'll also take Bella's beatings since I wouldn't want to get sued for assault *and* harassment." He smiled to hide his misgivings about the plan blowing up in their faces.

"For this kind of money, you can beat me all the way to the bank." Parker smiled at his friend and imagined a big payoff for their years of hard work and belief in each other.

"I need to make some calls Miles. Holler at you later."

"Later Parker." Miles watched as Parker left the room.

For the remainder of the day and well into the evening, Miles worked in his study. He flipped off his headset and looked at his watch as he considered calling off the date, but he had agreed to it, so he went upstairs to dress for his outing with Isabelle.

Bella was still at work in a spare office she used at the estate when she worked late. She hadn't bothered to change out of the simple black tailored dress with the matching black heels she'd worn to a press conference earlier that day. Her hair was in a messy bun atop her head.

It's going to be another long night. She sighed as she looked at her computer screen.

Miles came downstairs and into the room, donning a custom-made suit.

"Help me with my cufflinks, please. I couldn't find anyone to help me put these things on." He rushed into the room and threw the jacket to his black designer suit on the chair. "You don't want me to be late for my first date with Isabelle, do you?"

"Of course not, but wait a sec, please." She held up her hand to stop him. Standing in the middle of the floor, he frowned while waiting for her assistance.

"Where's Mr. Curtis or your stylist? I thought he was the one in charge of keeping you sharp."

"Mr. Curtis and my stylist have both left for the day, and Carrie is off. For your information, I dress myself—well most of the time, except when I'm wearing these cuffs."

"I'm almost finished responding to this email." She typed the last sentence. "Finished."

"Why are you still here anyway, Bella? It's late." She looked up from the papers scattered before her and placed her glasses on the desk.

"Why did you change the time of your dinner date is a better question. You should have been gone by now if you planned to arrive at her place on time."

"Isabelle changed the time. She wanted a later time for our date since that's when all the young and famous folks hit the town. She said she wanted to see and be seen by the pretty people. Ms. Bronson also told me she knew we would be the best-looking couple in the room, and she didn't want anyone to miss us."

She rose from the work piled up before her. *So Isabelle doesn't think this is only for publicity?* A negative charge of energy coursed through her as if she'd been shocked in the heart. *Where did that come from?* She rubbed her chest and tightened her lips.

"Bella, do you have to look like helping me is painful and the last thing you'd want to be doing? I have other things to do too, and it wasn't like I asked you to arrange this date." He snorted.

She locked her gaze on him and smiled to hide her irritation.

"I know this was my idea, Miles." She hastily closed the distance between them.

"I don't mind helping you; it's just hard to get back into a rhythm when my concentration is broken."

"So, I'm a distraction to you now?" He rolled his eyes.

"No, you're not." She looked up at him and noticed his slight frown disappear as he extended his arm while watching her delicate hands with their recently manicured red nails reach for his cuffs.

"Ouch." An electric shock surprised them both when she touched him, causing her to release his wrist. She looked up into his soft brown eyes and found him staring into her brown eyes as if they were both seeing each other for the first time.

"It's electric!" Miles quipped, and they both responded with nervous laughter.

He extended his wrists once more, and she fastened the cuffs slowly this time.

"You smell good, Miles. Women like it when men put in the effort on their first date."

"Thanks for noticing. Does this suit also meet your approval, Pimp Bella?" He looked at her with a half-smile, then turned slowly in a circle for her viewing.

This man is fine; his muscles under that shirt and oh...that tight ass.

She shook her head, trying to rid it of the image of a naked Miles, which had popped up, often when she least expected it, ever since that day he'd discovered her in his bedroom.

"So what do you think? I'm waiting." She let out a breath and wiped away imaginary sweat from her brow.

"You already know you look good. And yes, I agree that the suit is perfect for your date tonight."

"Well thank you. I'm sure you want Ms. Bronson to give me good reviews after all the money her father paid me to make her happy."

"You're a professional. Either enjoy yourself tonight or pretend that you're having fun. As your publicist, I'm asking you to put on a great performance if you have to. You know how to make people happy when you hit the stage, and I have no doubt you'll be successful tonight one way or another."

The pang in her chest hit her again.

Is this what heartburn feels like?

"Excuse me, I think I need a drink of water." *And some antacids.*

"Are you alright Bella?" He placed a hand on her shoulder.

"Yes Miles, I'm fine. I probably need to take a short break, but I have a ton of things to do before the tour starts in two weeks. Enjoy your date with Isabelle." She turned to head for the kitchen.

"One more thing before I leave for my *date*. I would consider it a favor if you would let Mr. Curtis tell cook to prepare breakfast for you. He's concerned about you. You come in early, work through lunch, and stay late. He had me hire a nutritionist last year when I was running myself down while touring. The meals cook prepares with the help of a professional dietician have improved my stamina, both physically and mentally."

She ran her hand through her hair and avoided eye contact with him, but he drew closer to regain her attention.

"Please don't be embarrassed. Mr. Curtis would never repeat what he saw the night of the storm."

"It's kind of Mr. Curtis to offer his help, but I don't want to be a bother or act like I need special treatment." She looked up at him.

"It's no problem, and you didn't ask for special treatment. I'll tell Mr. Curtis you'll be taking your breakfast here at work. I'm off to my date; have a good night." He turned to leave the room.

"Have fun Miles."

"Bye Bella."

She sat at her desk for a moment after he left, and the pain subsided.

Whew. I'm glad I'm feeling better. A message popped up on her computer screen and she scrolled down to view posts of some of Ari's most ardent fans and haters.

She's posting again? Click.

```
@Revenge123: Still like breaking
hearts pretty boy? How are you
going to feel when I put a
bullet in your ass?
```

"Shit," she muttered under her breath. *I need to alert Bradley to the increasing number of violent threats against Miles on social media. Miles might not be concerned about this, but Bradley will be.*

Click. *Forward to Bradley.*

Click. *Delete.*

Click. *Block all new posts from @Revenge123. Done.*

```
Bradley: Thanks, Bella, we're on
it. Saw the post an hour ago.
```

Bella: Have you reported it to the LAPD Threat Management Unit? This isn't the first time @Revenge 123 has posted on the page.

Bradley: We're on it. Thanks.

Click. She scanned other sites and nothing too exciting was trending today. She'd also placed notification alerts with keywords on her computer for widely trending articles from sites regarding morbid things such as celebrity deaths or accidents, but those sites were quiet too. The app that she discovered in one of her marketing journals allowed her to be notified when her keywords, such as *celebrity* and *death* were mentioned. She also had a cross reference with the keyword *hip-hop,* since performers from that genre didn't always receive coverage in the regular press.

She never wanted Miles to appear insensitive, especially if a cultural icon passed and he didn't mention it at one of his shows. Keeping him in the loop was her job and she planned to perform her duties well.

CHAPTER FIVE

Her limbs jumped under the covers. Both disoriented and startled by her phone ringing on the desk, she struggled to awaken from a deep sleep. Bella shook her head and squinted toward the direction of the red numbers on the clock at her bedside: 2:00 am. She patted the desk by her bed in the dark, searching for her ringing phone, and located it. With phone in hand, she pulled back the covers and sat up to listen to the person calling at such an obscene time of morning.

"Darien, I need you to get me out of this now. Call me, and I'll say something came up at the studio. This date isn't working out. She's too clingy, and she asks too many questions. I've had enough of Isabelle for one night."

"This is Bella, not Darien." Her fatigue made it difficult to mask the irritation in her voice.

"Bella?"

"Yes, Miles. It's me. You dialed the wrong number." With her faculties returning, his words began to sink in.

"Don't ask Darien to give you an exit call. She'll see right through it." She yawned and struggled to get her words out. "We promised her a date, and we have to keep our word. You know, in this town, a promise or handshake broken can be the death knell to a business. Please don't do this to me—I mean to AriMusic." With her brain now awake, she looked back at the clock and attempted to assess the gravity of the situation. "It's two in the morning, an appropriate time to take her home and end the date as a gentleman who respects her and the time. Just take her home."

"Okay, I'll get the check and take her home. I don't know if I can take a whole week of her."

"Let's deal with this one problem at a time. I'll figure something out."

"Good night, Bella"

"Goodbye, Miles." She flopped back in bed and looked up at the ceiling.

Look at the bright side. Corey has been busy with his stores and at least you don't have to deal with him and Miles at the same time.

She let out a deep breath of uncertainty and placed her hands on her head.

I'm not sure how much more of working with Miles I can take.

She arrived at work later that morning, prepared to get by with more than her usual two cups of coffee throughout the day. Unable to return to sleep after Miles's call, she'd stayed up, staring at the ceiling in her bedroom until she'd solved the Isabelle dilemma.

Mr. Curtis, always the professional, greeted her when she came into the kitchen for coffee. Instead of the usual one cup of coffee in the morning, he had cook prepare a green smoothie and placed it on the table with a straw beside it.

"I hope you like it," he told her, pointing to the glass.

"Thank you, Mr. Curtis, but I don't want to inconvenience you."

"No problem. You work hard, and you're good at what you do. You've changed things around here for the better while juggling a ton of things and bringing calm to a situation. Things are more professional since you've convinced other members of the executive team about the need to stick to a schedule, and I want to do this for you."

Mr. Curtis was a man of few words, and a compliment from him meant a lot.

"Thank you. I appreciate it." She sat and placed her straw in her smoothie.

"Yum." She closed her eyes to savor the flavor. "This is good."

Miles walked into the kitchen, just as she was opening her eyes, in the same suit rumpled by a night and morning of wear.

"Good morning everyone."

"Good morning." She smiled, acknowledging his presence.

Mr. Curtis returned the greeting and left the room after placing a smoothie in front of him on the other place setting already on the table. Bella remained quiet.

"Aren't you planning to say something or ask me how it went?"

"I'm trying to enjoy my smoothie, but since you insist, how did it go?"

"I took her home as you suggested, but not before she told me she planned to come to the studio to hang out with me today. I don't know if I can take having her around for hours."

Bella yawned and tried to make her stretch small.

"I'm sorry if I'm boring you."

"You're not boring me. I only got a few hours of sleep. Someone woke me up at two in the morning, remember?" She rubbed her eyes.

"Sorry about that. Feel free to go home early today and bill me for the time starting at two this morning."

"Thanks. I'll see how the day goes. One good thing came out of my sleepless night though. I think I've solved the problem with Isabelle for the rest of the week. Can you agree to at least an hour of your time tomorrow to show her around the studio? I'll have activities arranged to occupy her while she's here, but I may need your help tomorrow evening if things go as planned."

"What things?" His eyebrows furrowed and released.

"Just trust me on this one; I haven't worked out all the details yet."

"Okay, I'm tired; I'm going upstairs to take a nap." He turned the glass up to his mouth to finish his smoothie and licked the green moustache on his lip before he took the empty glass to the sink.

"By the way, I didn't sleep with her if you're curious about why it took me so long to get home. I hung out with some old friends who were in town."

"I wasn't curious about how you spent your free time. It's none of my business who you sleep with."

"Just thought you wanted to know, that's all. We can discuss your plans later." He yawned and left the room.

By midafternoon, she was coasting on fumes, and the coffee wasn't keeping her awake. Giving in to her fatigue, she decided to go home early to rest, but she knew her drive would be in bumper-to-bumper traffic.

Should I take a nap here or just go home?

There was music blaring outside of her office and footsteps of staff members walking back and forth. It was only a matter of time before she experienced an interruption from someone: Miles, Darien, or whomever.

I've got to get out of here. With her pocketbook and keys in hand, she hurried out of the office and slipped out the back door to her car.

Traffic wasn't bad by LA's standards, and once she finally arrived home, she parked in her driveway and shuffled with lead feet into the house, where doing the laundry and other chores she had ignored were waiting for her attention. She began undressing as soon as she got to her bedroom and fell on the bed face down to take the long nap her body craved.

She woke up and raised her head off her pillow, a bit confused, but the calm pink walls and the softness of her comforter reminded her she was home, safe in her bed. She yawned and took a quick shower before returning a few emails and telephone calls to finish the day's work.

Sitting at her computer with a towel rolled into a turban on her head, she couldn't contain the big smile spreading across her face as she clicked on the email from José Saunders, Ari's self-proclaimed biggest fan and the president of the LA branch of his fan club.

José: Excited about the momentum building about the concert. Thanks so much for the tickets for the San Francisco and Vegas shows. You know I'll be there. Let me know if I can help in any way to promote the tour. I'm available and here for you girl.

Hearing from José was something she looked forward to, and she returned his message, filled with smiling emojis, but she clicked on a few more emails with trepidation, concerned about the growing number of menacing messages sent to Ari on his social media sites. There were the familiar messages from women in love with him, willing to have his baby and spend their lives with him, the ones angry that he hadn't returned their messages and reminding him they were going to f*@# him up, and the more ominous ones from deranged men convinced Ari had slept with their wives or girlfriends, and he was going to pay for ruining their lives.

She'd spoken with Miles about the growing amount of hate mail from the latter group, but he shrugged it off again and thought it was the bad part that came with the territory of being famous. She forwarded the additional messages and emails to Bradley, with asterisks in front of the messages that concerned her. It didn't lessen her concerns that she was surrounded by alpha males on the executive team whom she thought took the threats too lightly. She also shared them with Darien, an ally who often agreed with her assessment of situations.

"I've been a part of this industry for a long time, Bella," he'd told her. "You can't let haters stop you from focusing on the music."

"Yes, but haters can kill those producing the music," she recalled telling him.

She powered down her computer and got up to heat up one of her favorite quick meals: garlic seasoned steak in baby potatoes and veggies baked in foil packs. She took one of the packs out of the freezer and placed it in the oven to slow bake while she went to the bathroom to finish taking care of her hair, silky and soft after a half hour of letting the conditioner set in.

The aromas of cooked meat and sautéed veggies coming from the kitchen filled her room and she took one last look in the mirror before leaving the bathroom to enjoy an evening meal with wine and a little TV. It was good to laugh and zone out in front of a comedy show. The time zoomed by, and she looked at her phone, realizing it was getting late, so she called her mother on her way to her bedroom and talked briefly before getting under the covers for a delicious slumber.

"Bella, there's a good chance I'll get awarded a consulting assignment with a firm here in Texas. The assignment could last for a month or possibly longer, but I still plan to try to get home as soon as possible so we can talk in person."

"Mom, I'm so excited for you. Does the assignment sound interesting?"

"Yes, I'll work with architects designing fire safety installations for a firm that's expanding. Wish me luck."

"Good luck, Mom."

"Good night, my sweet girl."

"Good night, Mom." She pulled the covers to her shoulders and settled in for a night's rest.

"Babe, you know I wouldn't call out another woman's name while I'm kissing you. You misunderstood me. I said *Belle* baby, not *Bella*. Talk to me Isabelle. I'm sorry."

Her cell to her ear, Bella couldn't believe he'd woken her up again, this time clearly intoxicated. "What the hell, Miles? It's three in the morning. Do I have to arrange your contact lists, so you won't wake me every morning?"

"Bella?"

"Yes, Bella, not Belle or Isabelle."

"Oh shit. I must be drunk. Isabelle is so pissed off with me right now. I guess I solved the problem of having her come to the studio." He laughed, still slurring his words. "She doesn't want anything to do with me."

"This isn't funny. What happened?"

"She came to my VIP booth at the club and began kissing me. I guess she thought I called her Bella, and she started screeching and stormed off."

"Were there witnesses?"

"No, we were alone at the time."

"Were you discussing business and that's how my name came up?"

"We were, and that's right. Bella is your name." He laughed again. "Damn, I'm lit."

"Stick with me, will you? We can say you've been so busy working on the tour, and I've been working closely with you regarding the details of the tour. It was an honest mistake. I'll talk to her assistant in the morning. I'll handle it, and you'll apologize."

"But it wasn't a mistake. I was thinking about you when she kissed me."

There was a pregnant pause as she repositioned the phone at her ear and shifted her weight in the bed. *He has definitely had too much to drink.*

"Miles. Listen to me. You'll apologize, and we can say it was the alcohol. You're drunk."

"I may be drunk, but I still know you're a desirable woman. Any man, drunk or sober, can see that. I'll call her now and apologize if that'll make you happy."

"No, no. Let me handle this."

"It's late," he replied, still slurring his words. "I can do this; trust me."

"Miles don't contact her. Go home, and I'll meet you there later this morning. We can discuss the plans for her studio tour then. Don't you want to know what I've planned?" She bit her lip, hoping she had distracted him.

"Sure, I can have my driver swing by your house on our way home and pick you up. Be ready in thirty minutes." He ended the call.

"Miles, Miles?" She couldn't believe this was happening again—she was about to get ready for work at three in the morning. This was probably going to be her last tour with AriMusic.

"This job is going to kill me." She threw the covers back and stomped to the bathroom.

His limo arrived at her home exactly thirty minutes later. She crawled into the limo casually dressed, hoping the alcohol would have him sleeping soon, but he remained awake and chatty, not his usual character.

"Did you know that I normally put on a show with lots of fireworks the night before the launch of my tour? I don't want to change that, and you don't need to do anything for it. I enjoy doing it myself, and the staff likes that they have the night off. See, I can ignite the fireworks myself."

He opened his palm and fire shot out from his hand. Bella leaned back away from him, afraid.

"Don't be afraid; I'd never harm you. I know how to control my condition. I've had it since birth."

"What condition?" Her jaw dropped following his disclosure.

"It's a genetic anomaly, one that allows me to produce fire."

"You were born that way?" The alcohol he'd consumed allowed her to ask questions and get answers he would have never divulged if sober, she hoped.

"I wasn't aware of my power until I was six or seven. My parents took me to the National Institute of Health to study and diagnose me. There's no treatment for it, but they did help me understand how to control it."

"Oh, so that's why you like fire? It's like a gift to you?"

"A gift or maybe a curse?" He cocked his head to the side. "So, what do you think? Do you think I'm a freak?"

"No. I think you have a freakish amount of talent, and I see it as a gift you've shared with others. You make millions of people happy."

"Thank you, but I was talking about my fire thing, not my musical talent. What you think means a lot to me."

"I don't know what to say Miles...I'm still processing what I just saw."

"I understand." He nodded as they both looked ahead in silence.

There was no traffic, and they arrived at the estate in record time. The driver pulled up the driveway to the entrance of the house and Miles pressed the button to lower the privacy window to speak to him.

"You can leave now and come back later today to pick up Bella when she calls to let you know she needs a ride home."

"Yes sir." He nodded and got out of the car to open the door for them.

Miles stumbled out of the car and grabbed her hand as she exited the limo to lead her to the front door.

"I have something to show you."

He released her hand before pulling his arm back and hurled a huge fireball into the sky, which exploded into a burst of colored embers cascading from its center before falling from the sky to the ground as gray flecks cooled by the night air. She stepped back toward the estate in shock and covered her open mouth as she looked at him and saw the glow of the flames from the fireballs illuminating his handsome face as they descended from the sky.

"Please stop it."

He stumbled and turned toward her. "You don't like it?"

Wide-eyed and grasping her throat, she backed away from him.

"I wasn't expecting it, and I need to get out of the night air. My throat is already a bit scratchy."

"Okay, let's go inside to discuss your plans. We can talk in my office."

She followed him to his office, took a seat on the couch, and he sat next to her. Gathering her thoughts, she hesitated and prepared to tell him her plans to communicate with Isabelle's people, but she was distracted by the motion of his head weaving despite his attempts to fight sleep. His head fell hard on her shoulder, and she tried to wake him, but he was fast asleep. Pinned to the arm of the couch on her left and him on her right, she sat on the couch for a few minutes to ensure he was asleep before grabbing his hands to touch his skin, warm and a little flushed.

Wow, he can produce fire. Wonder what that feels like? He stirred and she placed his hands by his side before her eyes became heavy.

The time on her phone was 8:30 am, four hours later. She looked up as Parker entered the room, frowning at her and Miles, who was still asleep and snoring as he lay with his head on her shoulder and his arms around her on the couch. They were still both fully clothed and stretched out with their legs and feet on the table in front of the couch.

"What the hell are you two doing? Explain."

"Help me, Parker. He's heavy, and I can't move him without waking him."

"Miles, get up." He yelled and shook Miles's shoulders. "Why are you and Bella asleep in your office?" She rolled her eyes at Parker.

"Thanks Parker. I could've done that. I was trying not to wake him."

Miles stretched and smiled as he looked up at her before responding to Parker.

"Isn't it obvious? We were tired from a long night of work, and we took a nap. What's the big deal? Are you and your dirty thoughts the real problem?" He yawned and straightened his body, relieving Bella of his weight. "Nothing happened, Parker."

"That's right; nothing happened." She eased off the couch and stood up. "I need to freshen up before starting my day. Excuse me." She hurried out the room before Parker could ask more questions.

Walking as fast as she could down the hallway, she intended to make her way to the spare office to get away from them. On the way there, she saw her name on a sign on the door of the office just before she reached her usual space. Curious, she opened the door and was surprised as she looked around the room. It contained a large mahogany desk with a gold nameplate on it embossed with her name and position: Bella Wahlberg, Chief of Marketing and Publicity. Her new desk was larger and had three monitors on it to allow her to view stats and different social media sites simultaneously. There was a meeting area with three chairs in front of her desk to receive business associates and guests.

She walked around the office and found a private bathroom with a shower had been installed, complete with marble on the floor and walls. She saw the change of clothes she always kept at the office had been placed in the small closet off the bathroom. She couldn't believe her good fortune. Maybe after the tour kicked off, things would settle down and she could enjoy her job again.

Bouncing with joy, she hurried to her desk and sat in her new brown leather chair. Her screen was on, with prompts to log in and change her passwords, and it lit up with a message after she typed in her security info.

```
Parker: Hope you like your new
digs, and congratulations on
```

```
your bonus and new position if
you accept it. You earned it.
```

What? A new position, an office, and a bonus? I wasn't expecting this. What's there to think about? A steady paycheck and a little more security? I'm definitely taking the job.

```
Bella: I accept the position if
we can agree upon salary and the
expectation that I can assist my
mother with her business, within
reason of course.

Parker: I think we can make it
work. Welcome to AriMusic.
```

She spun around in her new chair, ecstatic over her new digs and the additional money in her paycheck. She looked in the corner, at the boxes filled with her research data and marketing items sent to her from numerous vendors that required her approval before they could be used at the tour sites. The black keys of her new, faster computer were sleek to her touch as she ran her fingers across them, eager to surf various media sites. She became so immersed in work, she forgot to immediately thank her new boss. Instead, she sat up straight and squared her shoulders against her chair to face the task of contacting Isabelle's people. She typed in the first of many messages, and an hour later, the studio tour was back on.

Next on her to-do list: contact Darien and other staff members to make sure Miles stayed on site. She spoke to the recording engineers and producers at AriMusic, and they agreed to provide new arrangements for some of Isabelle's songs. They were some of the best in the business, and if they couldn't create a hit, no one could. Isabelle needed to be marketed differently, and a new sound couldn't hurt. She got approval from Isabelle's people to have her music remixed before placing her plan into motion. Isabelle was under contract, but her father owned the company.

Miles was still unhappy about spending time with Isabelle, and despite that, she knew convincing him to go along with her plan to sing background vocals on her song wouldn't be easy, even if it got him out of the agreement they had with her father. She'd leave the future legal issues to Parker and NeNe to iron out if the song generated significant profits. The plan had to work, and she needed to get Miles out of his obligation to Mr. Bronson before he blew the deal. Tired after a second day of little sleep, she called the driver to take her home and planned to thank Miles for the new office first thing tomorrow.

She got home and called her mother. They were sharing events in their day when the phone beeped, alerting her of another call.

"Mom, that's Corey on the other line."

"Okay sweetheart. We can talk later. I love you."

"I love you too Mom. Goodbye."

"Goodbye Bella."

She clicked over to accept Corey's call.

"Hey Bella. I just wanted to hear your voice before I went to bed."

"Hey, Corey. It's good hearing your voice too. How are things going?"

She heard him sigh before answering. "Negotiations have stalled, and it's going to take longer than I expected to close the deal. I'm sorry, but I won't be able to come over tomorrow. I know you've been patient with me, and I hope you know I'm doing this for us Bella, for our future." He yawned.

For us Corey? Or for you and your ambitions? She stared at the phone.

"Bella, tell me you understand."

"I understand Corey, and I know we'll be able to spend time together soon."

"Thanks Bella. I think I'd better get off the phone. It's been a long day."

"Good night Corey."

"Good night Bella"

After pressing the end call button, she decided to send out a final message before silencing her phone and calling it a night.

```
Bella: Parker messaged me about
the job offer.
Miles: Do U accept it? U
discovered it before I could
talk 2 U about it.

Bella: I accept it and thank U.
I appreciate your confidence in
me, but I'm turning off my phone
tonight. I need some rest and
please don't call me after
midnight if it's not an
emergency. Thanks, your humble
and loyal employee.

Miles: U R welcome, humble and
loyal employee. Pick up if I do.
Did U like your office?
```

Bella: I did. It's fantastic.
I'll share the plans I have to
get U out of the agreement with
Mr. Bronson later. Again, thank
U and good night.

Miles: Ok. Good night for now.

Bella: Don't. I'm not kidding.

Miles: All right, you've earned
the night off.

She was tired, too tired to reflect on all the things happening in her life. Miles had disclosed more personal information in his drunken state than he ever had sober. She had a new, big office, had averted a crisis with the Bronson family, and managed to maintain her sanity. She knew she had to slow things down somehow before fear, the part of her she tried hard to hide, caused her to run far away. Her blood pressure had been high on her last visit to her doctor a few months ago, she was chewing antacid tabs like candy, and she knew she needed to rest.

Pulling the covers around her, she settled in her bed, refusing to think about anything more, especially anything that had to do with her job. Hoping to be comforted by sweet dreams, she closed her eyes and drifted off to sleep.

This was not a good morning, especially with the start of the tour looming before her. She woke with a slight headache, felt a little warm and dizzy, and needed to go to the bathroom frequently. Having missed several appointments in the past two months, she knew she needed to reset her priorities and see her physician, who, thankfully, had an early morning appointment available for her before heading to work.

"Thanks for seeing me, Dr. Jones." She pulled the thin patient gown around her and rested her stocking feet on the small black step at the bottom of the examination table.

"I had a cancellation this morning and was glad I could work you in. I've been your physician for a long time, and I'm concerned about you. It's not like you to miss your appointments, especially during a medical workup." One of the nurses knocked on the door and came in to assist while he performed an examination on her.

"Get dressed, and I'll come back to share the results. In the meantime, Ms. Adams, please bring Bella an electrolyte drink to consume while she's here."

"Yes Dr. Jones."

Moments later after she had consumed the drink the nurse brought her, he knocked and entered the room. Nervous about the results, she held her breath while he flipped through her chart.

"I see you've missed several appointments, including your last two scheduled appointments, so let me share your results now that you're here. Your EKG was normal. Your diastolic blood pressure has been over ninety-eight on several readings within the last month, much higher than I like to see, especially in young people. It needs to be around eighty." He repositioned his glasses.

"Bella, it may be uncommon, but young people can have a stroke, and I don't think you should take your blood pressure lightly. I told you there were common reasons for hypertension in young women, pregnancy being one of them." She held her breath.

"You're not pregnant."

"Thank you doctor. That's a relief." She blew out a breath.

"You have a urinary tract infection that needs to be treated, and I'm going to switch your birth control pills, since some pills can cause an elevation of blood pressure."

"Yes, and I've modified my diet—less salt, and I've been getting more exercise."

"Good, but your blood pressure is surprisingly low today, probably because of the urinary tract infection, which is probably causing the increased urination and dehydration."

"I can't win," she sighed. "Are you going to start me on antibiotics today?"

"Yes, and I'm going to insist that you rest. I've shared the data with you since your teen years that early parental loss can make you more vulnerable to chronic effects such as depression, loneliness, stress-related conditions, sleep problems, and headaches. I think there are things going on in your life that may be making it difficult to stabilize your readings, and I'm wondering if the fluctuations in your blood pressure are coming also from stress, so I'll give you an antibiotic, vitamins, and place you on sick leave for a week to get some rest. You look tired, and you can't keep going on like this."

"No, Dr. Jones. I have to work. I'll take the antibiotics and try to manage my stress better. I just started a new job, and my boss is starting the Fire God World Tour in two weeks."

"Where are you working?"

"I have a new position with AriMusic. You remember I was a consultant with them, and I was recently offered a full-time position."

"Congratulations, but tell me the truth—have you been a little depressed lately?"

"A little weepy around the anniversary of my father's death and his birthday, but I'm functional. I go to work, and I'm still handling my business."

He chuckled. "I remember there was a song you liked when you were a teenager that talked about handling your business."

"You have a good memory." She smiled at him.

"I also wanted to thank you for writing the blog about the effects of early parental loss and mentioning my practice in the article. Several patients came in for an assessment, so I guess you believed me when I told you that it would be good if you added your personal experiences to the narrative. The British princes have done a lot to destigmatize seeking care, and in your own way, so have you."

"I'm glad I could help."

"Before I leave, let me share that your nasal passages were also a little inflamed. Anything new in your environment that could be setting off your allergies?"

"I think I'm reacting to the fumes from the glue and carpet fibers in my new office."

"Take a few paper masks to cover your mouth and nose, or better yet, find another office—at least until the room is aired out. I'll also prescribe some meds for your allergies."

"Thanks, I'll take a few masks to wear if I start coughing and sneezing a lot or camp out in another office as you suggested, but my office is so nice."

"I'm glad you like your new position and your new office, but I still feel you need to take some time off to see if it helps with your blood pressure. Your pressures have either been too high or a bit too low today. I want you to call if you don't start to feel better in a few days and come back for your follow-up appointment."

"All right, I hear you, and I'll follow your recommendations. Thanks for working me in."

"You're welcome, and I'll see you soon. The nurse will have the prescriptions for you after you get dressed. Goodbye, Bella."

"Goodbye, Dr. Jones."

She got samples of the antibiotics and took the prescriptions for her allergy meds and birth control pills, along with the paperwork for her short-term leave.

I really don't want to take time off. She knew she should go directly home but chose to go to work, despite recommendations to get some rest. *I'll only stay for a few hours then go home, rest, and work from there.*

She'd received text messages from the producers at the studio and Darien while she was at the doctor's office, assuring her the plans she'd set in motion yesterday were proceeding better than they expected. The sound engineers remixed Isabelle's original tracks, and the producer placed timed markers on the music where they thought Miles could add background vocals. He didn't have to think about anything. All she needed to do was convince him to sing in the designated places on the tracks and sing the hook with Isabelle so that it would sound like a duet.

How difficult could it be? And besides, didn't he want out of the arrangement with Isabelle's father?

She planned to make it clear to him how so many people not only went out of their way to ensure Isabelle had a great time and disturbed him as little as possible but also got him out of two of his three dates with her. Isabelle had declined the second date, happy to spend time working in the studio with the engineers and her assigned producer, who had released a snippet of the remastered song on social media, igniting a storm of interest in her music.

> **Darien:** Isabelle's people called to tell her they were on their way to pick her up, and she left with them in a rush to do interviews on several social media platforms. Third date canceled just as you had hoped. Ms. Isabelle has no time for Miles.
>
> **Bella:** Thanks for letting me know another star is born. ☺

She pulled into the estate, a little worn from the effects of dehydration and low blood pressure, which had improved a little before she left the doctor's office. On her way back to her office, she contemplated how to get Miles to do his part.

Hitting the intercom button on her desk phone, she called the engineering booth and spoke to one of the assistants.

"Ben, can you upload the track the sound engineers finished and labeled 'Izzy'?"

"Sure, Bella, I'll get on it right away."

He knocked on her door a few minutes later.

"Come in."

"I just wanted to make sure you knew the track was loaded onto the system and is ready for download."

"Thanks."

"Are you all right? I noticed there was no activity on it after I sent the file, and you don't look well."

"It's just a headache."

"Hope you feel better." He closed the door behind him.

Feeling dizzy again, she laid her head on the desk to recover but fell asleep.

A notification pinging on her phone awakened her, and she lifted her head to look at the message. The digital time in the corner of the phone revealed an hour had passed. She felt her forehead—still warm with fever—and laid her head back on the desk.

I'll find Miles in a few minutes. I need to feel a little better before I consider sparring with him.

CHAPTER SIX

Miles glanced up from the monitor to see Mr. Curtis standing in the doorway.

"Yes, can I help you?"

He proceeded into the room and stood at his desk. Mr. Curtis had worked for his parents as their butler, but he was more of an estate manager and confidante to Miles.

"You nor Parker were answering your phones this morning, so Bella called earlier to tell me she would be late coming in today. She went to her doctor's office and didn't want the cook to prepare breakfast for her." Miles looked up from his computer and turned off the music.

"What's wrong with her?"

"I don't know, and I didn't ask. I looked out the window, and her car is parked outside, but I haven't seen her. Can you go to her office and check on her? She's more forthcoming with you."

"You think?" He snickered but was also concerned. "Let me call her."

"I would prefer if you go to her office and see her for yourself."

"All right. She's probably working hard. Why don't you prepare lunch for her and meet me in her office in a few minutes?"

"Okay and thank you. She's a good person and I think she may be working too hard. Most people don't have your stamina, and they need a little more rest. It concerns me how much time she has been putting in lately. I'll go and have cook prepare something for her now."

"Knowing you, it has already been prepared." He got up and walked to her office. The door was closed, and she didn't answer his knock. He turned the knob and peeked his head in the door.

"Bella?" He found her asleep with her head on the desk and a paper mask covering her mouth. She attempted to raise her head and her eyes were glazed over. He walked quickly toward her desk just before Mr. Curtis came in with a tray of food.

"Bella, what's wrong?" Mr. Curtis placed the tray of food and drinks on the table and grabbed her favorite drink, filled with electrolytes and minerals, which she had every afternoon with lunch.

"I went to the doctor this morning, and my blood pressure is a little low."

"Why are you wearing a mask? Do you have an infection?"

"Yes, but—"

Miles and Mr. Curtis recoiled. Miles saw the masks on her desk, grabbed one for himself and the other he handed to Mr. Curtis. He couldn't take the chance of getting sick weeks away from the start of a worldwide tour.

"I'm not contagious, Miles. I'm wearing the mask because of my sensitivity, I guess, to the fibers in my new carpet and fumes from the glue." He pulled down the mask and sniffed the air.

"I don't smell any strong odors, and I'm not allergic to fibers, but Mr. Curtis, will you make sure her office is aired out starting today?"

"Yes sir."

He covered his mouth and nose with the mask anyway after he noticed the prescriptions on her desk.

"I don't want to be too forward, but if you have an infection and low blood pressure, why are you here?" Miles felt her forehead, and she was warm to the touch. Mr. Curtis donned his mask before lifting her up in the chair to help her drink the electrolyte solution. They watched her drink it slowly, hoping she found some relief from the coolness of the drink. She put the glass back on the tray without consuming all of it.

"Bella, I'll get your prescriptions filled if you'd like."

"I have samples of my antibiotics, and I've taken a dose, but I haven't gotten the others filled. I'd appreciate it, Mr. Curtis." She handed the prescriptions to him.

"Is there anything else you want me to do before I leave to get your medicine?"

"No, thank you."

"Can you bring her some water, and I'll stay with her until you return. If we leave, I'll call you to let you know that she's home with her mother, and you can have her meds delivered there." Mr. Curtis left them alone and returned with two glasses of water and placed them on the tray.

"Please don't call my mother. She's out of town on business, and she'll come rushing back home to be with me."

"Okay, but first drink up." He scratched his head as she drank some of the water and contemplated what to do next. "You need someone to stay with you. Let me call— what's his name—Corey?" She rolled her eyes and held her hand up to stop him.

"I tried to contact him earlier, but my calls went to voicemail. He's busy."

"Too busy to care for his sick girlfriend? He's special, isn't he?"

"Miles, he doesn't know I'm not feeling well and let's not get into a disagreement about Corey right now."

"Fine, but you need someone to stay with you—and I'm adamant about it."

She straightened up in her chair and grabbed the glass to finish her drink.

"I appreciate your concern, but this is making me feel better and I can get home by myself, but before I leave, I need you to listen to a song they remastered for Isabelle today."

"Later, after I help you get home." She pulled away from his attempt to assist her out of the chair.

"Please Miles, just listen to me."

"Alright Bella, who is they? And why would I be interested in Isabelle's music?"

"You're interested because you'll be singing on the track. I had the music formatted and—"

"No, Bella. Hell no. This isn't a good idea."

She bit her lip to stop from bursting into tears. In her current state, she was no match for him.

"Why do you want me to do this?" He backed down, not wanting to upset her.

Her head was heavy, and despite feeling dizzy again, she tried but couldn't quite explain her plan; her thoughts were too scattered, so she lowered her head, feeling defeated.

"Why do you want me to do this?" Despite her frustration, he relented.

"To get you out of the obligation to Isabelle's father while offering him something that would please him. You do want him to allow us to use his venues for marketing the concert, don't you?" He placed his hands on his hips and thought about it.

"All right, I'll do it, but by the time I get you home and settled, it will be late. I'm not leaving you to play with some mediocre music."

"Then I'll stay." She lifted her head a little higher, but he shook his head no. He couldn't agree to her request.

"This is important to me. I'll drink a little more while you sing. You have a couch in your office, and I'll sit there while you listen to the music. It shouldn't take long."

"Bella, this is crazy, but I'll do it if you tell me why you came in when it's obvious, you're not well." She repositioned her mask and began coughing but proceeded to answer his question.

"I have a strong work ethic, and—" She started crying and didn't stop until he took her into his arms as she sobbed, overcome with emotion.

"I'm not sure why this is so important to you, but let me listen to the song first and I'll do it, okay? Please stop crying. Why don't you drink some water and relax."

As he helped her sit in the chair, he stumbled and flipped over the tray, causing the water and electrolyte drink to spill on him.

"Miles, you're all wet." He looked down at his shirt, drenched with water and sweat from his own discomfort and took it off after placing the glasses back on the tray.

"Come to my office with me and I'll get someone to clean this up. I'll shower and change there, and then we can listen to the music." She nodded and coughed again before placing the mask over her mouth and nose.

He placed his arm around her to help steady her while they walked out of her office.

Shirtless, he reached the door and opened it, surprising Parker on the other side of the door before he knocked.

"What the hell? Better yet, forget it. I need to go home to my family." He turned away but stopped after it registered to him, they were both wearing masks.

"What's the matter?" he asked, facing them but covering his mouth and nose.

"You shouldn't stay here. Bella's sick and possibly contagious. I'll take care of her and make sure she gets home."

"I'm not contagious, Miles. It's my allergies that have me coughing." Parker turned his attention back to Miles.

"I still don't understand why you're not wearing a shirt, but I don't want to stay to hear your explanation, risk getting infected, and take something home to my family. We'll talk tomorrow. I hope you feel better, Bella."

"Did you need to talk to me about something?" She lowered the mask from her mouth.

"It can wait until later. See you both tomorrow." He turned to leave, and they continued on their way to Miles's office.

She was asleep on the couch when he returned from his shower, and he was happy he had gotten out of his promise to listen to Isabelle's tracks. He was planning to take her home when her head rose from the couch.

"Not so soon, Moore. You promised to listen to the music, and you should have a master list of all the music recorded in the studio on your computer. Check today's list. It should be labeled 'Izzy.'"

He sat down as he was told and, after pulling up the music, clicked on the song and turned up the volume. Sitting back and listening to the first draft, he was grateful the remastered version was good. Humming the music running through his head, he paused the tracks at the positions marked by the producers and started singing the first take into the microphone.

She listened as he added his voice to the background vocals and sang the hook. It took a little longer than they planned, but he completed the first takes.

"This is just a preliminary recording, and we'll finalize it in the studio tomorrow. I have to admit it—I like the remastered version."

She sat still on the couch; her cough quieted after leaving her office. Mr. Curtis returned and came in through the door, which was left ajar with her medicine and a glass of water on his tray.

"Excuse me, but I left the written instructions from the pharmacy for your meds in the kitchen. I'll be right back."

She opened the bottles and took the meds before he returned.

"Did you take one half of the dose of your allergy med? You're supposed to increase it to the full dose tomorrow. I remember your pharmacist emphasized that you should take the full dose tomorrow because of possible side effects."

"Oh my goodness, I took the whole thing! I guess I didn't read the instructions on the bottle correctly." She fell back on the couch and, within minutes, felt drowsy and too unsteady on her feet to stand.

"Bella why don't you stay here and I'll open this couch, which is also a queen-sized bed. You're too unsteady on your feet and I don't want to risk you falling."

Mr. Curtis helped him. "Sleep well Bella. I hope you feel better." He prepared to leave.

"Thanks for everything Mr. Curtis." She waved goodbye.

Miles was about to leave his office when she opened her heavily lidded eyes.

"Please don't leave me."

"I'm here for you Bella."

Unsure if she was delirious from her fever and not aware of what she was saying—or if she really needed him—he decided to stay through the night with her. They were fully clothed, and he knew nothing was going to happen. She was sick, and he didn't want to risk getting whatever infection she had, so he placed his mask back on his face and made sure her mask still covered her mouth and nose before settling in beside her to get some sleep.

He woke up the next morning, and despite struggling to open his eyes, he felt uneasy from negative vibes filling the room. He finally blinked his eyes open and found Parker staring at him with a frown on his face.

"Again, dude? This is the second time I've found the two of you sleeping in bed together, and I'm getting a little sick of it."

The loud noise roused him from a sleepy to a fully awakened state, but Bella didn't move.

"Technically, you've found us asleep one time in bed together," he answered through a full stretch and muffled yawn.

"Always the jokester, aren't you?"

Justin came in and stopped in his tracks at the sight of Bella still asleep on the couch and Miles propped up on his elbows.

Darien walked in seconds later. "Miles, I called Bella and I can't find her. She's not answering her cell, but her car is—"

Reagan came into the room and stopped behind the men, still staring at the two of them. "Bella! Oh, I'm relieved to find you." Reagan's high voice finally roused Bella from her sleep and she blinked, trying to wake up.

"Are you alright? Why are you wearing a mask?"

Bella rose from the bed and held her head.

"You don't look well, and your eyes have this weird glazed look. Did you really let Miles take care of you? He's not a doctor. I'm calling your mother."

"Reagan, stop with the questions, please." She held up one hand and pleaded with her friend. "Don't call my mother and stop yelling; you're giving me a headache." She looked around the room at everyone staring at her.

"Can I please have some privacy while I get my things?" Bella retorted.

"Technically, this is my office. I don't know why I should leave." Miles looked at her, trying to gain control of the situation.

She looked back at him and said nothing. Reagan finally broke the silence.

"The men can leave, but I'm staying to help you," she insisted. "Do you need to go to the bathroom?"

"Place a mask over your face if you plan to stay with her. I can't have you sick too, just weeks before the start of the tour," Miles barked and rubbed Bella's arm to show his concern.

"It's my allergies, low blood pressure, and a non-contagious infection, guys." She snatched the mask off her face.

"All right, it's allergies." Miles matched her irritation.

"I'll leave for now, but I'll be back to check on you. Do you need anything other than some more water to take the rest of your medicine and maybe a smoothie? I'll have Mr. Curtis bring them to you." His tone softened.

"That sounds good. Thank you." She didn't look him in the eye.

Parker paced the floor as he looked at the others in the room.

"Miles, I need to talk to you in my office alone. Justin and Darien, let's reschedule and meet in an hour." They nodded and left as Miles headed for his desk.

"Mr. Curtis, can you bring Bella a smoothie and some water?" he called over the intercom.

"Sure thing Miles. I'll get cook right on it." Mr. Curtis responded.

"Thanks Miles." She offered a faint smile.

"Don't worry about her. I'll help Bella," Reagan reassured Miles before he followed Parker, who had refrained from speaking until they were behind closed doors in his office.

"I hope you don't plan to treat Bella like your plaything of the moment, and I don't like what's happening between the two of you."

"What are you talking about Parker?" The two of them circled each other.

"Stop it Miles. You can't play me, and you know exactly what I'm talking about. Please don't mess her over like that shithead producer who screwed over my sister. She thought he loved her, but he used her to get a job in the music industry." He ran his fingers through his hair. "You remember she became depressed and suicidal after he broke off their engagement. Bella is sweet like my sister, and if you don't have good intentions dude, leave her alone. I don't want you to hurt her." His anger was palpable but mixed with pain, causing Miles to pause.

"You're my best friend—and you think I'd do something like that?" He rubbed the stubble on his cheeks and chin to gather his thoughts before he spoke.

"Save it Miles. You and I have done a lot of things together, and I know your past with women more than anyone." Parker crossed his arms over his chest as they faced one another.

"Fair enough, but you know I was angry about what happened to your sister. I think it's ironic that I helped blackball that shithead—he never worked in the music industry in this town again—and now you're helping me make sure Scott Hansen, that bastard at World Music, doesn't blackball Bella. They're not happy that some of their artists have signed with me, and I don't want his anger at me directed towards her. She works here now, and we look out for each other at AriMusic, so yes, I may be a little more protective of her."

"Alright and yes, I'm grateful that you helped me, but don't try to deflect my concerns with talk about the bastards in this industry. I think you don't know your intentions when it comes to Bella, and by the time you discover them, it may spell disaster for you both."

"Parker, I'm asking you to leave this alone and let us sort this out."

"Fine, but what is *this*? And if *this* doesn't work out, what if she sues your ass for harassment or Corey tries to beat your ass or some shit like that? Don't say you weren't warned."

"That's a reach, but your concerns are duly noted," he snorted. "I'm leaving now."

"Good. I guess we're done." He pulled out his phone and checked the contacts. "I've texted the name and number of the nurse we have on retainer to you. Let me know if you think we should hire a professional sitter to stay with her while her mother's away. You're sure she only has allergies, low blood pressure, and some non-contagious infection? She looks bad."

"That's what she said, and I also think she's run down. She's been working very hard, but I'll make sure she gets home and is quarantined if she really is contagious. I don't want the tour members getting sick."

"You said that last night Miles."

"Yeah, but she needed me last night."

"And you needed to be her knight in shining armor coming to the rescue?"

Miles returned to his office and found Reagan by Bella's side.

"Can you give us a moment alone, Reagan?"

"Sure. I'll be outside to take you home after I gather your things from your office, okay, Bella?"

"Thanks, Reagan." She left the room and closed the door as Bella turned her head to face him.

"What had Parker so upset? I don't get it?"

"He thought I needed to do the right thing and address something with you."

"What is it?"

"He's concerned about your relationship with shithead Corey and so am I."

A wrinkle formed between her brows. "That doesn't sound like Parker, but it clearly sounds like something you would think—bringing up concerns about Corey. You want to do this now, when I'm not feeling well? Go for it."

"Well, aren't you concerned about a man who isn't there when you need him? Has he returned your calls or is he too busy?"

"I haven't checked my phone, but let's be clear. I appreciate all you've done for me, but my relationship with Corey is my business, not yours." She tried to get up from the couch but swooned. He grabbed her arm and helped her sit down.

"You deserve better. That's all I'm saying. I'll take you home."

"I don't need you to do that for me." Her throat was dry, and swallowing was still difficult.

"You need someone and he's not here," he responded quickly.

She rose too fast and stumbled on her feet again. "Oh, so who's being the dick now?"

"Okay, but it seems you have a dick who's here for you and a shithead who's not. Your choice."

"I choose neither then. I can't do this with you now." She grabbed her head and yelled for Reagan.

"Reagan, can you take me home now?"

She entered the room with Bella's things in her hand. "Sure, Bella. I can take you now." Reagan offered her a hand up.

"You both can take the limo." Miles got up and left the room without waiting for her response.

CHAPTER SEVEN

Less than a week had passed since Bella went on convalescent leave. She agreed to Miles's plan for private care a few hours a day with Sarah Dover, one of the health care aides on retainer for AriMusic, under the threat he would call her mother.

"Don't you think it's a bit much, Miles? I can take care of myself," she'd relayed to him over the phone when they'd discussed the idea of home care.

"I'm concerned about you, Bella, and I don't need someone or something else to worry about," he'd told her. She was feeling better and told him she didn't want her mother to worry or to end her contract with her new client in Texas, thinking it was better her mother believed she had a cold and a flare up of her allergies.

"Alright, you don't want to worry your mother, and I don't want to worry about you, so we have a deal and I'll not let her know the truth," he had promised her.

Miles gave her a few days to get better before calling her again, and she surprised him by agreeing to a short visit. She gave him directions to her house, located in the gentrified part of Highland Park, now a mecca for artists and those wanting an ethnically diverse neighborhood with a collection of trendy shops, galleries, and restaurants nearby. The traffic during the day added a little more time to the trip than he had expected, but he was enjoying the drive in his sporty Audi R8.

He rounded the corner on a street landscaped with Californian oaks, fern pine trees, and jacaranda trees with showy purple flowers, and he noticed bright lilacs growing in Bella's neighbors' yards. Unlike his estate, the street was brightly colored with flowers and trees in bloom.

The GPS announced his arrival, and he parked in front of a 1930s craftsman-style dwelling; it had been renovated but still retained lots of character. The home was painted in earthy colors of brown, tan, and green, and there was a large front porch with tapered columns and exposed rafters. A big welcome sign was attached to the side of the door.

He took off his shades, silenced his cell, and before getting out of the car, he looked in the rearview mirror one last time at the goofy smile he couldn't wipe off his face even if he wanted to. He missed her and couldn't wait to see her again. Grateful she had a forgiving nature; he'd apologized during their last phone call for his remarks about her boyfriend. Thinking he was helping her, he'd shared his impressions of Corey, but he knew in hindsight he had overstepped his boundaries and needed to make things right.

With the bouquet of red, orange, and purple flowers he'd purchased for her, he headed up the brick walkway and rang the doorbell. Sarah answered the door and invited him in.

"She's expecting you, Mr. Moore. I'll let her know you're here. Please have a seat."

"Thanks, Sarah." He entered the room, filled with multiple bouquets of flowers. Unaccustomed to the heavy fragrance of all the flowers, he began coughing.

"I'll be back with a glass of water for you and a vase filled with water for the flowers," she told him before exiting the room.

"Thank you, but I'd appreciate it if you take them and make sure she gets them later."

He handed her the bouquet.

Way to go man, I guess she won't need more flowers. He looked around the room, which looked more like a floral shop than the front room of a home.

Sarah left and returned promptly and handed him the glass of water.

"Miss Wahlberg is on her way. She saw the flowers you brought and was delighted. I need to check on something in the kitchen," she shared before leaving again. He nodded and drank from the glass before placing it on the table. Instead of taking a seat, he walked around, viewing one vase after another of beautiful floral arrangements of pink, cream, and yellow roses, carnations, lilies and baby's-breath. He also took the time to look at the cards of get well wishes from the Bronsons, Parker, Darien, the Bakers, members of the Fire God Tour, Mr. Curtis, and a separate arrangement from Corey.

He read Corey's message: *Get well and we'll be together soon. I'm making plans for us.* There was even an arrangement from Bosco and his handlers. He didn't recognize some of the other names on other cards.

Where's my arrangement?

He'd requested an arrangement of red roses to be delivered to her earlier in the week but didn't see it.

I guess I didn't get the memo to send light-colored flowers or pale-pink roses. Even the arrangement with Bosco's name on it had pink roses in it.

"Aren't all those arrangements beautiful?" He turned toward Bella's voice and greeted her with a light embrace.

"Yes, they are, but I sent an arrangement earlier this week. I don't see a bouquet of red roses or a card from me.

Red is my favorite color and I thought you could use something vibrant to brighten your day."

"That arrangement of two dozen roses is in my bedroom on a table where I see it first thing in the morning, and it's the last thing I see at night. It's simply gorgeous and thank you for the arrangement you brought today. Sarah is placing them in a vase now." He smiled and stood close to her. "It was nice of you to come. I know how busy you are."

"No problem. I needed to take a break and check on my number-one girl."

She smiled. "Thanks for your concern, and please, make yourself comfortable."

She pointed to a set of chairs in the living room, the room decorated with a combination of modern and French-styled furniture. The walls in the comfortable yet stylish home were painted a modern blue and trimmed in white.

"All these flowers aren't kicking off your allergies?"

"No, my medications have helped control my coughing and sneezing."

"I'm glad to hear it. Lots of people have missed you in your absence." He took a seat and looked down at his feet before facing her. "I'm sorry if I hurt you. I didn't mean to be harsh but—"

"I've forgiven you already. Let's not rehash it again, please." Her eyes pleaded with him, and he nodded in silent agreement to change the subject.

"So, tell me, how's it going with the preparation for the tour? There's a little more than a week left before you kick it off."

"Thanks to you, things are going well. You were so ahead of schedule, and the rest of us had to play catch-up. Darien placed additional meet and greets in my schedule to help promote Isabelle's song, which is continuing to climb the charts. They told me you planned everything—the media story about us being a short-lived couple, the collaboration on the song, and even her break-up with me. Darien found the notes for the promotional plans you made for the tour and I signed off on all of them."

"Thanks. I hope you didn't mind the slant on the media story about her dumping you, but female fans are more sympathetic to a heartthrob who is dumped, and she insisted we spin it that way."

"I didn't mind. I knew I had some hell to pay for calling her by your name." They both laughed and he looked at his watch, knowing he didn't plan to stay long and needed to let her know some things while he still had the nerve. He just wasn't sure how to say it.

"Is something wrong?"

"I need to let you know how much I've missed you. I found myself heading to your office to share something with you only to remind myself you weren't there. You've brought something different to my business, my music, and my life, and I want to thank you. I like how you just get things done and don't worry if it's your job."

Her chest heaved, and she took in a breath to absorb the moment.

"Say something, Bella; I'm not getting a good read on your facial expressions."

"Thank you; I wasn't expecting that from you."

"Why? Because I'm a dick?"

"No." A little nervous laughter escaped. "It's because you have high expectations for yourself and those around you. I've seen you rehearse a short section of music over and over until it was exactly what you wanted."

"I can be demanding, but it doesn't mean I'm blind to the efforts of those who go above and beyond what's expected of them. People often tell me how sweet you are, and I agree, but I also see someone with a lot of business savvy. You know your stuff, and you have a great way of handling people. You're my secret weapon."

"Secret weapon? What does that mean?"

"It means you're the one I call on when I'm under siege and need to win a battle. You're helping the business grow faster than I expected at this point in my career."

"Thank you for acknowledging my contributions Miles. Oh, by the way, forgive me for not properly thanking you for the bigger office and the bonus."

"You earned it. Parker showed me the revenue increases for the last two quarters, which were directly related to your efforts in securing lucrative contracts." She blushed in embarrassment, uncomfortable with the praise.

"I spoke to the case manager assigned to your care, after I made sure you had signed the papers giving him permission to talk to me of course, and he assured me you weren't contagious or a business risk. I need my voice."

"I understand. The healthcare team is also here to protect you and your business. I get that. Would you like some tea?"

"Sure."

She poured him a cup of hot water from the teapot she'd placed on the table just before his arrival and handed him the cup while he looked through the box of tea to choose a flavor. He dunked a bag of chamomile tea in the hot water and smiled at her as she poured the hot water on a bag of English breakfast blend, dipping the bag and darkening it to her taste. He noticed how much she seemed to enjoy the aroma as she sniffed it before placing the bag on a saucer on the tray, then stirred it before she spoke. "Can I change the subject?" He looked up from his cup. "Something has been on my mind too, and I wanted to talk to you about it while I had the chance."

"What is it?" He sipped a bit of his tea, then gave her his full attention.

"It's personal, but I thought you've asked me about my background, and I wanted to know more about yours. Shouldn't one disclosure beget another disclosure?"

"Is that biblical or something you made up?"

She laughed. "I made it up, but don't change the subject, I want to know more about your genetic condition."

"Oh, that. There's not much more to tell. I was diagnosed when I was six or seven, and I don't know how to feel separate from it or to be *normal*. There are a few hundred people in the world with the same anomaly, many of whom have died tragically by fire because they didn't learn how to manage it."

"How did they discover you had it?"

He finished his tea and placed his cup on the table.

"My uncle discovered me emitting fireballs from my hands and told my parents. They researched it, and I ended up at the NIH undergoing tests. My parents had the money to move to Maryland with me, and my father worked in Washington, DC, while the doctors studied me. They told us I have the rarest form of the anomaly. I can create intense fireballs in addition to small flames, I tolerate smoke inhalation, and I can bear high levels of heat without burning my skin. I had to see my medical team routinely for a year, but I give them some of the credit for encouraging my talent. To pass time during my visits, they had me singing and dancing for the staff and the other patients. I performed at the holiday parties and saw how happy it made the kids hospitalized with severe burns. Not all forms of the anomaly come with the proteins in the skin required to protect the person from burns.

"I see, and children you may have can inherit it?"

"Yes, but I won't be passing it on because I don't plan to have children."

"Never?"

"No, never." She sat back to absorb how adamantly he spoke.

"So, what was the worst part of it?" She tried changing the subject.

"I found the behavioral therapy part of it the most tedious, but it helped me to deal with my feelings of estrangement from others, and it gave me the chance to process the fact that I was different. To this day, my arrogance at times is really my anger at not fitting in. The therapy allowed me to get a handle on some of the anger. I used to have fits of rage and set things on fire during my adolescence."

She reflected on his disclosure. "We're not that different from each other, you know—I mean when it comes to fitting in with others."

"What do you mean? Everyone on the executive team wants to spend time with you. Mr. Curtis has breakfast for you to get his Bella time. Parker sees you as a sister, and you are besties with Reagan and Darien. Even Bosco comes in your office and sits at your feet. He responds to some of the commands from you just as fast as he responds to commands from me. I saw the card and flowers his handler sent you. Since you've been gone, he mopes around looking for you. I know he misses you." His sad eyes reflected it was also his truth. "Everyone has Bella time except me. I'm constantly told I'm the boss and to be careful about our relationship."

"It's strange, Miles, but I once had a conversation with my mother about you. I told her you had an easy way with everyone except me. I thought I didn't fit in. Remember when you constantly called me Belsa?"

"Let's not revisit that part of our past. It wasn't one of my finer moments."

"For the record, you do get time with me. You're in my head throughout the day as I try to think of ways to promote AriMusic."

"I'm just in your head?" He tilted his head and smiled.

"You're always in my head," she chuckled.

He sat back, observing her. *Should he accept he wasn't in her heart, or was it that they both weren't ready to admit it?* He wasn't sure what his heart was telling him about her, or maybe it was just him who wasn't ready to accept he was falling for her. Either way, he was confused about the feelings he was developing for her.

"I don't want to tire you out, so I'd better leave. When are you planning to come back to work?" He leaned forward, eager to know.

"I'm planning on coming back in a couple of days."

"Good. Let me know if you need anything." He stood, leaned over, and embraced her longer than the usual goodbye hug, then pulled back, looking into her eyes.

"Please don't share my medical history with anyone. Even Parker doesn't know about my genetic anomaly. I'm surprised I was so open with you."

"Really? You're kidding. You haven't told Parker?"

"No, and that's why we've been friends for so long. He respects my privacy, so he doesn't ask, and I don't tell."

"You can trust me to not tell anyone and thank you for trusting me. It means a lot to have you as a boss, and I hope one day we can be friends."

"We're already friends." He gave her a slight smile and offered his fist in a fist bump. "Do you mind if I use your bathroom before I leave?"

"Sure, there's one down that hall around the corner and on your left."

"Thanks." He walked down the hall toward the bathroom as she had instructed. He relieved himself and was on his way back to the front of the home when sunlight from a room just beyond the bathroom shined a pink light onto the cream-colored walls of the hall. Curious, he peered inside and saw the picture of a little girl with spots of paint on her face, smiling and looking up at a large man who smiled with his whole face at the little girl. There was also a picture of the two of them on a motorcycle. On the table in front of the bed, a large bouquet of red roses sat just as she said.

"You're lost?" came a voice behind him.

"Sort of, lost in time. I guess I got turned around on my way back."

"You live in a mansion three times the size of this home, and you expect me to believe you were lost?"

"All right, I'll admit I'm more curious than lost. The pink hue shining in the hallway seemed so different from the colors in the rest of the house. My uncle is an architect, and the designs and color palettes in homes have always interested me. Was your bedroom a project you shared with the man in the picture? I'm assuming he was your daddy."

"Yes, that's my father." She came into the room, closer to the pictures, and touched the image of her father. "This room is a replica of the room he designed for me when we lived in Texas. Reproducing the room here in California was the way my mother chose to make me feel comfortable in our new home. She has been begging me for years to remodel this room, but I haven't gotten to it yet."

"Is it your attempt to hold on to the memories of your daddy's love?"

"Should I call you Therapist Miles?" She tensed her shoulders and placed her hand on her hips.

"And, it hasn't escaped me that you called him my daddy instead of my father. I know the room looks like a little princess room, but I assure you that I'm fully grown." She jerked her head toward the ceiling.

"I'm not judging you. This is your home, and you have the right to decorate it as you choose, but if I may, can I share something with you?"

"Sure, go ahead," she relaxed her shoulders. "I'm a big girl; I can take it."

"Any man would be weakened by the sight of this room. It's not made for adult action, if you understand what I'm saying. It's making me limp right now."

Despite herself, she burst out laughing.

"You're being silly, but Corey once said something similar." She rolled her eyes and pushed him toward the door. "Let's not get you stuck in traffic. Follow me. I wouldn't want you to get lost."

She walked him to the door, and they hugged goodbye before he returned to the car and pulled off from the curb.

CHAPTER EIGHT

She had returned to work, medically cleared by Dr. Jones, and was way too busy preparing for the launch of the tour to entertain the critical thoughts running through her head, as they were relentless and judgmental.

"Miles, the flowers you sent are in my bedroom. I look at them every morning..." and *"Miles, you're in my head all the time..."* and worse still, *"Miles, one day we can be friends."*

She sat at her kitchen table and covered her face with her hands. It was a good thing he wasn't a master of subtlety. He didn't seem to get that she was spilling out her feelings about him, however conflicted they were. How could she not have kind feelings for someone who had been so caring?

Corey was her man, but she couldn't deny it anymore. He hadn't been there recently when she needed him, and Miles...dear Miles...had showed up for her. She loved Corey, and he had explained profusely why they hadn't spent more time together lately. She understood how important acquisitions of new stores were to him, and he told her the negotiations had stalled. It was true he had been more attentive to her throughout most of their relationship and he was a Steady Eddie, but was she *in* love with him?

She hoped Miles hadn't seen her flushed face after she'd discovered him in her room. *Even if I sleep in a room once made for a little girl, I'm a woman by any definition. I make my own decisions, earn my own money, and have all the physical attributes of a woman. He said he understood the room was a link to the first man I had ever loved, my father, so why should I feel embarrassed?*

She tapped her foot in frustration, fully aware that, beneath her cool façade and the game face she wore in public, she was dealing with the chronic effects of early parental loss that Dr. Jones had spoken to her about many times. She finished her breakfast, put away her dishes, and went to turn on the radio in her bedroom to listen to a little music and traffic news while she finished putting on her blue dress with matching heels. One of her old favorite songs came on, and she started rapping, her mood lifting as she put on her clothes and danced around the room.

"Makin my own money,
Girl, handle yo' business.
Lovin' on my honey,
Girl handle yo' business.
Tables are a turnin',
And all o' my haters,
in their own hells
are burnin'
Ain't none o' yo business,
How I handle my business."

She grabbed her bag and turned off the radio, finally ready to leave for work when her phone rang on the table and a picture of Darien illuminated the screen.

"Hi, Darien, what's up?"

"Hey, Belles. I'm sorry to tell you this, but NeNe Moore, Miles's cousin and lawyer, is asking if you can meet with her in the next hour. I know this is short notice, but trust me, you want to find out what she wants and move on. To be fair, she had to change her schedule at the last minute to accommodate Miles's schedule. NeNe may be direct, but she's good people. She and Miles have always been close, and she loves her cousin. She has been in New York over the last six months involved in a big case, and it was unusual that he hired you without vetting you with her first."

"Alright, tell NeNe I'll meet her in an hour. Text the details to me. I was just on my way out the door. I guess it's better to get it over with rather than spend the day fretting over what may happen when I meet with her."

"Great. A driver will be waiting to take you to her hotel. Bye, girl."

"Bye."

A tall, gorgeous woman with the most alluring green eyes answered Bella's knock at the hotel room door.

"Hello. Are you Bella Wahlberg?"

"Yes, I am."

"Good. I'm NeNe Moore; come in." NeNe closed the door behind them and Bella looked around the nicely appointed suite, perfect for business and pleasure.

"Thanks for coming on such short notice. I know you're busy attending to final details for the tour. Have a seat. Can I offer you something?"

"No, thank you." She took a seat and prepared for the vetting process. She knew the meeting was part introduction and part information gathering for NeNe. Based on information from Darien, Bella knew NeNe was territorial when it came to Miles, and she expected her to share her opinions and concerns. *The downside of working for a business with family members as employees, I guess.*

NeNe gave Bella a folder.

"This is a bio on Miles. I've met your mother, and I'm sure she did some research on him before taking the consulting job, but I wasn't sure if she'd shared any of it with you. Has she?"

Bella didn't have an opportunity to answer before NeNe continued her courtroom-style examination. Bella remained seated with her hands on top of the folder.

"I know a few things about you—such as you've signed a nondisclosure agreement as a part of the terms of your employment, you've been around Miles long enough to know he has a small inner circle, and you're aware his people are very loyal to him. Is that correct?"

"Yes, I would say that's true." She maintained eye contact.

"And you've proven your loyalty, according to those same people, by repeatedly going beyond the call of duty. I want to thank you for your service to the organization."

"Sure NeNe, if I may call you by your first name. I was just doing my job."

"Of course Bella, please call me NeNe. Miles is my client, but more important to me, he's family. I would do anything for him, including protect him from himself. Open the folder. We can talk as you review the high points."

Bella did as she was instructed.

"Your mother may not have told you that Miles was kidnapped at birth, taken from his mother's womb by disturbed people. He was only held by them for a brief period, but it took a lot out of her worrying if her baby was still alive. She kept him close to her, and as an only child for quite a while before his sisters came along, he found comfort in his music, performing for the family; and in studying science. One day, he created a chemical reaction, which resulted in fire and he's been fascinated by fire ever since. Several years ago, he disappeared for months to view volcanic eruptions and other natural phenomena in every corner of the globe. We lost contact with him and, at one point thought he might have been dead—it scared the family to death. He's been very successful in his career, and this would be an unfortunate time to worsen his obsession with fire. We can't risk him making a bad decision to disappear again because of his addiction to fire, and he would be sued for breach of contract if he missed a performance. Many of his venues are indoors, and this amount of firepower has never been used indoors before. I've shared my concerns with him, but his response was, 'No guts no glory.' She paused and let out a deep sigh before continuing as Bella shifted in her seat under NeNe's scrutiny.

"I've been involved in negotiations on a very complex case in New York, and it's a little late for me to change things for this tour, but I just don't want him to continue the theme of the Fire God on subsequent tours. I'm sure you can understand why you shouldn't encourage him to use all these dramatic fire displays in his act, especially with all the concerns about terrorist activity, don't you? We wouldn't want people to get hurt at one of his shows, especially if the fire displays fall into the hands of evil people who use them as weapons to possibly hurt others."

"Of course, I don't want people to get hurt either. We can agree on that." She narrowed her eyes and tried to soften the sharp tone of her voice as NeNe continued.

"I understand you took the fact that his records are, excuse the pun, *blazing* up the charts along with the reviews of how *hot* Ari is right now to come up with the tour's name. You were the first to recognize that his fans know he loves the color red and red shirts sell out when he comes to town, also that questions about jewelry with rams on it have been trending on social media for quite some time. I thought you needed to understand the origins of his love affair with fire if you're going to work closely with him."

Bella listened to NeNe and made a mental note to research the possibility of developing a jewelry line to go with the tour. She steadied herself and closed the folder before addressing NeNe's concerns.

"Thank you for arranging this meeting today and I take it as a compliment that you've shared information with me only people in Miles's inner circle should know. I knew he had a genetic condition, but I didn't know as much as you shared today. Please understand I don't take concerns for him and his fans lightly. I'm in charge of marketing, and you're aware he likes when each of us on the executive team shares our opinions with each other. We have a very cohesive team, but I'm not the production manager, nor do I design the shows."

"He told you about his condition?"

Bella returned the folder to NeNe, who stood with her mouth open at Bella's disclosure.

"Yes, he did."

NeNe wrinkled her forehead. "You're not encouraging him to tell others, are you?"

Bella gasped. "Of course not—I haven't talked to him about anything like that. Why would you ask?"

"My uncle was concerned about Miles possibly doing a disclosure."

"I don't think you're aware, NeNe, that I lost my father, who died fighting a fire. Because of that, I could never encourage a compulsion for fire, and I don't understand his condition so I would never lend an opinion on how he should live with it. I have panic attacks sometimes with unexpected exposure to fire and to lightning strikes. It's true that I named the tour, and I gave him recommendations on how to promote the tour, but I think you already know Miles is his own man. No one makes him do things he doesn't want to do. If you can't control him, certainly you know I can't. He gave my career the break I needed and I'm thankful for the opportunity to share my skills with his organization. I'd never hurt him."

NeNe didn't respond to her right away, and Bella looked at her as she tented her fingers to her mouth while contemplating how to respond.

It must be a family trait. She had seen Miles respond in the same manner.

"You make good points, Bella. Miles is his own man and more than capable of making his own decisions. I'm sorry for your loss. Have you shared your history with him?"

"Yes, NeNe. He knows." She chose not to share how he came to know her history.

"I have a few more things to discuss with you before we finish. Parker shared some concerns he had with me. Bella, has Miles ever made you feel uncomfortable or harassed in his presence?"

"No. Why are you asking?"

"For legal purposes, I need to know the answers to these questions."

"Has his language ever been sexist or inappropriate in your presence?"

"No."

"Did your new office or bonus come with any strings attached by your estimation?"

She shook her head and stared at NeNe, unprepared for the turn their conversation had taken.

"If you're asking if I have ever had concerns about any type of harassment, the answer is no. Tell me, why are you really asking me these questions?"

"Alright, full disclosure; Parker said he found the two of you in bed together."

Bella blew out a long breath to manage her irritation.

"Did he also tell you I was fully clothed and sick at the time on a couch that yes, opened into a bed? We don't have a sexual relationship, NeNe, and he's never made me feel uncomfortable in his presence. This is personal for Parker. I've heard from people in the organization he's been on a crusade since his sister's disastrous relationship with her boss, but since he's so concerned, could you convince him and Miles to provide the funds for training the staff and for upgrading the policy regarding harassment at AriMusic? The organization has grown, and I would hate to deal with the negative publicity from a harassment case, especially if we've never addressed these issues with the staff before something bad happened."

"Good point, and I agree we could do better in regard to risk management for a growing company. That's all I need to hear, so...I guess this thing with you and Miles is a case of two people possibly falling for each other even though one of you is already in a relationship? Parker seems concerned about that too."

Bella leaned back in her chair; lips drawn.

"My bad. I'm just his lawyer, not the matchmaker." NeNe relaxed and held her hands upward, demonstrating her intent to stop her line of questioning. "That was all I needed to share with you, Bella. Do you have any questions for me?"

"I can't think of any." *I just want to get the hell out of here.*

NeNe held up her index finger. "I do have one more for you. Are you planning on accompanying him on the tour?" She placed the folders back in her briefcase.

"No, Wahlberg Fire Safety Consultants has some other projects that could use my attention, and Miles has allowed me to help them as much as I can. I probably won't get to see any of Miles's concerts on this tour."

"It's always good to see the end result of your work, but this won't be his last tour. I think you could benefit from talking to the vendors and getting some valuable insights from them. Please consider attending at least one show."

"That's good advice. I'll look at my schedule." Bella rose from her seat and extended her hand. "Goodbye, NeNe. It was good to finally meet you."

"It was good to finally meet you, too. I hope we can get together again when I'm in town in the future." She walked her to the door.

"Goodbye Bella." NeNe closed the door. Relieved an elevator was available, Bella proceeded with haste down the hall and got in just before the door closed. Unable to take a deep breath until after she got back into the limousine waiting for her in front of the hotel, she was glad her meeting with NeNe Moore, Esq., was over. After her departure from World Music, the last thing she wanted to do was get on the bad side of another music exec or his lawyer.

NeNe is as intimidating as Miles can be. Hopefully, she's less intimidating when you get to know her. Bella soothed herself with the fact she'd made her point that Miles had the right to make his own decisions regarding his performances.

She sat deep in thought for most of the ride and only broke her train of thought when the car came to a stop in front of one of the state parks.

"Why are we here?" she asked the driver, whom she thought was taking her to the estate.

"Mr. Moore is waiting for you," he answered. Miles opened the door from the outside dressed in hiking gear with Bosco by his side. She was surprised to see him and had no idea what he had planned. Looking around, she saw a full-sized camper parked beside the limousine as she took his extended hand and exited the car.

"So, you survived the famous NeNe Moore interrogation. Turn around and let me see if you're still in one piece." He twirled her around. "Nice! She didn't take a chunk out of your ass."

Bella laughed. She had on a blue dress, pearls, and heels—not dressed for a day in the forest. "Why did you have me brought here if you knew I just left the appointment with NeNe?"

He pulled her in the direction of the camper. "I thought you might need to commune with nature after your time with her. Bosco and I are going on a short hike, and I'm requesting the pleasure of your company."

Bella waved her hand down her body to display she wasn't dressed for the occasion.

"Come with me, Bella. There are hiking clothes for you in the camper. You can change in there while Bosco and I wait for you out here."

"Do I have a choice to accept or refuse the invitation?" she asked playfully as Bosco began circling around the two of them.

"No, you do not, and Bosco isn't taking no for an answer."

Bosco nudged her leg.

"He wants to walk, and he's impatient to get started."

That figures, after all, he belongs to you. Bella leaned down to give Bosco a hug and to stroke his back. "Well, since Bosco went to all this trouble, I guess I'll go along."

He led her to the camper, and it didn't take long for her to change her clothes. She came out of the camper dressed in a cotton shirt, hiking shorts, and black hiking boots.

"Where did you get these boots? They are so comfy, and they fit perfectly," she asked while lacing them up.

"Darien picked them out for you and I only insisted that they be black. They look good on you," he said, tossing a light backpack to her.

Bosco started up the trail ahead of them, looking back only once to make sure they were behind him.

She had hiked this trail before and knew the slopes were mainly gentle ones and the scenes picturesque. He held her hand the entire time they climbed up to the summit.

She loved climbing up the Santa Monica Mountains, with the rolling, rounded hills and low mountains nestled near the Pacific Coast that stretched into Hollywood. Large swaths of grasslands spread out before them. It wasn't shaded along parts of the path, so Miles dug into his backpack and pulled out hats and sunglasses for them.

An incredible display of wildflowers, blooming in bright spring colors, surrounded them. She looked at him, and he was smiling as he looked around at the nature on display. She pulled away from him to grab her cell out of her left back pocket.

"I want to take a picture of you. I don't see you smile like this too often, and I want to capture this moment."

"I'll agree only if you let me take a selfie of the two of us. If I can get Bosco to stay still, I'd like to take a picture of us with him in it too."

"Okay, let's do it."

Bella took a picture of him alone, then they posed for a series of pictures, including some with Bosco. She was happy he'd planned this day.

"Let me hold your phone." He took it and programmed additional personal numbers in her contacts and sent the selfies to himself before giving back her phone and grabbing her hand as they continued up the hill together, with Bosco running in front of them. They reached the top of Sandstone Peak, with its views of the Pacific Ocean and the Santa Monica Bay. She looked over the hill and spotted Bosco licking the face of a man she didn't know before the man walked toward them with Bosco in tow.

"What took you so long?" He extended his hand to Miles.

"Bella, this is Carl Jones, Bosco's newest trainer and one of his handlers. Carl, this is Bella Wahlberg, my new chief of marketing."

Carl smiled in greeting. "The helicopter is waiting for the two of you over there. I'll go down the hill with Bosco and see you both back at the estate. Good to finally meet you, Bella." She waved goodbye before Carl trotted down the hill with Bosco running happily behind him.

Miles led her to an area where they sat and sipped water.

"There are protein bars in your sack if you want a quick bite." She pulled out a bar while he lay on his back, looking up at the sky and at the Pacific Ocean stretching out before them. She sat cross-legged on the ground, munching on the bar.

"I have one more surprise for you. We'll need to fly over to the area where I have the surprise. Are you okay in a helicopter?"

"Yes, I've been in a helicopter before," she replied and went willingly with him.

The afternoon with him has been so great, but this isn't a date; he doesn't have time for dates, and I have a boyfriend.

She hurried to the helicopter with him, and the blades started to rotate, causing them to duck as they got in the back. His gorgeous smile returned as he motioned for her to buckle in and put on her headset before they took off for the flight over LA. It was a cloudless day and the sky was blue, its beauty unimpeded by the effects of smog as they flew over the city's iconic sites, including the Santa Monica Pier, the Griffith Observatory with its spectacular views of the Pacific Ocean, and downtown LA past the Sunset strip. They touched down outside a garage, and the rotating blades slowed as the helicopter prepared to come to a stop. He helped her out of the helicopter, and they walked hand-in-hand into the garage, filled with expensive cars and motorcycles.

"Mr. Moore, your cycle is ready. The helmets are on the table beside the bike."

Miles nodded and walked past a row of pricey bikes. He stopped in front of a shiny titanium one.

"Is that an Ecosse Titanium Series FE? The last of the Heretic series?"

She had a few surprises of her own. He widened his eyes and opened his mouth, speechless.

"Yes, it is."

Bella walked slowly toward the bike and reached out to touch it. She rubbed the handlebar, then the seat, before walking around the bike and taking in the artisanship of the expensive ride.

"I'm impressed by your knowledge of bikes. This is a custom-made Ecosse for two riders. I wouldn't have guessed you knew bikes. When did you become interested in them?" He gave her a helmet to put on.

"My father owned a Harley. We took care of it together and read magazines about bikes. He took me for rides, especially when Mom was at work. Motorcycles are part of the fond memories I have of my father." She took the helmet.

"I want to take you on a ride, but I don't want it to get too dark before we make our way back home, so we need to get going. We should change into some jeans first. Two pairs should be in the bathroom over there. Are you interested in a ride?"

"Interested? Let's go."

He pointed to the room labeled *Male*. "Darien was informed that the female bathroom was out of order today. Do you mind if we change together? There are separate stalls in the bathroom."

She was feeling a little frisky. "I've seen the goods already, Moore."

"So, you have, Wahlberg. Let's get going."

They changed into the dark jeans and boots that were located in the stalls. Bella liked the black riding jacket that complimented her outfit and put it on before joining him at the side of the bike. While she was still walking toward him, he threw his leg across the seat and moved up on the fine leather upholstery to allow space for her. She got on with a little help from him as the bike's motor revved up just before he moved it out of the garage and onto the road.

He drove for a short distance at an even, moderate pace, moving carefully as they merged into traffic. She heard his voice through the microphone in her helmet.

"Hang on Bella, I'm about to take you on a ride."

She tightened her grip around his waist. The quick acceleration of the bike pushed her off his back, but she settled into a comfortable position after repositioning herself on the seat and leaned her head to the side against his back, relaxing with him as the driver. It wasn't long before he opened up the bike full throttle for a couple of miles to show her what it could do. She smiled at him as he looked at her in the side mirror and slowed back to a moderate pace, as traffic was increasing on the roads leading back to the estate. When they arrived at his home, he cut the power to the bike, and they both got off before coming out of their jackets and taking off their helmets.

She felt so exhilarated from the ride that she threw caution to the wind, sprung into his arms, and placed a kiss on his lips. He kept his grip around her and deepened their kiss. She belonged to another, but in this moment, she surrendered to the whim to kiss him. While the two of them were kissing, Darien came out of the house, jaw dropped in surprise that the two of them were impetuously locked in a long embrace.

"So, Bella, you enjoyed the ride?" he asked.

She heard him but chose to take her time ending the kiss, and it felt as if Miles was in no rush to end their embrace either. She finally came to her senses.

I'm kissing my boss.... I'm the chief of marketing, and I'm kissing him in front of another employee. Hell. She bit her lip, now surprised by her impetuous behavior and backed away, placing her hand above her heart, which was beating so hard she was convinced it would burst out of her chest as she struggled to catch her breath.

"I'm sorry. And...yes...Darien...I did enjoy the ride." She looked at Darien, eyes wide, and sucked her lower lip back into her mouth. She didn't know what to make of her feelings. It was too confusing. She kept her gaze on Darien, but she felt Miles's eyes still on her.

"Don't be mad at me, Bella," Darien said as he took her hand. "He swore me to secrecy, and he signs all the checks around here." She loosened Darien's grip and turned to Miles.

"Yes, he does." At first, she couldn't look into his eyes as she tried to erase all the initial excitement she'd felt out of her voice. "Miles, thank you so much for such a fun time. I'm sorry I took up so much of your afternoon. I know you have tons of things to do, and I should be getting home."

"It was my pleasure to spend my day off with you Bella. It was relaxing, pleasurable, and I'm not sorry we spent more time together having fun. I should thank you, so please don't be embarrassed that we kissed each other. We're human and got caught up in the moment."

She knew he'd blown off a day of rehearsals and interviews and called him on the lie. "Miles, it wasn't your day off. I had interviews lined up for you."

He shrugged his shoulders. "Darien, Justin, and Parker did the interviews. I'm the boss, and sometimes it's my day off when I say it's my day off. I'll be available to answer questions tomorrow at the meet and greet, and I'll be available at my birthday party. We both know it's really a press party. Don't worry about it."

"Okay, I won't worry, but I should go. Can I get a ride home?"

He nodded.

"I'll call for the ride," Darien assured her and began walking toward the house to call for a car.

She chatted with Miles a bit more before the car came around to meet her.

"The driver should have the outfit you had on earlier today. See you later."

"Goodbye, Miles, and thanks again." She got in after the driver opened the door and hurried back to his seat to drive her home.

Miles watched the car travel slowly down the hill. Darien had told him he thought Bella would be perfect for him if they had met under a different set of circumstances, of course with his trademark statement, *but it's none of my business.*

They waved goodbye to each other a final time, and the car disappeared from view. His phone rang, and he answered it while walking toward the house.

"This is NeNe."

"I know."

"Did Bella say anything about our meeting today? If so, remember there are two sides to the story but often only one truth. I admit I focused more on you than on the usual banter about the job."

"I didn't expect any less of you." He snorted.

"You brought her into the inner circle without discussing it with me first Miles, and I wanted to get some sense of why she deserved to be there."

"Bella didn't say anything about the meeting." He was quiet as he listened to her response.

"Oh really? What is it about the two of you holding your cards close to your chest? You're still not saying much about her, and she didn't let you know how well she held up under examination? I need to see you tonight to discuss some interesting points she brought up."

"Sure, let's get together later. Why don't you bring your nosey ass over to the house at seven tonight?" She snickered and then her voice took on a more serious tone.

"I'll be there, but are you all right? It's not like you to keep anything from me. We've held each other's secrets and concerns since childhood. I sense your feelings for Bella are...complicated."

"Yes, NeNe. I'm good, we're good, but it's none of your business how I feel about Bella. I don't ask about the men in your life."

"Advantage point to Miles."

"See you soon NeNe. Goodbye."

"See you soon, cuz. Goodbye."

CHAPTER NINE

Although there were several details to wrap up before the tour, Bella decided to work from home again today. The other team members didn't seem to mind since she responded so promptly to all of their text messages and email requests. She convinced herself she was more efficient working remotely since there was a flurry of activity as members of the band, the dancers, and technical support people spent most of their time at the estate in the final days before the tour. The U.S. leg of the tour kicked off in 24 hours, and the members of the tour, especially the new members, buzzed around like little bees with smiles constantly on their faces.

To her relief, not only had the charity gala last night been a huge success, but Corey had been able to take a break from the main store to escort her to the dinner and dancing part of the evening. While billed as a charity gala, with champagne fountains, a silent auction, and guests in formal wear, the event was really a fancier version of meet and greets for VIP ticket holders at Ari's concerts. Bella had arranged enough events to know Miles had little tolerance for cocktail party chatter; therefore, she arranged it, so he only had to spend two hours with patrons and supporters who had paid big bucks for the personal meet and greet with him.

Determined to stay focused on her work, she had planned to spend as little time as possible with Miles; she didn't want to be alone with him since she was still sorting out her feelings regarding their kiss.

What does it mean? And what does it say about my feelings for Corey?

While pondering those thoughts, she also wondered about the hints Corey had dropped while dancing with her at the gala last night.

"I'm so glad you've been so understanding about the extra time I've spent at work lately. You know I'm doing it for our us and our future, even though I'm not worried about finances. As a man, I think it's important to take care of your family."

"Our future?" she had asked.

"Yes, it's time we start talking about our future together." He had led her back to the table after the song ended, but she was too busy putting out fires to ask additional questions at that time.

"Do you like yellow gold, white gold, or platinum jewelry?" he had asked just before she needed to leave their table to schmooze with the executive members of Bronson Media to ensure the radio and television stations in the tour cities were ready for upcoming media blitzes.

"Platinum," she had answered, but she was baffled that he seemed to be making plans for the two of them yet distancing himself from her with the excuse he needed to work. She knew she loved Corey like a dear friend with exclusive benefits, but she wasn't sure she wanted to be engaged to him.

Get your head back in the game Bella. No need to worry about Corey right now.

She would figure out what Corey's actions meant later. An urgent text from Darien appeared on her phone:

Darien: Bella, I noticed you
aren't a member of the online
community in the Miles's World
app yet. Download it on your
computer and your phone
immediately. It's mandatory that
you have it when we go on tour.
It's how we talk to each other.
Miles is requesting, correction,
insisting you attend his
birthday party so make some time
to talk to him alone. No Corey
tonight. Bye Bye.

Bella: Why no Corey? He can't
come anyway. Too busy at work.
What time with Miles?

Darien: Any time until midnight.

She huffed, knowing there was no way she was going to be able to avoid Miles tonight and she shrugged her shoulders; at least they would be busy during the meet and greets. Her mind continued to wander despite her attempts to return to her work.

At first, Miles had been annoyed by the number of messages she'd received requesting more introductions with him than he normally allowed, and it took a lot of effort to convince him to let her expand his schedule. However, he had agreed after she'd sweetened the pot by letting him know that she would handle all the arrangements for the media meet and greet and then he could spend the rest of the night partying with his friends and tour members to get hyped up for the concerts.

"You've probably been told I'm normally pumped before a tour, and I have interesting ways of settling down just before I go on the road," he had told her at the gala.

"I've heard rumors, but there's nothing wrong with changing things sometimes, is there?" she had responded to him, hoping he wasn't about to ask her to plan a wild party.

Getting girls lined up for you before a tour isn't in my job description...no way, that's Darien's job.

The clock on the kitchen wall seemed louder than usual as it ticked away the time and added to the tension. She had to admit, this week had been nerve-racking, and her blood pressure had creeped up a little despite adhering to Dr. Jones's recommendations. She still had a few hours before the party and spent the remainder of the afternoon communicating with vendors scheduled to sell merchandise at three of the first few venues on the tour.

Miles should be pleased with his entire team. We've all been working so hard...and in twenty-four hours, the tour begins.

Darien sent Bella another text, telling her to expect a box with an outfit he'd picked out for her at a local boutique.

Darien: I wish I had time to design something for you but acting as your stylist will have to do. Miles let me design some of the outfits for the tour thanks to you. You're my girl and I want you to look GOOD. Promise me you'll wear it.

Bella: Promise.

Darien has a great sense of style. Besides, what girl in her right mind turns down a free outfit?
She got another text. This time it was from Reagan.

Reagan: Will be late tonight. Something has come up with my family. Have fun and see you later.

"Bummer." She sighed. "I was hoping to hang out with Reagan tonight before they leave for the tour."

Her doorbell rang, distracting her, and she got up to look out the window at the truck parked in the driveway. She grabbed her purse along the way and opened the door for the delivery man standing on the porch with a package in his hand.

"Package for Ms. Bella Wahlberg?"

"Yes, that's me." He handed her the box and waved away her attempt to offer a tip. "Thank you, ma'am, but it's not necessary. I've already been paid."

"All right then, thanks."

Eager to discover what was in the package, she hurriedly closed the door and walked back to the kitchen, where she placed it on the table and opened the box covered with a cream satin finish tied up with a large red bow. There was cream-colored tissue paper neatly lining the box and a card inside from Darien.

This dress may be a cliché for any other girl, but since you once told me you don't own a little black dress, let me be the first to present you with one. The silver accessories are located on the side of the box. See you soon. Love you, girl, Darien (Present paid for by Miles, but I'll bet you knew that).

Bella pulled back the tissue paper and lifted up a gorgeous black, strapless, form-fitting dress with a sweetheart neckline.

So much for dressing like a conservative businessperson.

She looked at the clock and noted she had just enough time to take a nice warm bath to help calm her nerves, put her hair up in a high ponytail, and apply her makeup. The dress complimented her curvy shape and toned shoulders, with the hem hitting her thighs at just the right place. Her stiletto silver heels and accessories matched perfectly as she viewed herself in the mirror and smoothed her dress one last time.

It took a moment to gather her things, including her keys, before she headed out the door. *Settle down, girl; it's going to be fine.* She soothed herself while walking to her car. Darien had offered to send a driver, but she knew if she drove, she could sneak out when she was ready to come home and, hopefully, avoid time alone with Miles. She also wanted to be at the estate early so she could organize the press introductions before the invited guests arrived.

The drive over wasn't bad, and Mr. Curtis greeted her at the door then returned to directing the house staff while Bella went to her office.

After settling in, she checked over the introduction list for the press who were assigned to speak to members of the tour, who were scheduled to arrive in about an hour.

The music was getting louder, and the home was starting to fill with the evening's performers, who had arrived early and been ushered to the rooms in the studio wing of the home. The grand entrance hall and the executive wing were set up with bars and a ballroom for dancing. Bella moved from her office toward the grand hall just as Parker and Darien came down the stairs. Parker almost bumped into Darien, who had stopped on the steps.

Miles appeared at the top of the staircase dressed in a custom-made black tuxedo, which accentuated his athletic build. Darien told Bella that he was the one who had convinced him to wear it, knowing that photographs in the tuxedo in the press and on social media would undoubtedly lead to a fashion house endorsement or maybe even his own clothing line.

She looked at Miles, who was busy trying to fasten his cufflinks, awed by how debonair he looked. He secured the cufflinks, this time without assistance, descended several steps, and came up behind Darien and Parker, unaware they had stopped in their tracks. He almost tripped on the stairs at the sight of Bella standing in the grand hall. Silently, the three walked downstairs together.

Since she wasn't comfortable being the center of their attention, she lowered her eyes and gazed down at the shiny marble floor. Unsure what to do with her hands, she fisted them behind her back and stroked her fingers with her thumb.

Darien broke the silence with a high-pitched whistle. "Bella, you look fantastic."

"Thank you, Darien." She smiled at him.

"May I get a glass of wine for everyone to get this party started?" Parker asked as he turned and waited for an answer before he went to the sitting room, where a bar was set up.

Miles nodded but didn't break his gaze from Bella, who kept her eyes focused on Darien. She wanted him to stay with her and grabbed his hand to thank him for the dress, but he whispered in her ear before he slipped away.

"You're beautiful, Bella."

"Thank you, Darien, and you're a wonderful friend. I couldn't have done a better job picking out this dress." She tried to take his hand again, but he stepped away.

"I'm going to help Parker with those drinks."

Miles moved closer and planted a kiss on her cheek. The guests hadn't arrived yet, and they were alone together. He spoke to her for the first time since their kiss.

"Bella, I love that dress on you." He flashed her a dazzling smile.

She smiled back and noticed that he was reaching into his jacket, but before he was able to pull something out of his breast pocket, the dancers and backup singers came out and encircled him, dancing and singing Stevie Wonder's version of 'Happy Birthday.' More people joined in, pushing her farther away from the center of the hall. She slowly slipped away as Miles gasped in surprise at the growing number of well-wishers. She saw him searching around the crowd, but she was now out of his view.

Darien and Parker returned, each with two glasses of wine, and made their way through the crowd. Bella attempted to motion to Darien from the periphery of the crowd, but he couldn't see her. He became distracted when the door opened and NeNe appeared, a naturally beautiful and confident woman who commanded everyone's attention in her sexy green dress and gold accessories. Bella stood still, observing NeNe as she pushed to the center of the room and gave Miles a kiss on the cheek. She watched the people dancing free style while others joined the merriment in choreographed moves, which were probably part of the show.

This isn't your world, Bella. Don't kid yourself, Miles would never be happy with you. It's love not lust that sustains relationships. He could never love you.

She didn't feel much like dancing and instead went back to her office. She looked at the picture on her desk of her and Corey at his store and composed herself; taking in deep breaths, before returning to the party. The photo ops and meet-and-greets she could do with no problem, but a large unstructured gathering with a mixture of the creative types and LA's young socialites, she wasn't so sure. She wasn't just a fish out of water, she was a fish desperately seeking water. She knew the expectations and the goals of her business interactions. As she scanned the room, spotting some women in tightly clad attire in a not-so-subtle attempt to get the attention of the guest of honor, she understood some of them also had goals they were trying to accomplish.

NeNe also had her share of suitors in one corner and seemed comfortable with the attention she was getting. She and Parker eventually disappeared together before Bella could talk to her. Bella grabbed a drink from one of the trays carried by waiters walking through the room and realized she had been so busy working the last seven months that she'd failed to develop a close relationship with anyone besides those mainly on the executive committee: Parker, Darien, and of course, Miles. Sure, she had developed close relationships with Reagan, Mr. Curtis,

Bradley, and Bosco, but she didn't feel like one of the gang.

Members of the press, hoping for an interview with Miles, started to arrive. Bella decided once the interviews and the official press meetings were over, she would leave after members of the press left. The rest of the night had been planned for partying, and she wasn't in the mood for a party—nor was she planning to say goodbye to Miles in person. She wasn't trying to be rude, but she knew he had more important things on his mind, and besides, they would be in touch during the tour. The thought reminded her to put the Miles's World app on her phone.

After a few hours of schmoozing and socializing, she returned to her office to gather some papers before leaving for home. She was relieved that the press meet and greets had gone so well and she was ready to go home to get comfy. She had her things in hand and was about to close the door to her office when she bumped into Miles.

"Going somewhere? It's not polite to leave without saying goodbye to your host. Will you join me outside in the garden?"

"Sure. I was planning to say goodbye to you," she lied.

He led her to the lush garden where they could be alone.

"Bella, you are beautiful tonight, and I love your outfit." He leaned in to kiss her on the cheek again and pulled a small velvet-covered box out of his breast pocket.

She didn't want to accept any expensive gifts and was about to tell him he had already given her enough when he told her, "Bella, Corey spoke to me for a few minutes at the charity gala last night while you were attending to business. It was an interesting conversation, and he said he wanted the lyrics to my song 'Ram It.' I was curious, since I don't have a song called 'Ram It.'"

She stiffened as he continued his story and opened his hand to give her the box.

"I meant to give this to you as a welcome aboard present after you accepted your position, but life got in the way, you got sick, yadda, yadda."

She looked at the box and hesitated before she took it and opened it. Inside was a gold bangle bracelet with heads of rams on either side of the top of the bracelet.

He took it from her shaking hand and placed the bracelet on her wrist.

"Corey said you like to say, 'Ram it, ram it' when the two of you…you know. I'm no prude, but I thought it was inappropriate of him to share such intimate information with me, and I thought you should know about it."

She blinked, stunned by what he was saying, and she backed away from him. She needed space to process the information. Silence hung between them as they stood still, the moonlight framing her face. Her earrings twinkled like the stars in the darkness, lit by the glow of the moon and by the illuminations from globes of soft light from the light posts scattered throughout the garden. The vision of her loveliness was soon replaced with one of anger as her chest heaved.

Puzzled by her response, he cocked his head slightly. "What's the matter?"

"You're telling me you and Corey had a conversation last night, and he asked for the lyrics of a song called 'Ram It'? Is that correct?"

"Yes, Bella, that's what I'm telling you."

"And is it correct he shared with you that I repeat the phrase 'ram it' when he is fucking me?" Her hands drew tight in fists and she felt the pain of her nails pressing in her palms.

Corey dislikes Miles and he's made that clear, but would he go to this length to make sure Miles understands that he's the one having sex with me and not him, humiliating me in the process?

He raised an eyebrow at her use of the f-bomb. "Yes, Bella. According to Corey, sometimes you say, 'ram it harder.'" His expression was flat, his voice monotone.

She tried to speak, but no words came out, so instead, she frowned, covered her mouth in disbelief, and her back stiffened in a hostile pose. Finally, she found her words and spoke with feigned resolve.

"I'll come and get my things after you leave on tour." She grew more confident as she spoke. "I will *not* be the butt of sexual jokes or be embarrassed by my clueless boyfriend. He has this foolish notion that, if you as an artist can say anything that comes to mind, including speaking about your past sexual conquests in your lyrics, then so can he. He thinks you welcome his vulgarity, and now you're sharing his vulgarity with me? I don't know where we go from here Miles—personally or professionally. I just know I can't stay here."

"Bella, listen to me."

"I have to go." She turned to leave while he continued talking.

"You can't quit on me. Your resignation won't be accepted. Do you hear me?"

She saw some of the valets taking a break around a fountain at the back of the house. She walked at a fast pace toward them and called out to the man who had parked her car earlier and told him she needed to leave. He quickly got up to retrieve her car while she waited.

"Bella, please let me finish." Miles ran behind her, trying to reach her, but the other guests discovered their birthday boy, and women in short, tight dresses came quickly to surround him.

"Come on, Ari. Let's party." She overheard a woman clad in a tight body dress say, showing plenty of cleavage.

She turned away from the scene and didn't look back to see if he was pursuing her.

The house was dark when she returned home; she turned on a few lights to make her way to her bedroom, where she took off her outfit and let it fall to the floor. She slipped into bed and slammed her fist into her pillow, feeling anger, hurt and confusion about her future. So many thoughts ran through her head and she couldn't settle down to sleep.

She knew she was good at her job. She'd given Corey advice and helped increase sales at his stores when his marketing team couldn't seem to figure out how to do it, and she'd regularly contributed so much to the AriMusic organization that Miles had given her the position as a member of the executive team, but now she was confused.

"Maybe my efforts aren't good enough and I'm a joke to him," she said to the pillow. She raised her head and looked around her room before drawing her conclusion.

"I deserve better from both Corey and Miles. At the very least, I deserve some respect." She slumped back down. *But who's going to give me back the dignity I've lost?*

She ignored the text from Miles asking for a chance to explain, and she didn't answer the text from Darien. A picture sent of the three of them—her, Miles, and Bosco—lit up her phone. She couldn't look at it without spilling tears, but at least she felt safe in her place of refuge.

Her phone buzzed again, and at first, she avoided looking at it, but out of the corner of her eye, she glimpsed the image of her mother on the screen and accepted the call.

"Hello, Mom." She wiped away her tears, turned the phone away from her face and tried sniffing without her mother hearing it.

"Hello, my sweet girl. Are you all right?"

"Yes, I'm better. My allergies have been driving me crazy and, you know, getting over a cold."

"I hope I'm not calling you too late, but I thought hearing your voice could help me settle down. I've tried getting some rest, but I've been tossing and turning for close to an hour."

"What's wrong, Mom? Is the position not going well?"

"The position is going well, but I'm worried about you. My mind kept coming back to you, and then I started thinking about therapist Bob; you remember, the therapist you had as a little girl after Daddy died?"

"Sure, I remember him."

"Well one day I went to see him because I was concerned how shy you were becoming; you know what he told me?"

"You haven't shared this with me before. What did he say?"

"He told me I should love you, be there for you, but not worry about you. He said you were a little fighter, but because you weren't as quick at being assertive and telling people when to back off, you would let others throw a few more punches at you, leaving you at times feeling battered and bruised, but just like any other prized fighter, you could go the full rounds with the best of them."

"He said that about me?"

"Yes, Bella, and over the years I've come to appreciate that while I might question how you do things, I respect you as a young woman who knows what she wants and has the courage to achieve her goals. I've had friends tell me their daughters whine, pout, and vent all the time, but not you, my sweet girl. You handle your business." They both laughed at the reference to the song.

"Mom, I'm all right and even when things don't go as I plan, I know I'm going to be all right. I have the best mother in the world, and I love you so much. Don't worry about me."

"Thanks, Bella. I'm feeling better, and I hope your allergies calm down. Well, I'll let you get some rest."

"I love you, Mom."

"I love you more. Goodnight."

"Good night Mom." She settled down and fell asleep.

Michele Sims

CHAPTER TEN

Bella called Corey the next morning. "I'm beyond anger Corey, I'm pissed that you would say such things to my boss of all people. Have you lost your mind?"

"Bella, let me explain. I can come over right now."

"No, you may not. I'll let you know when I'm ready to see you. I wouldn't be able to tolerate looking at you right now." She hung up, and despite his repeated attempts to talk to her in person, she waited an additional two days before she agreed to meet with him and only decided to arrange a time to get together after he threatened to come to the estate to talk to her. She had returned to work after Darien called and reminded her, she could be mad with Miles, but she was still under contract, and besides, her anger had subsided after he left on tour, and there was no risk of running into him.

"Corey, I'm ready to have a rational discussion with you," she told him over the phone. "There are things I need to get off my chest."

"Bella, I knew I made a mistake asking for the lyrics to 'Ram It' when Ari responded to me with a quizzical look on his face. I'm ashamed to admit it but...I thought you started saying ram it when we made love because you were fantasizing about him. I looked up his songs online after my conversation with him, and he doesn't have a song called 'Ram It.'"

"I'm not buying it, and somehow Corey, I feel like you knew he didn't have a song by that name when you asked him." Her response was sharp and direct. "Please don't insult me with your attempts to play clueless and dense. You wanted to assert yourself and let him know we were sleeping together—as if he didn't assume that. The fact of the matter is, for the second time, your insensitivity was an embarrassment to me, and your behavior has negative repercussions for me and my career." She stopped for a moment in order to avoid getting angry all over again. "You hurt me, Corey, and I won't tolerate this."

He quickly interrupted her. "Bella, let's not do or say anything we'll both regret." His voice changed to a lighter and more playful tone. "You know the new restaurant that just opened you wanted to try?"

She didn't answer.

"Well, my family knows some of the partners in the venture, and I was able to get us reservations. Say you'll come with me tonight. Bella, I'm sorry, and I want to make this up to you. You don't have to dress up for our dinner tonight. We can do that later. Just promise me you'll be ready when I pick you up after work. The restaurant won't be as crowded, and we can take our time talking about our differences and enjoy a fine meal. Does that sound okay? Please don't make me grovel, but I will if I have to."

"We have a lot to talk about, and it might as well be sooner than later. Pick me up after work tonight and we can talk over dinner. I'm agreeing to dinner and nothing else. Afterwards, you can drop me off at the house. I'm expecting my mother back home tonight, and I need to turn in early. I have a busy day planned tomorrow."

"Okay, I agree to your terms, and I'll be there this evening to pick you up for negotiations and dinner."

"Save the sarcasm, Corey. Goodbye." She hit the end call button on her phone and resumed taking care of matters at work.

He arrived at the estate to pick her up and attempted to kiss her, but she turned away before he could plant his lips on hers. Most of the trip downtown was spent in silence, and she looked out the window at the passing scenery. Time could heal wounds, but enough time hadn't passed, and hers were still raw. It also hadn't escaped her attention that he still hadn't apologized for his actions. They finally arrived at the restaurant, and Corey remained the perfect gentleman.

The restaurant was opulent, with crystal chandeliers and ornate mirrors throughout the space. She viewed her reflection and noticed the scowl on her face, which refused to soften despite his attempts to show his remorse. They were quickly seated at a table set with a fine white linen tablecloth, beautiful porcelain accessories for their condiments, silverware gleaming to perfection, and crystal stemware that seemed to dance in the light. Bella excused herself to freshen up before the waiter came back with their menus. Her anger had resurfaced at seeing him again, and she wanted to calm down and gather her thoughts.

She returned and stopped short of taking her seat. In her absence, her wine glass had been filled with a wine she hadn't chosen, and salads had been placed on the table.

"I hope you don't mind; I took the liberty of ordering for both of us. I declined the bread basket since Mother has already started ordering dresses for you."

She cocked her head to the side and sat down. "Why would your mother order a dress for me?"

"Never mind. Try the dressing I sprinkled on your salad. It's delicious."

She took a small bite of her salad, put down her fork, and wiped her mouth with her napkin. She didn't want to waste the moment filling her mouth with food instead of having a frank discussion with him if he was to remain her boyfriend.

"Bella, let me be the first to say something. First of all, I'm sorry if I hurt you, but to be honest, I can't tolerate you working for Ari much longer. I know you've been faithful to me, but you just can't see that he's into you. Men like him use women, eventually get into their pants, and then discard them. I won't be able to live with the fact that he'll seduce you, and then you'll come running to me like some consolation prize. I have my pride."

"Is that so?" *You're incredible Corey. And what I didn't see were all your insecurities.* She looked at him momentarily, trying to stave off sarcastic thoughts.

The waiter returned with the dishes he'd ordered. She'd wanted fish, but a plate of beef sliced into thin strips was placed before her and a steaming lobster tail was placed before him. She attempted to contain her anger as she picked up her knife and fork, but before she could cut a slice of her meat, he took one slice of beef and then another off her plate.

"Oh yeah," he said as if enjoying an orgasm. "This is sooo good. Do you want a piece of my lobster?"

"No thank you." She returned her attention to her meal and looked hard at the beef, curled up like a small, limp penis, much like Corey's. She looked up at him and back at her meat and began slicing it into smaller pieces with vehemence and malice.

"Corey, you don't have a say in my job decisions or in how long I choose to keep my current position." She felt the muscles in her jaw tighten.

"If you're going to be my wife, I do have a say, and my position is final. I don't want you working for Ari, and I can help you secure other lucrative contracts. My family has clout, and the Baker name will open doors for you. I may even be able to help your mother with her fledgling business." He took another bite of the beef off her plate. Her hand shook as she realized she wanted to castrate him. She dropped her silverware onto the plate, and the loud clang startled them both so much that she placed her shaking hands in her lap to guard against her hostile impulses to harm him.

"You haven't even asked me to be your wife. And why do you think I would ever consider marrying an insensitive boor? You disgust me right now Corey. You're arrogant, and you're being a dick."

"Bella, you'd better watch your language. Maybe Ari's lifestyle and his coarseness are starting to rub off on you."

"Our problems have nothing to do with Ari. They are about you, your insecurities, and my refusal to call you on your shit earlier in our relationship."

She grabbed her bag and activated the rideshare app on her phone to locate a driver. At that moment, it was as crystal clear as the glistening glasses before her: she could never return to a relationship with him.

"I assume you will be settling the bill. Good night, Corey. We're done." She pushed back her seat and left a stunned and open-mouthed man seated at the table as she sashayed out of the restaurant.

"You'll regret this!" He was talking to her ass at that point as she was done with their face to face encounter.

She endured a flurry of calls from Corey over the next several days. Some of the messages he left were contrite; others were angry and laced with profanity. She was concerned he would come to her home or begin stalking her. She had never seen this side of him.

"Go ahead if you want to be one of Ari's bitches," he said on one occasion. She eventually had to block his number in order to get a break. He knew just how to hurt her. She'd confided in him earlier in their relationship that she'd worked so hard in school to make her mother proud of her after her father's death, despite her mother's reassurances that they were going to be all right living on her father's pension and benefits. As an anxious child, she'd still worried how her mother was going to pay the bills since she chose to give up her career and be a stay-at-home mother.

The cost of living in Los Angeles was a lot higher than life in a small, rural Texas town, and her parents were proud of their profession, but Bella knew the pay wasn't what motivated them to place their lives on the line. She'd been the recipient of a full scholarship she'd maintained with hard work and diligence in school, and she was determined to do anything to advance her career except sleep her way to the top. She knew of women who used men to reach their goals just as quickly as some men used women as sexual objects. Her father had always reminded her of how proud he was of her and had heaped praise on her when she made good grades. She never wanted to dishonor his memory.

It was his voice—*Bella, I'm so proud of you*—that had motivated her to graduate at the top of her class. She'd shared those memories with Corey, and now he was using them against her. He knew she could never be one of *Ari's bitches,* or anyone's sexual object for that matter, for any reason.

She needed a break following all the activity at the estate in the days preceding the start of the Fire God Tour, and now, on top of Corey's badgering phone calls, she was feeling worn down. Most of the members of the tour and the support staff had already left but making sure the promotions in each city were under control, including arranging television and radio time, was still a headache. She decided to leave her office and go out to the garden on the grounds of the estate near the pool to enjoy some sunshine and quiet solitude. After finishing her sandwich, she closed her eyes for a few minutes of downtime and opened them to find Corey standing over her with furrowed brows and a frown.

"Why haven't you returned any of my calls?" She refused to answer him; she didn't want to cause a scene in front of the landscape workers who were now standing nearby.

Her face and name were attached to the AriMusic Company, and she didn't want anything to cast a negative light on the tour. She stood, ready to leave, but he took her by the elbow and led her to a small square with a petite fountain decorated with flowers and greenery located behind them. The square was off the walking path, and the sounds of the gurgling water muffled their conversation.

"Corey, let go of me. I need to get back to work." She attempted to pull away from him.

"I told you, Bella, I don't want you working for Ari anymore." His anger was palpable as Ari's name rolled between his lips. She attempted to loosen his grip once more, but before she could pull away, he abruptly moved back away from her and fell on his elbows with his legs up to protect himself. Bella turned and saw Bosco launching toward Corey. He was on a leash, but his handler was nowhere to be seen. Just as she had seen Ari do on many occasions, she held up her hand before her. Bosco leaped in front of Corey with his snout to Corey's nose then settled on his haunches at Bella's command to await further instructions. He snarled but made no effort to attack him.

"Apologize, Corey," she demanded. "Apologize for all the threatening and derogatory messages you left on my phone."

"I'm sorry, Bella, but you drove me to this moment of insanity." She rolled her eyes at him.

"Tell me, when did you F yourself to dog sitting?" He turned up his lips and snarled, despite his compromised position. "Aren't you smart enough to realize that you have to maintain control of the dog on a leash. You can't just let him run free."

She couldn't contain her anger any longer.

"Demonstrate," she ordered Bosco, having seen his handler use this command, and he displayed his full set of sharp gleaming teeth. Corey let out a high-pitched scream and attempted to scamper away on his elbows and butt. Two young men working for the landscape company captured the scene on their cell phones and snickered as they watched a frightened Corey on the ground. They turned and laughed with each other as they continued with their work.

She took control of the leash.

"Sit Bosco." He nuzzled against her side as she stroked his back and she turned her attention to Corey after calming Bosco.

"Corey, hear me this last time. Don't call me anymore. Don't visit me at my home or my job, and don't come within fifteen feet of me. I told you we were over. One more thing, don't ever call me a bitch again or the world will see who the bitch really is. I'll try my best to block any video of this incident that may have been uploaded by those guys over there."

She pointed to the two employees trying to put away their phones quickly, and she knew she couldn't guarantee they wouldn't upload the video, but she hoped Corey didn't know that since he didn't have social media savvy. The men left before she could identify them, making it difficult to back up her threat.

"I think it's time you left, don't you?" He got up off the ground and walked swiftly away.

"You'll regret this someday Bella. I promise you will."

She returned to the bench with Bosco and continued to pet him until she saw that Corey had gotten into his car and driven away.

"How did you get here, boy, and where's your handler?"

Carl Jones, one of Bosco's handlers, slowly came out of the shadows of the trees and tall manicured bushes.

"Carl, I thought you had already left on tour with Bradley and other members of the security team? Why are you and Bosco still here?"

"The tour is still in California, and sometimes Miles comes home when he's still in the state or in Vegas to sleep in his own bed. A fringe benefit of having your own jet, I guess. Usually, he stays at the estate, but for some reason he's holed up at his apartment in the city. I came here to get a few more things for Bosco." He took Bosco's leash and wrapped it up in his hand.

"We were on a walk, and I could have stopped him, but he's very protective of you. He has good instincts, and he must have felt you were in danger. I would stay away from that guy if I were you." He prepared to leave with Bosco. "By the way, I paid those guys a handsome fee to send the video to my email, and I'll forward it to you for good measure. You might want to send some shots of the incident as insurance of what may go online if he continues to stalk you. No man wants to be seen as a bitch."

"I'll consider your advice, Carl."

"I've got to get back downtown. Are you going to be ok?"

"Yes Carl, I'm fine, and thanks for everything."

"No problem. See you soon."

She waved goodbye to both of them and got up to go back inside. After the incidents of this week, it was clear to her that her relationship with Corey was irreparably damaged, but she was relieved to be out of the middle of a testosterone war. Corey was out of her life, and Miles was keeping some distance from her.

CHAPTER ELEVEN

A little more than a week had passed since the start of the tour. Seven concerts down and too many left to go. Despite her anxieties, the tour opened to rave reviews. The promotional plans had encountered a few hiccups, but none that couldn't be solved with a few phone calls.

She dragged herself out of bed, glad it was Saturday. After a quick shower, she dressed in her usual hiking gear for a short midmorning hike and went to the kitchen to prepare a smoothie. She opened the blinds to sunlight flooding the kitchen while she took in a deep cleansing breath. Basking in the warmth of the sun, she looked out her window at the gorgeous day. The yellow sun shone brilliantly, and white fluffy clouds drifted lazily across the clear blue sky. She turned her attention to the garden in the backyard and saw small brown birds gathered around multiple bird feeders hanging from the limbs of trees, their heads bobbing as they picked at the seeds before flying off one at a time. A smile crossed her face just thinking about getting out and enjoying a bit of nature.

She went to the freezer, got out her usual mixture of frozen fruits, kale, and spinach, and placed them in the food processor. Settling at her desk, she logged onto her computer while the food processor made loud whirring noises and scrolled to her commonly visited sites. Her attention returned to the sound of the processor, and she got up and stopped it before pouring out the green concoction in a glass and consuming it through a straw. She settled back at her desk and resumed surfing the net.

Click. She scanned one more page and there was the usual stuff about celebrity sightings and trends. She was about to shut down her computer when her phone rang. She got up to retrieve her phone where she'd placed it last night, still connected to the charger.

"Good Morning, Bella, it's Darien. I…have another favor to ask of you."

"Darien, don't you dare ask me to do something on my day off."

"I'm expecting a package—a very important package—and I asked the courier to drop it off at your house. Someone has to sign for it."

"What about your boyfriend?"

"He's out of town. Please, Bella, say you'll be home to sign for it. I wouldn't ask you if it wasn't important."

"I have plans, and I don't care to change them." She pursed her lips.

"You don't care to change them, but you can change them?"

"Why didn't you get the package sent to you?"

"It's a long story, and we're too transient right now to have things sent to me on the road. Please say you'll be home between noon to one o'clock so I can confirm your address."

"Okay, but you owe me."

"Thanks, Belles. You know I love you."

"Yeah, right. Goodbye."

"Later."

Bella returned to her desk, and instead of powering off the computer, she decided to surf a few more sites and defuse her irritation.

Click, click. Glaring at the computer screen, she furrowed her brows. *So I'm everybody's trusted assistant— the girl Friday now?*

Click, click. *I'm the chief of marketing, not an admin assistant. I'm going to have a long talk with Darien. We're friends, but he needs to respect my position.* She still had time to get in a short hike before noon if she left now. She finished the last bit of her smoothie and got up from the computer.

Her phone rang again; this time it was Charlie Ferguson, a friend from grad school. She smiled and accepted the call. It had been a while since they'd last talked.

"Hi, Bella."

"Hi, Charlie. I'm surprised to hear from you."

"Yeah, it's been a minute. Sorry it took me a while to get back in touch with you, but I hear you've been busy since we last talked; heard you landed a sweet position with AriMusic."

"Yeah, I'm the chief marketing officer."

"Congratulations girl. Hey listen. I have an unexpected layover at the airport, and I was wondering if I could stop by your place and we could catch up with each other. I don't want to camp out at the airport for the next five to six hours. I know it may be asking a lot but...I was wondering if you could toss me a kernel of news about the Fire God Tour. I'm working for an entertainment magazine, and it would help my career if I could get a small scoop before the other media outlets."

"Yes.... Sure, we can get together today while you're in town. Do you remember where I live?"

"Great. Yes, I remember where you live, and if I can impose even further—do you have anything to eat? I flew in from Europe, and I'm starved. Your mother was such a good cook, and her leftovers were always so good. I'd love seeing her again."

"Mom's not home, but I can place some steaks on the grill and maybe throw some veggies on the side."

"Sounds great. I'll catch a ride and be over there in about an hour, depending on the time it takes to return a few calls and traffic."

"I'll be at home waiting for you. Bye, Charlie."

"See ya soon." She ended the call.

Chill, Bella. She rubbed her temples and closed her eyes. *Friends sacrifice for each other, don't they? I'm not sure what I can tell Charlie, and I want to be there when my friends need me, but do I need to sacrifice for Darien and Charlie on the same day? Damn, I guess I'm not going on a hike today.*

She blew out a breath and got up to walk outside for a few minutes to enjoy the serene scenery in her backyard. Warm sunlight streamed through lush green trees, and the branches blew in the breeze while the birds danced and splashed around in the bird bath. She smiled as a pair of large monarch butterflies lit upon the low-lying lantana plants blooming with bright yellow flowers. She wrestled with her desire to stay outside but eventually went back in the kitchen and closed the door behind her, resolved to try again tomorrow to spend some time relaxing by herself.

She walked to the freezer and pulled open the door, tucking her head in the icy box to look at the various cuts of meats wrapped in labeled white paper. She moved the wrappings around, alternately flexing and rubbing her fingertips while she attempted to locate the neatly wrapped package labeled as two sirloin steaks and another package with frozen chopped vegetables. She unwrapped the package and placed the steaks in the microwave to thaw before laying them on the grill and ran the veggies under warm water to thaw them out while the grill heated up. The microwave buzzed, and she washed the steaks one more time before patting them dry and placing them on the hot grill, which sizzled with the steaks and veggies seasoned with her mother's homemade marinade. The aromas filled the room, and she did a little happy dance as she started anticipating a shared meal and good conversation with an old friend.

She was about to turn the steaks when alerts from the app on her computer started buzzing. She clicked on the site and a picture of a man with his face turned to the side was bloodied and disfigured. He was lying on the ground, completely still and clad in a black leather jacket and leather boots with a small silver letter A on the buckles. He had the same coloring as Miles, and his hair was the same color and texture. People were yelling, "He's dead!" and hugging each other while others had their cameras out. Police and fire fighters were on the scene, clearing the way for ambulance personnel, and someone leaned over and covered the body with a sheet while women wailed, and others hugged each other and sobbed. A big caption appeared on the screen: *Ari is dead*. The other sites started flashing the same news.

This must be a mistake or just a sick joke. Bella took a seat at her computer and began clicking through the articles, which were posting so fast, she couldn't keep up with them. Surely, she would have been one of the first ones to know this if it were true, so she ignored it, but she couldn't ignore the pressure squeezing her chest.

I'm the chief of marketing for AriMusic and of course someone from the executive team would have contacted me by now but...what if Miles was sick of my shit and had accepted my resignation? They wouldn't call me if I had already been fired and was the ex-chief of marketing. Was that the reason he avoided coming back to the estate?

Click, click.... Click, click. She went to one of her most trusted sites.

Breaking News: Violence on the Streets Of San Francisco. Unconfirmed reports at this time: the hip-hop star Ari killed in alleged gang violence.

She covered her eyes and began shaking her head. *This isn't true—I need to put this rumor to rest before all hell breaks out.*

She grabbed her phone to call Miles, hoping the sound of his voice would put an end to the vicious gossip, and she let it ring until it went to voicemail. Then she tried another number and again, no answer. She texted a message, looking intently at the phone, willing the three transcribing dots to appear, telling her a message was coming, but she received no return on her message.

Despite her disbelief, she began breaking a sweat, and with each second, her internal tension increased as her heart raced, and her skin heated from dilated veins rising to the surface. Her vision narrowed a little, making her feel like she was going to pass out, but she gathered her wits as she decided to call other members of the team.

"I'll get Darien on the phone," she said out loud as tears clouded her eyes, but she refused to give in to her worst fears.

Stay calm. Call Darien. He's on tour with Miles and should know what's going on.

He'd said nothing about Miles when they'd spoke earlier, she reminded herself, and she focused on her breathing as she placed the call—again, no answer.

She texted him. She got no response.

"What the hell! Calm down and call Bradley," she barked and took in more deep breaths. "If his security chief doesn't know he's dead, then we're all in trouble." A nervous chuckle escaped from deep in her throat as she placed the call, and the phone rang too many times for her comfort before someone finally answered.

"Thank goodness you picked up Bradley. This is Bella. Is Miles alright?"

"Hi Bella. This is Bradley's assistant Ben. Bradley has the rest of the day off and he isn't available. Why are you calling about Miles?"

"Haven't you seen the news? It's being reported that Miles has been shot and he's dead. When is the last time you heard from him?"

"Bella, I can't share with you info about Miles's whereabouts. He's a big boy and I'm sure he's fine."

She was seething. "Can you check on him and get back to me?" she pleaded with him.

"No, I can't share information with you."

"You can't or you won't share information? Or are you just being an incompetent jackass?" Her heart was thumping in her chest as she spoke.

"I don't know who you think you're talking to you little ho, but I'm ending this convo right now. I just started this job, but Bradley told me you have trouble staying in your lane. For the record, if Miles wanted you to know anything about him, he would have told you himself."

"Did Bradley also tell you, Ben, that you may not have a job since you don't know who I am?" She abruptly ended the call and pushed the chair from her desk to calm her breathing and stop her vision from narrowing to black as she slowly paced the room. She placed her hands on the counter to steady herself and began moaning, "No. Dear God, no. Not again. Why is it that the men I love are killed and taken away from me?"

A mixture of gray and black smoke from the burning meat filled the kitchen; she looked over at the grill and grabbed the tongs.

"Ouch!" She placed her fingertips in her mouth, reddened from touching the hot tongs, and walked quickly to her large utensils drawer to get another set of tongs. Small flames were shooting up from the grill, charring the meat beyond repair. She pulled the meat from the grill with the second set of tongs and threw it in the trash. The onions and peppers, now reduced to blackened shreds, fell through the iron bars of the grill while more smoke filled the room and irritated her lungs. She cupped her mouth and nose with her hand and turned her head to cough before pressing on the button for the exhaust fan to draw out the smoke.

Feeling frustrated, she slammed the tongs on the counter and stomped her feet. Why wasn't she hearing from anyone at AriMusic if Miles was dead?

No, no. This can't be true. Miles can't be gone.

Confusion clouded her mind as flames shot from the gas grill, and she reached to turn it off, but a loud booming sound followed by sparks coming from the oven caused her to back away. She hit the emergency red switch on the wall to cut the power to the stove and prevent a raging fire.

Her anger was turning to sadness as she looked up at the ceiling, trying to ward off the thoughts running through her head on auto-loop.

Daddy's not coming home, Bella. He's gone. Daddy's not coming home, he's gone. He's gone.

The doorbell rang, followed by pounding on the door, but she couldn't will her body to move forward. She didn't want to hear more bad news. Her phone rang, and she rushed toward it, violently pushing the phone and papers on her desk on the floor.

I don't want to hear that he's been killed. She paused, trying to prevent the pull of past repressed memories. *No Bella, stay in the moment, in the here and now. You're not in Texas anymore.*

She had been productive and even happy for many years, but overwhelmed by too many triggers: the fear of another deep loss, the leather jacket, the boots with the buckles and silver letter *A*, the gray smoke, and the smells of charred meat in the hot kitchen—her body shook as she backed herself into a corner in a wide-eyed panic while cold sweat ran down her face, plastering her hair to the sides of her face.

She had been awakened by loud claps of thunder and torrents of rain falling on the roof on that fateful night, a lifetime ago. She jumped when a bolt of lightning hit the ground outside of her bedroom window, causing every nerve in her body to fire and vibrate with fear. The night light she left on every night was out, and she opened her eyes to an eerie darkness, except for the brief illuminations of lightning, making the limbs on the trees look like skeletal ghouls knocking on the windows.

"Mommy, where are you?" She remained hidden under the covers, but the urgent need to pee made her run to the bathroom. She finished using the bathroom and hurried out with the intent of seeking the safety of her parents' bed but was caught off guard when she ran into Mrs. Casper holding a flashlight.

"You scared me!" she screamed and held her chest. "Where's Mommy?"

Mrs. Caspar was a kind and thoughtful woman most days, but at night, her wild, thick hair and narrow face could be unnerving, especially in the dark.

"Your Mom had to answer an emergency call at the fire station, and I'm staying with you until she gets back." They both turned their heads to the sound of sirens blaring, and the bright red lights from the fire engines briefly lit the house.

"Go back to bed Bella. Your mother should be home soon. Go now."

"But Mrs. Caspar— why was Mommy and Daddy working on the same night?"

Mrs. Caspar frowned, and Bella realized she wasn't going to get any answers from her. She went back to her room and hid beneath the covers to avoid seeing the scary stick figures, just like the ones in the Halloween house she visited with Daddy.

The booms of thunder and the sizzle of lightning travelling across the sky kept her pulse racing and heart thumping until finally she got some relief from sleep. Her eyes opened and she yawned when she heard the sound of her mother's voice saying good night to Mrs. Caspar, who often stayed in the guest room when she babysat for the family.

Bella threw back the covers and ran out of her room into the hall but was assaulted by the strong but familiar smoky smell of her daddy's jacket and trousers, a signal he had returned home from fighting a fire. She walked down the hall, curious to see a light was on in her parents' room.

A cold chill ran through her body, causing her to wrap her small arms around her shoulders, embracing herself as she walked slowly toward the light and to the sounds of sobs growing louder as she got closer to the door, left slightly ajar. Bella slowly pushed the creaking door open and saw her mother seated on the bed, clinging tightly to her father's black leather jacket while she rocked her body and cried. Her father's black boots covered in soot and two or three little dark red droplets on top were placed at her mother's feet. She stopped before pushing forward into the room.

"Mommy, why do you have Daddy's jacket and boots? He won't be safe without them. Why did you and Daddy have to work tonight? You told me you never schedule both Mommies and Daddies from the same family on the same night." She walked further into the room and sat beside her mother.

"Bella, please sweetheart; too many questions at one time." Her mother lowered her head and continued sobbing. Bella placed her hand inside the palm of her mother's hand.

"Why are you crying?" Her mother looked up at her and hugged her tightly, causing Bella to cough, irritated by the smoke smell creeping into her lungs. After placing the jacket to the side, Joan looked at Bella with tears streaming down her face and she began to cry reflexively from sympathetic but still unknown pain as a heavy feeling of dread and sadness descended upon her.

"Where's Daddy?" She looked around the room, her heart pounding so loud in her ears she had to strain to hear her mother's response.

"Daddy's not coming back, Bella. I went to the hospital to see him and he didn't make it. He's gone, and we won't ever see him again."

She recoiled from the news, balled her fists, and pressed them against her eyes to hold back the stream of tears coming from a deep sadness coursing throughout her body and threatening to overwhelm her. She placed her arms around her mother's waist and her body shook in despair.

"Daddy wouldn't leave us. He promised me he would be back."

Hadn't he promised he loved her and would never leave her? She had believed those false promises made so long ago. For years after her father's death, the only promise she clung to was to never allow herself to feel that kind of pain ever again.

"Bella, what's wrong?"

She felt warm, strong arms around her as she focused her hazy vision on her surroundings, the computer on her desk, and the overturned chair lying on the floor. Assaulted by the awareness of the smells of smoke and torched meat, she coughed and squinched her nose. Turning her head slowly, a distinct cologne of sandalwood mixed with a masculine smell of musk calmed her wildly beating heart as she pulled away and looked into soulful brown eyes. *Miles.* She stared at him as sobs came out from deep within her, and she leaned into his embrace. He held her close and tried to kiss away her tears.

"Miles, Miles, I thought you were dead, Miles."

"Why would you think that?" He held her tightly around the shoulders.

She pointed to the computer which was still flashing news of his murder, and he saw a picture of himself above the caption announcing his death.

The Alt Knights probably sending me a message. I hate how this has affected Bella. He frowned as he looked at the screen.

"It's alright Bella. I'm safe." He comforted her as she hugged him around the waist.

His phone buzzed in his pants' pocket, and while pressing her head against his chest and stroking her back with one hand, he reached to grab it and placed it on speaker before setting the phone on the table.

"Bella's not answering her phone Miles. She said she would be at home."

"I'm here with her now. She's upset about the news of my untimely demise." She looked up and pulled away from him to wipe her tears away.

"Don't joke about it, Miles. It's not funny."

"Hi, Bella, it's Darien. Why didn't you answer your phone?"

"I don't know. I'm confused right now."

"What's wrong?" Darien asked. "Miles, I heard something about you getting killed today. I can't believe how far some people will go to start a buzz. Bella, you didn't believe it, did you?"

"Let me call you back later, Darien. Make sure the jet is ready when I call. I need to talk to Bella right now. Bye."

"Bye Miles."

He ended the call and looked at her as she calmed in his arms. Her clothes, damp from sweat in the hot kitchen and from the experience of a full-blown panic attack, stuck to her skin like a wet, smelly blanket. She was coughing from the cloud of smoke still inhabiting the room, so he attempted to get her up and guide her out of the kitchen before he shared the reason for his unexpected visit, but she surprised him by pushing away from him. He observed in silence as she looked around before she broke the tension in the room.

"I promised Darien I would be home to receive his package. I need to call him back and tell him I didn't get it." She pushed her damp hair back from the sides of her face and looked about the table, trying to locate her phone.

"Don't worry about it. He was in on my plan to surprise you. I'm the package you were supposed to receive, but why didn't you answer the door?"

"I must have zoned out." She coughed again and choked on the dry lump in her throat. "I thought you were dead."

"I get that."

"I shouldn't have gotten caught up in the drama, dammit. I know about the reality of false news in this business. I'm still your chief marketing and publicity officer, correct?"

"Of course you are. What made you doubt that?" He came closer but didn't touch her.

"Not one of you answered my calls except Ben, and I have to be honest…I called him a jackass."

"Ben has been fired, Bella. A staff member heard him talking to you and reported it to Bradley, who canned him immediately. My network of security associates also wasn't comfortable with him. Enough about Ben—I'm concerned about you. You're in the privacy of your own home and your actions were an authentic response to what you thought was true. I'm not as concerned about a mini-meltdown—I mean panic attack—as much as I would have been if you showed no emotions to thoughts I had been killed. I knew about your anxiety before I hired you, and I prefer having someone who cares about her job and me as a person rather than hiring a fake-folk automaton like the ones I run across in this business every day. Let me be honest with you Bella, I have so many faults that I find comfort in a motley crew. You can't know how much it means to me that you care…you really care about me."

"Yes. I really care about you Miles, not just as my boss, but as a person." Her skin heated and she smiled at him.

"I care for you Bella, you know…as a person." She laughed and rolled her eyes.

"Thanks—" he watched as she seemed to struggle to find the words to say. "Thanks for the vote of confidence and for membership in the motley crew, but you can rest assured I would have pulled it together and done my job; I always do."

"I don't question that, but what else happened?"

"What do you mean, what else happened?" She scanned the room some more. Her papers were flung everywhere, but she found her phone located in the corner on the floor.

"There's more to it, Bella. I can feel it, and don't try to deny it. Let's go into another room away from the smoky smell and talk." He took her hand and led her to the living room, where he guided her to the couch with him instead of the chairs.

"Talk to me, Bella."

"I don't want to do this right now." She looked at her hands in her lap. "I don't want you to think less of me even though you say you understand. Nor do I want your pity." He took her into his arms, and she rested her head against his chest.

"I don't plan to give you pity. It doesn't help, and seldom does anyone want it. I just want to understand you a little better. If I need to cancel the concert tonight to stay with you I will."

"What? You can't do that!" She leaned back off his hard chest and stared into his eyes.

"I'm waiting, Bella. You know patience isn't my virtue." He laid his hand on her head and pressed her back to his chest. "I'm worried about you." He kissed the top of her head and stroked her hair, breathing in the scent of her lavender and vanilla scented shampoo.

"I don't want you worried about me when you have to hit the stage tonight, so I'll talk. I used to have nightmares about my parents burning in a fire when I was a little girl in Texas every time either one of them had to answer an emergency call and go to a fire at night. Mom was concerned about me and my fears, which became a reality after my father's death, so she gave up her career and moved to California to help me heal since I couldn't tolerate the frequent thunderstorms in Texas. They triggered my anxiety, and thunderstorms rarely occurred here. When I thought you were killed, and with the smell of smoke…." She cried a little more and buried her head in his chest while he grabbed her a little tighter and rocked her in his arms.

"Bella, I'm so sorry you were upset, and it hurts me to see you in so much pain." He pulled her chin toward him and placed a chaste kiss on her lips. She placed her hand on his cheek and offered him a slight smile.

"I'm feeling better now that you're here." She looked into his eyes. "Why were you trying to surprise me?" Her phone buzzed in her pocket, and she lifted it to look at the text message.

Charlie: ETA-10 minutes

"Oh no. I completely forgot about Charlie." She popped up and placed her phone back in her pocket.

"Who is Charlie, and why is he coming here?' He stood up and frowned, his face close to hers. She backed away, widening the space between them.

"Charlie Ferguson is a friend of mine, and he's coming for lunch." She placed her hands on the sides of her head and turned in a tight circle. "My plans for lunch are ruined and I promised I'd have something ready."

This is some shit. I'm here, and she's worried about lunch with some other dude.

"And what kind of friend is Charlie?"

"Miles, I don't have time for an inquisition, but to answer your question, Charlie and I went to graduate school together, and we haven't seen each other in years. We were close when we were in school, but time and distance have gotten in the way."

Good, he's trapped in the friend zone. I can deal with that.

"Don't take this the wrong way, but you don't look like you're ready for company. Why don't you freshen up—you're a bit ripe—and I'll greet Charlie."

"Thanks for the offer but...the kitchen...." He turned her in the direction of her bedroom and urged her on her way.

"Go. I'll handle things out here. Hurry back."

"You're right. I could use a shower." She sniffed the air around her body. "I'll be right back."

He took out his phone on his way back to the kitchen and made a few calls, hoping to salvage lunch. For the right price, he was certain the Tex-Mex restaurant he'd passed around the corner could help him. Once he finished the call, he looked over the mess. The owner assured him they would have the food delivered and set up in the backyard.

He made another phone call to Mr. Curtis and finished his conversation before heading to the front door to answer the ringing bell—a welcome distraction from his fantasizing about the water running down Bella's naked body, in the shower down the hall.

A tall man with dark brown hair and brown eyes, satchel in hand, stood in front of him, wide-eyed with a blank stare on his face. An easy smile spread across his face after Miles extended his hand to him.

"Charlie Ferguson?" He shook his head. "Bella was expecting you. Please come in. I'm Ari." Charlie continued shaking his head like a bobblehead doll.

"I know you're Ari—the megastar Ari. Where's Bella? Did she arrange this meeting for me as an exclusive with you? Several sites are recanting the story they streamed this morning. Bella said she would answer a few questions about the tour, but she didn't tell me she had arranged to let me be the first to break your account of the false story instead? Wow, this is the break I've been hoping for," he babbled.

I'd better cover for Bella. He looked in the direction of the hall—she hadn't come out yet.

"I also agreed to answer a few questions about the tour and specifically about the next two concert dates. Come have a seat so we can talk." Miles led him to the seating area.

"Is Bella planning on joining us later or is it going to be just the two of us?" He pulled his pad and pen out of his satchel.

"She should be out shortly. She's freshening up a bit. Have you heard the identity of the man who was killed?"

"Yes, I have." He opened his pad and reviewed the name he'd written down earlier. "It was reported his name was José Saunders. The authorities think his murder was gang related. Did you know him?"

Bella walked into the room, refreshed and smiling. She wore her hair in an updo with curvy tendrils on the side and had changed into a mint green dress and matching sandals. Both men rose from their seats, and Charlie greeted her, lifting her off her feet in a tight embrace. "You're the best. I can't believe you did all this for me."

Miles took her by the arm after Charlie released her and directed her to the seat beside him on the couch.

"I was telling Charlie we agreed to give him a scoop about the concert, but since I wasn't aware, I was going to die today, I agreed to give him my first post-resurrection interview."

He smiled, Charlie belted out a laugh, and Bella shot him a *watch yourself now look* with her brows drawn and a twisted smile plastered on her face. He cleared his throat and continued.

"Charlie, Bella doesn't always get my humor, but as I was saying, I wanted you to be the first to get the word out about our commitment to seeing the hip-hop music genre continue to evolve. I will be releasing a personal statement sending my condolences to the family and friends of one of my greatest fans, José Saunders. I've spoken to José many times, and he wasn't associated with gangs."

"It was José who was killed today?" Bella placed her hand over her mouth and teared up. Her hands trembled a bit when she placed them on the couch by her side. Miles eased over to comfort her and placed his hand on top of hers, drawing Charlie's attention. She looked at him and smiled tentatively before placing her hands on her lap.

"Yes, you knew him too? It was reported he was shot in gang related violence." Charlie leaned in closer to her.

"I did know him. I answered many of his emails and phone calls. He was the president of one of Ari's largest fan clubs, and he worked with us on several community-based projects for AriMusic. José wasn't a violent person, and he wasn't involved in a gang." Her chest heaved and her eyes glistened.

Miles straightened himself on the couch, and he slid a little closer to her. He handed her a tissue from the nearby box to wipe away her tears.

"Bella knows how passionate I am about the music. The genre has lost two musical giants to gun violence— Tupac and Biggie—and many others that haven't commanded much media attention. That's why my company, AriMusic, is committed to developing new talent and minimizing the unhealthy competition among artists that not so long ago plagued the hip-hop community. AriMusic promotes not only club hip-hop but conscious hip-hop music with political and social themes."

Miles smiled at her before turning back to Charlie.

"I plan to give the local authorities my full support in finding his murderer because I'm tired of there being initial interest in murders associated with the hip-hop community only to have the case fizzle and be placed in the unsolved cold-case murder file. We can't be complacent about the deaths of young people on the streets of America. So please print that my concerts will be a tribute to José. We'll place flowers in the two reserved seats in front of the stage tonight and give some of the profits to organizations that promote peace and unity in their communities. Bella, can you help with the press releases?"

"Of course, I'll be happy to do it."

"Charlie, I only ask that you vet your articles with her before they go to print. Bella is my chief marketing officer, and normally, all my press releases go through her." Charlie wrote as fast as he could and looked up to nod his head in agreement as Bella offered a faint smile at both of them. Miles grabbed the phone buzzing in his pocket and scrolled his messages.

"Ari, I would love to work with Bella again." Charlie's stomach growled, and he grabbed his abdomen. "Sorry about that, but I haven't eaten much today." Bella attempted to get up but sat back as Miles extended his arm to block her from leaving the couch.

"No, I'm sorry I took up more of your time than I intended with the interview. You must be hungry, so let's eat. The restaurant around the corner set up a lunch for us in the backyard. They left a message on my phone. Lunch is ready. I told you I had a few surprises for you Bella." He looked over at her.

"I'm starved," Charlie announced. "Bella, which way to the bathroom?" She pointed to the closest bathroom at the end of the hall. "If you'll excuse me, I'll be right back."

He walked away and left the two of them on the couch.

"I told you I had this." He leaned closer and pressed his finger on his cheek. "Place it right there." She turned his chin and placed a kiss on his lips before planting another on his cheek.

"I don't know how to thank you for everything you've done today. Charlie helped me land an internship early in my career, and I appreciate you doing this for him."

"I did it for you, Bella, and you can thank me by agreeing to give me a chance. Please give us a chance, Bella." His phone buzzed again, and Charlie returned from the bathroom.

"I need to take this. Don't wait for me to start lunch. I'll meet you both in the garden."

"Are the two of you together?" Miles heard Charlie ask as he walked away.

"Shush, Charlie, he's my boss, not my boyfriend," Bella quipped.

Miles smiled as he walked away to take the call.

I'm not your boyfriend now, but I hope to be soon.

CHAPTER TWELVE

Miles was on the phone with Mr. Curtis again, confirming his earlier requests. He made another phone call, this time to Parker. Time was passing quickly, and the calls lasted longer than he intended. He promised Parker he would be at the concert venue tonight in plenty of time for a review of the song playlist and the sound check. The flight from LA to San Francisco was only an hour and a half ride.

"You know we're under contract to have you here at least two hours before the start of the concert."

"I don't want to brag, but I am a professional and I've done this a million times, Parker. Chill, bro. I'll be there. Bye."

He ended the call and wandered out to the garden to join Charlie and Bella. Charlie had finished his meal and was dabbing the corners of his mouth with his napkin.

"I'm sorry, Ari. I couldn't wait any longer. The food was good. Thank you." Bella placed her utensils alongside her plate.

"Yes, thank you. The food was very good, and it was thoughtful of you to arrange this. I told Charlie that I burned the original meal and you salvaged lunch for me. You're the best Miles. We saved some for you. Come, sit and eat."

"You're welcome, and I'm glad you and Charlie enjoyed the food, but I'll have something on the plane. I need to start making my way to the airport in a little bit."

"Ari, I have a flight leaving today too. If you don't mind, I'd like to catch a ride back to the airport with you. I got a notification from the airlines while I was returning from the bathroom that I could leave on an early flight and I've checked in already." He waited for an answer, but Miles paused.

"Charlie, I'll call and have a car pick you up in the next few minutes. Bella and I have some unfinished business to discuss, and we'll need a private car to the airport for our talk." He took out his phone to make the call to arrange the transportation.

"Thanks, Ari, but I planned to help Bella clean up before leaving." He listened to Charlie and spoke to his employee on the other end.

"You said you checked in already for the earlier flight, and I wouldn't want you to miss it." He completed his plans on the phone and then directed his comments to Bella.

"I've arranged to have a cleaning crew come over to clean the kitchen and the backyard. A security detail will be on site to lock up after they leave so you don't have to worry about anything. My crew is on their way, and they're licensed and bonded." Bella tossed her hair to the side and cocked a single eyebrow.

"Thanks Miles, and I have a few things I need to discuss with you too."

I sense a little irritation, but at least she didn't refuse to come to the airport with me.

Charlie raised his eyebrows. "Wow, it must be nice to have people take care of so many things for you. How many people work for you?"

"Yes, it's convenient, and I value their services. I have a privately held company, and I don't give out information such as the number of people I employ."

"Sorry, I didn't mean to pry. It's just that my readers want to know as much as they can about you. I see how close you are with your fans, but I've noticed you generally don't talk about the business side of your organization."

"Good observation, Charlie. I prefer to keep the attention on the music." His phone buzzed again, and he looked at the message. "Your driver is waiting out front for you."

"Ari, let me walk Charlie to the door and I'll be back soon."

"Sure. Charlie, it was good to meet you, and I hope the information we'll release to you for your article will be helpful." He shook Charlie's hand before he departed.

"Goodbye Miles, and thanks." He followed Bella into the house.

Miles took a seat and looked at the fajitas still hot on top of the warming plate.

This does look good. I should try some of it. He grabbed a plate and placed a small amount of food on it while he awaited Bella's return.

He bit into the combination of strips of beef, peppers, and onions on a warmed tortilla and closed his eyes, relishing the taste. Bella returned with her pocketbook and keys in hand, prepared to leave, and remained standing after reaching the table.

"I don't want you to be late, and I'm ready to go to the airport when you're ready."

"Sit down. We have time. The plane leaves when I leave and not a minute before." He cleaned his face and hands hastily with a napkin before pulling out a chair and dragging it closer to his. She sat down and waited for him to say something.

"Let's talk." He pulled a small, black, felt-covered box out of his pocket and gave it to her. She took it, examining the outside.

"Go ahead." She pulled open the box and her mouth widened in surprise.

"Do you like it?" His jaw relaxed as he awaited her response.

She looked at the contents: an 18-carat gold pendant charm of a ram with diamonds encrusted in its horns and small diamonds in its eyes on a gold chain.

"It's nice. I see you like to give ram's head jewelry." A faint smile appeared on her face.

"Yes, my astrological animal sign is the ram, and I use the symbol in gifts to those closest to me—you know, those in my motley crew."

"Of course, I forgot it's the sign for Aries." She looked at the pendant again. "It matches my bracelet...so, you didn't give me ram's head jewelry to make fun of me?" He placed his hand on her arm before he answered.

"No.... No, Bella. Your reaction all makes sense now. I wasn't trying to make fun of you then, and I'm being sincere now. I want a do-over. The last time I gave you jewelry, things went terribly wrong. I apologize if you thought I was disrespecting you, but I wanted to give you another piece of jewelry as a member of my inner circle and speak to you about my feelings. I'm falling.... I'm falling...." She squirmed in her seat and interrupted him.

"Miles, I appreciate your generosity, but I don't want things to move too fast between us. Do you think it was a good idea to give Charlie the impression we're an item? He asked if we were together while you were returning phone calls. He knows me, so he didn't think I was sleeping my way to the top, but others may get that impression. I also told him I recently ended my relationship with my boyfriend."

"So there's no chance of you and Corey getting back together?"

"No, not ever again in this lifetime, and I really don't want to talk about him."

He tried containing the faint smile as he took the box with the pendant out of her hand and placed it on the table. He took her hands and released a deep breath before looking into her eyes.

"You say you're worried about others, but have I ever given you the impression I care what others think?"

"No, but I'm not as free of the judgment of others as you are." She looked down and away. He gently turned her head back to face him.

"This is between us and no one else. I think you care for me, and I care for you. I'm having problems expressing my feelings right now, but I'm asking you to give us a chance to get closer and maybe we'll grow comfortable with each other…as lovers."

He looked at her as her lips twisted in a cynical smile.

Oh no, things are going south again. He held her hands tightly despite her attempts to pull away. She rose from her seat, causing him to return to his feet.

"Why do you need another lover?"

"Bella, please." He released her hands and ran his fingers through his hair, exasperated. "I don't have other lovers."

"That's not what *On the Inside* said," she jested.

"Give me a break. You know that publication is rubbish. If I had someone call and tell them I made love to you and five other women on the Golden Gate bridge last night, they'd print it." He pulled out his phone, pretended to dial a number, and looked at her with a devilish look in his eyes.

"Don't you dare." She swatted at his phone, and he flashed her his boyish grin. "Miles, I mean it. Don't start rumors I'll have to clean up. Let's go to the airport, and on the way, we can talk about your security detail in light of the number of threatening emails I've been reviewing for you and sending to Bradley...and of course, because of what happened to José today." Tears welled up in her eyes.

She didn't resist him taking her into his arms and placing a kiss on her forehead. The cleaning crew came around to the backyard while they were still together in an embrace.

The crew chief came toward them, and Miles slowly released her.

"Good afternoon, Mr. Moore. We're here and ready for further instructions."

"Mr. Williams, you've spoken to Ms. Wahlberg before, I presume?"

"We've spoken at the estate. Good afternoon, Ms. Wahlberg."

"Good afternoon, Mr. Williams. Thanks for helping me at such short notice." She deferred to Miles to direct the operations.

"This is Ms. Wahlberg's home, and I've assured her you'll do a great job cleaning the kitchen and taking down everything in the backyard." Bella handed the keys to Mr. Williams.

"Let me show you the kitchen Mr. Williams." Miles placed his hand in the small of her back as she guided them back to the kitchen.

"Yes ma'am, but before that, I need to ask, Mr. Moore, if you still want us to arrange with the hotel staff to have your whirlpool bath cleaned every night in your rooms while you're on tour? Darien hasn't gotten back with me about the matter and we can have it cleaned more than once a day if that's what you desire."

"I won't need those services for this tour, but thanks for maintaining contact with the hotel officials at all of our stops." *Groupies in the whirlpool for fun nights are over.*

"That's my job, sir. I've already looked around the kitchen, and I don't have any questions. Seems like a straightforward job to me."

"All right then. Ms. Wahlberg and I will be leaving for the airport."

The traffic was heavier than usual as they creeped back to the airport. Miles sipped his small glass of wine, and Bella looked over her papers after she declined a drink, telling him she and Charlie had enjoyed a few shots of tequila at lunch while he was returning calls.

"So, are you going to give us a chance to get closer? Again, I'm sorry about the misunderstanding regarding the jewelry. I would never intentionally ridicule you, and I had problems expressing my feelings earlier, but you probably guessed I'm not good at telling people how I feel about them."

"I think you're good at expressing your feelings once you have clarity." She looked up at him.

"Well, I'm clear that I've never had to share my personal feelings with anyone before now and talking about my feelings isn't my thing. I'm one who shows people I care about them by the things I do instead of the things I say. The truth of the matter is you know more about me than most people. I've kissed you as passionately as I know how, I sing about you, I write songs about you, and I had nightcaps with Isabelle and her father instead of having my fireworks show just for you. Oh, and don't forget I sent you flowers. I've been there for you. What more do you want me to do?" She moved away and placed her papers on the seat between them.

"Miles, stop trying to corner me. I didn't know about the songs dedicated to me, but I'm grateful you've been there for me, and you don't have to hit me over the head with a big stick of reminders." She spoke through pursed lips to control her mixed emotions and she took a breath before continuing.

"What I want is for you to know I'm not interested in being just your lover. You have many of those—just like all the cars and other toys you own. I'm glad you're alive, but I don't want my fear of losing you to cause me to plunge into a relationship we'll both regret. And by the way, what's the deal with the whirlpool bath anyway? Is that where you and your groupies make out?" She looked at him and frowned.

"Temper, temper, Ms. Wahlberg." He took a sip of wine. "You're shooting daggers at me with your eyes." He paused. "You heard me say I won't be needing cleaning service in the whirlpool because I won't be using it to relax my sore muscles."

"So that's the line you're going to tell me?"

"No, it's the line I'm sticking with. How does it help me to win your confidence if I'm stupid enough to talk about my past behavior with groupies? You already know I have a past."

"That's fair enough. Let's change the subject. Anyway, what I really need to talk about is your reckless disregard for your safety. You can't ask me to consider having a personal relationship with you when you don't follow the security plans in place to protect you."

"What are you talking about?" He set the glass down in the side compartment.

"When you're with your fans, you go directly to them instead of maintaining some distance or staying in the zone Bradley and his security detail carve out for you. I may not be staying in my lane by telling you this but, you're driving everyone including me crazy with that. You don't see all the death threats and creepy letters of unrequited love you receive. I don't think you should consider having a Night with Ari promotion anymore. Many of the women who spend time with you think you're in love with them, and some are angered by photos of you with other women. They write that they're going to hurt you and the other women. It's frightening how scary some of your fans look on paper."

"A little jealous are you, Bella?" His voice was calm and his gaze steady.

"Don't patronize me, Miles. It's irritating when you make fun of everything." She boldly met his eyes, answering him in a rush of words. "You're not taking me seriously, and I refuse to accept this behavior." She turned away and looked out the window as he placed the papers to the side and moved in a little closer.

"I'm sorry, Bella. I have a bad habit of making a joke out of things when I'm challenged. I get what you're saying, but I don't want to distance myself from my fans.

After all, I do all this for them. My performances are for them, and besides, Bradley is always nearby. You know he doesn't leave town until I leave town." His voice became less mocking and his tone more contrite. "Forgive me?" He pulled her into his arms. "I'll do better. I promise. Please don't freeze me out."

She stayed in his arms but pulled out her phone and quickly typed out a text.

"You need to take care of something more important than talking about us?"

"Jealous, Mr. Moore?"

"I can't say I've ever been jealous before." He shrugged and dismissed the thought.

"What do you call all your questions about Charlie earlier today?"

"I wouldn't call it jealousy, maybe curiosity and a need for male dominance. I'm not hiding that I want to be the man in your life."

She chuckled at his honesty, and he hugged her tighter, happy to see her beautiful smile again.

"Come to the concert tonight."

"Miles, you know I can't. We need to take it slow. We'll have time to sort out our feelings when you get back."

"But Bella—"

The driver rolled down the dividing window. "Sir, we're almost at the airport. I'll park inside the security area at the private strip because there's a crowd formed outside the gate."

"Thanks. That's life in LA. There's always a celebrity coming in and going out and crowds to greet them." He grabbed his dark shades and gave an extra pair to her. He wrapped her in his arms again and pleaded with her one more time. "Come with me please. We can talk on the plane and after the concert." She shook her head as he looked at her with puppy eyes.

"You're so beautiful Bella. Can I kiss you one last time?"

"Yes I would like if you kissed me. You're going to be gone and I'm not sure when I'll see you again."

He kissed her, hoping to work his magic as he grabbed her around the waist, causing her dress to gather around her hips, revealing a hint of her round ass before plunging his tongue into her mouth. Almost immediately, he had to pull his hand away from brushing against her soft breasts. He was surprised by his heart pounding and his pulse racing, which caused him to move closer to the door and rest his head back against the headrest.

Panting, he struggled to regain his breath, and his heart skipped beats, excited with lust. She looked at him, puzzled by his reaction, and touched his flushed skin before wiping away the sweat forming on his brow.

"Please…say you'll come." He struggled to speak as he looked at her.

"No, Miles, I can't go with you. You've worked hard, and you should enjoy this time. Are you all right?"

He grabbed his chest, still heaving as he fought for his breath. "Wow, it felt like my brain was short circuiting when I kissed you. It felt so good, too good, touching you." She widened her eyes in disbelief and pulled a towel out of one of the pockets to give to him.

"Here, take this. You have lipstick on your lips, and you don't look like you're ready for company." She leaned forward to wipe his face and giggled after he swatted her ass playfully.

"You're making fun of me?" He took the towel and wiped his face before putting on his shades.

"No, I'm enjoying seeing your vulnerable side. It's endearing to me."

He took her into his arms one last time and placed a kiss on her forehead as the car came to a complete stop.

"You call it vulnerability, but I call it excitement. Caressing you is like holding TNT, and you know how much I like playing with fire." He kissed her again, but this time avoided touching her breasts.

"Stay in here. I'll come around to open the door." She unwrapped herself from his arms and placed her hand on his bicep.

"No, Miles. We shouldn't display any affection or physical contact in front of your fans." Her voice was firm and determined. "It will only aggravate those who don't understand Ari is just your public persona." She raised her voice to be heard over the screams of fans that could be heard through the raised dark tinted windows and the closed heavy doors.

"Fine." He moved farther away from her.

"Tuck in your shirt. It's hanging out of your pants."

He straightened his clothes before exiting the car.

She put on her sunglasses, opened the door, and climbed out of the limo on the side away from his fans while he opened his door to the scene of people screaming and jumping up and down behind a chain-link fence.

"There's always a group of fans at the airport for a chance to see a star, and any star will do," Miles mumbled to himself as he looked around at the crowd.

"It's Ari!" The crowd yelled and he tightened his lips as he looked at Bradley and his security force standing at the door, surrounding him on all sides instead of waiting for him at the foot of the stairs leading to the plane.

He popped out of the limo and instinctively moved toward the crowd to be among the fans but stopped and looked over at Bella, who pushed her blowing hair behind her ears. He raised his glasses to look at her as she bit her lip and met his eyes before quickly looking away. He was about to take another step closer to the adoring crowd but stopped again and waved at them instead while moving closer to the plane. He paused to wave goodbye to her, and she waved back, rewarding him with a bright smile. He placed his hand to his ear mimicking a phone handset.

"I'll call you tonight." He hoped she read his lips as he ascended the plane and waved one last time before disappearing inside the door with his security detail behind him. He pulled out his phone once in his seat and texted Bella as he looked at her out of his window standing beside the limo.

> **Miles:** We're not closing the door until I see you're safely inside the limo and heading back home.

> **Bella:** I'm going back to the office to finish a little work before I go home.

> **Miles:** I'll call U tonight.

> **Bella:** Okay, Thanks for being a little more observant about safety measures in place to protect U. Don't take it out on Bradley. I texted him to meet us at the airport and to have a

prudent safety plan in place once we arrived.

Miles: So, U ambushed me?

Bella: Yes, and imagine if U were ambushed by someone who hated U?

Miles: I'll admit I prefer the ambush by someone who cares for me.

Bella: Later.

Miles: I'm out.

Bella told the driver to take her to the estate and buckled up as the limo drove off and the engine from the jet fired up. She had a lot to think about and didn't want to go home to her empty house and face the possibility of revisiting her fears about Miles being gone. She liked having him around, and it was true her feelings for him were changing.

As the limo made its way through traffic, she grabbed her phone and looked through the AriMusic's sites at the usual posted messages: messages of love, messages of hate, the why don't you call me Ari messages. It was easier to look at the messages when she didn't have romantic feelings for him. *Can I continue to do this part of my job as his lover?*

She placed a finger to her cheek and rolled her eyes upward. She wasn't sure, but she knew they both had to change if things were going to work out for them. She made use of the time in traffic making personal calls, assuring the vendors at the arena Miles would be there so they could start setting up the merchandise. She sent out press releases quelling the rumors and assuring the fans the show was still on for tonight.

The driver navigated the busy streets and eventually arrived at the estate, directing the car up the long driveway to the back near the kitchen. She was thirsty and decided she needed a drink of water before heading to her office. She gathered her things out of the limo and walked into the estate, heading for the kitchen, where she was greeted by Mr. Curtis, who was busy doing inventory.

"Hi, Bella, I was expecting you." He came toward her and handed her a glass he retrieved from the refrigerator.

"It's for you. Miles called and told me you were coming to work. I thought you could use some nutrients after your scare this morning. It's a small smoothie."

"Thanks, I appreciate you so much, Mr. Curtis. It was an eventful morning. Oh, something is in my eyes." She teared up and stretched her eyelid, pretending to rub out the nonexistent foreign object.

"You're welcome. I have something else for you. Miles told me to give this album to you when you returned to work." He handed her a light blue album cover with Prince's name on the top in pink cursive writing above a picture of the artist. She turned the cover over and looked through the lists of songs.

Staring at the album, deep in thought, she paused before she spoke.

"I don't understand; why did he want me to have this? Are you sure he wanted you to give it to me? It looks in pristine condition."

"I'm certain he did. This album means a lot to him because his father bought two copies for him after he attended his first Prince concert when he was ten years old where Prince did a lot of cuts from his earlier albums, especially this one. One copy he played until all the grooves almost disappeared and the second, he maintained in his private collection. The copy you have has never been played. I recall when he was younger, his parents struggled with helping him control his temper and his father tried to get him interested in playing the guitar as music therapy, but Miles would have no part of it. He heard Prince play the first song on the album, 'I Wanna Be Your Lover,' and he was bitten by the bug. He listened to that song over and over, and almost drove all of us crazy after hearing it for the tenth time. When his mother complained about the sexual content in the lyrics and forbade him listening to it, he started playing the next song over and over, 'Why You Wanna Treat Me So Bad?' His parents knew he was a phenom when he learned to play the guitar solos faster than his father could play them. I think he wanted you to have something he cherishes because he loves Prince's music, he loves his parents, and he…. I shouldn't interfere. Did you enjoy your smoothie?"

She put down her glass, got up out of her seat, and placed her arms around his shoulders.

"Thank you for caring about us. I promise you I'll do my part to figure things out between us." She returned to her seat and finished the last drops of her drink before going to her office for a little time at the computer. She took the album with her and looked at it while she sat at her desk. Maybe she'd get it framed; it definitely deserved a place of honor in her office.

She tried getting some work done, but she kept pondering the talk they'd had before he left. *Why did he tell me he didn't have his fireworks show because of me? I had nothing to do with his decision to cancel the show. He chose to have dinner with Isabelle and her father the night before he kicked off the tour? I knew about the earlier arranged dates, but I knew nothing about the nightcaps with Isabelle and her father until he told me today.*

She opened several messages and read the communications from Mr. Bronson, telling her of his plans to invest more money in promoting tickets sales at the venues he owned. The Fire God Tour was selling out ahead of each scheduled appearance and she loved being a part of the success of AriMusic, but there were times when she felt overextended. She thought about talking to Miles and Parker about increasing the number of people assigned to promote the tour, but she didn't want to have to go on tour with them to supervise the new employees.

Things will work out; I just have to hang in there. She'd planned her promotional events months ago, and Mr. Bronson had agreed to make members of his staff available if necessary. Looking through the social media sites, she noticed several of them had recanted the story about Ari. She teared up again as she thought it could have been him dead on the street. She couldn't shake off the nagging feeling maybe José wouldn't be dead if he hadn't been dressed like Miles.

She used her Miles's World app to send a message to Miles, thanking him for the album. She also sent a message to Bradley.

```
Bella: I sent the official list
       to you with all the authorized
       backstage and VIP passes. No one
```

```
else should be added to the
list.
```

He replied immediately.

Bradley: We're on it, Bella.
Don't worry.

She looked at the wildly popular #WheresAri thread of submissions and chose three fans to receive the fan package for the week based on the votes they'd received from other fans. Some of them went all out to look like Ari. Next month, she would pick the top five submissions to win tickets to the show and fan packs. She rationalized that if looking like Ari had something to do with José's death, she would pick several people, some at random in unexpected giveaways, instead of making one fan a possible target. She had considered ending the contest, but José had loved it and had encouraged her to continue it.

She hadn't made time to look at all the features of the app before now, but since it was quiet and there was little chance of an interruption, she clicked on the menu button and a shortcut called "Surf the Web" popped up. Right clicking on it, a drop box came down, revealing recent sites she assumed Miles had searched. She wasn't surprised she had access to the information since Darien had told her Miles approved linking his account to hers in the event, she needed to respond on his behalf on his media sites. He had access to any employee's web search if they used company equipment, and he didn't mind if she knew his web search history, at least not the ones he searched using the Miles's World app.

The usual sites she thought he would search popped up: expensive fast cars, sites of recent volcanic eruptions, advances in musical equipment, and a few fantasy sex sites. She shrugged, unfazed he had watched sex videos, although she was curious that he visited one site multiple times. She looked at the line containing the site and warred in her mind if she should click on it.

Oh, what the hell. The little devil sitting on her shoulder won and she opened the site.

She was surprised he only visited one French site and viewed multiple vignettes of a man's fantasy of watching another man having sex with a woman. Using what little French she could recall; she gathered the man in the storyline was the husband of the woman having sex with many different lovers. He watched them, and each vignette ended with the husband's fantasy of joining in and banishing the lover before he had sex with his wife.

Odd, but to each his own. These scenes don't do anything for me, but who am I to judge?

She clicked off the site and continued with her work, looking at the marketing merchandise and choosing from the selection of t-shirts, jewelry, and Ari bobble heads. She had spoken to some of the vendors personally and was struck by the fact that so many people earned a living from Ari's concerts and other celebrities coming through their town. She rubbed her eyes, sore from hours in front of the computer.

So much for a day off and a hike up the canyon. She stretched her tired limbs and yawned then closed her eyes for a little power nap.

Three hours later, she woke up with Mr. Curtis standing before her.

"Why don't you stay in the guest room just to the right of the stairs? Your car was left here for you, I guess Miles arranged it, but you look too tired to drive home. I can have a meal sent to your room if you'd like.

"I am tired and hungry." She stifled a yawn.

"Good, and don't forget, it's almost time for the concert. We have satellite TV in several of the bedrooms with the app on it recording the concert and mirroring it on the TV. You can watch the concert here and avoid Miles's irritation if you tell him you missed the concert because you fell asleep again or got stuck in traffic. He told me you've never seen him perform live before."

"You're right." She stretched her arms. "I wouldn't want to upset the maestro."

"There are changes of clothing and toiletries in the bedroom next to Miles's suite. Don't worry; he won't show up tonight. You're safe." She bit her lip and attempted a smile.

"I thank you for the hospitality. I've been so busy lately." She rubbed her forehead. "I need to look at managing my time better."

"I've seen others do this job Bella, and you're doing it a lot better than many. It'll get better after the first two weeks the tour is on the road. Things generally go smoother after the initial wrinkles have been ironed out."

She got up from her desk and headed upstairs to the room Mr. Curtis told her was available; to get ready for a night in bed watching the concert while he left for the kitchen to alert the staff to expect her for the night. A wide grin spread on her face, and she felt a bit of an adrenaline rush as she hurried out of her office and up the stairs to prepare for a night of entertainment with the incomparable Ari Moore.

The wonders of modern technology. You gotta love it.

The blue light from the television provided enough light to find the phone ringing on the desk. A glimpse of the lighted face of the clock showed it was 2:59 am. She struggled to grab her phone before it stopped ringing and saw the picture of a smiling Miles from the day they hiked the canyon together on the screen. She hit accept call and sat up in bed.

"I'm still alive."

"Not for long. I plan to choke you, Moore. It's three o'clock in the morning."

"Did you see the concert?"

"Yes, I did, and I saw some of the positive reviews online. You put on a great show and you're an excellent performer, but I don't understand, where do you get all that energy?"

"You had me so horny, I had to burn it off somehow. It's not often I get to sit with you in the back of a limo and hold you close."

"Right, blame me…. Thank you for being there for me today, and for the album. I saw the title of the first song, and I wondered if that was why you gave it to me. Are you using it to try to tell me something?" She covered her mouth to muffle her yawn.

"I gave you the album because I flubbed my lines like some schoolboy when I tried to tell you my feelings. The song kept running through my head while I was on the plane, and even though I couldn't put my feelings into words, I remembered when I fell in love for the first time—not with a girl but with music, and I've been committed to her ever since. Prince did a better job talking about sex and love than I can. Most of my adult life, a good lay has been what I sought."

"We're confessing now Miles?" She laughed.

"That was the old me, Bella, but now that I'm discovering what true love is, I'm having a little difficulty finding the words to express what I feel for you."

"We're both struggling to express our feelings, but I've always heard when people tell you about themselves, believe it the first time. I don't want to be just another woman you lay with for a couple of times and then what? We won't be able to work together when the lust is gone because surely, it will disappear." She took in a deep breath. "This conversation is way too deep for this time of morning, so let's change the subject. Why did you blame me for canceling your fireworks show?"

"Because I left the party early and went downtown to meet with Isabelle and her father to please you. Didn't you arrange the meeting? Instead of playing with fireworks the night before the first show, I was having nightcaps with them. I'm not mad about it, and I actually enjoyed spending time with her father. He's a great businessman, and I learned some things from him."

"Who called you to arrange the meeting? I had nothing to do with it."

"Isabelle called me."

"Oh, I'm not sure about her intent, but the meeting the night before the first concert was news to me too. I didn't arrange it."

"I don't know her intent either, but I don't want to spend more time talking about her. We need to talk in person and not over the phone about us because I'm not so eloquent over the phone, and I won't lie that I've fantasized about having sex with you."

"So you just want my body?"

"That's not what I said, but it's late."

"Yes, it's late. Goodnight."

"Good night. Sleep well in my bed."

"I guess you're correct in that I'm in one of the many guest beds you paid for."

"Of course that's what I meant. Good night, Bella."

She pressed end call. He was right. She was in one of his beds, cozy and comfortable. She fell back asleep, too tired to sort out complicated matters like her feelings for him or how he knew she was still at the estate.

In the quiet of the early morning, her back arched as she awoke from a delicious dream of Miles making love to her. She wiped away the sweat from her brow and blew out a breath, imagining Miles igniting her passions. She looked about the guest room, much more masculine in its appeal than her pink room. Her body heated with the fantasy of seeing his nude body again, and her physical response to him answered some of her questions. Sure, he was attractive, and she lusted for him, but was she ready to admit she was falling in love with him? She settled back under the covers and closed her eyes, hoping for another salacious encounter with Miles Moore.

Michele Sims

CHAPTER THIRTEEN

"Mom, you promised me you would remain calm."

She jerked the car into park and cut the motor.

"We'd better get inside. The traffic coming from the airport was heavier than I expected, and I don't want us to miss our reservations. You remember how hard it is to get a table at this place."

"Fine, but you're paying for the meal, young lady. I can't believe you didn't tell me all the things going on in your life. You could have told me over the phone."

"I promise to tell you everything, but let's get going." She locked her arm around her mother's elbow and walked with her into the restaurant.

"Table for two. The reservation should be under the name Wahlberg." She told the hostess, who found the reservation and escorted them to their table.

"Bella, are you telling me Corey came to your office and got into an argument with you?" Joan opened her folded napkin and laid it across her lap in a huff. "He called me several days ago and asked me to speak to you. His version of the story was Miles was having a negative effect on you, and he had come between you two. He thought you were worried about money and that's why you were keeping the job instead of quitting as he'd suggested. What is really going on?"

"There is no two of us anymore. He was calling me multiple times throughout the day and night and threatening me over the phone. That's after he shared intimate details about our sex life with Miles." Joan opened her mouth and absently took the menu from the waiter who had come to serve them.

"I'll have a glass of wine immediately, no, make it a bottle of your best white wine."

"Mom, since I'm paying, can you make it a glass of their best white wine? I'm not drinking since I have more work to do at home."

Joan looked at the waiter to make sure she had his attention. "Young man, make it a glass of white wine, but if I point to my glass at any time, I want you to fill it."

"Yes, ma'am. I'll return with the wine immediately." He came back, filled her glass, and took their food orders.

"The specialty salmon dish here is very good, Mom. You want to try it?"

"Sure, I can tell already what you have to share shouldn't be received on an empty stomach."

"The wild salmon, medium well-cooked for two please."

"Very good choice, ma'am."

Joan looked at Bella and shook her head. "This is reminding me of the time I thought we needed to talk about sex and birth control, and you told me you had already begun discussing the matter with Dr. Jones. We were frank and open with each other then, so lay it on me now." She picked up her glass and took a big swallow. "Oh, that's good, Bella. You should try some."

"No thank you, but as I was saying, my relationship with Corey is over, and that's not all. I'm starting to have feelings for Miles, and he said he had feelings for me, and—"

"Wait, is this the part where you tell me you're pregnant and you don't know who the baby daddy is?"

"Mom, please! I'm not pregnant; I haven't had sex with Miles, although I kissed him twice."

"You meant he kissed you, right? Is that what had Corey so out of control?"

"We don't need to talk about Corey; it's over and I don't care what he told you. Miles didn't come between us, and I kissed Miles, but he did return my kiss." Joan blew out a breath.

"I had concerns about taking the contract position in Texas for six weeks and having a prolonged absence from home, but I never thought I would return and find out that Corey was stalking you." She took two more swallows of wine and emptied her glass. The waiter returned and filled it again while Bella frowned at both of them.

"Fix your face, Bella, frowns lead to wrinkles. I've had a long day, and it doesn't seem to be getting better any time soon. At the very least, I'm enjoying my wine, and this very interesting conversation. So how did you get Corey to stop calling you?"

"We're back to Corey again? Mom, I know how polite he was with you, but maybe we don't know everything about him. Miles's dog, Bosco, stopped him from threatening me, and I have a video of it."

"Let me see it."

Bella handed her the phone, and Joan, after placing her hand on her chest, froze as she viewed Corey's face, contorted by the angry exchange with Bella.

"This is disturbing. So...so that explains why I saw pictures of you and Corey together online at the charity ball but none of the two of you at Miles's birthday party." She handed Bella her phone.

"Bella, I can't say I've ever seen Corey look so angry and then so frightened in a matter of seconds. Bosco doesn't play, does he?"

"I'm glad he was there. I was so angry with Corey; I could have hurt him myself."

Joan chuckled. "I like your bravado, but don't get it twisted. The two of you should continue to stay away from each other."

"He hasn't contacted me since that day." Bella assured her mother.

"I'm glad to hear it, and before I forget to tell you, I loved the dress you had on at the party. It didn't seem quite your style, but it fit you so well."

"Darien picked out the dress, and Miles purchased it."

"Well, that explains everything. Quite a cohesive, albeit enmeshed group you all have, but I will say that it was always my impression that Miles picked people who were not only competent, but people he genuinely liked. His management team seemed to really care about each other, but I digress, you told me you and Miles have started kissing each other?"

"Yes, a motley crew." She smoothed out the napkin in her lap before continuing the conversation with her mother. "I sense the disapproval in your voice Mom."

"It's more concern than anything else."

"So much has happened, and I'm still trying to wrap my head around it. NeNe interviewed me *after* I got the job, but I realized she and Miles have been close all their lives, and she needed to mark her territory by sizing me up. I figured if I wanted to stay on Miles's good side, I needed to be cool with NeNe."

"So you've got a read on NeNe, what about Miles? You know most office relationships don't work, and if this…this situation doesn't work out, where do you go from there?"

"I'm ambivalent about my feelings and about continuing to work at AriMusic. I also understand if it doesn't work out between us, there's no other place for me but out the door. I know the stakes are high." Her phone pinged with several messages.

"Please forgive me. I need to respond to these messages."

"No problem sweetheart. For better or worse, we don't do nine to fives. Miles hasn't demanded that you tour with him, and it's only fair for the team to be able to get you when they need you."

"Yes, I appreciate how flexible he's been." She scrolled through the messages.

Justin: Please address issue online about Miles and one of the dancers. He's not hitting it, and the rumors about him having sex with one of them are starting to irritate him and cause dissension among the dancers. It's a few of the new crew members putting rumors on social media and causing problems, but it's too late to fire them and get replacements. I've addressed it internally, and I hope you can put a spin on this for public consumption.

Bella: Have you talked to Reagan about this?

Justin: No, Reagan is out for a couple of days with an ankle

> **sprain. I didn't want to bother
> her with this while she was
> focusing on healing.**
>
> **Bella:** Got it. I'll address it
> tonight.

She scrolled through another message, this time from Darien.

> **Darien:** I need you to talk to
> the Bronson people. Isabelle
> thinks it would be good for her
> publicity and for Miles if she
> made a guest appearance at one
> of the concerts. Not!
>
> **Bella:** I have her father's
> direct line. I'll talk to him,
> and you should consider this a
> non-issue. It was our initial
> agreement that Isabelle would
> have time to spend with Miles
> before the tour and not
> afterward.
>
> **Darien:** I knew I could depend on
> you. Thanks.

Their salmon dinners arrived, and the hot plates were placed in the front of them.

"Thank you for your patience, Mom. I've really missed you, and I'm so glad you are back home."

"It's good to be home. The meal does look good. One more glass of wine young man." She pointed to her empty glass. "Let's enjoy our meal and we'll talk more later."

Bella was grateful for the time with her mother, filled with laughter, wine, and good food. They decided after returning home from dinner to delay further discussions about their future until they both had the benefit of a good night's rest.

Bella got up early to work at home, but before pouring through reviews and emails, she looked at articles about José's murder case. There still were no leads, and she wondered how much interest the authorities had in solving the murder. The articles in the general press too many times blamed his death on random urban violence, but a headline on a popular hip-hop site caught her attention:

If we can't solve Biggie and Tupac's murders, what hope is there for solving the murders of less well-known African American males? It made her wonder: if Miles had been shot, would there still be a lack of interest in solving the case? She knew Bradley wasn't too happy about her multiple emails about Miles's safety, but she hoped he understood that her intentions were good. She shot him another email to ask if he had heard anything about José's murder from contacts he had on the police force before she turned her attention to reviews about the tour:

Ari brings the sizzle.
One word can only describe this tour: Hot.
The New Master of Hip-hop is Electrifying.

She knew how hard he'd worked to make the tour a success, and he didn't need to deal with unnecessary distractions. She addressed the more blatant rumors and had granted a few online bloggers interviews with her about the tour. She couldn't believe six weeks had passed since she'd last seen Miles. The time apart gave her the needed space to realize she wanted more from him—more than she thought he was willing to give.

She was shocked as she looked at the video of his concerts, showing him still body surfing with his fans. She shot off another text to Bradley, and a message came up on her computer with his response, surprising her.

> **Bradley:** Don't know about José's murder. U know I'm busy with the tour, and I don't have time to follow up on a murder case.

Another message came in from him and she glanced quickly at it.

> **Bradley:** Doing my job. Too much traffic in this lane Bella.

Maybe he's having a tough day. Providing security for Miles has got to be stressful. She shrugged and continued to respond to questions from the merchandise vendors along the tour stops.

"Good morning Bella." Her mother entered the room and poured a cup of coffee.

"Good morning Mom." Bella took a sip of her coffee.

"Have you thought more about your career plans?" Joan took a seat at the kitchen table as they sat in their bathrobes to discuss finalizing their business plans.

"Mom, you know I've been torn about staying at AriMusic, but after his antics at his concert last night, I've finally made up my mind. I can't stand by and watch him flirt with danger anymore."

"What are you talking about, dear?" Joan blew over the top of her mug, containing hazelnut cream flavored coffee. She drew in a breath as the aroma filled the kitchen with a creamy scent.

"I thought I wouldn't have a chance to catch the show, but I was able to see a bit of the taped performance on my computer this morning, and I'm glad I did. After his first set, Miles lunged into the crowd off the stage and body surfed. He was eventually carried back stage by some big burly guys. I thought I was going to die when I saw him leap off the stage. He could've been trampled or hurt someone if he landed on them."

Her mother looked at her over the top of her glasses, her mouth open. She placed her mug on the table before she spoke.

"Baby girl, sometimes you amaze me. Despite your methodical approach to problems, you can be so gullible sometimes. Miles staged that part of his show with Bradley's help. Those guys weren't fans. They were part of his security detail planted in the audience to catch him."

"I know that members of security are planted in the crowd, but what about the push from the crowds and the hordes surrounding him? Somebody could have a gun, and Mom, this day and time, crowd surfing isn't safe."

"I hear you, but his security team isn't about to lose their handsome five-figure paychecks by dropping Miles on the floor or letting the crowd get too close. Believe me, he was safe."

"So, is that why Bradley seemed to blow me off when I texted him to complain? In so many words, he told me he had everything under control, and he seemed a little perturbed with me of all things. In one of his latest texts to me, he wrote, Miles wasn't effing anyone so what else did I forbid him to do?"

"Effing anyone dear?"

"You know what I mean…having sex with anyone…fucking," she said in hushed tones. *God this is hard. I really need to talk to Darien or Reagan instead of my mother about these things.*

"Bella, we work for Miles; he doesn't work for us. He's grown, and I fear you're trying to control him to treat your anxieties. Corey tried to control you and how did that work out?" Her eyes hardened as she looked at Bella, who focused her gaze on Joan and winced after biting her tongue to avoid saying anything else, but it came out anyway.

"If you'd stopped Dad, maybe he would be here with us now."

Where did that come from? She covered her lips, stunned by the words coming out of her mouth.

"Mom, forgive me, I'm tired and stressed. Of course I don't blame you for Dad's death." She looked up to address her mother and lowered her head again before raising it slowly to search her mother's face for her reaction.

"Bella, there's no need to apologize, but it's time we have this discussion, woman to woman. I know you don't blame me, but maybe you've idealized me being a strong woman who could tell your father what to do. Your father was a good man, one of the best, but he drew the line at being told what to do. He didn't have to go in to work the night he died, but he insisted, despite the fact I had someone to cover the shift. Your father was a risk taker and lived life on his own terms. We wouldn't have been together for twelve years if I had tried to control him, and I wouldn't have his greatest gift to me: you." Bella got up to hug her mother and sat back in her seat to continue their talk.

"I can always count on you to understand me, so am I being awful to worry about him? I feel I'm drawn to risk-taking men, romantically and platonically; even Corey was a risk taker. He plunged his trust fund into his venture with the stores. Miles is clearly a risk taker, and I found out that Charlie is also involved in a start-up venture while working for his father's media business and learning it from the ground up."

"How is Charlie doing? I haven't talked to him or his father in ages."

"He's fine. He and I completed a series of articles about Miles for his magazine. He said sales were unbelievable."

"Bella, you're a risk taker, but in a different way. All of these men see how you're able to invest your time and energy believing in their dreams without the benefits of having a sure thing for yourself. You're drawn to the vision of building something or making it better—taking a risk. Well, relationships offer no guarantees either. There's always the element of risk that you may get your heart broken if things don't work out. So, I'm asking you to think about this. You both have feelings for each other, and he told me over the phone that you fell just short of blasting him out about his risky behavior around his fans. He must care for you because I've seen him fire others for less than insubordination. My dear daughter, I'm telling you: Don't continue to mess with his head, especially while he's on a strenuous worldwide tour. You either decide to give the two of you a chance or move on."

"I hear you, Mom, and I appreciate your advice. You know how much I value your opinion. You're my mother, and you've always been there for me. I'm okay with your plans to move back to Texas, and it's time for me to make some decisions about my life." She folded her arms while Joan leaned in to listen.

"I've weighed my options, and I'm staying here in Southern California, even if I put in my resignation at AriMusic. I'm no longer the little girl who cowers every time it rains too hard—well just *some* of the time when there's severe lightning. In the meantime, I promise you I'll be professional with Miles and not string him along. I understand what you're saying. Corey tried to control me, and I refused to submit to his demands. You can't love an adult and try to control them at the same time. It's not being kind, and it's not love."

"You got it." Joan nodded her head in agreement. "What are your plans today? Are you sure you don't want anything for breakfast?"

"No, thank you, I'm good. I have a lunch date with Darien, and I need to make some calls before I meet him downtown." Bella got up and placed their mugs in the sink. She ran her hand through her thick hair.

"I need to do something with my hair before I go. I'll be in my room if you need me."

"Enjoy your day. I'll be in town for a week, and we can talk more later."

"Thanks, Mom." She blew her a kiss before returning to her room.

❧

Bella hadn't been able to tell Darien before he left with the tour about her conversation with Miles at his birthday party. She was embarrassed, but she knew although he was loyal to Miles, Darien was truly a good friend who listened and never judged her.

They met over lunch on one of his return trips to LA to spend time with his partner before the tour went to Vegas, Texas, the East Coast, and then overseas. She showed Darien the bangle Miles had given her and told him about the pendant he gave her during his surprise visit. She had intended to throw the bangle away or maybe take it to a pawn shop, but she'd received so many compliments about it, she continued to wear it. She enjoyed the pendant too, but it didn't complement the outfit she had on today: a high neck, skater-styled blue flared dress.

"Bella, Miles told me about the misunderstanding between the two of you over the bracelet. We thought you knew Miles gave everyone in his inner circle ram's head jewelry."

"I didn't make the connection that the ram was his astrological sign. It just seemed too much of a coincidence that it also could have referred to something I said to Corey that he shared with Miles."

He pulled out a gold necklace with a ram's head pendant from around his neck.

"He gave this to me, and Parker has a watch with a ram's head etched on the face. It was an unfortunate coincidence that you turned the ram into something dirty." He broke the seriousness of their conversation and threw his head back in a hearty laugh.

She could laugh at the incident now that time had healed her bruised feelings. She threw a piece of bread, from the basket on the table at him and his laughter was so infectious, she soon joined in. He wiped his eyes with the backs of his hands and looked up at her with a bright smile, which slowly faded and was replaced with a look of concern.

"Let me get real with you, girl. You know Miles has feelings for you and he thought he was doing something nice. I don't know which of you two social misfits are going to drive me crazy first but; I hope you realize you both care for each other before it's too late."

"I hear you Darien." She moved the food around on her plate.

"Have you been watching the live feeds of the concert on the links I've been sending to you? Bella, you've got to make some time to see him live."

"Yes, I haven't missed a single show. They're all fantastic, and Miles is a great performer. He comes alive when he uses fire in his shows, and it's obvious he absorbs the energy of the crowd and radiates it back to them. His shows are really fantastic, but I still have concerns about how often he comes down from the stage into the crowd. The crowd always goes wild, and there are safety risks. You know artists have been hurt, and he has his share of deranged folks who write to him regularly." Darien cocked his head, his eyes softening.

"I agree that some of his fans are downright scary and they travel in packs but try not to worry so much. We've got his back." He reached out and touched the back of her hand. She let out a puff of air, not wanting to be a Debbie downer, and smiled with a lift of her shoulders despite her concerns.

"Enough of the morbid stuff. I've been communicating with him as one of his biggest fans in the backstage chat room of his app, giving him lots of fan love and sometimes he replies. The app is a great idea. It allows his special fans to have a backstage look at Ari's world, and I'm happy how fast the number of followers he has on social media has grown."

She paused and tilted her head slightly. "I have a question for you, Darien. What do the signals he seemed to be giving the roadies mean when he's on stage? I don't see him respond by raising one or two fingers in the air as much as he did during his concerts six weeks ago. Now, he usually responds with a fist in the air."

"Those are 'groupie signals,'" he answered, making air quotes with his fingers. "Miles doesn't ask for groupies as much as he did on other tours. He spends his time adjusting songs for the concert, or he's lost in his world of fire. He's either throwing fiery darts, choreographing the fire segments of the show, or practicing his archery with his newest bow and arrow set. At the start of each show, he sends fiery arrows extraordinary distances to targets around the stage. It adds a little magic and mystery to his shows."

"How does he pull it off?" She hoped she could get him to share what he knew about Miles's talent.

"Who knows? He worked with some theme park engineers for placement of the targets, but even they can't understand how he creates the fire. Why don't you come to one of the shows next week in Las Vegas or the show in Texas? The concert in Texas is at a large arena with very high ceilings and your mother has approved the plans. It'll be safe."

She shook her head, and he shrugged his shoulders.

"Oh well, I tried to get you two together to talk to each other."

"Maybe we should just stick to business, Darien."

"Okay. Did Parker tell you if the terror level is increased, more shows in Europe will be canceled? We've added more shows in the U.S. as a buffer if things get more dangerous since all of us are concerned that so many people have been killed in Paris, in Manchester, and throughout Europe at concerts. The thought of all this violence, affecting the music industry also here at home just sickens me." He lowered his head and rubbed his forehead with his hands.

"Despite the challenges of beefing up security, he said the tour has been a success, and we're still on track to make millions in revenue. The merchandise sales are brisk, and all of your recommendations have been great moneymakers. You're going to get one big commission check."

"What commission check are you talking about?"

"Your contract includes a commission clause. All of your ideas that make money for the organization result in a commission for you. Conversely, too many bad ideas will get you fired because Miles doesn't suffer fools. You should start to see the proceeds from your hard work in a month."

She was pleased she would get a bonus check soon. "Oh, before I forget." She handed him an envelope. "These are copies of Miles's personal health information. I think the insurance underwriters for the tour requested them but somehow they ended up in my possession."

She didn't tell Darien she'd reviewed the information. *I'm too curious for my own good.*

According to the report, he was healthy and should be able to deal with the energy demands of his shows. He didn't have any STDs, and his physician had also documented they'd discussed safe sex practices.

"Any idea who sent this to you? And why?"

"Not a clue."

"Let's just keep this between us for now." He patted the envelope and looked at his watch. "I'm rejoining the tour in Las Vegas tomorrow, so I'll need to be getting back to the estate. Can I give you a ride or did you drive?"

"No, thanks. I think I'll sit out and enjoy the weather before going home. Miles has been concerned about my late-night rides home from the office, so he assigned me a limo driver. He also gave me free rein to play with some of his toys, and I relax some days using his archery set. My father taught me how to use a knife and bow and arrow when I was little, and since then, I've been pretty good at archery. I even won a couple of junior-level awards."

"Okay, Daniella Boone, frontier woman. I'll leave you to enjoy the afternoon sun. Don't forget what I said about you and Miles. You're the only one who's played in his sandbox with his toys, so that should tell you something about his feelings for you."

They hugged, and he paid the bill before he left. Bella pulled out her phone and saw she had a text from Reagan.

> **Reagan:** Hey Bella. Call me when you can. Thinking about you.

Bella hit the return call icon and Reagan picked up on the second ring.

"Hi Reagan. What's up?"

"Bella I just wanted to hear your voice so you could tell me how much you miss all of us." She giggled and Bella shared in the laughter.

"Actually I do miss all the activity around the studio, but I've been keeping busy."

"Sorry we couldn't hook up a bit more before I left with the tour, but my Mom was having a hard time accepting that I'll be gone from April to November." Bella remained silent for a bit. She knew Reagan was close to her mother and this was her longest tour with AriMusic.

"I understand. How are you?"

"I'm fine…. No girl, better than fine. At first, I was concerned when you cancelled a large portion of the VIP and backstage passes. The last publicity secretary did that and he was threatened by some of Miles's fans, but not having to deal with bumping into so many people backstage as we make costume changes or having a bunch of people around consuming the food and drinks for the tour members has been a blessing. All the dancers and the musicians said to tell you thank you. It's good having someone look out for us." Bella beamed as Reagan spoke.

"You're welcome and tell the performers I said thanks for their support. Marketing a great product like a polished show is always easier than trying to promote a show where the performers don't look happy to be there. Justin is great at providing the polish for the show as the tour manager, but he couldn't keep up with all those passes that were floating out there. Something had to be done."

"I agree. This tour is too long to deal with one big hassle after another. I really miss you girl, and I wish you'd reconsider joining us."

"I'll think about it."

"Don't think too long. Girl, gotta run. Got rehearsals. Bye Bella."

"Bye Reagan."

She ended the call and was in the process of returning another call when she heard her name. She looked up to see Isabelle standing there.

"Bella, I haven't had a chance to thank you for all you've done for my career. The producers at AriMusic remixed a few of my songs, and I've been on top of the charts ever since. May I sit down?"

"Sure. Have a seat." Isabelle lifted her dark shades from her eyes to look at Bella as she sat across from her and placed her oversized designer purse on the table beside her.

"I also wanted to tell you something else. I had my father meet with Miles to get his opinion about maybe Miles and I getting together as the new *it couple*, for publicity of course. I thought, who knows? Something real may develop between us." She flipped her long hair. "My father is a shrewd judge of character, and you know what he told me, Bella?"

"No, I don't." She silenced her phone and waited for the answer.

"Silly me." She giggled. "Of course you don't know what he said. He told me Ari was a decent man enjoying his youth, but he loved another and not to waste my time. The public would see right through it and know we're not really an item, but imagine a man not wanting to be with me?" She played with her hair and arched her back in a sensuous pose.

"I thought about what he said, and it didn't take long for me to guess the person he loved was you." Bella's jaw dropped in response.

"You must be mistaken." Bella shook her head.

"Don't deny it, Bella. You know it's true, and I can't tell you how often he called me Bella instead of Isabelle." She rolled her eyes before continuing.

"He often had the look of a man in love when he mentioned your name, and his voice always went higher when he spoke of you. You know the signs when a man is into you. He showed those signs, the sexy smile when he spoke your name, and I noticed his quick response to a text from you."

"Isabelle, he was probably returning a business text from someone."

"No, it was from you. He told me and my father he needed to answer your texts. I won't embarrass you by asking if you love him. Men like Ari can have sex every day with many women if they want to, and you've been good to me, so I'll share this with you." She leaned in closer and spoke in a whisper.

"Did you know he turned down all of this after I threw myself at him?" She ran her hands down her body like a model on a game show displaying her goods and shook her thick hair from side to side. "Only a man in love with another woman would turn down the chance to have sex with me." Bella's eyes widened as she listened to the confession.

"Thanks for sharing, Isabelle. I don't know what else to say." She smiled inwardly.

"Say you'll give him a chance. Underneath his megastar persona, he's just a man in love with a woman— you. Give him a chance." Her phone buzzed, and she looked at the time on the display.

"Gotta go." She got up and waved goodbye with one hand while balancing her oversized bag on the other.

"Bye bye, Isabelle." *Only in LA.*

She shook her head and resumed scrolling through her phone messages. This was the third time today someone had shared advice to give a relationship with Miles a chance. The unlikely coincidence caused her to tremble, as if an imaginary chill had settled in the air.

I'm afraid I'll lose myself if I just let it happen. Am I ready for a relationship with Miles? She looked at her wrist with the gold bracelet dangling from it and, opening her palm, she stared at it as her inner voice gave her a reading from the universe.... *The problem isn't if you should or shouldn't trust Miles but if you've grown to trust yourself.*

CHAPTER FOURTEEN

Bella looked at her phone as it buzzes with several text messages from her friend Tyler Morgan, who had worked with her during her fellowship at World Music. She recognized that the phone calls she'd gotten earlier this morning were probably from a phone extension at the World Music complex, but she had decided to ignore them.

I wonder what's going on. It's been quite a while since I last heard from her.

She powered off her computer and responded to the message.

```
Bella: What's up?

Tyler: Trying to get in touch
with you. 911

Bella: Calling now.
```

She placed the call and Tyler picked up on the first ring.

"Bella, I've got to make this quick. You know there's still a lot of anger around here about the way you were treated by the marketing division and the employee development division, especially after it was discovered that Scott Hansen was trying to blackball you after you refused his offer to come back to World Music."

"I heard about his attempts to get the radio stations to refuse to play songs by AriMusic artists and to try to block interviews I arranged for the new artists, but I've handled that and I'm moving on."

"Bella, he's not going to stop trying to ruin your career. He's angry at you that some of the artists left World Music and went to AriMusic to work with you. But despite that, there seems to be something personal he has against you and Ari. I know you don't want to play his game, but a woman's gotta do what a woman's gotta do. An employee who I can't name has passed on some information to me that I'll pass on to you. I'm tired of how things are done around here, and I've got another offer in New York. It's time for me to get the hell out of here. This place is toxic, and I know there may be repercussions, so I'm taking some insurance with me and I wanted to leave some of it with you."

"Alright, but I'm not sure what you mean by insurance."

"You'll understand when you get the package. A personal courier I hired is on the way, and he's been instructed to give the package to you and only you. I know you're at work because you work all the time, girl. You were always the first one there and the last to leave." She laughed.

"Well, I'm still putting in the hours. You know it goes with the territory."

"Nothing wrong with working hard, but it's never cool to let someone else take credit for your work. Bella, you inspired me to stand up for myself. Gotta go. Someone is coming this way." She spoke in a muted voice.

"Okay Tyler. I'll be waiting for the package. Bye and thanks."

Bella finished reviewing and signing new marketing contracts. It was the end of another successful week, and she had a meeting with Parker to discuss the tour going forward. He flew out to the first of the Vegas shows after their meeting.

Several hours later, one of the receptionists came into her office announcing she had a delivery, and Bella requested that she direct him to her office.

"Ms. Wahlberg?" He came in dressed in a courier uniform from one of the local firms.

"Yes, how can I help you?"

"I've been hired by Ms. Morgan to deliver this package to you only." He handed the sealed brown envelope to her. "She said you would be expecting it."

"Yes, I was expecting a package from her." She took it from him, and he backed out of the room.

"I know my way out. Have a good day."

"You too." She wrinkled her brow and returned to her desk to look for a letter opener and found a jackknife her mother had given her from her father's collection that she kept in her drawer. Bella opened the envelope and turned it upside down, spilling the contents. Her jaw dropped as numerous pictures of a naked Scott Hansen engaged in sexual poses with a groupie known to her from her numerous requests for VIP passes with the new artists. Three VIP passes for several of the World Music new artists tours were also included in the packet.

"Scott and Angel Howard? Who would have guessed? Why that sanctimonious bastard!" She shook her head and turned away from the photos, her lips drawn in disgust.

Tyler said I needed insurance, but I would never blackmail anybody. Not even a snake like Scott Hansen. I need to think about this before I act.

She gathered the contents and threw the envelope to the side.

After finishing up for the day, she gathered her things. She didn't know what she wanted to do with the photos yet, but she thought it best to copy them and lock the originals in a safe in her office. With a few errands to run before going home to watch Miles's show tonight she hurried out to her car with her bag containing her *insurance*.

Traffic was the usual Southern California gridlock, but it was good to get behind the wheel and not depend on her assigned driver all the time. Besides, she needed the time to clear her head. Miles may not have liked it, but she wasn't going to surrender her freedom and depend on his drivers any more than he chose to give in to her requests to be more cautious. She arrived home and returned a few calls, including one to her mother.

Joan had suggested to Bella before she returned to Texas that if she didn't want to stay in her position with AriMusic, she could head the California division of the Wahlberg Fire Safety Consulting firm while she extended the company's presence in Texas, or she could start her own marketing business in California. Joan had made multiple contacts during her last assignment and thought it was a good time for an expansion of the company in Texas. Bella shared in her mother's excitement because she had landed a few more clients, but she still hadn't decided if she planned to strike out on her own or become the president of the California division of her mother's company.

"I'll be watching the live stream of the concert tonight," Joan reminded her before ending the call.

"Me, too." They said their goodbyes, and Bella prepared for an evening of entertainment.

She sat cross-legged on her couch with a bowl of popcorn in her lap. She was wearing her comfortable "boyfriend" sleep shirt and her hair was up in a messy bun. The show started, and she bounced to the music along with the crowd; Miles didn't disappoint his fans. She wasn't sure how he was able to give such a high-energy show night after night.

The show ended with a number that pleased the crowd, and he left the stage with the audience screaming for more. While the band continued playing, and the background singers were still onstage, he returned with his guitar and took the chair placed on stage for him. The lights went down to a single spotlight directed on him and he started playing while the dancers swayed slowly to the music.

She bounced up and down in anticipation that he was going to sing the unplugged version of the song "No More." He looked back at the band before beginning the first few chords of the familiar song. The silence was broken by applause from the audience, which grew louder and louder. She let out a few screams as she joined in with his fans.

He looked back at the band and stopped. Following his lead, the band abruptly stopped after a few notes. The people in the audience screamed out in unison, "We want more."

Bella absorbed the energy of the crowd through the screen and started jumping up and down. "No More, No More," she yelled.

He looked up from his guitar and, instead, started playing an impromptu reggae song while the dancers swayed as if they were on a Caribbean island enjoying a day of fun on the beach.

Miles sang lyrics to a song he'd penned that was influenced by his love of reggae music, and Bella stopped clapping to listen. The band was still playing, and the dancers were still swaying to the music, but all eyes on the stage were focused on Miles. Her eyes widened, and she covered her mouth with her hands while staring at the image of Miles, who she swore was staring back at her. She couldn't believe what was happening. The unexpected continued to unfold as he turned quickly to his right side. He was seated stage left, and a female fan who had broken his line of defense was barreling toward him. Bosco appeared out of the shadows, and Miles stood and motioned to Bosco with an outstretched hand to sit. With Bosco obediently settled on his haunches, Miles then looked at his fan, who had also stopped. Her eyes were filled with tears, and she was covering her face with her hands. He looked like he was assessing the situation, and Bella also saw she didn't have a weapon in her hands, and her pants were skintight without pockets.

She could see Bradley in the shadows, spitting out expletives on the split screen.

He was shouting so loud backstage to his crew; she could make out a few of his profanity-laced words coming in over the feed. She was grateful the recordings were internal and only for a few of the AriMusic employees and consultants.

The audience stood in anticipation as the fan slowly walked toward Miles, and he comforted her in an embrace while the two of them spoke to each other before addressing the crowd.

"Teresita, is that your name?" He kept one arm around her shoulder and spoke into a handheld microphone in his right hand while he turned her to face the crowd.

"Call me Terri."

"You told me your boyfriend's name was Luis?"

"Yes, Luis Rodriguez."

"Terri doesn't want to wait anymore, Luis Rodriguez. Come on, Terri, let's call him out."

Miles sang the chorus with Terri, and she surprised the audience by singing the tune in key. Other members of the audience tried to get on the stage, but a security force of tall men with thick ropes for biceps held them back. The crowd morphed their chant into Miles's lyrics: *I don't want to feel this pain, my Bella. I love you, my Bella….* Some yelled out his name while others yelled out the names of those who hadn't returned their love.

He released Terri, and the guards escorted her off the stage while he made his exit. He held up his hand in a fist and yelled: "Good night, Las Vegas!"

Bella sank back into her couch, her forehead wet with sweat, her heart pounding, and her breath shallow. *Did Miles just tell me he loves me?*

Her answer came quickly. Her mother called first. "Did you catch the show, Bella? I think Miles told the world he loved you. Are you okay?"

Before she could answer the question, a text came through:

```
Darien: 911. Call me! It's cray-
cray around here.
```

"Mom, I have to call you back. Something has come up. I'm okay. Bye." She ended the call and called Darien on FaceTime. He answered immediately and ran his hands through his hair. He was pacing while an angry Bradley spewed saliva and threats toward members of the security team in the background.

"Why was Bosco the only one at his post tonight? Does Ari pay y'all to enjoy the show or keep him safe? How in the hell did a 120-pound female get past all of you?" He kept his hands on his hips and leaned forward, barking like a drill sergeant. Veins popped out of his neck while the guards stood at attention. The band and dancers scurried away from the tension backstage as they cast their eyes downward and ran to the changing rooms. Miles was nowhere in sight.

"Darien!" someone yelled out in the background.

"Gotta go, call you back later," he told her before ending the call.

Another text came in before she could respond to Darien.

> **Parker:** We need to talk, Bella.
> I don't know if I'll be back in
> town as planned. Have to fix
> what happened tonight.

She wasn't sure what to do. She felt Bradley was right in being upset about the security breach. She had expressed concerns about keeping Miles safe for months. She paced with her phone but calmed down, relieved he was safe and not currently in danger.

She tapped the corner of her lips with her phone while thinking but held it away from her to see what was causing the active vibrations. Her auto-alerts were going wild with messages from the fans leaving the show about his encore performance. She clicked on the comments:

You don't have to wait any longer, Ari. I'm here for you, one fan wrote.

Be my baby daddy, Ari. We shouldn't wait any longer.

Crying and tasting my salted tears. Ari was perfect with Terri; A fan for life.

Ari's music in the background/Girl in my arms/Getting some tonight.

Bella couldn't keep up with the comments coming in, and Ari started trending after a fan uploaded a few seconds of the performance. She read a few more of the comments and started crying too. *Miles would never admit he has a tender heart for those in pain. He heals others through his music.*

She decided to text him to congratulate him on his performance. Her hand was shaking, making it difficult to finish the text.

> **Bella:** Your performance was fantastic. You're a man of many surprises. Did U plan the encore?

She didn't have to wait long for a response.

> **Miles:** Not planned. Thought about doing 'No More,' but this one seemed right.

> **Bella:** We need to talk. I've gotten clearer on things. Need to see U.

> **Miles:** Say when.

> **Bella:** Soon. Love U.

She hit send and forgot she ended her text the same way she ended her texts with her mother and Darien. She tried to clean it up quickly.

> **Bella:** Sorry. Meant to say,
> Loved your show tonight.

> **Miles:** Love U too. Sorry, meant
> to say, love all that U do.

Bella placed her phone to her heart and lowered her chin to contemplate what just happened. *Did I just reveal my true feelings to him or were we just responding to a moment of high emotions?*

Darien texted her a few minutes later.

> **Darien:** The universe must have
> shifted, and I think you had
> something to do with it. Miles
> is cool, and Bradley and his
> team's jobs are secure for now.
> On to the next show. Love U.

Parker sent her a text of thanks. His plans to be with his family were back on. She continued to receive many texts, including one from Bradley thanking her for not saying "I told you so," and he mentioned his plan to close all the gaps in security, even ending the crowd surfing. Pictures of a smiling Miles at the backstage meet and greet she'd arranged with fans flooded her phone.

CHAPTER FIFTEEN

Bella was busy at her desk, looking at the new posts of Miles painted in a knitted red, black, yellow, and green hat. Red flames painted on a black background gave it an updated look and she had sent a few of the pictures to Miles before her meeting with NeNe, who came in just after she hit *Send.*

"Good morning. Thanks for meeting with me today. I wanted to run a few legal questions by you in regard to new marketing ventures." NeNe took a seat.

"Good morning Bella, but before we talk legal matters, let me acknowledge something. I underestimated you. You're one smart, shrewd, undercover badass. No—not just smart, you're brilliant."

She looked at NeNe. "Thanks, NeNe…I think. It's nice to be called smart, but a badass? You've got me pegged wrong. I'm not aggressive." She crossed her arms over her chest as if to block the words from getting too close to her heart, which thumped after she heard NeNe's description of her.

"No, no, I think I'm right. You're uncompromising and tough. Beneath that sweet exterior of yours is a cat that would scratch a person's eyes out if threatened. Don't get upset by my observations. I'm just saying you're no pushover. And, by the way, did you miss the other things I said? Like brilliant for one thing. You can handle Miles's tough exterior because you can see past it and he doesn't intimidate you. I should involve you in some of my tough legal negotiations. I can't believe you made him wait. Can I ask if it was after the first or second encounter between the two of you?" She knew NeNe was never one to shy away from direct questions, so she decided to be straight with her.

"We haven't had sex, at least not together, if that's what you're asking."

Her mouth dropped open, and Bella couldn't believe no sound came out of it. NeNe gripped the arm of the chair and leaned forward.

"Get outta here! How did you know Miles needed someone to tell him no? The boy gets too much cherry thrown at him, and you realized not giving it up was the way to go. Let me say it again: Brilliant."

She wanted to tell NeNe her decision to maintain some distance from Miles wasn't a scheme or grand plan to get his affection, but NeNe wouldn't let her get a word in edgewise. She sat back, nodded, and accepted her compliments. When she finally got her turn to talk, she had NeNe's attention for no more than a second before the woman's cell rang.

She listened as NeNe accepted the call and invited her Aunt Lecia to come to the house. She told her she would be at the estate for an hour, then ended the call.

"Look, Bella, I'll be quick. The boy loves you. You may not be ready to admit it, but you love him, too. He poured out his heart in front of tens of thousands, and he's willing to wait for you, but you need to talk to him. Oh, by the way, my Aunt Lecia is in town to meet with the board members of the burn unit here in Los Angeles. She's the representative for Miles's charitable foundation, and she's also his mother. I want you to meet her."

Bella grabbed her chest and gasped for air. "NeNe, don't you think you've crossed too many lines to mention? It's not up to you to introduce the people in Miles's life to his mother. Maybe he doesn't want her to meet all of his employees, even if I'm a member of his executive staff." She struggled to catch her breath. Scared and irritated by NeNe's actions, her mind raced about how she would handle her meeting with Mrs. Moore. NeNe joined her hands together and placed her forefingers to her lips. Silence fell between them as bright green eyes stared at soft brown ones.

"I'm not introducing you to my Aunt Lecia as Miles's associate, a member of his inner circle, his friend, or his lover." She snickered. "Oh, I forgot, the two of you aren't lovers. I'm not introducing you based on your relationship with Miles. I'm introducing you as *my* friend. You are a woman to admire, and she could probably use your help in marketing for the family's charity funds. Please forgive me if I've been too forward with you today, but my intent was to tell you thank you for being there for Miles. I love him, and I want the best for both of you. Enough of that, let's go over some legal issues."

Mr. Curtis stood at the door with a beautiful Dominican woman who was middle age. With thick, brown, wavy hair and soulful brown eyes, she was alluring and smartly dressed in a blue business suit and matching blue leather pumps. Bella tried to swallow the lump in her throat as she gazed upon the beautiful woman who had passed her good looks, on to her son.

"*Tía* Lecia"—NeNe rose to greet her with arms open wide and a big grin—"I'm so glad you came. Let me introduce you to my friend Bella Wahlberg."

Bella rose and extended her hand.

"Pleased to meet you," they both said in unison.

"I've been in meetings all morning. Will the two of you please excuse me while I go to the restroom to freshen up?" Mrs. Moore explained.

"Sure, Tía." After her aunt left, NeNe returned to her seat and looked at Bella, who was biting her lower lip. "Don't worry, my tía is warm and friendly, and you're a kind person. The two of you will love each other."

She nodded and tried to take a deep breath to slow her wildly beating heart. Her fears were realized when NeNe answered her ringing phone again and advised the person on the other end to tell the judge she was on her way. Mrs. Moore came back into the room, and NeNe rose to apologize for skipping out on them.

"The two of you should get to know one another. You have a lot in common. I'm so sorry, but I have to be in court for a ruling. I'm happy this case will finally be over."

"Please excuse me, Mrs. Moore while I ask NeNe one more thing before she leaves."

Bella grabbed her by the elbow in a friendly but firm manner. At a loss for words to express her anger, she growled at her the entire time.

"You'll be fine, Bella. Bye-bye."

She feigned confidence as she held her head high and walked with a steady gait when she returned to her seat behind her desk. She hoped Mrs. Moore couldn't hear her knees knocking or her heart beating out of her chest. She placed her slightly trembling right hand on the pulse on her neck to calm down, but when one of the housekeepers dropped something outside of the door, she was so startled, her nose flared, and her lashes fluttered.

"I must have had too much caffeine this morning."

"Maybe we're both on the verge of a panic attack, and it's not the coffee," Mrs. Moore began. "I left earlier to settle my nerves. I was concerned Miles might be mad at me for getting together with you without his knowledge. He has always hated when I meddled in his affairs, and I don't need to give him another reason to be angry with me. He can be fiery when he's crossed the wrong way. He won't argue with me, but he'll distance himself, which, for me, is worse."

Bella started to calm down and collected herself. "Thanks for being honest with me. I didn't want to make a mistake, either. NeNe said she introduced me to you as her friend, not Miles's friend."

"That sounds good, but he won't buy it. He talks about you all the time. He said you're very pretty, but he didn't tell me you're gorgeous."

Bella felt the blood rise to her cheeks.

"I suffered from panic attacks in the past, Bella, which is the only reason I noticed your subtle signs."

"Thanks for reassuring me, Mrs. Moore, that my signs aren't quite so obvious. I've been trying to cope with my symptoms, and Miles has been a comfort to me during instances when triggers such as storms come up. He and I haven't seen each other for weeks, and I needed some distance and time to sort out my feelings and.... I don't know why I'm going on and on about things, but I know I don't want you to get the wrong impression of me."

She sat back in her chair and wiped the nonexistent wrinkles out of her skirt, trying to do something with her hands to settle down. Mrs. Moore looked at her, nodding and allowing her the chance to get it all out before speaking.

"Please call me Lecia. I know the stress of having a relationship with a successful musician. Miles's father was a very popular jazz musician when we met, and it took me a while to admit I loved him. There will be some folks bent on keeping the two of you apart; they won't win if you commit yourselves to each other. Don't be offended, but Miles told me you can be aloof, distant, and protective of your heart."

Bella opened her mouth wide and cocked her head to the side.

"Don't worry, Bella, I know he was describing himself. I've known him for twenty-six years. NeNe tells me you have a quiet strength. She's very perceptive and reads people well. I think Miles's yang has finally met the perfect yin." She looked at her watch. "My son has spent more time communicating with the family in the last four months than he has in the last four years. We all agree it must be the 'Bella effect' on him. I want to personally thank you. You helped him realize the importance of family."

"Lecia, why do you think I'm the reason he came back to you? We've never talked much about your family."

"He told me about the night he spent with you."

Bella blinked and jerked her head back. "I don't know how else to say this, especially since this is our first meeting, and you're his mother, but Miles and I are...not sleeping together." She stuttered over her words. "This—this is really awkward."

"I wasn't referring to a sexual encounter, Bella, and yes, it's awkward to talk about my son's sex life on any level," she assured her. "What I meant was he said he could see the pain on your face when you spoke of your father, and he wanted to make the pain go away. He realized from spending time with you that he had taken his family for granted. As I said, I know about living with a famous musician, and Miles could be with a different woman every night if he wanted to, but his heart has chosen you."

Bella thought about the clothes in the bedroom closet where she slept and the women who were at his party.

"It's my observation that he's more than physically attracted to you and he wants a relationship with you. Consider my advice to you, Bella, if you let a relationship with him naturally evolve: You may share his time and talent with the world, but never your bed and the details of your relationship." She paused and stared off into space. Her tightened jaw and closed lips spoke more of her experiences than words. She turned her attention back to Bella and smiled before rising from her seat and looking around the room.

"You have a very nice office."

"Thank you, I like it." Bella had personalized her space and mounted the framed Prince album on the wall.

"Is that from Miles?" Lecia pointed to the album.

"Yes, it is. He's a Prince fan and so am I."

"Now, I know it's serious if he parted with that album. I must have heard him play it fifty times. The Prince concert was a turning point in his life, and that album was a cherished gift from his father. I'm no therapist, but I think he wanted to share a token of some of his own father's love with you. He told me you lost your father in an accident. I'm sorry for your loss."

"Thank you." She choked up not just because of the reminder of her loss but because she felt the sincerity of Lecia's sentiment in her condolences.

"Cade, my husband, is a great man and a great father. I'll tell him we met, and I hope he'll get the chance to meet you." She looked at her watch.

"Well, it's off to another scheduled event before I say more. It was my pleasure to meet you, Bella Wahlberg." She looked into her bag before getting up and handed her a business card, which Bella took and thanked her.

She held on to the card as she came around the desk, and Lecia reached to embrace her.

"I like what Miles has done with the house. You know he added the two newer wings to the original house; he always breathes energy into any space he occupies. Well, I'd better be on my way. You have my card. Call me any time."

"Thank you, and it was nice to meet you, Lecia."

"Same here, and we must get together again to talk about marketing ideas for the charities."

"I look forward to hearing from you," Bella told her as they walked to the door. "Have a safe trip back home."

"Thank you. You take care." She watched as Lecia walked to the limo that was waiting for her and waved goodbye before closing and leaning against the back of the door for a moment. Her mind was boggled by the events of the last twenty-four hours. *I need to talk with someone.* She thought about Darien and Reagan; both were friends who cared about her, but they were busy with the tour. She remembered she owed her mother a return call. *I'll catch up with her, and we can talk things over.*

She collected her things and couldn't wait to get to the sanctuary of her own home. She locked up her office, walked to her car, and activated the Bluetooth option to talk to her mother in Texas while she drove.

"Bella, I'm so glad you called back. I need you, honey." Her mother's voice came over the speakers, filling the car. "I need you to do me a favor. One of my prospective clients has a teenager, and she is dying to see Miles in concert. Can you get her front-row tickets and a meet and greet with Miles? I think if we could swing that, I'll be able to close the deal."

She frowned at the steering wheel. "Mom, why don't you ask Miles? You know how to get in touch with him. He's headed there to play a concert in your city."

"I called him, and he wouldn't commit to another meet and greet. I called Darien, and he said he's not willing to get on Miles's bad side. They're all still walking on eggshells after the incident in Vegas. Please honey, I wouldn't ask you if I wasn't desperate. I need you."

"Mom, you've never needed me. It has always been the other way around, I'm the one who has always depended on you."

"Bella, I don't have time to discuss that fallacy right now, but if you don't already know, I will tell you this: If it wasn't for you, my sweet girl, I wouldn't have gotten out of bed in the first year after your father died." She heard her mother choking up as she continued. "You got me through the worst year of my life, and you've been a source of joy to me since the day you were born twenty-four years ago. Just promise me you will think about calling him."

Bella was stunned to hear her mother believed *she* had helped her. Her mother had always been *her* rock. "Okay, Mom, I'll do it for you."

"Please do it quickly, Bella. The concert is this week. Call me if you get the backstage passes for the meet and greet."

"I'll try, Mom. Goodbye." *I really don't want to owe Miles another favor, but my mother needs my help. Darn, I didn't tell her I met Miles's mother today. I'll tell her later.*

She arrived home, kicked off her shoes, and put on yoga pants and a crop top of the same material. After checking her mail and then placing a load of laundry in the washing machine, she grabbed her laptop and sat down to check her social media sites. Distracted, she put the computer down and started pacing the floor while biting her fingernails, uncertain what she was going to say to him.

"I guess I've stalled long enough, and something will come to me. Hi, Miles, how's it going?" She cocked her head playfully to the side.

"Listen, I need you to do me a favor." She shook her head.

"No, No.... I just needed to let you know...."

She stopped pacing and grabbed her phone. She'd promised her mother she'd call Miles, and she had to keep her word.

"I know what I'll do. I'll use the app to ask him for time for a meet and greet."

She held her breath and connected with him. She was surprised by his immediate response.

Bella: I need to place another meet and greet in your schedule.

Miles: RU coming to make the introduction?

Bella: Wasn't planning on it.

Miles: Wasn't planning on another meet and greet. The answer is yes if U do the

introductions, stay for the
entire concert, and spend the
night at my hotel. Not asking U
to stay in my room, but U must
stay wherever I'm staying.

Bella: You're driving a hard
bargain. I'm hesitant, but I
agree to your terms. I will need
2 additional front row seats and
at least 5 minutes for the meet
and greet time before the
concert starts.

Miles: Agreed. See U in 2 days
at the concert. Don't change
your mind. I won't agree to
reschedule the meeting.

Bella: Fine. Approve the
additional meet and greets for
my Mother and her guest. Darien
knows how to get in touch with
her.

Miles: Done.

After Bella closed out the app, she texted her mother to
let her know Darien would handle the arrangements for the
backstage passes, then she went to her bedroom to start
packing. As she stood in front of her closet, trying to decide
what to pack, her cell pinged. She checked the screen; it
was a message from Darien's assistant, Lisa James.

Lisa: I'll be making plans to
send the jet for you, and I'll
ensure your guests are taken
care of and enjoy their time at
the concert.

Miles is a man used to getting what he wants when he wants it.

Her phone buzzed with another text, this time from Bradley.

> **Bradley:** I just got a message from Lisa James. She said U authorized more passes. I thought U said NO More Passes? Explain please.

> **Bella:** Passes are for my mother and her guest.

> **Bradley:** I see.

Bella pressed the phone call icon to talk to Bradley.

"Bradley, I have to be honest. I now see how so many passes got issued. I know I'm contradicting myself but…she's my mother."

"Bella, I understand, and I have to man up and also be honest. You were right to ask us to limit the list. It's a security issue and the tour members are happier that there are less people backstage. I've even heard it from word on the street that World Music has recalled many of their VIP and backstage passes. Not sure why since many of their performers like the raunchier side of the business." Bella bit her lip before she continued.

"Bradley I'm going to need your discretion about a matter."

"What is it?" She heard him breathing as she contemplated how to tell him about the pictures.

"I need your help to authenticate," she paused. "I need you to authenticate some pictures of an exec at World

Music. He's been trying to make trouble for Miles, and I need to know if these pictures are real or they are maybe photoshopped and fake."

"So, I'm guessing the pictures show him in a compromising situation?"

"Yes Bradley, they do."

"I'll send a member of the security detail assigned to guard the studio to get them in about an hour and then I'll begin an investigation of the matter."

"Thanks Bradley. I have copies of the photos here at my home."

"No problem. I'll get back to you as soon as possible. Goodbye."

"Goodbye Bradley and thanks."

"No problem Bella."

She knew she had to tell Miles about the photos now that she had shared the news with Bradley. She finished packing her clothes and placed mace and a small jackknife in her suitcase. She'd carried them for protection ever since Corey had ambushed her.

CHAPTER SIXTEEN

The jet was luxurious and the ride smooth as silk. As planned, she arrived in Texas several hours before the concert. She went to her mother's corporate suite and spent some time with her, catching up on lighthearted matters and discussing pressing things like the details of pending contracts before getting dressed for the show. She told Joan the terms of the meet and greet tickets included her staying at Miles's hotel to attend the afterparty. She didn't know if there was a party planned, but she didn't want to get into a discussion with her mother about his request to stay the night in the hotel with him.

"Bella, I have a quick meeting with my prospective client, so I'll need to leave and meet you at the concert venue."

"Sure, I have the backstage passes for them." She handed them to Joan.

"You can come back any time if you want to stay here with me tonight. I know you have to attend to business, but if you can, I'd love having a little girl time before you return to California."

It's the taking care of business part I'm worried about, Mom.

"No, Mom, I have a room at the hotel with the tour staff. I don't know what time the party will wrap up, and I don't want to inconvenience you, so I'll probably have to call you tomorrow."

"Suit yourself, but you know you can come back anytime. There's a pull-out couch and you probably won't disturb me." Bella smiled but shook her head, firm her answer was no. She'd made a deal with Miles and hoped she hadn't made a bargain she couldn't keep to land her mother coveted tickets to the concert tonight.

Her mother grabbed her bag and hugged her before running out the door for her meeting and to deliver the tickets.

Lisa James had arranged a time for a car to pick her up, but she requested the chauffeur arrive early so he could give her a tour of the town. It had been years since she'd been back in Texas, and she wanted to visit a barbecue shack that had been getting good reviews on the Travel Foodie site she followed.

She went to the bathroom to freshen up before her pick-up time and grabbed her travel bag before going downstairs to wait for her ride. She got out of the elevator and took a seat in the lobby. Leaning forward in her plush chair, she saw the chauffeur exit the car with the Fire God Tour VIP sign on the side. He came inside, and she waved to him to alert him that she was the one needing the pick-up. His professional demeanor was impeccable as he introduced himself, promptly picked up her small travel bag on the floor and led her outside to the car.

"Can you give me a city tour and maybe stop for some barbecue?"

"I'm sorry, ma'am, I have strict instructions to get you to the venue on time," he responded in a British accent.

"I don't want to be late, either," she assured him.

"I'm willing to oblige your request, but my continued employment with this company depends on getting you to the meet and greet not one minute late."

"You have my complete cooperation. I also have a business obligation that requires me to be on time." Her mother's contract with her new client depended on it.

"All right, we should be able to do a quick tour."

The chauffeur relaxed, and Bella enjoyed the tour of Houston, feeling good to be back in Texas. He knew about the barbecue place she wanted to try and drove her there. She wasn't disappointed. The food she ordered for take-out was delicious, and since they were pressed for time, he didn't mind her filling the car with the aroma of fine Texas barbecue. She was careful to avoid dripping sauce on the leather seats.

He took her to the hotel where she would be staying with Miles, to freshen up one more time before the show; and he told her he would wait for her in the circular drive. Bella went to the front desk to check in while the bellman grabbed her bag out of the car.

"Aren't you with the AriMusic entourage? We were expecting you."

"Yes, I am." She showed him her credentials.

"A room has already been reserved for you, Ma'am, on the executive floor."

"No, thank you. I'd like to stay on the floor with everyone else in a standard room." She'd agreed to stay in the same hotel with Miles, but she hadn't agreed to where in the hotel she was staying, and a standard room was fine.

"All right, but Ms. James told me to let her know when you checked in."

"That's fine," she responded and took the key from her. She found her room and waved at several of the dancers in the hall before preparing herself for the concert.

Later that afternoon, she was back in the town car, dressed and ready for a night of partying. She had on her black skinny jeans, her black sequined top, a black leather jacket, and black leather ankle boots. Her makeup was dramatic and heavier than she customarily applied it: cat eyes and bright red nails with ram-head appliques on her forefingers completed her appearance.

Darien texted her on the ride over to the venue to tell her his assistant would meet her and her entourage for the meet and greet at backstage door number five at 6 pm.

She looked around for her mother. A white stretch limousine arrived, and two excited teenaged girls jumped out from the backseat and ran toward her.

"Bella Wahlberg, is that you? Your mother told us to meet you here. She said to tell you she couldn't make it. I'm Ashley, and this is my friend Katie. My daddy's driver will meet us after the concert." They looked at each other and started jumping up and down, screaming in excitement and holding on to the passes around their necks as if their lives depended on them.

"Yes, I'm Bella. Come on, we can't be late. Ari has to prepare for tonight's show." She led them to the back door and rang the bell. The girls were still shaking their hands to contain their excitement. Seconds later, a member of the security team answered the door. He recognized her and said hello, but he still looked at his clipboard to confirm that she had three backstage passes. She was wearing her company-issued Fire God Tour concert badge, which had her credentials on it. He opened the door wider, and she saw Bosco, who came running to her while the security guard summoned an escort to assist her and the girls.

"Hey, buddy. I missed you too."

Bosco wagged his tail and circled around her. He paused to let her rub his head and stroke his back until his handler called, and he went to him.

If Bosco is here, then Miles is nearby. He lets Bosco roam with him to settle them both before he goes on stage. She followed her escort to the room for the meet and greet. Ashley and Katie were walking with their arms wrapped around each other's elbow and giggling behind her.

They approached a door with a large gold star and crimson flames stenciled on it. The escort knocked and heard the one-word instruction: "Enter."

She opened the door, and there was Miles with a headset on, looking down at sheet music on a music stand. He turned around to greet them and flashed a bright, sexy smile at his three guests. He took off the headphone set and placed it on the stand.

Bella pushed the starstruck Katie and Ashley into the room and introduced them to him. They both hugged him and giggled with each other. He gave Bella a chaste kiss on the cheeks, took pictures with them, and signed autographs. Lisa opened the door this time without knocking first and listened through her headset to someone communicating with her.

"Girls, I'm here to take you two on a tour backstage." The opening act was a popular local group, and she told them they would have a meet and greet with them. The girls jumped up and down, screaming again. She assured Bella and Miles she would stay with them the entire time.

"I'll also personally escort them to their front-row seats." She directed the girls to follow her and they hugged Bella and Miles before they left.

"So this is how you planned to get some private time for us?" She smiled at him.

"Yes, Bella, it was planned. I wanted a few minutes alone with you. Thanks for coming tonight. I've kept my part of the bargain. Are you prepared to keep your part of our agreement?" He came closer to her but didn't attempt to touch her. He surveyed her face, the clothes she was wearing, and breathed in the smell of her perfume.

"I've missed you, and I didn't think it would take this long for you to visit me. Does this mean you're willing to give us a chance and maybe you really don't blame me for your breakup with Corey, now that you've had more time to think about it?"

She bit her lower lip and swallowed hard before she spoke. "At first, I was angry and confused, you know…about the misunderstanding with the bracelet, but I don't hold you responsible for what happened between me and Corey. You didn't break us up; he did it by himself. However, as I said before you left, I didn't think it was wise to jump into another relationship so soon after the breakup, and my time away from you wasn't about a failure to forgive you but a need for clarity." He kept his eyes on hers but didn't close the distance between them.

"I initially thought I needed you or Corey to give me my dignity back, but I realized after thinking about it, I never gave my dignity away. I'm stronger than that. The two of you were caught in a pissing contest for whatever reason, and I needed to get out of the middle. Corey was inappropriate with you on more than one occasion, and he refused to accept responsibility for his behavior. I also know after our last visit together, you have feelings for me, and I can't deny any longer that I have feelings for you."

She extended her arm to show him the bracelet on her right wrist and the ram's head temporary appliques on her nails. He smiled and grabbed her forearm, kissing it all the way down to the back of her hand. Bella arched her back slightly, the electricity of his touch warming her body. He placed her arm by her side and moved in so close to her, she heated up a little more and her chest heaved under his close gaze.

"Let me be clear Bella: I want you, and I have to admit I didn't always fight fair. I waited and capitalized on Corey's blunders, and I'm glad I don't have to spar with him anymore. I prefer to spend my energy building a relationship with you."

"I'm sure Darien told you Corey and I broke up, before I told you."

"He did tell me, and that's part of the reason I came back to LA to see you and to confirm your relationship with him was over, but too many things were happening at the same time. It's hard to stay focused when you arrive at someone's home and they're trying to burn it down. You know I like fire, Bella, but maybe that was going a little too far to impress me." He chuckled.

"Always the jokester, aren't you, Miles?" She laughed and punched him on his forearm. She took a step back, her smile slowly fading away. She recalled the fear she felt when she thought she had lost him, and she was no longer afraid to have a serious talk about the two of them pursuing a relationship.

"You've been there this past year when I've needed you most. I won't ever forget it. You're a good man, Miles Moore." She reached up and ran her hand along the side of his face as he leaned in and closed his eyes. He opened his eyes as she moved her hand away.

"I'd do anything to ease your pain."

"Thank you, but I shouldn't risk embarrassing myself by saying much more, especially when you have a show in the next hour, and I'm here to enjoy a great show." She bounced with excitement, trying to lighten up the mood in the room.

"I've seen every concert on the tour on live stream, and you're fantastic on stage. By the way, I'm the fan who refers to herself as your favorite fan on the Ari app. I may not have visited you, but I left personal messages for you."

"I've known it was you for months. I had your IP address tracked and it either had to be you or a stalker with mad hacker skills—so I was glad to discover it was you. My hope that we could be together has come true and you've made me very happy tonight." He pulled her into his arms for a kiss that was interrupted by a knock at the door.

"One hour until show time," the stage manager called out.

She returned his deep kiss and caressed his face before she pulled away from him. She grabbed her things and blew him a kiss on her way out the door.

"Break a leg." He smiled at her and pretended to catch her kiss.

Her escort was waiting for her outside the door, and they were on their way to her seat when she encountered a scene backstage.

"There's the bitch who thought she could keep me from Miles." Angel Howard pointed at Bella and hissed while members of security held her, blocking her from advancing toward Bella.

"Did you really think I would turn in all of my passes? I have several under different names. Miles and I go way back, and this VIP pass could only be revoked by him." She smiled and held up the pass, while the other two women accompanying her, crossed their arms and puffed out their chests, despite the guards attempts to hinder their push to get further backstage. Darien came upon the scene and stood between Bella and the women.

"I'm so sorry Bella. I forgot about the platinum passes that Angel still had. My bad, but I'll handle this." He turned to Angel as she struggled against the security guards.

"Angel stop it. This is a bad look for you." Darien held his hand up close to her face.

"Miles, baby. Miles, it's me." She screamed, and Bradley, with a thick envelope in his hand, came running up to the crowd of tour members gathering and standing behind Bella in a show of support.

"Lower your voice before I throw you out on your asses." He got into Angel's face and frowned at the other women. "Miles hits the stage in less than an hour and I'll not have you get in his head."

"It's not that head I want. I like the other one better." She threw her head to the side and took a step back as the other women laughed with her.

Bradley held onto the envelope with a firm grip.

"Are those the pictures I sent you Bradley?" Bella turned her attention away from Angel.

"Yes, all the copies of the pictures and the original passes are inside." He patted the envelope. " I was on my way to place these photos in a safe place and review them with you later, but I can tell you now that they are authentic. Face recognition technology proved it was the two of them and the pictures were taken in his office." He looked at Angel and snarled.

"That's good; give them to me. I've decided how I'll handle this, and you can release her." Bradley handed over the envelope and the guards looked to Bradley before they released their hold on Angel and her friends.

"Please, the rest of you can go prepare for the show. Everything will be fine," Bella urged the tour staff, and they slowly backed away, leaving her with only Darien and Bradley by her side as she faced Angel and her friends. Bella moved closer to Angel, lowering her voice for a more intimate chat as she pressed the envelope containing the rigid plastic passes.

"Yes Angel, I had your passes revoked, and your antics tonight won't change that, but I have something better for you."

"You're not going to blackmail me with some photos Bradley just gave you, are you? I have witnesses." She placed her hands on her hips but kept her voice low.

"Please, Angel." Bella let out a breath. "I have no plans to blackmail anyone. What I plan to do is to hand over to you several coveted backstage passes for World Music tours. I understand your passes with them have been revoked?"

Bella had her suspicions about Angel and her current relationship with World Music, and she could tell by the glimmer in Angel's eyes that it was true, despite her attempt to hide it.

She's acting desperate to return to Miles. Bella focused her gaze on Angel's eyes, wondering how the woman had gotten herself into this situation.

"Here, these passes are for you." She handed the sealed envelope to Angel, who looked at it, then squeezed the contents.

"I don't have anything to open this envelope, and besides, I don't trust that you would give anything of value to me." Angel frowned but didn't give the envelope back.

"Please, let me help you." Bella reached for the small jackknife in the pocket of her jacket and leaned closer to Angel, placing one hand on top of hers while she exposed the blade and slashed the top of the envelope in one quick flick with her other hand, causing Angel and her friends to flinch.

"Hell, Bella—Daniella Boone—you got skills." Darien and Bradley looked at her wide eyed with amazement.

"Yes, I do have skills." Bella closed the blade and placed the knife back in her jacket.

Angel lowered her shoulders and her hands shook as she looked at the contents of the envelope, then pulled out one of the passes to view. She fingered through the envelope but didn't pull out the pictures, nor did she seem surprised.

"I knew that bastard was up to something." She looked up at Bella.

"And now you have insurance that your passes won't be cancelled."

"Ahh, yes. That and other things." Her mouth remained open as she stared at Bella.

"Angel, these pictures were taken of you in his office and could have been used to manipulate you." Bella continued to plant seed for thought.

"You're right Bella. He could've been trying to control little ol' me." She batted her eyes and shrugged her shoulders as she smiled.

I doubt it. He's just a freak. Bella pursed her lips.

"Angel, you need to leave. Take your guests with you and never come back. You're not welcome at AriMusic events anymore." She was tired of this exchange and didn't want Miles to come out of the dressing room and have to deal with this mess.

"Don't worry about it. I don't need Miles anymore. I have bigger fish to fry, and besides, Scott never liked that I slept with Miles. You can have him all to yourself with all his secrets." She smiled and turned to walk away, followed by her friends.

"I'll see them out." Bradley escorted them to one of the backstage exits.

Bella let out a deep breath and pressed her hand against her chest before leaning against the closest wall.

"I'm so sorry Belles. I thought I had revoked all the passes. It slipped my mind that Angel had one of the platinum passes for family members and close friends, issued only at Miles's discretion. Can you forgive me?" He placed a hand on her shoulder and searched her eyes for an answer.

"There's nothing to forgive Darien. It was an honest mistake." She turned her head and blew out another breath before looking into his eyes. She had handled the situation on pure instinct, but it worked out better than the best laid plan.

"I have guests waiting for me in the front row. I'd better join them before they get worried."

"Let me walk with you. Are you sure you're okay?"

"I'll be fine." He walked with her to the VIP section and left her to join the girls already in their seats. The opening act took the stage; they were good, but it was clear the crowd hadn't come to see them. Bella smiled at the girls, not letting on that she had just been involved in a near catfight backstage.

The excitement was building, and the crowd started chanting, "Ari, Ari," just after the opening act finished their set and while the roadies set up for the next act.

Fifteen minutes later, Ari hit the stage, and pandemonium broke out. Large men lined the aisle to prevent a rush to get to him. People were screaming, cell phones lit up the night, and the music started playing. Ari stood in the shadows of smoke and fog swaying to the music and taking in the sight of 30,000 people screaming his name, "Ari, Ari." The dancers were on the stage performing their choreographed moves while he ran to the end of the platform and broke into a popular song center stage in front of Bella. She was jumping up and down with Katie and Ashley. He pointed to nameless females in the crowd with their arms flailing, and they responded by screaming and placing their hands on the sides of their faces.

"We love you, Ari! We love you, Ari!" they chanted.

Bella accepted that Ari belonged to the world, but Miles belonged to her. He was so sexy on stage; it caused most of the women, including her, to climb out of their jackets, feeling the heat of wanton desire. She looked around and saw women arching their backs and rolling their hips. Ari had his hands above his head and wore a sly smile as he moved his hips from side to side. He was making love to thousands of women at the same time, and she was a part of the collective fantasy of having sex with him. She saw the roadies making the hand signals, and she knew when he raised his right fist in the air, it meant no groupies tonight. She planned to tell him she needed to see his fist in the air every night.

He closed out the first part of the set with the popular song, "House of Shame." The 30,000 fans in the arena joined him in singing the hook. A video of a roaring fire flashed across the back of the stage while the crowd chanted:

> Take the vanity of violence
> and break it down;
> The bedroom of bigotry,
> burn it down;
> No room for intolerance,
> tear it down;
> Bullies can't hide,
> burn it down.

He dropped the mic on the floor at the end of the song and walked off the stage. The lights went down, and people started screaming and clapping again. Ari was on fire.

After the concert, Bella escorted the girls to the backstage exit and waited with them for their limo to make its way past the other VIP cars. Despite tears of joy and squeals of delight, they were able to say thank you and give her hugs before getting in their car. Her mother sent her a message on her way back to Miles's dressing room, telling her Ashley had contacted her parents and told them it had been the best night of her life. She told her she was hired as the new safety consultant for the family's company, and Bella sent her mother a text.

Bella: Congrats Mom and I'm glad the girls had a great time. I'll be attending the after show parties with the crew. Gotta work. Catch up with you later.

Joan wasn't the only one who had scored a professional victory. She got an email alert from Parker telling her he'd signed a contract earlier that day with Electronic Tunes to upload the live version of some of Miles's impromptu songs. She shimmied with delight, as she was the one who had convinced Parker to sign the contract, noting they had nothing to lose with the deal and much to gain.

A girl has got to give herself props sometimes.

Ari's sales continued to rise, with people downloading the song to their phones. He was trending at the number one spot on all the streaming services, and she was going to get paid!

Miles was wiping the sweat off his brow with a towel when she entered his dressing room and gave him a kiss on the lips.

"You were fantastic tonight. Like…wow. I loved the performance."

"Thanks." He got up, and thinking he was about to embrace her, she leaned forward, but he smiled and playfully swatted her on the butt with his towel, then squeezed her buttocks before she by reflex pushed him in the chest, causing him to sway off balance.

"What's that for?" She rubbed her behind. It didn't hurt, but the wave of desire spreading through her body as her core clenched and her panties became wet in response to his touch, surprised her. He backed away from her, still rubbing his chest.

"Gosh Bella, you're strong. I was just playing with you."

"Sorry, I didn't mean to push you so hard. I know you must be tired."

"I'm not too tired to discuss the fact that Bradley came in while you were saying goodbye to the girls and told me all about the pictures and your encounter with Angel. Why did I have to hear about it from him and not from you? He was under the impression that you had at least told me about the pictures. You don't think anything is going on between me and Angel, do you? It's over and has been for quite a while."

"No Miles, I don't think there's anything between the two of you now, but what were you going to do about her showing up here minutes before the show? I planned to tell you afterwards." She averted her gaze, then turned back to face him as she placed her outstretched hands on his chest with care this time. He relaxed his frown while she talked fast, trying to make her point.

"You probably had your headset on, finishing your final preparations for the show. What did you want me to do? Run back into your dressing room yelling, 'Miles, help me! Angel is here and she's gonna get me!'" That got a laugh out of him, and she smiled, relaxing her shoulders.

"To answer your question—" he moved in a little closer and, this time, placed a kiss on her lips.

"I would have given the pictures to my network of friends to vet, but to his credit, Bradley did come to me after the pictures were vetted for authenticity. They are definitely pictures of Scott Hansen and Angel Howard. Now I understand why his vendetta against me felt so personal, but what was your angle?"

She backed away from him and thought about it while he explained his concerns.

"Bella, you know Scott is a powerful man who can be dangerous in his abuse of power. For a person who likes to be cautious in her actions, I'm surprised you handled it the way you did. You're aware he's not going to be happy about it, and how can I protect you if you don't level with me?"

"I don't need your protection Miles. I understand Scott better than you think I do, and I know he's someone who likes to pretend to be moral and upstanding—the good guy. I didn't plan what happened tonight, but I went with my instincts and took advantage of the opportunity. Scott is a hypocrite, but he's no fool. He's not going to mess with Angel because he's got more to lose than she does, and even if Angel slips and tells him she got the pictures from me, he's got to know I still have the originals. FYI, I know that you've had your lawyers and men in dark suit meet with his people. I still have friends at World Music, and the word is that there was talk of a lawsuit and/or retribution if he didn't stop interfering with your business. So Miles, you handle things your way and I'll choose my way. The pictures I have are only the tip of the iceberg, and Mr. Hansen doesn't like trouble. He knows that what World Music did to me and other female professionals was wrong, but I don't want to file a suit against the company. This isn't the town where it's a good thing to have too many enemies."

"That's fine, but in the future, we handle things like this together. I don't want anything to happen to you because of me. I couldn't live with that, so promise me."

"I promise. I'll come to you first."

"Good, that's settled." His smile returned. "In the meantime, we need to join the cast at the tour party. They're probably wondering what's keeping us."

"Us? As in you and me?" She stood still as he took her into his arms.

"Yes, you and me." He took her hand, leading her out of the room to the area filled with well-wishers, and kept her by his side at the celebration party to mark the end of the tour of cities in Texas, now a little over two months into the tour. Many people came to congratulate him, and they repeatedly heard comments about his phenomenal performance. She tried to loosen his grip when she noticed how many people were looking at their joined hands.

"If we're going to do this, tonight is as good as any to let people know we're a couple," he spoke quietly to her.

They had never before displayed physical contact in public, but she nodded, still uncertain about their decision.

Parker came over to them and whispered in her ear. "Miles has discovered his muse, and it's you. Are you sure you know what you're getting yourself into?"

"I'm not sure about anything right now," she whispered back as Miles spoke to a few more people who had come to congratulate him.

Parker turned to look at his friend. Despite his consumption of liters of electrolyte water to attempt to refuel himself, he looked beat. Parker patted him on the back. "Go and get some rest. Darien and I'll stay to host the party."

She agreed with Parker; Miles needed to rest, and she knew he would leave if she wanted to go. "I'm really tired. Can we leave?"

"Are you sure you don't want to stay? I'll be all right."

"No, Miles, I've been up since early this morning." He finally agreed to take her back to the hotel. They said goodbye to the throng of well-wishers, and he summoned his chauffeur.

He kissed her relentlessly during the limousine ride to the hotel and resumed claiming her mouth in the elevator on the way to her room. He pressed her against the smooth mahogany wood lining the elevator, her arms draped around his neck while his were tightly around her waist. She tried in vain to move from his embrace, but he grabbed her hand before she could hit the button to her floor.

"Miles, we're going to miss my floor if you don't hit nineteenth floor."

"You're staying in my suite at the top of the hotel. Remember our deal?"

"But what about my things?"

"They've already been moved to my suite."

"A deal is a deal, and you did your part." She relented and thought it best not to argue with him or say anything further about the move.

Once inside the luxurious dwelling, with its commanding views—a far cry from the standard room she'd booked downstairs—he continued the conversation.

"Bella, I'm too tired for small talk, so I'll come right out and ask you bluntly. Will you stay in my bed tonight?" He came close to her, lowered the zipper on her sequin top, and stopped midway, just past her baby girl pink lacy bra. "How many pink bras do you own? I've seen many of them peeking out from under your clothes, and I'll bet you have on pink panties too?" He rolled his eyes when she shrugged.

"Maybe and maybe not. I don't choose my underwear with you in mind."

"I understand that, but I do prefer things that turn me on. That being said, I promise I'll behave tonight, even if you're not wearing panties. I won't touch you if you don't want me to. Besides, I need a little sleep tonight, but afterward, no more pink underwear. It doesn't do it for me." He waited for her answer.

"Were you assuming that at some point tonight we'd have sex?" She knew she was asking a loaded question. He paused and cocked his head, looking unsure of how to answer it. He opted to let her continue the conversation.

"I saw your signal on stage—no groupies tonight—and I won't be your groupie surrogate. You know you have the ability to burn the drawers off any woman, but I'll keep mine on tonight, and we can see what happens tomorrow. Where's the guest bedroom?" She kissed him softly, and he pointed to the bedroom beside his.

The doorbell rang, and he loosened his embrace before going to the door. He opened it, and Bosco came bounding in, delivered by one of his handlers, who left after a brief good night to them. He rubbed the dog behind the ear, and Bosco responded by licking his face before heading to the food Miles pointed to, waiting for him in the kitchen. She thought it must be their routine. Smiling as she watched, she couldn't help observing the exchange of affection between the two of them.

"Good night you two. I'll see you in the morning."

"Good night Bella." He waved and she went to her room.

Her bag, she discovered, was on the floor at the foot of the bed, and she took out a few things and went to the bathroom to take a shower, before changing into a sheer long white cotton nightgown. She was about to climb into bed when she heard Bosco whimpering at the door. The second she opened it, he nudged her on the leg and turned, knowing that she would follow him on his way to Miles's room. His clothes, now strewn across the room, made a path to his bed, where he was prone, naked, and asleep.

Bella stood over him, admiring the muscles in his back and his ass when, suddenly, he started thrashing and sweating in the bed. She waited until he'd calmed to press her hand on the mattress close to his side before touching his hair, still wet from his shower, with tender strokes. She moved her hand slowly side-to-side along his shoulder blades and down his back before lowering her head to lay light kisses down the middle of his back. His breath slowed as he calmed to the tender sound of her voice, barely above a whisper, and her heart thumped, skipping a few beats, as if it was anxious she was about to reveal its secrets.

"I think I finally understand you Miles. You're a very complex man, but you have a tender heart. The feelings I've developed for you scare me, and I'm afraid I'll make the same mistakes your mother did by smothering you with my love. I don't want to risk suffocating you, but I can't deny it anymore—I love you. I love you so much but, I'm so scared you'll run away from me too, and it will shatter me." She was about to get up off the bed when he reached for her wrist.

"Don't leave me, Bella. Stay with me tonight." He turned over and revealed his thick erection. She had been going on her instincts for the last two days, and she couldn't deny that she was aroused by the body of this sexy man, who had told her he wanted to build a relationship with her. She had no regrets about wanting him, but she wouldn't throw caution to the wind either, as her brain raced through the facts-healthy male, test results negative, no STDs—so she unbuttoned her nightgown and slowly let it drop to the floor.

His pupils dilated with desire while she salivated, looking at his hardening cock, and as he sat up, beckoning her to him, she was emboldened by lust and burned with desire. She wanted him and needed to claim every aspect of him. He was her Miles, not the mercurial Ari who belonged to the world.

"Don't hold it against me, but I want you more than I want sleep right now. I'm safe and I haven't been with anyone in months, but I think I should get a condom before we move forward."

"I want you too." She licked her lips as her heart tried to beat its way out of her chest.

"Okay." He hurriedly grabbed several flavored condoms out of the drawer and had her help him cover his cock.

"Touch me. I don't bite unless you want me too."

"Maybe you can give me a few nips later." She kissed his lips, deepening their connection with her tongue, and she got on top of him to lay hot kisses down his chest and slowly down to his groin. Rubbing her cheeks along his soft manscaped hair, she hesitated and looked up at him. He looked uncertain of her next move and sat still as she lowered her head and continued her exploration of his body, seizing the length of him in her mouth. She straddled his legs as she moved her head up and down his shaft, hollowing her cheeks to squeeze him tighter and tighter.

Placing him in a tight grip, she pulled on his thick girth as he started moaning.

"Bella, my angel baby. My angel of light. My true angel. I'm coming." The muscles in his abs flexed as she looked up and saw his face contorted with the tension of sweet agony before he arched his back and fell back on the bed in orgasmic ecstasy.

He seemed to be fighting for breath as she released him from her mouth. She stayed on her knees, straddled across his hips, and laid her head on his chest as he wrapped his arms around her shoulders. He raised her up to his mouth for a kiss and caressed her tenderly. After their breathing calmed, he lifted her off him and got out of the bed to discard his condom before returning to bed to spoon with her as he stimulated her hardened and exposed clit at the same time his cock grew harder.

"I know I came a bit fast because I haven't been with anyone in a while and you got me so worked up—I lost my mind in temporary overload, but baby, I'm ready now to give you pleasure."

He caressed her breasts, covering and massaging them with his large hands.

"I missed you so much. Did you miss me, Bella?"

She responded and groaned as he smiled and continued to lavish her breasts with his attention.

"Yes, I missed you a lot."

The heat of his breath, his soft voice in her ear, and the touch of his magic fingers traveling down her body and now rubbing and flicking her tender clit was causing her to tingle with pleasure. She had never felt so turned on and she wanted more, needed more of him. Quivering under his touch, her abdominal muscles tightened, and her breathing became shallow. He asked another question while rubbing her breast with his other hand.

"Do you love me, Bella?"

"Yeah, oh baby, yes," she responded between shortened breaths in a deep, husky voice. He kissed the side of her face and smiled against her cheek.

"I'm yours forever. Do you belong to me?" Her body, hot with the fever of passion, was trying to speak volumes to him, and she rolled her hips as he continued laying his hands on her.

"Yes, yes." They both moaned, and she whispered, "I love you," as she got closer to the brink of climax.

"I love you so much, Bella; say those magic words again." He kept his voice low, deep, and melodic. With fingers wet from her juices, he touched her clit again with firm, slow, circular motions, inserted a finger inside her, and with a few quick thrusts, she exploded, screaming in ecstasy. He held her a bit longer then reached over and grabbed another condom off the nightstand as she calmed in a moment of quiet bliss.

"Are you up for another round?"

"Hell yeah." *I hope he gives it to me hard.*

"Good, because baby, I need to be inside of you." He continued to spoon with her, hugging her tight and planting kisses down the side of her neck and along her shoulder. He ran his hands down the sides of her body and bent her over as he planted kisses down her back. He gyrated his hips and rubbed his cock firmly against her butt while running his hands down her thighs.

"Are you ready for me, baby?" He gently turned her body and hovered over her before he positioned himself at her opening, then slipped inside with ease.

"Yes, Miles, I want you and I need you. I love you so much, babe; I'll always love you. I can't help myself." Her body shook as he thrusted harder and deeper inside of her. He placed warm kisses on her lips and claimed her mouth with his tongue.

With every thrust, his breathing got louder, and the warmth of it stimulated her neck while he massaged her breasts. His hands traveled the length of her body and hot with passion, he grabbed her buttocks and held her tight as he hit her G-spot with force.

"Oh, Miles," she screamed out and felt the warmth of his release. She listened to him panting as he struggled to catch his breath again. He rolled off her so that they were side by side, grabbed her tightly around her waist, and placed her head on his chest as they calmed and remained in an embrace.

She relished the feel of him as he held her against his firm chest.

"I love you so much, Bella. Make it a good luck charm and tell me for the third time you'll always belong to me and no one will ever come between us. I'll never get enough of hearing it," he implored, this time singing in her ear. She was too delirious to find her answer. "Do you love me, baby?" He pulled her chin upward and looked into her eyes.

Sensing he needed more from her, she looked up at him and smiled. "Yes, Miles Aridio Moore, I love *you* very much, without doubt or reservation and no one will ever change that. I've fought it, but it's true. I love you now and forever. I thought I knew what love was, but I've never truly been in love before." Tears of joy welled in her eyes. "I've been in love with you for quite some time, but I was afraid to admit it. I didn't want to end up on your long list of past lovers."

"What list?" He lifted a single eyebrow and a slight frown came upon his face. "The list of women I've loved is short because I've never been in love before. Wasn't it obvious to you that I didn't know how to love a woman? I do know how to lust after one, but before you, I never loved another. There will only be one name—a woman I love now and forever—tattooed on my heart, and it's yours."

"What makes you so sure it's love this time that you're feeling?"

"Hmm, good question, but after months of struggling with it, I've found answers. I'm obsessed with thoughts of no other woman except you and I've called other women by your name."

"Yes, I remember the drama with Isabelle." They both laughed before he continued.

"There's more; I've been more transparent with you, than I've been with any other woman, and I'd go wild when I thought too long about another man touching you. I want to be there for you Bella, in sickness and in health." He lifted her hands to his mouth and kissed them.

"I know I was awkward with you, Bella…int the beginning…but looking back on it, I wanted you even when I thought you were the Ice Princess."

She stroked his face. "If you wanted me, then why did you call me Belsa? You only made me angry."

He shrugged his shoulder and jutted his chin. "I guess I didn't know how to handle your coolness, but I was comfortable with the heat of your anger. I connect with fire and passion. By the way, could you wear panties that aren't pink or no panties at all?"

"You've got a deal. I'll wear other colors, but no more groupies ever, okay?"

"Deal. That will never be a problem," he promised, hugging her close.

"You were having a nightmare Miles. What were you dreaming about?"

He hugged her tighter, placed her head on his shoulder, and stared off into space.

"I was told the terror threat was raised to the highest level in Europe, and we have multiple shows there before the final show in Scotland on October thirty-first. The promoters postponed some of the tour dates, but my safety and money aren't what I worry about because I have insurance on the tour. I worry about the safety of my friends and my fans. They're like family to me, and I don't want anybody to get hurt. Also, what happened to José still haunts me and I can't shake it. I don't believe he died in a random attack or in a crossfire between rival gangs. I know I was the intended target."

"I'm not sure how you know that, but you've got a good security team. Send some of them well in advance of us, and call it wishful thinking, but I feel we'll be all right." She didn't share her mutual concern that he could have been the intended target.

He looked down at her. "Did you say *us*? Are you planning to come with me?"

"You're not leaving without me."

He hugged her tighter. "Bella, I love you. I don't know if I want to risk your safety. Let's talk about it in the morning." They got under the covers, and he stayed close to her all night. Bosco came in and fell asleep on the floor beside them.

"We both need to rest before round three." He wiggled his eyebrows.

"Good night Miles."

"Yes, this *has* been a good night." He yawned and fell asleep.

CHAPTER SEVENTEEN

She awoke and peered sleepily at a shirtless Miles clad in his pajama bottoms, smiling at her and stroking her hair. Smiling and breathing in the aroma of fresh coffee, she enjoyed a full stretch of her limbs. He'd kept his promise to be a tender lover, and after one night full of lovemaking, she knew she was spoiled for life. He took his time exploring her body and rewarded her for her patience. She thought she'd known what it was like to experience an orgasm, but found out last night what she'd been missing: the big O.

"We need to talk Bella. Here, I have some coffee for you."

"I need to go to the bathroom first." She pulled back the covers and scurried naked to the bathroom. She wasn't about to have her first morning after sex talk without fresh breath.

"Hurry please. I have something to tell you."

She peeked out the bathroom, mouth full of paste, brushing as fast as she could.

"Is something wrong?" She washed her face, looked around the bathroom, and spotted his pajama top which she put on and ran her fingers through her hair, comfortable with her reflection in the mirror. Rubbing the dark red marks on her breasts and abdomen left on her body from their night of heavy petting, she frowned and buttoned the shirt to hide the marks.

Could be better, she surveyed her face but ran out before he called again.

He patted the bed and repeated, "We need to talk."

She sat up on the bed and waited for him to speak. He gave her a cup of coffee sweetened with sugar and cream, and she smelled it, still hot with steam wafting from the cup.

"So, what's the rush?"

He sat in the chair he'd pulled alongside the bed, grabbed his coffee, and looked into her soft eyes before he spoke.

"I called my father earlier this morning and told him about us. My father," he smiled, "famous for his calm temperament, the same man who raised me and never hit or yelled at me." He gazed off as if he were looking at his father.

"I told him how in a drunken state, I shared with you information about my genetic anomaly, and the man went TNT ballistic over the phone. I've never heard him so angry. He had to hang up and call me back after he calmed down. He said he thought I made a mistake sharing information with you, but I told him you weren't a passing fancy for me, and I want to share my life with you."

She repositioned herself on the bed, uncomfortable she might have created conflict between him and his father. "So why was he so angry?" She fidgeted, not sure she wanted to hear the answer.

"My mother told him I was serious about you, and now he's concerned for your safety. He didn't agree with my decision to tell you my secret—at least not yet."

"I don't understand. Why is he concerned about me? I promised you I wouldn't share it with anyone, and I haven't, except for NeNe, and she already knew about it."

He got out of the chair and sat beside her on the bed, taking her into his arms.

"I've always had a lot of security around me, even before I became famous. My skills have been of interest to a lot of people around the world—not very nice people. Since my teens, there have been attempts to radicalize me, recruit me into numerous national and international terror and hate groups, and entice me with obscene sums of money to work for them. There is a bounty on my head on the Dark Web placed there by a group known as the Alt Knights."

"Really?" She placed a hand on his cheek.

"Yes, it's real, and I know this is heavy first thing in the morning, but you deserve to know the truth. Do you know how much damage people like me could cause to high security places? I can pass through security without a weapon and still cause an explosion. My father and uncle were both affiliated with an organization known as the Network, which is kind of like Interpol. After they realized the full implications of my powers, the organization has helped to keep me safe. They got intel that José's death may not have been an accident or a random act of violence, and my father was concerned that if you're associated with me as my new love interest and not just my girl for the moment, harm may come to you."

"Don't worry about me, Miles." She tried to reassure him.

"I am worried. My mother told my father she thought I was falling in love with you, but she wasn't quite accurate with her assessment. Bella, I *am* in love with you, and we're going to increase security around you."

"What do you mean 'increase security'?" She stared off, recalling incidences in which she felt she was being observed.

"So, it wasn't a coincidence Bosco intervened in my encounter with Corey months ago? Am I to assume you knew about it?"

"Yes, Carl informed me, and no, Bosco wasn't assigned to cover you. It just so happened he was at the estate with Carl picking up a few of his things while I was downtown at my apartment. The drivers I assigned to take you to business meetings were a part of your security detail, and they overheard some of the conversations you had with Corey. Why didn't you tell me he was threatening you? Never mind that for now, that's the past, and I don't have time to digress." He frowned.

"Is there anything else you need to tell me now that we're being honest with each other?" she asked, closing her eyes and rubbing the side of her face to take in the news of being followed by security.

"My father plans to send you more information about my condition, so check your email for info from Cadejazz. He said you should also expect a package by courier."

"Okay, I'll watch for it, but no more secrets." She rubbed his hands, which were a little wet from sweat and discomfort, the veins noticeably dilated. She recognized it as signs he was tense and sought to calm him. He looked at her and gave her a full smile.

"How can I plan your birthday parties and hide the presents I plan to buy you if I don't keep secrets?" He laughed to lighten the mood.

"Don't deflect, Miles; you know what I'm saying. We can have surprises for each other but no deceit. I'm also telling you I'm not looking back. We're in this together, but you have to keep me in the loop, and I promise to better communicate with you."

"I can only promise you I'll do my best."

"I guess that's better than lying to me."

"My sentiments exactly. Can I ask another question?"

"Sure, what is it?"

"Last night, was that the first time taking a man…in your mouth?"

"Yes, and I was a little uncomfortable with your girth. Why? You didn't like it?" He smiled, taking her into his arms.

"I loved that wicked mouth of yours. It was delicious, and I can't wait until you do it again. It was your eyes, not your mouth, that betrayed your secret. You seemed unsure, and I want to assure you—you have mad skills, babe." She smiled back at him and pressed her lips together before continuing their conversation.

"Thanks for the compliment, but as you said, you could tell I've not done it with anyone else, and I wasn't sure about what I was doing. I was surprised that I enjoyed it too, and I liked the flavor on the condom you chose. It was sweet like a lollipop."

"I'm glad you enjoyed it, and our lovemaking will be full of adventure. I promise you." His phone rang, and her phone pinged at about the same time. She stretched to get it off the nightstand alongside the bed. It was an alert from one of the morbid sites. She looked at it and covered her mouth; another fan dressed like Ari had been killed. The phone shook in her hand as she passed it to him to see the alert.

"Damn." He shook his head and accepted Bradley's call, placing it on speaker so she could hear.

"Miles, someone hacked into the MilesWorld app and sent a message to you. Let me read it to you: `You're next. How many people have to die before you agree to our terms?`"

"I'm not sure what terms this person is talking about, Bradley," he responded.

"I'm not sure about it either, so I followed the protocol and spoke to your father and his associates. We all agree that some of your upcoming dates need to be canceled. Are you aware a second fan of yours has been executed?"

"Yes, Bella shared the news feed with me. She's here with me now."

"Hi Bradley."

"Hi Bella," he responded, followed by an awkward silence.

"Bradley you can talk candidly in front of Bella. I've already shared concerns with her about possible terror attacks."

"Alright, if I can be honest with both of you, I don't think their deaths are a coincidence but were planned attacks to send a message to you. If those plotting against you keep killing your fans, I guess they think they'll kill your career. That's the only sense I can make of this madness. There have been too many terrorist attacks and random violent events throughout Europe recently, and now with the personal threats against you, we can't cover this detail as tightly as I would like. I can't say I really understand the nature of the threats against you, but our agreement when you hired me was to let the international team handle situations like this, especially since this is far beyond threats against other celebrities I've covered. Your father will give me further instructions while I'll look for leads in the social media posts on this."

"No, Bradley." She leaned toward the phone. "That's my job to sift through social media posts, and I can release our official response to the murder."

"At this point, the security issues make it my job to sift through the posts for leads, Bella."

"We're talking about two different things, Bradley." She felt she needed to make her point, so she sat up straight, shifting into an authoritative posture.

"Miles, it's your call. What do you want me to do? If I find some leads, I may need you to authorize publicity releases that may help lead authorities to the perpetrator. I have contacts in various police stations."

She looked at him, and Bradley stayed silent, awaiting his response. She noted his fists were tightening again, so she decided to end the impasse.

"Bradley, you're right. We need to work together. I'm not familiar with all the facts of this situation, and you need to take the lead on this while I get additional information."

Miles looked her in the eyes and nodded. "Yes, I think we should proceed with you, Bradley, as the lead on this while I bring her up to speed on the publicity side of this. Yes, that's what we should do."

"Sounds like a plan. Thanks to both of you, and I'll get right on it. I've already taken down the Where's Ari site, and we're retooling the MilesWorld app with additional security features."

"It sounds like you've got things covered." She nodded her head in agreement with his assessment.

"Thanks, Miles. I'll call you soon, goodbye."

"Goodbye, Bradley."

He ended the call and turned his attention to her while she got up and paced before him.

"I'll make sure things are handled correctly, Bella. Please don't worry, I've got this." She stopped in her tracks and turned to face him.

"No, *we've* got this. No one is going to threaten you and get away with it. You. Belong. To. Me. Do you know how much hell I've been through in my life?"

He nodded his head and watched while she resumed pacing. "No one is going to take you away from me. I may not get a happily ever after, but I deserve a happy for now."

"We both deserve it, or I'll die trying to make it happen." He rose from the bed to embrace her.

Her bravado fading, she trembled in his arms.

"You can't die. I love you, and I can't imagine living without you."

She looked up at the ceiling and lowered her head against his chest while snuggling tightly in his strong embrace.

She prayed she wouldn't have to suffer through the pain of tragic loss—not again.

Miles was napping before his performance that night and she didn't want to wake him while he slept soundly beside her, so she got up to use the bathroom and planned to get some work done. She was on her way to the front of the suite when he called out to her.

"Come back to bed, Bella. I'm awake." She returned to the bedroom and he took her into his arms, pulling the covers over them.

"Are you still worried about my safety after the second murder?"

"Yes, and I don't understand why you're not more worried."

"I'm saddened by it babe, but I'm not worried. I've lived under the threat of injury or kidnapping all my life, and my father and his friends in The Network have never rested until they've investigated and discovered the source of all threats against me. I'm not worried they won't get to the bottom of this, and I don't want you to worry about it either." He turned on the lights and looked into her eyes.

"Promise me, Bella, that you won't let the fear of a threat against me rule our lives. I'll see it in your eyes if you worry about it, and I won't have us live in fear. My parents gave me the gift of freedom to live my life as I choose, and I won't surrender it."

"I don't want you to compromise your freedom, and I'll try to contain my anxieties about your safety if you'll try to avoid unnecessary risks."

"What are you defining as an unnecessary risk? No sky diving or riding my motorcycle?"

"No, you like those activities, and I would never suggest that you live a sedentary life. That's not you."

"You don't understand the reach of The Network, and I'm not at liberty to talk about them, but literally, I trust those guys with my life. They have access to intelligence that I'll never have, even if I hired the best security team in the world, and that's why Bradley knows he is to defer to the instructions of The Network when they call. Bradley is excellent at what he does, but he's not on the same level as they are."

"You're right; I don't understand your affiliation with The Network, but I do trust you, and if you tell me not to worry, I promise you I'll do everything humanly possible to support your decisions regarding your safety."

"And I'll do everything in my power to keep you safe, Bella. I understand now why I've been drawn to you since the day I met you. You are kind, caring, and compassionate." He kissed her.

"Most of my life, others have viewed my kindness as a weakness." Her eyes tinged with sadness.

"No Bella, it takes strength and courage to stay kind, especially in a society where acts of violence are rampant."

"Do you really believe that kindness is a strength?" She leaned away from him and folded her arms.

"Yes I do because I know how much strength of character it takes to stop from slapping the shit out of some people, and I also know how easy it would be for me to incinerate fools who piss me off, like I thought I would do when I heard Corey had threatened you but… it was knowing that you would want to handle things your way that stopped me. You've made me a better man, Bella. I distanced myself from my family, which they at first thought was me being selfish and unkind, but it was because I thought being around them placed them in harm's way. Not visiting my family on a regular basis was the hardest thing I'd ever done, and I miss them even though they don't think I do. I tried to distance myself from you too, but I just couldn't stay away. I love you and I want to protect you, but it will never be at the risk of making you feel that I'm trying to control you." He shook his head and his chest heaved.

"I'm telling you Bella, it took everything I had to not intervene in the situation between you and Corey, but I thought about it and realized you had to make your decisions about him."

"Thank you for letting me handle it my way and for believing in me." She kissed his lips and stroked his cheek.

"I believe in us, and I know I found favor in the universe when I found you. Your love gives me strength and fills me with joy. I can't tell you how happy I am that you're going on the tour with me."

"I look forward to sharing this time with you. I missed you so much, and nothing will separate us. I won't let it." She squeezed his hands.

"Are you planning to use a superpower to keep us safe?" He laughed.

"Yes, and my superpower is my love for you that's strong enough to protect us both. I promise."

"Let's get some rest before I experience your love in action." He took her in his arms and smiled with an expression of pure bliss.

Michele Sims

CHAPTER EIGHTEEN

It's my day off, I've sold out every concert date in Europe so far, and now I'm in London on a cool, rainy day at the end of September instead of on the Amalfi Coast, soaking up some sun. I was looking forward to the tour stops in the Mediterranean; that's why I insisted on that schedule, but here I am in London one week earlier than I'd planned.

He took a sip of scotch and placed the glass on the table just as the door of the hotel room opened and the lights were flipped on.

"Shit, Miles, don't scare me that!" Bella picked up the bags she'd dropped on the floor after seeing him unannounced and seated on the couch looking up at her.

"You weren't expecting me, babe?"

"Of course not," she caught her breath and went over to kiss him before taking off her jacket. "I thought you were in Barcelona heading to the next stop on the French Riviera for the concert there."

"I was in Barcelona, and the last time I saw you, we were in Portugal on our way to Barcelona. You told me you would be gone no more than a day and you would rejoin me there." She snuggled in his arms and leaned against his chest, which was warm to the touch and exposed with his shirt unbuttoned.

"How long have you been here?"

"Long enough to take a shower and enjoy a drink."

"You're really hot. Are you all right?"

"I'm fine, Bella. I'm not hot, I'm horny. Maybe it's you who's hot. Why don't you climb out of some of those clothes?"

"You mean like my dress, shoes, and stockings?"

"Yeah, why not. What took you so long to get back to the room, and better yet, what delayed your return back on tour with me?" She disrobed down to her underwear and resumed her position next to him.

"I'm glad you asked." She smiled as he leaned back and a muscle in his jaw ticked.

"The International Marketing Conference here in London was fantastic, and yes, I did tell you I would only attend the keynote speech, but the opportunities for networking and the contacts I've made here were so invaluable, I knew you wouldn't mind if I stayed an extra day. I also got the chance to meet with NeNe and Parker, who were already here to confirm the marketing plans for the expanded tour schedule in London. Can you believe you're doing several days in the arena on the Greenwich peninsula? It will give you a chance to see if you like doing artist-in-residence gigs instead of extensive touring to different cities. Besides, all of your shows are almost sold out here, and the rave reviews from the other stops are contributing to the tour selling itself without additional dollars needed for publicity."

"That's great, Bella," he responded in a flat voice.

"Yes, it is, Miles, and I'm surprised you're not happier about the success of the tour." She got up and tried to straddle him, but he grabbed her leg.

"Excuse me, I need to use the bathroom."

"What's wrong?"

"Nothing, nothing is wrong other than a slight headache, and maybe I'm a bit hot."

"Let me call for some Tylenol."

"I'll find some," he said, and he went to the bedroom.

"Miles, you don't seem like yourself." She rubbed her arms before going to the bedroom to grab her robe. He was standing by the bed as she entered the room.

"Did you find some Tylenol?"

"Yes, I did." He came up to her and planted a kiss on her lips while she caressed his shoulders and biceps.

"Your muscles are so tight. Can I give you a massage?" He nodded, and she pulled him to the bed. "Take off your pajamas and lie down. I'm going to work my magic fingers on your shoulders and back. I'll be right back." She went to the bathroom and grabbed a bottle of essential oil and she warmed it by rubbing in her hands before she applied it to his taut muscles. She smoothed it over his shoulders in a firm circular motion.

"Is that good?"

"Hmm, yeah. That feels good."

She poured more oil in the center of his back and kneaded it into his skin while rubbing gently along his spine and, with firmer pressure, she rubbed the sides of his back and down to his round, tight glutes.

"Babe, you're so tense. Relax." Massaging the back of his legs, she was able to smooth out the knots in his thick calf muscles all the way down to the heels of his feet.

"Is there another part of your body that's tight and needs massaging?"

He turned over and loosened the belt of her robe before pointing to his raging erection. She took off her robe, laughing at him as he looked at her with puppy-dog eyes.

"Are you sure you need a massage there?"

"Yes, my cock is really tight." She took him into her mouth and massaged his shaft with her cheeks and tongue.

Sweat formed on her forehead, and her cheeks warmed as she took him in deeper, causing her to gag before pulling back a little. He closed his eyes, and her breath quickened as he continued thrusting in her warm mouth. He was approaching orgasm when, all of a sudden, she loosened her grip around him and pulled back, leaving him more frustrated and exposed to the cool air.

"What happened?" He opened his eyes and looked up at her.

"I don't know. Your body was getting hotter, and I was overheating to the point I thought I would pass out. I'm sorry." He pulled her into his arms and laid her on top of him while she recovered her breath.

"Are you all right? Maybe we should use the salve my father sent us since it's probably me burning with desire for you."

"I have a little bit of the salve with me. Most of it, I left in my things with the tour. I didn't think I needed it, but if you take your time, maybe we can enjoy the sex without burning each other with desire."

"I'll try," he agreed as he turned them on their sides and took his time trailing kisses down her neck and along her collarbone. He unfastened her bra and lowered his head to suck her breast and encircle her nipples with his tongue. He then grabbed her buttocks in firm circular motions, and after slowly moving down her body, he pulled her thong to the side to massage her clit with his tongue.

"Miles, you're starting to heat up again, and so am I," she told him in between breaths. "Your hands and that wicked tongue of yours are making me explode. Oh shit. I need you to make love to me now."

"With pleasure, my Bella." She lifted her hips and was about to take off her thong when he ripped it off and plunged deeply inside of her, panting with lust.

"I'm trying…trying to take it slow, but I can't."

She placed her hands on his ass to slow down his thrusting and began talking to him slowly.

"You missed me, baby?" She slowly rotated her hips, and he raised up his torso and lowered his head to watch himself thrust into her.

"Talk to me, Miles."

"I missed you—I missed you so much." She rotated her hips, contracting and relaxing her muscles while gripping him tighter.

"Oh, baby, you're so tight, so good. I can't hold out much longer." He turned her over on top of him and started thrusting faster while watching her facial expressions as she stimulated her clit.

"Yeah, baby, I love when you play with yourself." She threw her head back and let out a deep breath in orgasmic pleasure followed by his sexual climax. Tired and completely satisfied, she rolled off him and lay beside him until her heart stopped frantically beating.

"Bella, I'm so sorry. Does it hurt?" They looked at the red blotches on her torso and her back. "You look like you have a bad rash."

"No, it's not as tender as the first time we made love but, I think we still need to use the salve. I'll get up and put some on my body."

"Bring the salve to me, and I'll put it on you."

"All right." She returned to the bed and gave him the tube.

"Be careful not to use too much." She told him.

"I'll be careful babe." He applied it first to her back and shoulders, then to her neck and breasts, which were dotted with marks looking like hickeys or love blotches he'd placed along her body.

"It's a good thing it's autumn so I can cover up until the marks fade." She frowned and looked up at him. "Was it just lust or was it also irritation you were feeling that brought you here to London?"

He took in a breath. *Time to be honest.*

"I missed you so much, and even though I've told you not to worry too much about my safety, I was driving myself to the point of distraction when you told me you planned to stay in London another day instead of coming back to join me on the tour. I know you kept in touch the entire time, but when you didn't even get angry or mention it when I heeded my fans' request to crowd surf, I thought you didn't care anymore. I spoke to Bradley, and he said you hadn't contacted him either."

She cocked her head to the side and blinked her eyes.

"So tell me, Miles, how do I win? I'm damned if I bother Bradley with my concerns or you feel I don't care when I stay in my lane."

"Bradley may have been irritated by your concerns, but did I ever complain about it?" She paused to consider his question.

"No you didn't, but I don't want to place you in a position to choose between us, especially when I know he's capable of doing his job." She sat up, and he took her hand.

"I realized a long time ago that, in my life, the things that irritated me the most were often the same things I missed when they were gone. I loved when I no longer had to deal with my mother's overprotective nature, but after I was on my own, I missed her fierceness when it came to me. My mother would go up against anyone for me, and while you were gone, I missed you and how you would go up against anyone even if it put you at odds with them to look out for me. You're my ride-or-die chick. I love you and can depend on you no matter what, and I hope you know you can count on me. So yes, I was irritated when I thought you decided to distance yourself from me, and it didn't help when you told me yesterday the massage therapist here at the resort laid his hands on your naked body and gave you a massage."

"It was innocent, and he was professional." She kissed him and gave him a hug. "So you're telling me it doesn't anger you when I ask questions about your safety plans?"

"Not as long as you don't pester me about them. I've always known from the beginning that you weren't trying to suck up to me or care about me just because I was a paycheck for you. You genuinely cared about me. You know I run a family business, and when I spoke to my mother and NeNe about you, they both agreed that it sounded like your concerns were real and driven only by your desire that I stay safe."

"And driven by my love for you."

"Yes, we're fortunate to have found each other, and I love you more than life itself. Bella, I'm tired. Do you mind if I get some rest before we take in a little sightseeing while we're here? We can leave tomorrow to join the tour."

"I'd love to go sightseeing in London after you get some rest." She smiled at him.

"I was planning on a few days of fun in the sun in the Mediterranean during my time off, but I'm happy about seeing a little bit of London with you before the frenzy that will surely happen when the tour comes to town." He yawned and closed his eyes.

The Fire God Tour finished its stint in London and arrived in Glasgow, Scotland, in October, one week before the concert and after completing the eastern and most of the western European wings of the tour. There had been no new terrorists acts in western Europe for months, and the terror threat in Scotland had been lowered, but the security team remained on high alert. Parker's father, Henry, owned the controlling interest in the new Middleburgh Golf Club and Resort on the outskirts of the city where the tour members would be staying. Miles and Parker had a smaller share, but they were interested in doing their part to make sure the business venture was a success. The concert would be held at Glasgow Green, a park in the east end of the city and on the north bank of the River Clyde. Miles was excited to play at the same venue as the Dangerous World Tour in August 1992, and his ticket sales were on track to exceed 65,000 sold.

The temperatures in Scotland were warmer than usual and perfect for outdoor activities. The date of the concert coincided with the week of celebration of Samhain, and there would be fireworks displays, bonfires, and parties leading up to the concert. Tens of thousands of people were coming, and as expected, many of the partygoers had booked rooms in the resort. Henry thought having investors come in to see the resort during a period of full occupancy would help with his plans for expansion.

Miles joined Henry and Parker in the private dining room for an early morning breakfast and meeting with a prospective investor while Bella chose to spend the morning sleeping in. The tour members had arrived after midnight, and she wasn't in the mood for breakfast when he got up, dressed in business attire, and left the room.

"I'll join you later…maybe," was the last he heard from her as she moaned and turned over in bed.

A traditional full Scottish breakfast had been prepared and laid out in buffet style. He loved the Scottish breakfast of sausage links, bacon, eggs, potatoes, sautéed mushrooms, grilled tomatoes, baked beans, buttered toast, black pudding, porridge, and kippers. The bountiful breakfast reminded him of simpler times when he spent his summers with his grandparents in North Carolina. A server poured cups of tea or coffee for the men as they dug into their meals.

The meeting with the prospective investor went well, and Miles graciously consented to take pictures and provide autographed albums for members of the investor's family. They all shook hands on the deal, contingent on having the agreement reviewed by their lawyers before the new investor left them to attend another meeting. Miles finished his meal and sat conversing with Parker and Henry.

"Miles, what had you so irritated last week when you called to check on your marriage license?" Henry looked over his glasses at both Miles and Parker.

"I'll be damned, Henry, if I can please my woman despite my best efforts."

"So, what happened?" Parker asked with a mouth full of sausage.

"You remember I had Darien arrange for a private shopper and a stylist to come from Florence to our suite while we were in Rome, right?"

"Yeah, so what's wrong with that?"

"I had Bella's measurements sent to the private shopper and stylist and they both came to show her luxury items most women would die to have. I didn't want Bella to be bored while we rehearsed for the show, and she could have even gotten her hair and nails done in the suite. Anyway, there they are with fine Italian leather handbags, designer shoes, 18-carat gold jewelry, and couture dresses for her to decide on a piece—or all of the items if she wanted them. I wanted to spoil her. The next day I get the bill. I review it, and I'm pissed."

"She chose all of them, and now you're stuck with an exorbitant bill, right? Cheer up, laddie. Do you know how much money I've spent on Parker's mother, trying to keep her happy? Talk to your accountants and try to make it a business expense," Henry advised.

"That's not it." This time Parker put down his fork beside his plate while Henry scrunched his face and cocked an eyebrow.

"So, spill it, buddy. I don't want my breakfast to get cold while you tell the long version of this mystery." Miles took a sip of his tea and grinned.

"My sweet Bella told the women who'd spent hours shopping for her that while she appreciated all the efforts they made to find just the right things for her, she wasn't interested in getting anything right now. She has a closet full of clothes and didn't see the need to spend my money. I got a bill for their services and a nasty gram telling me to forget about calling them in the future. I had to make it right, especially after I saw all the beautiful things they had picked out for her, so I purchased the entire collection for our wedding."

"Man, are you sure both of you are ready for this? I mean this wedding you are hell bent on having. What if she refuses your proposal? Well, I doubt she would, but what if she wants a long engagement?" Parker picked up his fork and resumed eating.

"I've been a good boy, wouldn't you say? I've stuck to the security plan, I don't dive into the crowd anymore, and I haven't had as many fire effects in the show. I'm willing to do whatever it takes to make her happy. She knows the two of us belong together."

"Aye. Your Bella sounds like a fine Scottish lassie. I'm looking forward to meeting her. Did you share the results of my genealogic research of her family?" Henry ate a little more off his plate.

"She knows her father was a Scottish descendant of the Campbell clan. Her mother told me he often joked how lucky she was to marry someone distantly related to Scottish nobility. He told her she was the queen of his heart, and he was her king. I found this out when I approached her with my plans to ask Bella to marry me. I wanted her blessing, which she freely gave, and she told me if Bella wanted to marry me, she would support our decision. I don't think Bella knows the story of her family's royal connection or that her father wasn't kidding. They really do descend from a noble line. I plan to tell her soon, but first, how's it going with the marriage license?"

Miles had spoken to Henry after his time with Bella in Texas. He'd told Henry he loved her and wanted to marry her. There was no doubt in his mind that she was the one. She had made sacrifices for him and showed how much she loved him every day. He couldn't imagine a life without her.

Henry and Parker had both agreed to help him with the paperwork to get married in Scotland, the land of her father's people. He knew she might decide she didn't want a wedding on such short notice, but at least the paperwork would be completed and filed, before the required 28 days before the ceremony.

"I have the papers right here." Henry pulled the folded paper out of his pocket and handed it and a pen to Miles. He opened it, perused it quickly, and signed the document immediately before slipping it in his breast pocket.

"I know people at the registrar's office who can help us. They have paperwork with signatures on it that I produced for them, but we'll need to get these papers signed with both of your authentic signatures on them and filed at the office as soon as possible."

"I understand, and I'll take care of it." He knew Bella was fatigued and had difficulty with the demands of travel and sleeping in all the multiple hotels they had stayed in. He saw her sign papers she had given NeNe to review without looking through each document, and he planned to place the request for a marriage license in the next group of papers for her signature. If it passed by her attention, good; if not, he'd share his plans with her, but he wanted to keep his plans for a romantic dinner and his planned proposal a secret as long as he could. He looked up and saw her walking toward them.

"She's coming into the room now. We can continue this conversation later," he told Henry and Parker. They looked up and smiled as she approached their table. Miles loved the way her navy-blue jersey dress draped over her curves. He didn't recognize the matching tartan scarf thrown across her shoulders and knotted in the front. She wore her thick curly hair in a sleek style cascading down her back. *Damn, she's sexy as hell.*

They rose from their seats to greet her when she arrived at the table.

"Good morning gentleman. I'm sorry I couldn't come earlier. I was too tired after traveling to so many cities. I don't know how you all keep up this pace."

He greeted her with a kiss on the cheek.

"Bella, this is Henry Middleton, Parker's father and a great friend and mentor to me. Henry, this is Bella Wahlberg, my fia…my girlfriend." He stumbled over the introduction and pulled out a chair for her.

"I'm pleased to meet you, Mr. Middleton." She extended her hand.

"Likewise but call me Henry. You're a bonny lass, Bella." He shook her hand and beckoned all to sit down. "You're planning to see some of this beautiful country, I hope?" The server came over to refresh the tea and coffee and to encourage Bella to visit the buffet.

"Just coffee for me please," she responded to the server. "It depends on Miles's schedule. I would love to see some of Scotland, but this is a business trip."

"I've got some time, since we'll be here until the end of the week. This will be a business and pleasure trip," Miles added.

"Bella, Miles and my son told me about your marketing savvy at AriMusic. I would consider it a favor if you could meet with my marketing team and give us some recommendations about marketing the resort while you're here."

"Sure, it would be my pleasure, Henry. I'll be glad to help. I can also personally attest to how wonderful the accommodations are at this resort. I feel so refreshed after a night in the suite."

Henry engaged in a little more small talk with them before announcing he needed to leave to show Parker future plans for their other holdings throughout the United Kingdom.

"Oh, before I forget, Bella, I have the invoices for you to sign and some other papers from NeNe finalizing the marketing contracts with the new vendors." Parker opened his satchel hanging off the back of his chair and opened it to retrieve the papers.

"I'll take it. Bella hasn't visited the breakfast bar yet. She doesn't need to contaminate her hands." Miles snatched the papers out of Parker's hand before he could give them to her. He looked curiously at Miles, who smiled back at him but offered no further explanation for his odd behavior. Henry and Parker both said their goodbyes and left them at the table to enjoy time together.

"Did you sleep well last night?" He placed the papers in an interior jacket pocket.

"Yes, the bed was heavenly, and I'm feeling a little more rested. I don't know how you do it. Some days, the traveling from city to city is grueling, and other days it may be less tiring, but I've awakened confused and uncertain of where we were. You get so little sleep and yet you're still able to hit the stage and put on an electrifying performance."

"It's my job, and I've trained rigorously for this tour. You haven't been in training for this, but we can always hire a trainer for you for future tours or cut back on the lovemaking."

"Don't even think about depriving me of my exclusive sexual privileges as your girlfriend." She winked and sipped her coffee. "I love being with you, and modern conveniences allow me to work out of any space with a computer and an internet connection, but I'm not sure if life on the road is for me."

"Please don't say that. I need you with me." He looked at her, then grabbed a piece of toast from his plate. She grabbed the other piece and bit into it.

"I'm not saying I won't accompany you on parts of any upcoming tour. I'm just not sure about accompanying you on a full tour for months at a stretch, but we have time to sort it all out."

"You're right. Why don't you get something else to eat? I have a full day planned for us. There are hiking clothes in the room for you, including your favorite hiking boots. Your mother also gathered some additional clothes and had them shipped here."

"I'll have to thank her when I get home, but are you serious? We can go hiking today?" She smiled brightly, hoping it was true.

"Yes, hiking and few other things."

"Sounds great. I'll get a little something from the bar and we can go back to the room and change after I eat. First sightseeing in Europe, and now hiking in Scotland with you. I'm living a dream." She got up from the table and went to the bar. He saw her looking back at him while he quickly reviewed the papers before placing them back in his pocket.

I need to get these papers signed as soon as possible, but I guess it will have to wait.

He drank a cup of coffee while she finished her breakfast, but he still couldn't come up with a plan to keep his proposal a surprise and get her to sign the request for their marriage license.

I'll think of something later. I've got to get these court papers signed.

He pulled the invoices and contracts out of his pocket but kept the request for their license hidden.

"I need your signature on these papers, but we'd better hurry if you want to get that hike in. I've got some gorgeous sites to show you. Besides, NeNe has already reviewed the contracts, so you don't have to look at them too closely." He thought he could just hide the court papers among the stack of papers, but she began reading each invoice and contract.

"Come on, babe, I'm ready to go. We can drop off the papers with Darien, and he can have them delivered electronically back to NeNe today."

He decided to keep the court paper in his pocket, as he wouldn't have been able to slide it in without her seeing it.

"All right! Slow your roll. Relax dude and stop rushing me." He rolled his eyes as she signed all the papers except the request for their marriage license.

He enjoyed the extra time roaming the countryside of Scotland with her and listened intently as she recalled stories her parents had told her about her father's people, who once lived in larger numbers outside of Glasgow.

"Mom told me that my father's people were members of the Campbell clan, originally from the Scottish Highlands, who migrated to the lands outside of Glasgow."

He listened as if he hadn't heard the same story on the plane as they were heading to Scotland, but this time, her face brightened as she spoke, and he felt she'd never been so beautiful. Bella was so excited about walking in the footsteps of her ancestors that it gave him an idea he planned to share with Henry before surprising her tomorrow night with his proposal.

They hiked the seemingly endless trails, visited beautiful lochs and glens around Glasgow, and enjoyed the breathtaking scenery of central Scotland before returning to the resort for lunch and a little rest.

"This has been a glorious day. I can't remember when I've been this happy." She placed her arms around his neck and kissed him as he lifted her off her feet and took her to the bed, placing her gently on the mattress, then lying beside her.

"Bella, I'll spend a lifetime making you happy if you let me. I can't remember when I've been happier. I have my girl with me and my music. What more could I want right now besides a nap?" She wiggled her behind as he spooned with her.

"Girl, we've spent all day hiking, and you've got me tired. Let me take a nap and then I'll be ready for you." He kept her close as he snuggled against her warm, soft body and fell asleep.

The next morning, he encouraged her to enjoy a little girl time, shopping with Parker's wife Jen, Reagan, and a few of the dancers. They were in the bathroom preparing for the day when he presented his suggestions for places to shop.

"I didn't budget for shopping every day, and besides, the shipping charges to get things back to the States are expensive."

"Bella, uhmm, I have a private plane, remember?"

"I know, but I don't want the crew to be responsible for my personal things in addition to all the equipment you need for the tour."

He took off his towel from around his waist and put on his underwear. He saw her staring at him as he got dressed. "Like what you're seeing?"

She blinked her eyes and bit her lip. "Yes, and I'm having dirty thoughts about what I want to do to you, but I also want to see a little more of this beautiful country, not with the girls, but with you. Miles, I just don't think you have to spend a fortune to have a good time." He came closer to her.

"First Italy and now here in Scotland. I'm not asking you to spend your money. I have money *budgeted,* as you say, for you to spend as you wish. Do you have a hang-up about accepting money from me? If so, we need to talk about this."

"As you said, it's your money." She faced the mirror and focused on brushing her hair. "I have my money, and as my mother always told me, 'Bella, you're smart and resourceful. If you really want a few material things in life, be willing to get it yourself.'"

"Sound advice, but my father always told me a good man never thinks it's robbery to share his resources with the woman he loves. What's the use of having money?"

"I don't have an answer for that right now, especially since it's not a simple question." She placed the brush on the counter and turned to look him in the eye.

"Good. You have an account that has been set up to use as you wish. Just use the card I gave you earlier. It's not every day we get to visit Scotland, and you can purchase some things to place in the house to remind you of your ancestors."

"Alright, it would be fun to visit some of the quaint shops and pick up a few mementos." She turned to face him and sighed.

"Thank you, Miles. I don't want you to think I don't appreciate all you've done, but it's being with you and making memories, not buying things, that has made me so happy."

"I know, but I still want to share a few *things* with you. Is it wrong for me to share my toys?" He gave her his boyish grin and kissed her on the lips.

"No, I guess not."

They spent the morning together walking the grounds of the resort and enjoying a midday picnic, but he told her that after lunch, he planned to participate in a round of golf with Parker and his friends Fergus and Andy. He also hoped to get in some time fishing and sailing in a few of the lochs around Glasgow before they left Scotland.

Miles hired a cultural guide to work with the performers, some of whom would wear period costumes and traditional tartans during the show. According to mythology, Samhain was a time when the doorway of the world beyond opened to the land of the living, and supernatural beings, ghosts, and souls of the dead were allowed entry back into the mortal world. The cultural guide explained that Halloween had evolved out of the celebration of Samhain.

While Bella enjoyed her days shopping, spending time with Reagan, and visiting historic sites near the city, Miles spent a lot of time working with the engineers building the bonfires customarily used in the celebration of Samhain. It was the use of massive bonfires during the celebration that had sold him on hosting a concert date in Scotland. He was also happy to be a part of the Middleton family's financial venture into Scotland. They meant a lot to him. They were family.

"I have special plans for you tonight," he'd reminded her before he left.

He planned for them to spend the night together at the ancient castle located on the grounds of the massive estate at the end of a long, winding road at the edge of the Middleton family property. The castle, not as grand as the Cawdor and Edinburgh castles, was undergoing extensive renovations, and most of the work was largely unfinished except for the great hall and a few bedrooms. He'd shared his initial plan with her to stay a few days at the castle, but since it didn't have modern conveniences such as computers and internet wiring yet, she'd nixed his plan but agreed to spend one night there.

He told Bradley to make sure the perimeter of the property was secured, but he didn't want the team to stay with them at the castle and lessen their privacy since they would still be on the grounds of the estate. He wanted that one night to be intimate, spent completely alone with the woman he loved.

They had grown closer, first as friends then as lovers over the last six months, and he was surprised she loved sex in a hot Jacuzzi as much as he did. As her trust had increased and she'd became open to novel experiences during their sexcapades, he felt she was ready for new sexual adventures.

It delighted him that she no longer wore her baby girl pink underwear as often. They had a new color code for sex with each other to let him know how she wanted her lovemaking. He could take it any way it was given, but he knew if she wanted it sweet and slow, she wore white. Hot and spicy, give me the best you got, and she wore a red negligee. Black leather meant it was Dominatrix night, one of his favorite nights. He was happier than he had been in a long time, and tonight, he planned to ask her to marry him.

They left the group at the resort to enjoy a light dinner and wine in the castle. He had rented a vintage roadster to travel up the long, narrow road to the stone castle with its high walls. They arrived, and he took time to pull the top back up to cover the interior of the car; as the skies looked as if rain was coming. He grabbed his bag and went to help her out of the car. He was glad there would be no interruptions or prying eyes from members of his staff. She grabbed her bag and exited the car with his assistance.

He took her hand to guide her to the castle, but she resisted moving from her spot. He remained silent as she covered her eyes against the sun and the wind, which blew her hair into her face, and he stood watching her as she turned her head and looked up at the castle, gazing upon its rugged and stark exterior with its massive stone towers poised atop a small rising overlooking the breathtaking lake. The lush greenery surrounding the castle, the breaking of the dark waters against the shore below, and the blue-gray clouds in the distance provided a magnificent and stunning backdrop to the night he had planned for the two of them.

"This looks like the castle I dreamed about as a little girl. It's beautiful."

"If you think this is impressive, wait until we get inside."

Miles had visited the castle two years ago to walk the grounds and view the plans with Henry and Parker for restoring the edifice to its former glory. He imagined how it would look when it was completed, and as part owner in the venture, he hoped to provide their future guests with a perfect and extraordinary experience. He wanted them to feel like they had ventured back to a different time. He was anxious to get inside and tried to pull Bella toward the large wooden door against her steady resistance.

"Miles, wait. I want to take in this moment. This place is so beautiful—so majestic. The quietness and serene beauty of it takes my breath away."

She walked, one slow step after another, toward the massive door and stopped to enjoy the scenic view. He loosened his grip on her hand, finally agreeing to slow down. She was right. It was beautiful, and he was happy to share the castle with her, the woman he hoped to make his future wife. They had the entire night together, and he realized a hasty entrance wasn't the answer.

"Take your time. We have all night to enjoy the castle." He walked a step behind her, relishing a deep sense of satisfaction as she looked back at him with bright eyes and a wide smile. He wanted a lifetime of making this woman happy. Bella had given him more happiness than he could ever give to her with money and lavish gifts.

"The door isn't locked whenever you want to go inside." He moved to the side and let her take her time rubbing the rough chiseled stone on either side of the massive wooden door before she placed her hand on the black wrought-iron door handle. She pressed the lever and slowly pushed open the door to reveal the entryway to the manor hall. He stepped inside after her, and she immediately looked up at the vertical details of the room, which drew her attention to the high, vaulted-wood ceilings made of Scottish oak and carved with intricate designs. He was amused by her reaction as she looked around in awe, her mouth still wide open and eyebrows raised. She placed her bag on the floor, and he set his bag beside hers, then took off his jacket and laid it on top of his bag.

"This. Is. Awesome." Her declaration provided him the response he had hoped his guests would experience someday.

"So, you like it?"

"Like it? I love it. I feel like the lady of a grand manor already." He studied her expressions as she walked further into the room and looked from side to side, as if she couldn't decide where to cast her gaze. She walked past the oak-paneled walls, with impressive carved moldings. Medieval weapons were mounted on the walls, and knights' suits of armor stood guard in the corners of the expansive hall.

"Oh, this is so nice." She spoke in hushed tones and carefully placed her feet on the soft, plush tartan carpets scattered throughout the room. He stood with her and looked down as he pressed his feet into the thick wool pile.

"These are historical reproductions of the tartans once used in this home. Don't be afraid to walk on them. We want our guests to feel at home and not like they're visitors in a museum."

"You said *our* guests. Did you invest in this property with Parker and his family?"

"Yes, I did, and we hope to make it a memorable experience for all our future guests, but right now, I want to make more memories with you." He took her into his arms and kissed her.

"Do you want to see more of the castle before we eat?"

"I'd love to. I'll let you point the way."

He led her past the massive black candelabras, holding multiple white unlit candles, and pointed out the rich colorful stained-glass windows adorned with heraldic crests and framed with thick velvet curtains that puddled in a mass of fabric on the floor. He urged her to rub her fingers on the impressive tapestries, which pictured the lush Scottish countryside.

"If you're trying to impress me, you've hit the bullseye. This place is unbelievable."

"Believe it, baby. This night is all for you."

He escorted her to the other side of the hall but stopped before opening the heavy wooden door.

"This is the Crimson Room, with a replica of a historic marriage bed. It's where I hope to end the night with you." He threw back the double doors and took her by the hand so they could enter together.

An imposing mahogany wooden bed dressed in blood-red satin fabric adorning the mattress took up most of the room. The head and foot valances, made of crimson satin on top with a cream taffeta lining underneath, were tied to the carved four posts and drawn across the bed. He'd insisted on the custom-made feature of the head of a ram carved into the headboard. The bedding was complete with soft pillows covered in crimson red satin with gold trim.

More tapestries of romantic vignettes of men and women gazing at each other in pastoral scenes were hung on one side of the room. On the other side was a gilded crown more ornate than the one in her room. Mounted on the wall the crown provided a tent like structure for the matching thick cream and red colored fabrics streaming down from the crown and surrounding a settee, placed near a window overlooking the estate. She walked toward the bed and looked at the two oversized portraits of a man and a woman clad in formal Scottish attire; usual for the landed gentry of their day. There was a separate portrait of a younger adult male clad in a kilt, and smaller portraits of young children standing in front of ponies were mounted on the large wall on either side of the bed. He stared at her and was taken aback by her surprised reaction to seeing the portraits. She turned to him with her hand over her mouth as she tried to gather her wits to speak to him. She was silent as she struggled with her emotions.

"Look at their eyes and their noses. The older man in the portrait, the young man and the children all have facial features like my father. They look like they could be my distant relatives, except for the skin tones, which my father inherited from his Native American heritage." She pointed to the portraits.

"I'm surprised you noticed it right away." He moved closer to her while she looked straight ahead, unwilling to avert her attention.

"Bella, I didn't mean to upset you. I thought this would make you happy." She shook her head and dropped a few silent tears. "These people are distant relatives of early Moors of Scotland, some of whom served in the court of King James IV. Henry is quite the historian, and when I told him you had Scottish relatives, he commissioned some of the local genealogists to do a search of your family several months ago. Imagine our surprise when we found out you not only descended from the Campbell clan through your grandmother's paternal side, but you're also a descendant on her maternal side of Scottish nobility. These are paintings of the Laird Roderick and Lady Ledicia Dubh and their children…your relatives. We found their portraits in a castle museum in the Highlands and had them reproduced. I was going to surprise you with them when we returned home, but I thought this would be more of a pleasant surprise seeing them in this setting here in Scotland."

"What? You did all of this for me?"

"Yes, and I would do more if you asked." She moved closer to the bed, took off her jacket, and dropped it on a nearby chair as she touched the silk covering on the bed.

"Make love to me now." Looking back at him and at all the unlit candles surrounding the room, she stood still as he came closer, pulled back the covers on the bed and scooped her up in his arms, taking her breath away as he claimed her mouth.

Slowly, he placed her on the bed and, while on top of her, took in the smell of her sweet perfume of musk and jasmine while kissing her along her jawline and neck. Her skin heated up every place he touched her as he slowly undressed her. He took off her loose-fitting dress and discovered she was wearing no underwear.

"Oh Bella. Did you forget something?" His eyes widened as thoughts that his angel of light, his sweet Bella, could be so wanton for his touch. Ideas of all the things he wanted to do with her coursed through his head and ignited his passions.

"No, I didn't." She smiled as he got up, climbed out of his clothes in record time, and pulled a condom out of his pocket while fleeting thoughts of concern about her habits with her birth control ran through his mind. She would take it some days in the morning if she woke up in time, some days at night, and others not at all. They'd talked about it, and she'd told him she had her days and nights mixed up from the last six weeks of travel to so many different cities, mainly at night. He knew she wasn't consistent in taking her pill, but it wasn't going to stop him from having her tonight. He'd address it with her again later.

He slid the sheath on his cock and then his large hands traveled down the sides of her body, stopping to tickle her nipples with his thumbs, and with his heated tongue, he licked her belly until she giggled with delight.

"Give me more of you, baby," she purred.

"Be patient. You're going to get a lot of me tonight."

He laid her back against the pillows and spread her legs, smelling the sweet aroma of her sex before darting his tongue in and out of her center. She was wet with anticipation and leaned up on her elbows with her legs spread wide, giving him maximum exposure to her pink folds. Delighted by his foreplay, she threw her head back and closed her eyes. He planned to give her the first of many climaxes tonight, and he wanted to watch her getting turned on.

"Open your eyes," he commanded her. She was breathing heavily and struggling to keep them open.

"Take me, Miles. Don't make me wait any longer."

Her head fell back as he filled her with his thick, throbbing cock. He thrusted deep within her core, in and out, stimulating the places he discovered; and provided them both with maximum pleasure. She held up her breast for him to suck and arched her back in response to the pressure of his mouth pulling on her body.

"Oh, baby, you feel so good," he panted with pleasure.

"I love you so much, Miles."

His breathing grew increasingly labored, and he let out an agonized groan, causing all the candles surrounding them to burst into growing flames as he sought his release. The heat of the flames diminished as his warm semen squirted out in spasms.

"I love you too, baby," he replied as he rested a few seconds inside of her before grabbing his cock, wrapped in the condom, and slowly pulling it out. He removed the condom and tied it at the top before leaving the bed to put it in the trash. With haste, he jumped back under the covers and took her into his arms.

"Miles, the sex was great and the mood of the room perfect. Tell me, how did you do the thing with the candles?"

"I've worked at mastering my gift. It was with a sleight of hand I released fire balls."

"Yes, you did release the fire," she giggled.

"Only wanting to please you, my dear. I could stay like this with you all night, but I'm hungry, and I need to get some food in you. Let's get our clothes back on and go eat in the main hall. The food should be ready and smells delicious."

He helped her find her dress and the shoes he'd thrown around the room and then escorted her back to the main hall. The massive fireplace was lit to provide warmth, and hot food was on the table when they arrived.

"I thought we were here alone?"

"I wanted us to be alone at first, but I realized I'm not much of a chef, so I have a skeletal crew here with us, but they know to maintain a low profile. They're here only for the time needed to prepare our dinner then they'll return early tomorrow to clean up and serve breakfast."

He pulled out her seat, and she sat at the table.

"Thank you," she told him as he hurried to his seat across from her.

"Let's eat. You need to build up your strength for tonight." He winked.

They each removed the silver dome covering their plates, letting steam and a heavenly aroma escape and reveal plates filled with sliced filet mignon and vegetables. He had a larger portion of food, and he grabbed his utensils and dug in, aware he wasn't observing his customary habit of letting his guest take the first bite of food. Bella smiled and watched him savoring his food before taking her first bite.

"This is so good. I didn't realize how hungry I was." She took another bite of the tender meat and licked the juices off her lips.

"It is good. I'll make sure this is a standard part of the menu," he agreed and gobbled the food off his plate.

"Miles, thank you for everything you've done to make this evening enjoyable."

"You're welcome, and nothing but the best for my love." He puckered and blew her a kiss.

He'd instructed the staff that morning to make sure the décor in the room was romantic, with lots of flowers in crystal vases scattered throughout the room. There was a small table covered in white linen and lace that held more wine, an intricately carved decanter, two crystal glasses, and a plate of fruit and cheese. He was not disappointed by the efforts of the staff to help him make tonight memorable, and he smiled as he held up his glass to toast her.

"To my Bella, the queen of my heart."

"To the only king of my heart. May our love last throughout eternity."

"Yes, through eternity and beyond."

"Cheers." They finished their wine and dinner and he took her hand, leading her to a portion of the room where more candles were placed in the shape of a heart surrounding a thick sheepskin blanket with plush pillows on the floor close to the fireplace. She squealed with delight and kissed him, darting her tongue in and out of his mouth. The heat within him began rising as she pressed her hips against his while he grabbed her buttocks and ground his hips slowly against her groin. The delicious friction between the two of them started to ignite his passions again, but he didn't want to rush the time they had together tonight.

"This is so romantic Miles." She turned her head and looked absently into the fire, as he rubbed her back, content to spend this special evening with her. She leaned back and spoke to him, breaking his trance.

"You're not the only one with a surprise Miles. I have something special for you too. Don't worry, I cleared it with Parker's father before I had the crew assemble a few rows of fireworks in the clearing not far from the castle." She got up and retrieved their bags and his jacket, which were still at the door while he looked on. She placed her small bag on the floor closer to her, unzipped it, and produced a few fire rockets, which she gave to him.

He took them from her and lowered his head to look at them. His eyes were downcast until he looked up at her and toyed with the small rocket sticks in his hand.

"I thought you liked fireworks?" She was perplexed by his response.

"It was sweet of you to go to the trouble of having a small mounted display, but I like the professional-style fireworks, with plenty of power and pizzazz." He kissed her before finishing his thoughts. "I really appreciate your thoughtfulness, but this is child's play for me."

"Well, you haven't seen what I had set up outside. The rain seems to be holding off, so we can play with each other a little more, let it get a little darker outside, and then go have some fun with the fireworks." She licked her lips and ran her finger down his chest.

He placed the rockets on the floor and was about to take her in his arms again when he heard the sound of something or someone prowling outside the door.

"Did you hear that?"

She shook her head. "Hear what? It's probably a small animal—or maybe the staff is still here."

"I'm sure they're gone by now." He turned his head to the door. "I can't explain it, but I feel there's something weird going on. Stay here and let me check it out. Be good until I get back babe. I promise I'll be right back." He got up and began putting on his jacket.

"Miles, please don't go out there. It's probably nothing. Why don't we call down to the resort and let the staff check on it?" A little anxiety crept into her voice. "Better yet, we can light the fireworks now. Let me go with you."

"No, we can wait to light the fireworks later. Let me check things out. It's probably just the wind, but it's going to bug me until I know for sure. I'll be right back." He finished putting on his jacket and shoes and went to open the front door. After blowing her a kiss one last time, he didn't delay before disappearing into the early darkness.

"Miles—" she called out to him as a cool night wind blew into the room. She rubbed the goosebumps on her arms to calm her fears.

CHAPTER NINETEEN

Rummaging through her bag filled with adult toys she'd planned on using tonight, she viewed the black leather outfit, his favorite, with the matching boots she thought she would be wearing by now, and then, looking at the instructions on the black tape for bondage and sexual pleasure, she read that it was strong but touted to be safe enough to protect the skin during sex play. Attempting to keep her mind occupied, she pulled out the salve made from Silvadene, aloe, silica, and other things she couldn't pronounce. Cade, Miles's father had sent it to her months ago, along with information she found useful about Miles's condition.

He'd stoked her ire by repeating the mistaken belief that Miles had canceled his fireworks show before the start of the tour for her, but his father had shed light on why he did it by himself. He loved the opportunity to use his God given power at full capacity without having to explain his condition to anyone.

She found it interesting that the power in his hands could produce intense heat and damage to other people's skin if he touched them when he exerted his full strength. His father used the word "awkward" in his communication with her about sex, but he also encouraged her to use the salve lightly on her skin to protect her until his brain circuitry could compensate for his sexual feelings and control his heat production during their lovemaking.

Yes, awkward is the word.

Reviewing the part of the letter again about how Miles had to learn how to deal with the intensity of feelings produced by the combination of both love and lust which were new to him, she reflected on that morning after they made love for the first time, and a couple of times afterwards when he'd told her he thought his brain felt short circuited by his intense feelings of love and lust for her, and she'd noticed she had tender red marks on her chest. After she'd started using the salve, it had protected her skin during their heady nights of passion.

He closed his letter in telling her he appreciated she loved his son and was grateful he'd finally found out what it was like to love a woman.

Miles, where are you?

Sighing in frustration, she looked around the room at the weapons mounted on the walls: a medieval bow, a quiver filled with arrows, daggers, and a throwing axe. She got up and began pacing, anxious as time continued to pass. The wind was starting to pick up, and still he hadn't returned. The flames of the candles had burned out, and the fires in the fireplaces were slowly dwindling, causing the room to cool. She knew she had to do something, so she pulled out a shirt, underwear, and a pair of jeans from her bag and changed out of her light dress before slipping on her shoes and starting for the door.

She opened it and called out.

"Miles! …Miles!" He didn't answer.

Closing the door, she turned back to find her jacket and looked at all the weapons around her. She wasn't about to go out into the darkness unarmed. She found her jacket, quickly put it on, and went to the wall to take the quiver off the mounting. She placed it over her shoulder, slipped a dagger in her pocket, and took down the medieval bow before testing the strength of the string across it. She was more familiar with the American bow and arrow, but she could use this if she had to. She also placed the fire rockets in her pocket before heading back to the door to search for her man. She wasn't waiting any longer.

The roadster was where they'd left it, with the keys in the ignition and the top pulled up. She got in and started back down the darkened road as the wind calmed while she traveled at a slow speed, looking alongside the path. After rolling down the window, she yelled for him again, but he still didn't answer, and she stopped calling him as her fears increased. *Something's wrong.*

She drove a little more in the direction of the resort, looking on both sides of the path before she decided to stop the car, turn off the lights, and cut the engine. Gathering her weapons, she was determined she wasn't going down without a fight, even if it was possibly the last fight, for her life and their love. Armed for a possible battle, she got out of the car and bent close to the ground, moving lightly through the trees. There was no explanation for it, but she felt a comforting presence, a guide to help her find Miles. Her father always told her when they hunted together when she was about ten years old to be quiet and stealth-like. They were wise words, as she had no plans to be the prey tonight.

Moonlight beaming through the trees illuminated the darkness and aided her on the path to finding him. She looked up at the starry skies and hoped all that was good in the universe would help them survive, just before pushing back the underbrush off the path and looking at what appeared to be a body tied up and placed against a tree. She held her position, allowing her eyes to further adapt to the dim of night, uncertain if she was walking into an ambush. A few minutes went by, and the body, which looked like Miles, moaned and moved, but no one else came around him. She leaped across the distance, holding on to her pockets, containing the daggers, tape, and salve, as the bow and quiver bounced on her shoulders.

After reaching his side, she hugged him and took the tape off his mouth, then noticed his hands were tied behind his back with thick rope.

"Bella, leave me and go get help. I don't want you to get hurt."

"Shut up. I'm not leaving without you." She took the dagger out of her pocket to cut at the rope binding his wrists. After she freed him, she pulled out the salve and applied it liberally to his hands.

"We need all the weapons we can get Miles."

"I don't know what you're doing, but please, if you love me, go now before they return. These men are probably affiliated with the Alt Knights—and they're killers."

She was about to wipe the salve off her hands when she heard a voice and looked up.

"You're not going anywhere." The voice had an accent that didn't sound Scottish, and a man came out of the shadows, taking something out of his pocket. She saw the glint of his gun as he pulled it out and aimed it at her.

While standing as quickly as she could, she took an arrow out of her quiver and directed it at him. His laugh was loud as he mocked her.

"Stop! You're making me laugh. Do you really think you're a match for me, little girl, with your bow and arrow while I have a gun pointed at you? Put that thing down and stop playing with me." He took a long puff off his cigarette.

Its light illuminated his face in the dark while he pointed the gun at her with the other hand.

"Bella, please do as he says. Put down the bow."

She refused to change her stance and tried to keep her arrow pointed at him, but her hands shook with fright. He laughed at her again and exhaled the smoke from his cigarette.

"You probably can't shoot straight, you little whore. I dare you, but if you miss, prepare to die," he stepped back and cocked the gun. "I want to see lover boy watch you..."

Her blood boiled with anger as she steeled her nerves and steadied herself.

I'm nobody's whore.

"Die," was his last word as she shot her arrow, striking him in the chest—bullseye. He stumbled back and fell to the ground, and his gun fired in the air before falling out of his hand. She crouched close to the ground and was about to go retrieve the weapon when another figure approached, holding an automatic weapon and pointing it right at her.

"Stop right there. Don't think I won't shoot you."

"Don't hurt her," Miles called out to the unknown man facing both of them. "Bella, come back here to me. Now." His commanding voice shocked her, and the man holding the weapon turned slightly and stared at him. She dropped her weapons, stepped back with her hands held high, and moved behind him. She looked at his hands, which she had freed from the ropes, and realized he was still keeping them behind him.

"I could have shot your girlfriend for killing this man, but I didn't. How could I begrudge a doomed man one last hug or perhaps a kiss?" The stranger laughed and looked down at the dead man on the ground. "What a chauvinistic buffoon." He kicked the body and stamped out the cigarette, still lit on the ground.

"Let me make something clear: You make any wrong moves and the girl dies. How many people have to die, Miles, before you join us? José suffered before he died. Oh, how I wished it was you, but I have orders to spare your life," he spat. "Or, maybe I could kill her now and let you watch her die."

Miles turned his head and spoke softly to her as their captor laughed and sneered at them.

Miles turned his head toward her and whispered, "Is the fireworks display set up in the clearing over there to the left?"

"Yes."

"Stay behind me and hug me. Act as if you're scared. Keep behind me at all times."

"Act as if I'm scared? I am scared."

The captor looked at them, frowning. "Stop talking! Look, Miles, I have on a special vest, pants, and shoes made of state-of-the-art flame-retardant material, so don't go thinking you're going to throw one of them fireballs at me. I'll still have time to shoot the girl, and her blood will be on your hands."

"Stop scaring her." He turned to kiss Bella, and she hugged him around the shoulders while Miles grabbed the fire rockets that had dropped out of her pocket and kept them hidden behind his back.

"How cute." Disarmed by their display of affection, he lowered his gun a little. As he moved closer to them, Bella looked up and saw another figure in the shadows. The sound of a helicopter getting closer caught the man's attention and he looked up at the sky.

"That bird's coming for you and for the fine whiskey we stole from this resort. You know how-to live-in style—and so will I when I cash in on you." The wind pushed the strong smell of whiskey from his clothes in their direction. He stumbled a little over the roots of the tree after the sound of leaves rustling behind startled him as an emerging dark shadowy figure came into view.

"Probably a ghost of Samhain," he snickered while trying to regain some composure.

"Daddy!" Bella screamed. The man with the gun turned his head again, and Miles threw a fire rocket lit by an intense ball of flames, striking him in the chest and igniting his flame-retardant clothes, which were no match for the heat of a fireball intensified by the salve on his hands. He yelled in agony and dropped the gun, his arms and torso burning and flailing before falling to the ground, dead, while the shadowy figure stopped approaching them.

Miles struggled to his feet and placed his arms around her shoulders.

"Bella, we have to get out of here. There are others in the helicopter sent to kidnap me." He tried to get her to leave.

She refused to move and continued to yell, "Daddy, why did you leave me?" She struggled against Miles's attempt to get her to go.

"We have to go. Remember what the guide said about Samhain—images appear real. Your father is not here. Bella, I love you. Let's go."

She kept her eyes on the figure of her father, smiling and consoling her.

"Sweetheart, it's time. Let me go to my resting place and you go with him."

"Did you hear that? It's my father, Miles." She struggled against him.

"Bella, enough. We've got to go." The helicopter landed, and it appeared they had run out of time to get back to the car before being recaptured. Miles led her behind a stone boulder and stepped to the side before sending a second rocket ignited by a fireball in the direction of the explosives mounted on the fireworks display, which burst into flames before many of the rockets could fly off into the air. The force of the explosion hundreds of feet away knocked them back behind the protection of the stone and caused the helicopter to shake violently and fall over on its side. Engulfed by the fire while the detonation of rows of fireworks hanging from steel mountings caused a blazing show of red, white, blue, and green sparks to illuminate the darkness. The loud bangs startled her, and he took her hand and remained behind the large stones for cover. She looked at his face as he bent close to the ground, mesmerized by the awesome display of fire.

"You're right, babe. This isn't child's play, but we've got to get out of here."

He waited for the last sound of an exploding rocket before attempting to evade capture and wrapped her up in his arms to begin their escape to safety while she pointed the way to the car. They struggled back to the roadster, and he made sure she was safely inside before running to the other side. He got the car started and gunned the accelerator while she sat beside him, looking back at where the image of her father stood, now faded from view as they moved toward the resort.

"What did you place on my hands?"

"Your father sent a salve for me to apply to my skin, and he told me to apply it before we made love because your touches could burn my skin, especially when you were excited, but the risk of burning me would end once your brain circuits mastered combined impulses from lust and love. He knew you could handle sexual impulses of lust without love, but impulses of romantic love were new to you."

"Awkward," he looked at her and turned his attention back on the road.

"He also said the salve had a paradoxical effect on you if applied liberally; it intensified your fireballs, making them hotter and able to travel farther distances."

"He didn't talk to me about a salve before."

"You never mentioned you loved someone before." Her face heated, and she looked at her hands.

"He told me you admitted to *him* you loved me." He grabbed her hand.

"And I'd say it again and tell the world I love you if you wanted me to." She raised his hand to her mouth and kissed it.

"Miles, you believe I saw my father, don't you?"

"Bella, I think you honestly believe you saw him, and some things defy explanation. Whether it's the mystery of spiritualism, faith in a love that will never die, or belief in your father as your guardian angel. Although I don't know much about that or the mystical occurrences around Samhain, I won't question your belief that you saw him as long as you allow me the option of thinking it could also have been the alcohol we've been drinking all day."

"Fine, but I know what I heard and what I saw," she turned and looked ahead without further attempts at validation.

They got back to the resort, where others were waiting, including all the members of his security team. They'd heard the explosive blast and come running outside, witnessing the fireworks exploding above them. Just as the two of them were approaching in the roadster, he saw Bradley running toward them and brought the car to a stop in front of him.

"There was activity near the castle that alarmed all of us. We heard a helicopter approaching, and it sounded like it crashed, followed by a loud explosion. I knew you were going to set off fireworks with Bella—she told me about it but—it shouldn't have caused that much noise. Are you two okay?" Bradley asked as Miles stumbled while leaning against Bella for support.

"We're fine Bradley." He rubbed his head.

"I was about to dispatch someone to investigate the possibility of a crash when your father called with additional information from The Network. You've always instructed me that when he calls, answer it immediately. He said I should have been near you at all times, and my incompetence could've gotten you and Bella killed. Do you have The Network looking over my shoulders? They seem to be everywhere." He ran his hand through his hair.

"No, I trust your competence Bradley, but The Network has had a shadowy presence around me most of my life. I'll talk to my father and tell him it was my idea you stood down. He's angry with me, not you, but he's right. My desire to spend time alone with Bella without security close by was a lapse in judgment on my part. Let the men from The Network communicate with the local authorities." He placed his hand on Bradley's shoulder.

"I need you to follow their lead and also help security here at the resort calm the nerves of the guests. We don't want anyone panicking or venturing off near the castle."

"Sure thing; my men and I can also play a supportive role for the operatives with The Network since reinforcements are due to arrive any minute to cordon off the place and sanitize the scene near the castle if they deem it necessary. Your father told me not to talk to the local authorities and said The Network would handle them. What is this Network anyway? Is there something you need to tell me?"

Bella interrupted the conversation just as the rain was starting to fall.

"We need to get inside. A man attacked Miles, and he needs to be examined." She looked at the bruise forming on his head.

Parker had witnessed their arrival. Before he left, he told Bradley he was calling a nurse kept on standby during the resort's peak season to examine his friend. He didn't want to risk wasting time.

Bella insisted that Miles come inside with her to get off his feet, and she pushed past Bradley's security detail as she led him to a couch near a fireplace. He noticed she was shivering despite having her jacket around her.

"Can we please get Bella a blanket? She's cold," Miles asked, and a member of the staff came back with a blanket, which he placed around her before taking her into his arms to comfort her while she warmed up.

"Miles, what happened out there?"

"I'm not sure what happened, Bradley. I was investigating a sound coming from the woods. I turned my head, and the last thing I remember is being hit by someone. I was out cold until my angel came looking for me."

She remained quiet, allowing him to tell his version of the story. She knew he had confided many of his secrets to her as a member of his most intimate circle, but it made her wonder how much Bradley really knew about Miles.

"I was about to risk your anger by coming to the castle to tell you the concert tomorrow has been canceled," Bradley told him. "We were getting information from the intelligence community about a possible terrorist attack in the next twenty-four hours that could involve a suicide bomber. For your safety, and for the safety of your crew and fans, we can't risk it, so if Bella rescued you tonight, she's a hero. She thwarted a plan that could've resulted in the loss of innocent lives or injury to many people." Bradley kept looking at his phone at the slew of messages he was getting.

"Sorry, I need to respond to these messages from The Network, but we need to talk." Miles nodded and turned his attention back to Bella after Bradley left.

Parker returned with the nurse, and she cleaned the wound and placed Steri-Strips along the small cut above his eye. She did an alertness check and told Bella he had a slight concussion. Although he refused to be taken to the hospital, he did agree to be monitored. Before she left, the nurse urged him to rest, gave him something for his headache, and gave Bella instructions for the night, along with recommendations to call for medical assistance if they had questions or concerns.

Darien arrived to assist, and he and Parker encouraged Miles to return to his suite to get some rest, but he didn't want to go to bed until Bella agreed to come with him. She promised Parker and Darien she would watch him the entire night.

They returned to their suite, and while she helped him undress as he sat on the bed, he leaned to the side and took a small box out of his pants pocket.

"I have something to tell you and to show you."

"We can talk about anything you want—but in the morning, Miles." She tried, but he wouldn't listen, and he stopped her attempts to take off his shoes and pants.

"I know tonight has been disturbing to say the least, but like I told you when we were in London, let The Network handle this, and we shouldn't worry about it." He searched her eyes for a response.

"Are you serious, Miles? You could have been killed, and you're telling me not to worry?"

"I see the fear in your eyes, Bella, and you promised me you wouldn't worry. As I told you, I've lived under the threat of kidnapping all my life, but never has an attempt been successful since the time I was an infant. Can you bear this burden with me? Please, Bella, tell me you won't let this come between us."

"Miles, I'm only human, and there was a bonafide attempt on your life that we can't just ignore and move on from. I'm trying to be strong for us, but if you see the fear in my eyes, it's because it's there, but you don't need to worry that I would give up on us or even consider leaving you. I love you, and I'll always love you. Remember, I'm your ride or die chick." He chuckled.

"I never wanted our love to be put to the test, but since you're in it all the way with me, I have something else to tell you; it's important."

"Alright I'm listening." She sat beside him.

"I would get on my knees, but I'm afraid I'll fall over." He opened the box for her to see an engagement ring with a brilliant, large princess-cut diamond.

She placed her hand over her gaping mouth.

"Bella Wahlberg, will you marry me?" He was serious, his face drawn tight at first, but the delight on her face made him smile, revealing his boyish charm. She looked at the beautiful ring he removed from the box, and with a slight hand tremor, he placed it on her finger.

"Yes, Miles, I will marry you, but first, let me help you undress and get in bed."

"You're always wanting my body, which I will always gladly give." He winked at her.

She laughed and kissed him while helping him out of his pants and into a fresh pair of boxers. She undressed and snuggled into his arms, trying to get settled in bed.

"This isn't the way I intended to propose to you, but I'm happy you accepted. I've already picked out the perfect place for us to get married: a small church in a village near here. I was going to tell you tonight that the local registrar's office called and approved our request for a license. Henry must have pulled some strings so…surprise!"

"But Miles—"

"Let me finish Bella. A minister here in town has agreed to perform the ceremony, and we can get up tomorrow, get dressed, and be married in a small intimate affair, just the two of us and a witness, by three o'clock tomorrow." He kissed her and smiled.

"Surprise? I was hoping for a longer engagement after I heard you had requested a marriage license.

"You knew?" He raised his eyebrows.

"Yes, Henry let it slip when I met with him to discuss marketing plans for the resort. I knew you planned to ask me, but I didn't know when, and besides, you can't ask me to get married without my mother or your parents at the ceremony. I can't do that to them."

"You saw the request?"

"Yes, I saw it after I went to the courthouse and spoke to the clerk that Henry told me had a copy of the request with your name on it awaiting my signature. You have an additional copy of the request in case we couldn't make it to the court house. You're a *very* busy man Miles Moore." She gave him a side eyed look.

"Why didn't you say something?" His jaw dropped as he looked at her in surprise that the tables had turned on him.

"And ruin your surprise? No, it warmed my heart to think about the lengths you were willing to go to make me happy. Yes, I will marry you, but no, not tomorrow."

"Hasn't tonight shown us that time isn't promised to us? If you won't give me your hand tomorrow, I'll give you forty-eight hours." He closed his eyes and nestled her into his side.

"I'm tired, and I can't discuss this further."

She looked at him as he opened one eye then closed it again.

"I know you're tired, so just listen. I want a hand in planning our wedding. I love that you've gone to so much trouble to plan a ceremony for just the two of us, but I want our families to be there as witnesses, and I want to incorporate a piece of my Scottish heritage, since we're getting married in Scotland."

"So you want to nix my plans?"

"I can't do it in two days, but we can discuss it further in the morning." He looked at her, his frown deepening as he contemplated what to say.

He really isn't a patient man. She shook her head.

"Miles, I love you, and I'll marry you soon. Can we sleep on it for now?"

His frown slowly disappeared, as he turned her head and delivered a passionate kiss on her lips, while caressing her hips before they both fell asleep.

The next morning, he was up and out of bed before her, as usual. She'd slept lightly in his arms the night before and woken up throughout the night to make sure he was still breathing. She opened her eyes to sunlight streaming through their bedroom, yawned, and stretched before heading to the bathroom for a quick shower. Intoxicated by the smells of fresh bread and other sumptuous delights wafting through the room, she went to the front of the suite after getting dressed and heard him singing as he moved throughout the space. He looked up and greeted her with a smile.

"Good morning my fiancée. I had food brought to the suite for the two of us to enjoy a private breakfast together." He kissed her and directed her to the table, set with bountiful meats, assorted pastries, and fruits. She took her seat at the table and looked at him with her head tilted to the side, curious about the set of papers lying flat on her gleaming china plate.

"I need you to look over the papers," he told her as he took his seat opposite her.

"Are you feeling better?"

"Yes, I'm fine Bella, and I need you to review the documents before we discuss the contents."

She placed her hand on the fine vellum papers drawn up on letterhead with the name of NeNe's firm and address listed at the top and scanned the next few lines of the papers.

In the matter of the prenuptial agreement between Miles Aridio Moore and Bella Aliyah Wahlberg, no terms are deemed necessary or rendered.

Her chest heaved as she looked at the words of the brief document already signed by her husband-to-be. He handed her a pen to sign above her name, which had been typed on the document.

"We're a team, and you've proven that to me. I wouldn't be sitting here if it wasn't for you. You'll be my wife and entitled to enjoy the benefits of our joint labor, but sadly, you may also bear the consequences of my past behaviors and indiscretions. I love you and plan to stay with you for our entire lives. Baby, trust me, you'll earn every penny of the fortune we build together. Neither you nor any of our children will ever have financial worries. I promise to provide for you and our children, but I need you to sign the papers and then we can enjoy our breakfast."

Her head was swimming with his unexpected generosity and his veiled declaration that she would earn her keep.

What does that even mean?

Memories of her own anxieties about an uncertain future without her father; and when her mother told her of plans to sacrifice her career by leaving her job and relocating to another city because she was frightened by the storms, ran through her mind, along with thoughts that others might say she was a gold digger.

"This is too much, Miles, too much. First the wedding plans and now this? I won't start our life together being controlled by you." She bolted angrily from the room to the bedroom, where she locked the door behind her.

She heard his footsteps getting closer to the door of the bedroom.

"Please let me in. Baby talk to me. You've got me confused."

She heard his footsteps fade as he backed away from the door while she sat silently. Her phone started to ring within minutes of his departure, and the name Lecia appeared on the screen. She accepted the call from the one person who might be able to help her decide on how to handle her dilemma. She took in a deep breath before answering the call.

"Bella, sweetheart, Miles called and asked me to speak to you. Do you mind receiving some unsolicited advice? I also married into an affluent family, with all the complications that go along with it, and I can help you through this, but first, tell me what happened."

"He just presented me with a prenup agreement that wasn't a prenup. Why did he feel he had to a put a non-prenup in writing if he didn't think one was necessary? Last night, he insisted that we get married right away. Lecia, I'm confused. Is this part of a test? And if I pick the wrong answer, I fail?"

"No, I don't think he's testing you, and I'm glad, frankly, that the two of you didn't elope. Bella, I had to consider something similar before I married his father, and you need a voice in deciding the terms of your agreement with him, but trust me, if a Moore man tells you as his wife, you'll merit everything you get, the good and the bad that will come from your union with him, please know he's telling you the truth. My son walked away from his family's fortune because his freedom to follow his heart was more important to him than money. He's trying to tell you that what he's giving you is more important to him than money. He's giving you the thing he has protected all his life—his heart."

"Thanks for the advice. I'll work this out with him, and I think I'm ready to talk to him now. I thank you for calling me. Goodbye."

"Goodbye, Bella. I trust the two of you will come up with terms you both can live with."

Bella ended the call and took in a deep breath before getting off the bed, unlocking the door, and returning to find him sitting silently at the table. She pulled out her chair and took a seat.

"I didn't mean to upset you. My only intent was to assure you money will never be an issue for you or our future children. My father was an excellent provider, and I'll be the same for you and our family."

He rose from his seat and slowly made his way to her, taking her into his arms in a supportive embrace.

"Bella, I don't understand how you misunderstood my intent in presenting you a non-prenup agreement, but maybe I didn't do a good job of explaining myself. Let's promise we'll be patient with each other."

"I promise. I thought you were testing me, and I wasn't sure of the correct answer. We owe each other all the time we need to understand each other's intent, and I'm sorry I bolted on you. I should have asked questions instead of running out on you, so if we can allow ourselves a redo of this situation, let's sit down. I have some questions for you." They both took their seats.

"What is your first question?"

"Can money buy me your loyalty?" He took a breath and kept his eyes locked on hers.

"No, it cannot."

"Can money buy me your fidelity or commitment?" Her eyes watered as she spoke.

"Bella, I'm not sure the point you're trying to make, but if those are the things that are the most important to you, then I agree, you don't need the power of my money because you already have my loyalty, my fidelity, and my commitment to us. It's part of the package deal of my true love for you."

"I…I needed to hear you say that Miles. It's what's important to me." She looked down at the papers before her.

"It's important to me too, Bella. I just thought when we said we loved each other, all those things were implied and didn't need to be spoken between us."

"Miles, I don't want us to assume anything or risk, taking each other for granted."

"Other concerns babe?"

"Yes, I see you've made provisions, and you spoke of future children. Does that mean you're not against the idea of having children someday?" She looked up and stared, holding her breath.

"I've changed my mind about having children someday. I realized how important family is to you, so yes, I'm looking forward to being a parent—just no time soon."

He placed his hands atop hers on the table, and seconds later, she slid her hands from underneath his, to take the pen he'd placed to the side of her plate and began writing on the agreement in the space above her name.

I, Bella Aliyah Wahlberg, agree to the terms of the agreement in which none of the assets belonging to Miles Aridio Moore accumulated prior to the date of my marriage to him will be subject to the terms of our non-prenup. He will continue to own fully and outright all of his assets to be used by him as the sole owner. Any assets accumulated after the date of our marriage will be owned jointly.

She signed and dated the agreement before sliding the papers across the table for his review.

"I concede the fact that financial security for all the children we might have is also important, but I've always worked hard and earned my keep." *I'm nobody's gold digger.*

He silently reviewed the terms of the new agreement before placing his signature and dating the document.

"I accept your terms. Is there anything else about this agreement we need to discuss before my breakfast gets colder? Babe, I'm hungry."

She looked him directly in the eyes and decided against fighting fire with fire and sarcasm.

"No, baby, I'm satisfied." She offered a slight smile before chewing a piece of her crepe, and he nodded at her, offering a slight smile in return. He chewed on a large slice of bacon, then picked up a napkin and wiped his mouth before grabbing for his phone.

"Let me call Parker now while he's still at the estate. He told me yesterday he and Jen planned to go into town today." Parker accepted the call after the first ring.

"Do you mind coming to my suite to witness some forms? Thanks."

He ended the call, placed the phone on the table, and finished eating.

News of their plans to marry in Scotland passed from one member of the tour to the other, and soon, social media was buzzing about her unexpected nuptials to Miles, and for the first time, she took his and Darien's advice and didn't comment on anything about the wedding online.

I'm the chief marketing officer, and isn't it my job to direct the narrative? She refrained from commenting on the things she saw in the media, but it didn't stop her from looking at it.

She was angry about all the lies she read, but eventually she realized the storyline was too personal and the likelihood of the situation turning into an ugly affair if she responded was high. She shared her concerns as they prepared for bed.

"I'll stick with just the facts—the where, when, and how. You know, tell the story but not the full story. We can give your fans a little bit of information about how we met and why we chose to get married in Scotland," she tried explaining to him.

"No, I'm not interested in having someone pry into our private lives. We need to set the tone right now. Our private lives should remain private. Trust me on this. I've been in this business a long time, and you don't want to give anything to the internet trolls." He yawned and continued to state his position.

"I've agreed to give your friend Charlie Ferguson an exclusive on the wedding ceremony, with pictures of the reception but nothing more. I'm not willing to say anything before the wedding. You convinced me you and Darien needed more than two days to make wedding arrangements, but I don't want our special day turned into a media circus."

"Well, I've been a part of the 'media circus' as you call it, and I know how to manage it. I hope you don't think I can't see through your choice to give an exclusive to Charlie since it will help you and Parker market the resort."

"Do you think so little of me that you would accuse me of marketing our wedding for financial gain?"

"I think you're a shrewd businessman."

"Well, I learned some things from you, the best marketer in the business, and I didn't want you to think less of me by missing out on a golden opportunity."

"Caution about mixing love and business." She warned.

"Normally I am cautious in business, but I have no defenses when it comes to you. It's all about love."

"Well, I know your family's involvement in your business is important to you."

"It is, but let's not start *that* discussion. I'm tired, I want to go to bed, and hopefully it won't be too long before the wedding plans are completed." He walked with her to the bed and, pulling back the covers, he got in with her to finish their conversation.

"You're a quick study Miles, but if anyone is going to profit from my wedding, it will be me, laddie. A lassie has to pay her bills, and marrying you, Miles Moore doesn't come cheap." He looked at her and sighed.

"You're not paying for the wedding with money but with your life." She frowned, interrupting his laughter.

"Just kidding…it's my attempt at humor, and besides, the wedding has already been paid for. The Middleburgh staff has confirmed reservations for at least one year for weddings and family events because our wedding here has placed the resort on the map, and the Middleton family wanted to show their gratitude by throwing in all their resources at the resort to make our reception a success. If they didn't pay for it, then I would. I just need your sexy ass to show up and not leave me standing at the altar."

"No way, honey. You're stuck with me, but after tonight, I'll not share your bed until we marry."

"Really? Don't you think it's a little late for antiquated ideas? I've seen and tasted the goods and I don't need a ceremony to claim them." He frowned at her and clenched his jaw.

"I don't expect you to fight me on this, Miles. I've already reserved another room here at the resort, and I'm moving out of this suite tomorrow. I'll make the wait worth your while." She placed her finger on his nose and gave him a sly smile while he pouted.

"Good night, Miles." She kissed him and turned on her side away from him.

He grunted and came close to spoon with her for their last night together before the wedding. She moved out the next day as planned without much resistance from him.

Two days later, despite her best efforts, she was unable to convince him to give Charlie and his magazine a full exclusive interview to include a teaser of pictures of them together and a small blurb of texts and postings before the wedding. She thought if she offered something on social media, she could minimize some of the negativity popping up on various sites about them and start another buzz.

He remained firm that the time leading up to the wedding should remain as private as possible, and he tried again to press the issue of a ceremony at the courthouse or even a small intimate wedding outdoors, but she refused any plans to elope or to scale back the plans for their nuptials. With Darien's assistance, they were able to turn the concert event team into a wedding and reception team and plans for the wedding were completed not in the forty-eight hours he wanted but were on track to be completed in a remarkable six days. Their discussions were heated at times, but they both saw the benefit of a compromise. After a tiring day of looking at potential venues for the wedding ceremony and reviewing menus for the reception, they spent a quiet night enjoying tea in one of the private drawing rooms.

She had told him of her desire to get married in a castle, but not the one on the grounds of the resort after the planned romantic night of his proposal was interrupted by intruders. She knew if they rented another castle, it would only spark questions about their night together at the old castle, questions she didn't know all the answers to, and questions Miles seemed hesitant to answer. Instead of the small church wedding he had envisioned, he told her he had secured The *Glenlee*, a 19th century tall ship, one of only five Clyde-built sailing ships that remained afloat in the world.

"I'll do anything to make you feel safe, and I don't want any more negative memories to ruin our special day. I've spent a little time sailing and fishing since we've been here and being on the water has given me a new perspective; sometimes, serenity is sweeter than fiery passion. I'm looking forward to exchanging our vows on a historic ship in a calm port."

"I am too. The ship is beautiful and being on the water has always been calming for me."

She smiled at him to affirm he had made a good choice and returned to the thoughts slowly swirling around in her head in cadence with the movement of the spoon she absently swirled around in her hot cup of tea.

"Our love has kindled internal passions that far exceed the need I once had to witness the power of fire. My last show in Texas was a phenomenal success without the use of fire. Bella, you were right. I don't need the fire I once thought was necessary to ignite the passions of my fans. It's all about the music and the performance."

She continued stirring her tea as they sat in front of the fireplace. Still deep in thought, she didn't hear his last comments, nor did she respond.

"Are you listening to me? You seem deep in thought. Are you getting cold feet about the wedding?" She looked up from her cup and placed it on the table in front of them before joining him in his overstuffed chair. He rubbed her back as she nestled in his lap.

"I know now why you didn't want more media attention before the wedding. I fought with myself, but eventually I gave in and went on some of the sites. I stayed on social media longer than I should have, and eventually I entered the world of the trolls. It's different when the story is about you, and I see why you don't bother much with social media."

"It's a monster that's unwelcomed in my private world, but the music industry's expectations demanded I get used to having it around." He continued rubbing her back.

"I could keep it at a professional distance when the story was only about you, but now that I'm a part of the story, it has gotten harder. Most of the comments were supportive, but some were mean and cruel. A few of your fans wondered what I'd done to get you to marry me. Of course, there were the stories we had created a love child and that's why we were getting married, and there were stories of the sordid sex we were having. I kind of liked those stories. Still, there were others that said I must have cast an evil spell on you, and a few were the usual stories about me using sex as an undue influence on you instead of just doing my job."

She played with the buttons on his shirt but continued without interruption from him.

"There were pictures of me shopping and having lunch with Reagan, and the pictures were shot at the most unflattering angles. They made me look unattractive."

"Stop doing this to yourself Bella. You know how the game is played."

"I do but let me get it out of my system. There have even been Vegas sites set up for gambling on the amount of time we'll stay together." She looked up at him and met his sad eyes, glistening in the light of the fire.

"Bella, you know I can't shield you from all the ugly aspects of my world, so it's probably best we face it head on together. I intentionally waited to ask you to marry me until I was sure you were the one because I knew if you said yes, I would promise to remain married for life. I was raised that way, and I truly believe in the vows for better or worse and until death do us part." She felt the weight of his strong arms come around her back and grip her in a tight, protective embrace before he continued.

"I know it's difficult when it's personal, but we can't live our lives in a bubble or expect others to be happy for us. We'll have troubles just as all couples do, but despite the media hype, eighty-five percent of people won't care, maybe five percent will prove themselves true family and loyal friends, and the other ten percent will be happy about our troubles. Do you really care about the ten percent of people you don't know and will never meet? You're not the real target—I am. The trolls know the only way to get to me is through you. I love you, and if anyone hurts you, they hurt me." He kissed the top of her forehead, down her high cheeks, and planted his tongue in her mouth. She felt him sucking and pulling away her pain.

"I'm glad I shared this with you. No one will ever hurt you through me. I started out as your media consultant, and from the beginning, I've been protective of you even before I fell in love with you. No one will ever hurt you without reckoning with me first."

"I don't think anyone wants to reckon with you. You can be quite a force to deal with, especially with a knife and a bow and arrow," he whispered in her ear.

"I did what I had to do. This trip has helped me to understand I come from strong stock. I've always embraced my African American and Native American heritages, but now that I know more about my Scottish background, I feel more grounded in who I am. My mother told me about her family, and now I know more about my paternal relatives. I come from strong stock on both sides, and my people are survivors. I know painful things happen in life, but I also realize running from adversity isn't always the best choice. I want you to know I plan to enter into this union with my eyes open, and together we'll deal with whatever comes our way."

"Deal." He bumped the fist she held in the air. "Come sleep with me tonight. I don't want to take another cold shower."

"Patience, my dear. Only a few more days before the wedding, and tonight, I'll visit you in your dreams just as you told me I did last night." Frustrated, his chest heaved, and he arched his back, almost pushing her out of his lap.

"Why dream when I can have the real thing?"

"Hopes and dreams make life sweeter. You've made my dreams of the sweet life come true. My mother is coming in tonight, and we'll be spending the night together finalizing plans for the wedding. I want to show her my dress and spend some of this special time in our lives with her. I hope you understand."

"All right. I don't like being so close and unable to touch you, but I understand."

"Maybe I can get some lovemaking time before she arrives. Let's do it here, now. No one will disturb us if I lock the door." He touched her breast, and she fisted her hands then squeezed her eyes shut to diminish her sexual tensions.

"No," she jumped up off his lap. "Not before the wedding night, and that's my final answer."

A member of the staff came in to refresh their tea and to leave a tray of scones with a guest-favorite concoction of raspberry jam made at the resort. She also brought in specialty breads and small slices of coconut cake served on fine china plates decorated with yellow and crimson flowers trimmed in gold.

"Thank you, he was getting hungry." She cocked one eyebrow and took her cup from the staff member.

"Hungry for you, not food," he said under his breath as the staff member exited the room. "Alright Bella. I'll be patient for a few more days, and then, my dear, we'll be together for life." He smiled at her.

"Yes Miles, my lover and best friend, we'll be together until death do us part." She closed her eyes and leaned over to kiss him, her heart beating wildly as his tongue darted in and out of her mouth before he pulled away from her parted lips, leaving her struggling to catch her breath.

"You're not going to make it easy for me to keep my hands off you, are you Miles?"

"No. I love you Bella, and until death do us part, I hope to leave you begging for more." He offered her that sly smile she loved so much.

ABOUT THE AUTHOR

Michele Sims is the "author-ego" of Deanna McNeil and creator of the Moore Family Saga and the Fire God Series.

She loves writing hot love stories and women's fiction with multidimensional characters in multigenerational families.

She is the recipient of the 2018 RSJ Aspiring Author Award and first runner up in the Introvert Press Poetry Contest for February 2018. She is a member of the LRWA, in Charleston, SC, the From The Heart Romance Writers' online group, SC Writers' Association, and RWOWA.

She lives in South Carolina with her husband who has been her soulmate and greatest cheerleader. She is the proud mother of two adult sons and the auntie to many loved ones. When she's not writing, she's trying to remember the importance of exercise, travelling, listening to different genres of music, and observing the wonders of life on this marvelous planet.

Thank you for reading my book, The Fire God Tour. Book One of the Moore family saga, Seed on Fire, and book two, Playing with Fire are also available. I invite you to introduce the Moore family saga to fellow readers and share with others. If you enjoyed reading the book, please do me a favor and leave an honest review where you purchased it.

Sign up at michelesims22.com with your email address for updates and giveaways.

Your support is appreciated.